MINE INHERITANCE

MINE INHERITANCE

FREDERICK NIVEN

COLLINS
48 PALL MALL LONDON

" . . . the task of those to-day is the
development of the heritage already
secured by those who went before."

King George VIth, speaking in
Canada, May 30th, 1939.

FOREWORD

To prospective readers I should like to say that I have in various places, preparing David Baxter's narrative for the press, permitted him, without any commenting footnote, to put into the mouths of historic characters words which were actually written by them in letters or in diaries; and that, I think, is not culpable of me. Sometimes he appears as taking part in actions of which the records I have consulted tell without mention of his presence. For example: on the attack by the *métis* at Red River, when John McLeod a second time manned the small gun at the smithy, he had, according to his diary and to all other reports that I have seen, only three to aid him—Hugh MacLean, Archie Currie, James McIntosh. David Baxter, by his account, makes a seemingly forgotten fourth. But such differences from the archives that I have consulted are, I feel, trivial, when I consider the accuracy of his narrative as a whole.

Not much more than a century has passed since the last days of Baxter's epical story. The " little Christina " of it, living on into 1902, would then be aged eighty-five, and we may well imagine that often, walking in the city of Winnipeg amazingly risen on the site of scenes of which account is given in this book, she must have been aware of some passer-by nudging another to observe her and that she may even have caught the whisper of: " That old lady, there, was born on the day of the Semple Massacre."

The bibliography at the end will indicate the extent of my researches for evidence regarding the lives of the historic characters in Baxter's narrative. These researches make me able to vouch for its essential truth.

F. N.

PART ONE

CHAPTER ONE

I

I, DAVID BAXTER, for many years in the service of the famous Red River Settlement, have sometimes to remind myself that I was not present in the London home of its founder, the Earl of Selkirk, when Captain Miles Macdonell, appointed organiser and governor of the projected Colony, called on him there for final instruction before setting out for Red River. Very clearly, from Macdonell's account of it to me, is that occasion fixed in my mind.

That I take upon myself the task of inditing this record of the first British settlement in the Canadian west is due to the fact that I participated in all the stirring and desperate events of its early history, remaining there while several governors, in various upheavals, came and went, and that each governor in turn I served. With a prior incident relative to the Settlement—though I was not a participator in that—I begin this record because I feel that, on reading of it as it was vividly related to me, you will have fair impression of what led to all that follows.

It was in the spring, then, of the year 1811, that Thomas Douglas, Earl of Selkirk, and Captain Miles Macdonell—who, towards the end of the American Revolution had been an ensign in the King's Royal Regiment of New York, later a lieutenant, then captain in the Royal Canadian Volunteers—sat in the study of the earl's London house. On the table between them lay a map, lit by a shaft of sunlight from the tall windows.

"I have progressed some way," said his lordship, "since I first discussed with you, visiting you at your farm at Osnabruck in Upper Canada, my scheme further to help these unfortunate people who are being evicted from their homes in Scotland. It is my desire, my intention—more strong now than ever—to establish them in a part of the world where they can own their land, from which they can never be evicted, that will be an inheritance for their children."

He paused.

"I have therefore purchased from the Hudson's Bay Company," he said, his fingers tapping the map, "that large tract known as Assiniboia, and it is there, on the banks of the Red River, that I propose to found a settlement for these people. The Hudson's Bay Company retain judiciary rights over the territory. Already it has been brought against me that I am the chief shareholder in the Company, as though that fact makes my personal purchase of land from them in the nature of sharp practice. I may as well frankly tell you, Captain Macdonell, that it looks as if their enemies, the North-West Company, will be the Settlement's enemies too. Already that rival fur company has shown disapproval of my scheme. I want you to go out in advance of the first settlers, take over the tract of land from Mr. Hillier of the Hudson's Bay Company, start clearing for the farms, and instal yourself amicably with all concerned. *Suaviter in modo* will be your best maxim, I think, for the sake of all who will be eventually in your care. I must tell you that I anticipate a little antagonism even from Hudson's Bay Company officials out there. I am prepared to hear that many, not only in the North-West service, may look upon the venture as an intrusion. After all, what have they thought of all the years of their service?"

It was obvious that he was not merely meditating aloud, that he had made an inquiry. So Miles Macdonell sought for a reply and at last——

"Furs," he suggested.

"Precisely—furs," said Lord Selkirk. "Their duty to the Company is to procure furs. Must they not be dubious of any plans for a settlement of farmers, even in a small corner of the land? Might they not look upon the venture as an intrusion? Actually it is not so. Practically no furs are taken in the area to be settled, by the banks of the Red River below the place where Assiniboine flows into it. I realise there will be difficulties, and probably from within as well as from without. But most undertakings of value have their difficulties."

Captain Macdonell looked directly across the table and bowed.

"I am indebted to you, my lord," he said, "for entrusting me with this service. As I have told you, I think your plans should have happy attainment. My brother John, as you know, has been in the neighbourhood—in the service, by the way, of our rivals, the North-West Company—and he also agrees that it is excellent alluvial soil."

As he spoke he considered the face opposite him, the high forehead over eyes of candour, the face of a man of refinements and sensibilities. Raeburn's portrait, the Governor told me, well represented him and conveyed a sense of his height. Macdonell, one of a family of tall men, and Douglas were near of stature as well as in age. At their first meeting, that meeting at Osnabruck in Upper Canada, he had been greatly taken by the earl's character, and had then written a letter to his brother John telling of his admiration for his guest—of how, rebuffed by parliament when suggesting a scheme for the relief of the labouring poor of Scotland he was endeavouring to remedy the situation by personal aid. And that, his first impression of Lord Selkirk's character, was renewed when talking with him on that May day of 1811 in London.

"I am, of course, a Lowlander," said Selkirk. "We are of the border Douglases, but ever since my visit into the Highlands it has been impressed upon me that I might be of service to these poor people. They are in a pathetic plight. All is not as simple as it seems. I was amazed to discover how many of the chiefs who were evicting the crofters—aye, and even the tacksmen—talked as though they were averse to emigration of their victims. I tried to get inside their heads; I tried to be fair to them. I realised that since Culloden the condition of a Highland chief has changed. In the old days he was as a father to the clan. Even the most humble crofter considered that he had the same blood in his veins." A smile passed on his face. "You hear them talking up there of ' forty-second cushins.' "

"I know," said Macdonell, who, being a Highlander, knew well.

"They were all," said Lord Selkirk, "the chief's willing retainers. When he called all answered, whether for foray or defence, but they were answering not only him—they were answering themselves. He and they, in a sense, were as one. Then the old life ended. Culloden rang its knell. This generation of Highlanders does not bear arms."

"Unless for the Sassenach," remarked Macdonell.

"Unless for the Sassenach," agreed Selkirk, "and even when the Highlander bears arms for the Sassenach he does so at the desire of his chief."

"To be rid of him," said the Governor.

"It often seems so," replied his lordship. "But what I was coming to is this: The making of the Caledonian Canal cannot give employment to them all, and after that is finished—what then? Some of them, I gather from my inquiries among them, would as soon go to Georgia as to the canal. I speak from my own experience, Captain. I gave work on my own estate in the borders to some of these folks who were driven out of their small crofts to make room for the sheep. When this idea of a promised land in the west filled my mind I discussed it with some of them."

" With what result?"

" They told me—or almost all told me," replied Douglas, " they would as lief be thousands of miles from home as hundreds. It is a strange thing, but these folks, treated even as they are, seem to retain something that is less love of their land than of a spirit which, it seems to me, it symbolises."

" You have, of course," said Captain Macdonell, " Sir Alexander Mackenzie of the North-West Company against you."

" Yes," said Douglas. " Ecky of the North-West Company has pledged himself to put every stumbling block he can in our way. I am a little hurt," he added, " a little hurt that these Nor'-Westers do not confine themselves to saying that the scheme is ridiculous from the practical point of view, do not confine themselves to saying—even if it be an inaccuracy—that the Red River soil will not grow crops or that depopulation of the Highlands must be prevented. You have read my book so you know what my answer to that is, both by my own statistical researches and by consideration of Mr. Malthus's book on population. Oh, well!"

Miles Macdonell understood what was in his mind.

" It must be galling," he said, " to have them spread the view that you are merely wishing to exploit these people." He meditated briefly a moment and then said he : " As a matter of fact I think it would be excellent to have a settled community at the back door of our late rebellious colonists, a settled community between their back door, so to speak, and the great fur countries."

They had come very close in mutual respect during this talk. The shaft of spring sunshine had drifted across the table, across the map, and left the map. Lord Selkirk bent forward.

" A shadow is on my Red River Settlement," said he. " You will have your work cut out for you, sir."

" I am willing to take the burden, my lord."

II

It was at Stornoway, in the Hebrides, that I joined the expedition, being sent thither to do so by one Captain Roderick who was recruiting for the Settlement Scheme in Glasgow, reporting myself, as I had been advised to do, to Captain Macdonell. My home, by the way, was in Paisley, but in a youthful discontent and ferment, seeking change and escape from much that irked me, to Glasgow I had gone on hearing of the Settlement, of the recruiting for it there, and to offer myself for its service.

In the bay at Stornoway three ships lay anchored, the *Edward and Anne,* the *Prince of Wales,* the *Eddystone,* and beyond them a fourth, the convoy for these on their intended voyage to Hudson Bay, the *King George.* Already, before the voyage had rightly begun, there was trouble. At Sheerness they had lost seven days, waiting for the convoy; out of the Thames they had met adverse winds and put into Yarmouth; putting out of Yarmouth they had been driven back there again by storm; against contrary winds they had arrived at Stromness; and here, at Stornoway, was more trouble, not from the weather but from the men.

All manner of impediments were being put in the way of the fleet's departure, these, by much evidence, at the instigation of the North-West Company, that fur-trading company in rivalry to the Hudson's Bay Company. Its chiefs, with Sir Alexander Mackenzie at their head, were vigorously of opinion that a settlement of farming folk at Red River would mean eventually ruination to their lucrative trade. But at last all intimidations and frustrations were overcome and the fleet set sail.

The Governor, Captain Macdonell—tall, vigorous, with a long stride—I had seen frequently, very busy in his comings and goings between ship and shore during these annoying days, but beyond half a dozen terse words from him when I reported myself as *come aboard* had not had any speech with him. On the evening of the third day at sea, on the *Edward and Anne,* when I was watching the *Eddystone,* fairly close, climbing a hill of water and sliding down into the next hollow, the *Prince of Wales* bowing on her way and, a little way off, His Majesty's ship with a long pennant streaming, he passed down from the poop to the main deck for a brisk walk there, and was on the point of making a rightabout turn when he noticed me standing alone by the windward bulwark.

"What are you thinking, young man?" he inquired, coming to a halt.

"I was just thinking, sir, that we must look to them—the folks on the other ship—very much as they look to us, with the foam spurting over our bow."

"According to what I've been hearing we'll look a bit worse to them," replied Macdonell. "This vessel is what sailors call a tub. Have you ever been to sea before?"

"No, sir."

"Well, I have, many times, and sometimes I have been forced to recall the saying of one of the old voyageurs: 'We are as near to heaven by sea as by land.' How old are you, Baxter?"

"Twenty, sir."

"What are you coming out for?" he inquired with the faintest smile. "To make a way in life for the sake of some girl? Or—er——" he left the rest unspoken, as though awaiting speech from me.

"Really more to get away from one, sir," I answered abruptly.

He looked at me sharply.

"We hear of that often enough in the army," he said. "So you are running away from responsibility."

I was not slow to understand what he meant.

"No, no, sir, not that," said I.

"That's all to the good," said he, as though relieved, and he smiled again. "You have wearied of a fickle fair one?"

A youthful grin, I recall, was all reply I had to that suggestion.

"For myself," he went on, "I married when I was twenty-one. I believe in early marriage when there is true affection—and not only for its steadying effect. There are military commanders who do not care for ensigns or subalterns to be married. They think it makes them chary of risking their lives, but it all depends on the man— and the woman. After all, a soldier's wife knows that her husband is a soldier. She too has to be prepared for a sudden end to happiness."

He considered me from head to foot.

"I have been looking up the lists since getting to sea," he said. "I notice you are down, as you told me when you reported arrival, as a writer. You are down as willing to go on with those who have to prepare the way for settlement at Red River."

" Yes, sir."

" Well, I may have some work for you on the voyage, Baxter. There will be letters to copy and there are various documents that the Earl of Selkirk sent me for perusal that I should like to have copied before returning them to him. That will be something for you to do."

" Do you want me to assist you now, sir, with the copying?" I asked.

" I'll send for you when I want you," he replied, suddenly very much the officer, and wheeled sharply away.

In latitude 59°, 50^n, longitude 17°, 46^w (I made note of it in a small private log I kept), Captain Turner of the *King George* decided he had convoyed the three ships far enough upon their way. Ahead of us would be no dangers of enemy ships, only of the ice floes and the icebergs, and against these we would have to protect ourselves.

Already, by the time the King's ship left us, I had made friends with two young men who were to play their part as definitely as I in the story of the Red River Settlement : John McLeod from Lewis, three or four years older than I, employed by the Hudson's Bay Company, and John Bourke from Sligo, perhaps a year or two my senior, in service of the Settlement. Sailing on into the Atlantic we had a sense then very definitely as of sailing into a new world.

A month later, more than five weeks out of Stornoway, when coming on deck one day I stared into the north with amazement. An extraordinary light lay along the ragged edge of the world there. Between the ships and that horizon, as though elevated above the sea, adrift in air, there was a whiteness that was not of cloud. It might have been a vast cathedral of marble. In the undulations of the sea it slightly rose and fell as though buoyed up by a rising and falling of the air between the sea and it, but as I looked the mirage effect vanished. That white immensity dropped lower and was clearly of a mass of ice coming towards us on the long undulations. I watched that pinnacled ice island enormously drifting past. So engaged was I in contemplation of it that it was as though my spirit landed in a little cove upon its southern side, a sickle cove sculpt and smoothed by the waves. When they receded there was a radiance there of wet prismatic colours; when they swept up again she was just white and

B

glistening. All that day as we sailed north-westward we met other icebergs. There would be a twinkle on the horizon and still one more would rise and grow in bulk and bear down on us, sometimes in doing so achieving again that illusion as of drifting in air.

In late afternoon there was a fluttering of signal flags from ship to ship, with directions regarding procedure in the night—if the word *night* could be used in these latitudes. For as we sailed north the last of the sunset had scarcely faded from the clouds that hung over the western horizon when dawn came eerily up out of the sea to east. It appeared often as though we were tacking into the very precincts of eternal light.

Among this strangeness of sea and sky and the islands of ice I at times thought of my home in Paisley, of the flagged entries, the cobbled streets, the weavers in their windows beside the looms with flying shuttles. I thought of the house I had left, of my mother with her gentle sadness: Long ago, before I could recall, my father had gone away across the Atlantic to one of the American colonies and had never again been heard of. Her husband had gone, said my mother, in the hope of being able to do better there and if his hopes materialised was to send money home for the passages of herself and the two boys—James, then five, and I, then a baby. He must have died there, or have been killed in the forests by some unfriendly natives, she told us; but as I grew older ever and again I wondered if she believed that. A chance remark here, a chance remark there, and something as it were in the quality of her settled melancholy made me surmise that this explanation might be but her public one for our father's absence. As I grew in years I had an impression of her often as a woman not bereaved but discarded. By other chance remarks here, chance remarks there, from relatives, I had come by the opinion that my father had been somewhat of a scapegrace in his youth. There seemed more of determination not to tell me much of him when I made natural inquiries, than of inability to do so. As much by these refusals to speak as by those chance remarks, that suspicion had been increased for me. All that I knew for certain in the matter was that my father had gone to South Carolina, sent word of his safe arrival, and never had been heard of since. Mother made various attempts to trace him but all had failed.

I tried to put myself in her place. Not to know whether the father of her children was alive or dead : there must be a constant agony. To wonder if he was alive and had forsaken his family : there must be deep pain. Often when I came in and found her alone, I surprised sign of recent tears in her eyes.

A poor son I had been to her, I considered. There was no doubt that my brother's criticisms of me were deserved. Pondering on home during the voyage I admitted the truth of much censorious that James had to say regarding me. It was true that so far I had done little— next to nothing—to aid in my mother's support. James had progressed well, had his own cartage business between Glasgow and Paisley, was supporting mother. Nevertheless, I had wished that my brother would not rate me for my failure to obtain regular lucrative work. The charge was sound enough—I could not gainsay it—and the three years of seniority seemed to give James the right to censure; but in course of time, merely to avoid lectures, I became secretive regarding my comings and goings, and James, aware of that, was flattered thereby. My very avoidances of him he considered as tribute. I admired my brother's uprightness and at the same time was irked by his manner of being master over me. For myself, I had no desire to be master over anybody. When homilies were being delivered, I noticed, mother seemed to be on the side of her elder son.

When I was not yet nineteen it was discovered that—in James's word—I was "mooning" over young Janet Lennox, and more joy was tarnished for me. Let me fall short in any way and I would have it flung at me : "What would Janet think if she knew you for what you are?" I felt that there was a lack of grace in stabbing me with the question. But what a young gomeril I must have been! The worth of my devotion may be questioned by the fact that the frequent use of Janet's name made me wish her blue eyes and her dimples had less power over me. And I began to realise that, like James, she had pleasure in finding evidences of her power. In those days I could only understand in others what I experienced in myself, and to lord it over any was not in me. Even so I could have enough, too much, of what I did not understand. Janet's way was to raise my spirits and to dash them. I must never think I had her affection; when I seemed too sure of her she turned chill, she was My Lady Disdain. Once or twice the disdain had been too much for me and I believed myself discarded by her beyond any hope of pleading. Then she knew that she had gone too far and came fluttering back, chirping before me; and she was the one, by her complaints, who had been hurt by chilly treatment, and oh, how could I treat her so?

Thus it was that the announcements of Captain Roderick, appointed agent in Glasgow for the Lord Selkirk Settlement Scheme, had an appeal to me in a low fever! I would be gone from lectures. I would get away from these blue eyes and these dimples that made me too frequently demean myself against my will. Well, that was all over now, even to the last moment's regret when, because of tears in my mother's eyes, I was almost swamped by vacillation, had almost decided to remain at home. It was all over. And I told myself I had acted wisely.

Every day, as the ships voyaged on, I was employed upon the copying of letters and accounts for Captain Macdonell. There was plenty of work for me to do.

III

Head winds in the Atlantic, fog off Greenland and Labrador and in Hudson Strait, pan-ice joggling in the great inland sea of Hudson Bay, made ours the longest voyage in the knowledge of the ship-captains. It was in fact not only the longest passage but the latest arrival in the season so far known. Too late we reached York Factory to undertake the inland voyage that year by the linking waterways to Lake Winnipic and Red River. The journey would be slow because of all we had to take with us. Winter must not catch us on the way.

Not far from the Hudson's Bay Company's fort we built log houses for winter quarters (named Nelson Encampment, being by the side of Nelson River), and all the consolation that Captain Macdonell— Governor Macdonell—had for that irksome delay was that in the winter months, which were chiefly occupied in building boats in preparation for the spring and the thawing of the rivers, he had opportunity to know his men and to decide upon which to take on with him and which to discharge as proven unfit for his service.

It was with a sense of utter relief that on July 6th, sitting in one of the boats going up Hayes River, which thawed earlier than the Nelson by which we had encamped, we looked back and saw the metal roofs of York Factory, glinting in the sun above a cape and a fringe of trees, slowly eclipsed by that cape and forest tip. There were nineteen of us thus cheerfully continuing on our way. The Governor, after the testing of all through the winter by Hudson Bay, had selected twenty-two to go on with him, but three declined. They preferred to try to get work at York Factory or, if they failed to do that, to return home with those discharged, on the evidence they had given of the qualities during the past months, as not likely to make satisfactory helpers.

As far as the Hudson's Bay Company's post on Oxford Lake, Oxford House, we had the assistance of a few Company men who had come down thence to York Factory after the breaking of the ice. At Oxford House we found that there were bulls and cows owned by the Company, the lush grass of the lakeside their fodder, lush grass that turned into natural hay in the fall of the year. Unusual loads we took with us into the Indian Countries, such as hoes and harrows and the like; and some twelve-pounder guns we took also, these last carrying a hint that possibility of need, some day, to defend the Settlement from enemies had been considered. At Oxford House the Governor purchased a bull and a cow from the factor, our boats being large enough to transport them. The progress of our party, with much unwieldy cargo to transport over the portages or " carrying-places " where rapids had to be evaded, could be, you will realise, by no means as speedy as that of the famous Ermatinger's Express that carried no such cargo, by no means as speedy as that of the celebrated swiftly-paddled canoe of the Hudson's Bay Governor, Sir George Simpson, whom I was to meet many years later.

On the last day of August—the year was 1812—we drew in to the bosky bank of Red River, otherwise known as Summerberry River, a little way below where the tributary Assiniboine flows in from west.

CHAPTER TWO

I

IT was near where Assiniboine joins Red River that we were to meet the Hudson's Bay Company's prairie officers, Mr. Sinclair and Mr. Heney, who each summer came there in their carts to get incoming goods and to hand over outgoing bales of furs.

All did not go ashore at once—only the Governor and one or two of his officers. From the boat we watched them greet those who came down not over eagerly to meet them. And soon, though we could not hear a word spoken, we realised that something was amiss. We could see it by Captain Macdonell's pose. He raised his head; he thrust his chin out at the two to whom he spoke there. Mr. Hillier, formerly a lieutenant of the navy but at that time in the service of the Hudson's Bay Company, stood beside him. He had come all the way with us from across the Atlantic formally, at the appointed place, to hand over to our Governor the lands that the Earl of Selkirk had purchased for the Settlement. We saw Mr. Hillier shrug his shoulders and then nod his head up and down. It was as good as hearing him say, " Well, there it is—and it cannot be helped! "

Soon, with disgust in face and bearing, Miles Macdonell and his companions came down the bank again. By their orders the boats were rowed to the east side of Red River, opposite the mouth of Assiniboine, and there we made camp looking across at the North-West Company's fort, Fort Gibraltar.

There was no secret regarding what the officers had heard on arrival. They discussed it frankly, and at times with profanity because of their annoyance, before us. Orders had been sent by the Company in London, as far back as three years earlier, for a supply of pemican, the staple food of the country—dried and pressed buffalo meat which, so treated, keeps almost indefinitely—to be laid in store there against the coming of Selkirk's people. The order had been entirely ignored.

" It is not only ourselves," I heard Captain Macdonell say, " that we have to think of. We may have a party of settlers here almost on our heels because of our delay at Hudson Bay."

"We can only hope," remarked Hillier, "that their ships will be held back as ours were and that they also will have to spend a winter at the Bay. They can be fed there on Company's stores."

"And so increase his lordship's account!" ejaculated the Governor. "It is worse than what is called gross carelessness. It is gross heedlessness. These men had no excuse to offer even—no explanation. It was just, No, they had none. All that interests them is getting their trade goods in and their bundles of pelts out to York Factory, utterly uninterested in us. What can we say about it?"

"We can only say damn 'em and hope, as I remarked, that the immigrants will have to stay at the Bay for the winter and give you a chance to prepare for their arrival next spring."

"Oh, well," sighed Macdonell, "we have met the Hudson's Bay Company's officials in their camp here, and now we shall have to go and make a duty call on the North-Westers at their fort over there—pay our respects. We shall hardly find them less interested in our welfare."

"You may be able to buy pemican from them if they have a store."

"We shall see. Here are some Indians coming. They may help to provide. We may enlist them as hunters and fishermen."

Several Indians appeared close by, in the Indian manner as though suddenly created there. One of them drew nearer.

"How-do? Bo'-jour," said he, as though to let the white man know he was tri-lingual—had at least salutations of two white races as well as his own speech. He was attired in white men's apparel but his hair was in plaits on either side of his head and he wore moccasins. In his ears were shell rings.

"How-do? Bon jour," replied Macdonell, and held out a hand to his visitor. At the post of Jack River on the way he had engaged a Mr. Ishman as interpreter, he knowing both the Cree and Saulteaux tongues, but to have called upon his services then, I realised, would be to insult this linguist.

"You Boston men?" asked the Indian, meaning American as I quickly learnt.

"No!" replied the Governor very definitely with his antipathy to those he still thought of as the rebels. "Not Boston men."

The Indian nodded.

"You Nor'-West?" he inquired.

"No."

"You King George men?"

"Yes, King George men," replied Captain Macdonell.

To our visitor there was evidently a difference between a Boston man and a King George man but a difference also between a Nor'-Wester and a King George man for he remarked: "King George man more good than Nor'-West."

The Governor, I surmised by his expression, did not know whether that was inquiry or statement, and later I heard him say that he wondered if the fact that the North-Westers had followed the old French trade routes made them seem to the Indians, though talking English, less truly King George men than those of the Hudson's Bay Company. But—"Oh, yes," said he, warmly.

"You go far?"

"We stop here."

"Huh!" What that meant neither the Governor nor any of us, listening, could guess. "Maybe your people trade me. What you want? You want fur? You want robe?"

Macdonell wanted neither furs nor buffalo hides then.

"Some pemican," he said. "We want food—eat."

"Plenty whitefish now," answered the Indian, cheerfully.

"That would be good. Whitefish to eat now and maybe you make pemican by and by?"

"Maybe. I not know," and the Indian smiled. Then, as if dismissing all that, he added: "How old you?"

Captain Macdonell must have met Indians before, both in the Canadas and in New York State, and already had noticed, no doubt, what I was to notice later—that after a man has passed his youth they are wontedly curious regarding his age.

"Me forty-three snows," he answered.

The Indian frowned and thought a long while, muttering to himself, "Forty-three—forty-three." Then: "My name Peguis," he announced. "You pass my people's village near lake," and he pointed north.

"I saw tepees, wigwams, but no people," said the Governor. "My name Macdonell."

At that Peguis held out his hand again, considering our Governor with a level appraising gaze. With another of these Indian sounds in his throat he turned suddenly and departed.

"What about the possible pemican? What about the whitefish?" demanded Hillier.

"We'll leave it as it stands, as it lies," replied Captain Macdonell. "He won't forget. He'll be back with some of his people and the whitefish—whitefish, anyhow, I expect to begin with. There they all go off together, talking. He's telling them about us."

I I

It was not until the 3rd of September that at last he managed to get away to pay his respects to the officers of the North-West Company at Fort Gibraltar, near the mouth of the Assiniboine. Each day so far there had been something to prevent the visit, but at last, though time was wearing on, he succeeded. He was accompanied by Mr. Hillier and had John McLeod and myself in attendance. We rowed across Red River in the late afternoon, rounded the knob of bank into the Assiniboine, and landed immediately below the fort.

Up the bank we mounted where it was marked with a gouge of much coming and going and from there had a view of the plain, the wide expanse tufted here and there with clumps of brush and clusters of trees. Fort Gibraltar was set a little way back from the river, a palisaded fort. A few tepees were pitched near the gate and their occupants, with dark eyes, watched us.

"Some *métis* among these, by the look of them," remarked Hillier.

"What are *métis*, sir?" I asked out of my ignorance.

"It is just the French word for half-breed," he explained, "like *Noël* for Christmas," he added with a genial smile. "The French say *métis*, we say half-breed. Same thing. And both, I trust, without reproach, *sans reproche*," and again he smiled.

The gate was open. Beside it I saw a massive *métis* or half-breed in an attire part Indian, part from the trade room—buckskin and fustian. He had a red sash round his waist and from it a pistol butt protruded. He eyed us frowning as we approached.

"Is Mr. Willis within?" inquired Captain Macdonell.

The man cast back his head and lowering his eyelids examined him from top to toe in a manner that annoyed me. Within the palisade were several small houses, one, we discovered later, for the wintering partner (as the North-West Company called those who, in the Hudson's Bay, were styled factors), two for the men, a trading store, two "hangards" or stables, a blacksmith's shop, an ice-house where ice cut from the river was kept for the preservation of their victuals and the cooling of their drinks in summer, and above it a watch-tower that they called, with their French turn, a *guérite*.

The sentry indicated the chief officer's house with a pointing hand, then evidently decided he might leave the gate and announce us.

"Come this way, *messieurs,*" said he. "I shall go with you. What is the name?" he added as we drew near one of the houses.

"My respects to Mr. Willis," replied the Governor. "My name is Macdonell—Captain Miles Macdonell."

The door of the officers' house stood open and the sentry had no sooner stepped within and called, "A Captain Macdonell to see you," than Mr. Willis was on the threshold to greet us. He was a man of medium height, well built, yet with a suggestion of some bodily frailty, of recent, or present, illness in his appearance. That was a hearty enough welcome he gave us. There was no antagonism in his eyes. Somehow we all had the impression that we were expected. We presumed that our arrival had been reported by watching half-breeds and Indians.

"Captain Macdonell," said John Willis, extending his hand. "It is a pleasure to meet you."

"I am glad to be here, sir," replied Macdonell. "Allow me to introduce Mr. Hillier, late of His Majesty's navy, now of the Hudson's Bay Company."

They put their heels together and bowed to each other, then shook hands cordially.

"And one of the Company's young officers," continued the Governor, "Mr. John McLeod."

The physique of John McLeod engaged John Willis's attention. His eyes roved over him as he bowed.

"And Mr. Baxter, my secretary." A secretary, appointed by the Earl of Selkirk, was to come out that year, a Mr. Spencer, but I was so styled temporarily.

It was all, from the point of view of deportment, courtly. These preliminaries over, with a circling of a hand in air almost as though to put it amiably upon Captain Macdonell's shoulder, Willis led us along a corridor in which were odours of meat being cooked. We passed into a comfortable room where two men rose on our entrance.

"I do not know if I need to introduce you," said Mr. Willis. "At least you are namesakes—Captain Macdonell and another Macdonell, Alexander, often called Tête Jaune—Yellowhead."

The Governor smiled.

"Indeed we are related," he replied. "We are cousins, and not only cousins but brothers-in-law. How are you, Alexander?"

"Delighted to meet you, cousin," said Alexander, but there was little evidence, I thought, of friendliness or delight in his eyes.

Yellowhead had his soubriquet with reason, and he carried his head proudly. These Macdonells ran to size. He was as near as tall as our Governor and with quick alert movements—a dashing fellow, as McLeod remarked to me afterwards, talking of that visit.

The other man was heavy and dissipated-looking. A mountain of a man he seemed as he rose. There was a red glint in his eyes that were inclined to be peeping; his nose was short, his upper lip long, his chin heavy. I found him both repellant and interesting.

"And let me introduce Court Nez, one of the free-traders," said Willis. "Just Court Nez—known by no other name on the prairies and desiring no other name. Court Nez—Captain Macdonell of the Lord Selkirk Settlement Scheme, of which you may have heard; and Mr. Hillier, gentlemen, late of His Majesty's navy and now of our rivals," and he smiled tolerantly. "Mr. McLeod, and Mr. Baxter."

"Baxter!" exploded Court Nez, staring at me. "Did you say Baxter?" and he made a fresh scrutiny of me.

"Yes, Mr. Baxter," repeated Willis giving him a glance of anxiety. Court Nez laughed.

"Well, so far as that goes," he rumbled, "why the hell not?"

"Drunk," I considered. "And carries it not as well as might be wished."

"Be seated, gentlemen, be seated," begged Willis. He clapped his hands together and there appeared a young *métis,* by no means subservient of manner though prompt in his attention. "More chairs, Pierre." The chairs were brought and all sat down. "We were just having a dram," Willis continued, "before we dine." He wagged a head sideways at Court Nez and added, in a bantering voice, "He has his drams all the time. The rest of us usually wait till the day is getting on. Your cousin was joining him in one for an appetiser."

"Before you dine!" exclaimed Captain Macdonell, "I had not intended to arrive to pay my respects just before a meal."

"Oh, well, you'll stay to it anyhow," Willis invited him. "By the odours in the corridor it should not be long."

At that moment a girl passed through the room, which had two doors. She put a spell on me. She was clearly a half-breed but she was dressed in white woman's clothes though wearing moccasins which allowed her to enter so silently. Her hair was of a lustrous black, parted in centre, drawn back, and hung on either side of her face in thick plaits. But what caught me most was the velvet softness of her eyes. They met mine in a quick survey of all those who had arrived, and I had the impulse then—so strong that I had to hold myself in my chair to thwart it, so strong that I have never forgotten it—to be up and to follow her. I had heard the phrase "his head reeled" but had had no personal understanding of it till then. Janet Lennox had never affected me thus.

Court Nez raised his great head and laughed raucously.

"What's the joke?" asked Willis.

"Youthful bad manners," answered Court Nez, and casting back his head he laughed again, loudly, to Willis's embarrassment and continued speaking, addressing himself to me : "Aye, you have come to a great country, Mr. Baxter! Wild ducks, buffalo tongues, bear fat, saskatoon berries, fresh whitefish, Indian women. But be careful, young man, be careful."

I then was embarrassed and, I know, reddened. The Governor gave me a quick inquiring inspection while Hillier sounded Court Nez shrewdly and, by his expression, passed the same verdict upon him that I had passed earlier—had him mentally docketed as drunk.

A diversion was created by the entrance of another to introduce, Mr. Willis's chief officer, Benjamin Frobisher. There was again much drawing of heels together and bowing, and we had all just seated ourselves—Frobisher on a stool from under the table, that he found for himself—when the lad Pierre hurried in with more tumblers on a tray which he set down. Willis saw to the charging of the glasses and then, with a lead from him, they were all duly elevated with more bows one to another.

Frankly, to me such ways were somewhat new. I felt awkward but I watched and imitated the procedure. A few minutes later I was aware of the girl passing back, but because of the attention I had brought upon myself earlier at first sight of her, I forced myself to immediate contemplation of a bearskin rug at my feet.

" Can any one tell me," inquired Court Nez conversationally, " why the French half-breeds in this country are so much darker in complexion than the Scots half-breeds?"

" Are they so?" asked Hillier.

" My God, man," said Court Nez, " would I want any one to explain why they are so, if they are not so? *Bois-brûlés* they are sometimes called : burnt wood: charcoal. There you are! But no matter— forget my question. Another sip," and he raised his glass again and gulped.

John Willis turned to our Governor.

" Did you have a fair journey?" he asked politely.

" Not too bad," Captain Macdonell replied. " There was a storm on Lake Winnipic but we had a naval man with us," and he nodded to Hillier, " to give us confidence."

" Your Company has a shorter way than ours to travel into the Indian Countries," said Willis. " York Factory is, I suppose, about a third as far from here as Montreal, our headquarters and port. Of course, because of the length of our journey we break it always at Fort William. Mosquitoes, I suppose, especially ashore at the carrying-places, were your worst trouble?" and he began, merrily descriptive, to slap his cheeks and the backs of his hands as though slaying these pests.

It was obvious to me that he was working hard as a good host. He had felt, I suspected, the antipathy of Alexander Macdonell to us, the new-comers. Alexander, we discovered in course of talk, was visiting him from one of the North-West forts out on the prairie. Willis, I am sure, wished he would not look so sullen on his cousin and these men who had courteously come to pay their respects, and also hoped that his other guest—Court Nez, the free-trader—would not embarrass them further.

" Your Indians up there," said Alexander, " are all more or less subservient—tame. Down here it is a different matter. We have the warlike Dakotas fairly close, and we have the Assiniboines out on the plains. I doubt if they will be pleased to see farmers coming into the country."

At that moment Mr. Willis looked beyond his guests into the corridor, and nodded. Evidently he had received some sign for——

"Well, gentlemen, we will go in to supper," said he.

When we were all seated at table in the dining-room, Willis, as though with his best manners as a host, leant forward and addressed the Governor.

"Tell me," he said, "a little more of what I have only had rumours about so far, chiefly from Mr. Fidler of the Hudson's Bay Company while he was engaged on surveying the land close by. This Selkirk Scheme—tell me of it. The Earl of Selkirk has bought some considerable tract hereaway, has he not?"

"Yes, sir. Roughly, south from the middle of Lake Winnipic and the little Winnipic Lake—or Winnipigosis—to the height of land between the waters running to the Missouri and Mississippi and those running to Hudson Bay; and from the source of the Winnipic River westward to a line drawn down from where the fifty-second parallel intersects the Assiniboine."

"Grand God!" exclaimed cousin Alexander. "He has not bought much! And from whom did he purchase?"

"From the Hudson's Bay Company," answered our Governor, easily.

"The Hudson's Bay Company lays claim to these lands, then—sufficient claim to consider it can sell them?" asked Alexander, while Willis frowned anxiously from one to the other, feeling no doubt, as I did—as indeed I think all who listened felt—that there was a quality as of suave sparring in the talk of these two.

"Oh, surely, yes. By the original charter, cousin. I remember even the words of part of it," and lightly Captain Macdonell chanted : "'And all those seas, straits, bays, rivers, lakes, creeks and sounds, in whatsoever latitude they shall be that lie within the entrance of the straits called Hudson Straits together with all the lands, countries and territories upon the coasts and confines of the seas, straits, bays——' and so forth."

"The charter gives them not ownership but merely trade and commerce, does it not?" persisted Alexander.

"It begins by saying sole trade and commerce," agreed Captain

Macdonell, "but goes on, after having dealt with those matters, to say that the Governor and Company of Adventurers Trading into Hudson Bay are made and created the true and absolute lords and proprietors."

"I am sorry to press the point, cousin," said Alexander, "but did not that charter of the English king specify all straits, sounds, lands and what-not, got at through Hudson Straits not already claimed by any other Christian power?"

Court Nez threw back his head and laughed as though greatly enjoying himself.

"All without by your leave of the Indians," said he.

"Yes, some such words were in the charter," admitted the Governor in answer to his cousin, "words to the effect of '*lands not now actually possessed by any of our subjects or by the subjects of any Christian prince or state.*' The earliest French claim to my knowledge was that of Henry the Fourth of France towards the end of the sixteenth century. I have been refreshing my memory of all that, I may say, since receiving my commission as governor from Lord Selkirk. And I must remind you that it was in the reign of Henry the Seventh of England that Cabot, commissioned by that monarch, sailed out of Bristol and discovered the North American continent— the continent. Henry the Seventh of England well predated Henry the Fourth of France."

"Yes, yes, of course I know all that," said Alexander, and smiled. He seemed to me then amiable enough. "Columbus landed on an island. Cabot landed on the mainland. And, by the way, there is a legend that Norsemen were on the continent even before Cabot. So we might continue this erudite conversation! But what I am thinking of chiefly now is that the North-West Company, which I serve, is in a way successor to the old French traders who were here on these plains under the old régime."

"Yes, I suppose so," said Miles Macdonell. "That no doubt explains why the Indians—who know its history—look upon the Hudson's Bay Company's men as being King George men but do not look so upon the Nor'-Westers."

I saw at once that the terms of that agreement with him annoyed Alexander more than disagreement could have done. His eyes flashed. His body stiffened.

"But of course," added the Governor, "any possible, or impossible, French claims, by the fall of Quebec and the treaty of Utrecht need no longer be considered."

Pierre, who had been attending to the dishes and the plates, at a sign from Willis passed round, refilling the glasses.

"Let us have a toast, gentlemen," suggested Willis, "to the success of Captain Macdonell and his party."

Court Nez chuckled to himself over that. He appeared to be enjoying himself vastly. He rose to his feet, glass in hand. Frobisher and Willis rose also. Alexander looked at them as with contempt, then half-rose. The toast was drunk and when they were all seated again our Governor stood up and bowed graciously to his host and to the others.

"I appreciate the courtesy," he said.

He had hardly seated himself when Alexander spoke again.

"While agreeing with you," said he, "that by the Treaty of Utrecht the French claim went, and seeing it as possible—just possible—that some of the Indians hereabout may still consider the Hudson's Bay people a little more King George's, so to speak, than the Nor'-Westers, I fear you will have trouble with the aboriginal inhabitants who know nothing of the claims of kings of Europe to their land. They are an interesting people, you know. They have communal ideas. That any single individual could own a piece of ground is beyond their comprehension. They tolerate our posts because they are trading posts. Farther west they do not even tolerate posts. A leathern tepee, here to-day and gone to-morrow, is well enough, but to fell trees and build a lodge of wood—no. The tribes of the prairies here will resent any fencing and *No trespass* notices, so to speak. I think you would be well advised to urge your noble employer not to waste his substance on the project."

"Drink up, drink up," begged Mr. Willis, "and let us forget this. After all, as you say, Captain Macdonell, France—whatever it owned once—owns nothing here now, and I have no doubt the earl had legal opinion before completing the transaction."

Pierre, lounging against a sideboard looking on, was again active. The drained glasses he refilled at once. Court Nez emptied his immediately, signed to the half-breed to fill his goblet again, loosened his waistcoat buttons and, with glassy eyes, apparently gave himself up to reverie.

Anon, Alexander seemed to dismiss his captiousness towards his cousin, or at least appeared to hold no personal animus against him.

"By the way," he said, "your elder brother John passed east just shortly before you came."

"I knew he planned to resign this year," said Miles Macdonell, and in his eye there showed gratitude for this change of manner. "I wish I had met him here."

"How extraordin' religious he is," interjected Court Nez dreamily, reflectively, "stopping his canoe-men on Sundays for Mass. Aye, and he knows a good Madeira too. A fine honourable gentleman."

Frobisher and Hillier, I observed, exchanged a humorous semi-blank stare.

"I feel sorry, cousin," said Alexander, "that you are not, as he was, in the service of the North-West Company. It is too bad that you are with our rivals."

"Comfort yourself, cousin," replied our Governor, smiling and trying to return what might be sign of friendliness with sign of friendliness, "that I am not exactly with your rivals. I am here on behalf of Lord Selkirk to prepare the way for his settlers."

"That is worse still," declared Alexander, his voice acid again. "I wonder why he purchased such a large chunk of land? Does he expect to put farmers on all that at once?"

"I believe to begin with, and certainly for some time to come, there will be only a strip settled along the fertile bank of Red River, or Summerberry River as I believe some still call it," Captain Macdonell told him.

"Even so it is too bad, too bad! Farming is utterly opposed to fur-getting. I am sorry you have become involved in that foolhardy scheme."

Then it was that I felt suddenly, for myself, distracted and distressed, for as I looked round the table all who sat there were abruptly duplicated in my vision. I lost part of the conversation, but was brought back to it by Court Nez. There was something about this man that increasingly both fascinated and repelled me.

"Do these settlers of my lord Selkirk," he asked, "have to believe in the existence of the Holy Trinity?"

c

I tittered. I thought the question was merely in the nature of drunken nonsense and was, I suppose, by my own condition, in a mood to appreciate it.

"Wasn't that extraordinary of Lord Baltimore?" said Captain Macdonell. I wondered what he meant.

"He did that?" inquired Willis.

"Yes. In founding his settlement he had a stipulation that the settlers must believe in the Trinity. Lord Selkirk," he went on, with some dignity in his voice, addressing himself directly to Court Nez, "is one of the most broad-minded men I have met, and the most tolerant. He did me the honour to discuss every conceivable angle of the scheme with me. There is to be entire religious liberty. According to the creeds of the farmers they will be ministered to."

Court Nez began to laugh without opening his mouth, just shook, heaved, with suppressed mirth. Mr. Willis made a great show of interest.

"Well, cousin," said Alexander, "be he broad-minded or no, it seems to me he plans the beginning of the end of the fur trade."

"My dear Alec!" exclaimed the Governor. "Think of the extent of the land, the vastness of the land."

I pulled myself together and had no difficulty in thinking of the vastness of the land. I was filled with a sense of its vastness, aware of expansive Rupert's Land round me. Then I found that all were rising. There was much putting of heels together again and bowing. Alexander bowed stiffly. Court Nez ("known by no other name on the prairies, and desiring no other name," Mr. Willis had said when introducing him to us), with tumbler in hand stood in the middle of the room, a smile on his face that almost hid his small eyes in creases.

Mr. Benjamin Frobisher came to the door with us. Mr. Willis accompanied us to the palisade where I had a desire, I remember, to ask if the gates there, as at York Factory, were closed every night at eight o'clock, to prove to them, if they suspected otherwise, that I was sober. Then I said to myself, "No matter, no matter." We were bowed out with polite words of thanks for the entertainment by Captain Macdonell and Mr. Hillier, polite expressions of pleasure in having had them to entertain from John Willis.

"I trust you will be able to come over to-morrow," said Captain Macdonell, "to see the ceremony of taking seizen."

"Taking seizen?" inquired Mr. Willis.

"Yes, sir. Mr. Hillier here, in the Hudson's Bay service, and with the rank of magistrate, is to deliver over formally to me on behalf of the Governor and Company of Adventurers of England Trading into Hudson Bay, and I have to take over on behalf of Lord Selkirk. I propose to have the ceremony at noon. I shall be delighted to welcome you to witness it, and any of your officers you would desire to have accompany you."

III

In lack of any straight pine or fir such as we had seen, plentifully, northward, we had to be content with a slender young aspen as flag-pole for that ceremony of September 4th. William Hillier saw to the felling of it, the lopping of its branches, the peeling of its bark, and fitted it atop with a pulley.

Indians, their interest aroused by the search for that tall and slender tree, gathered round to watch the proceedings like children at a fair. Some of our men found occasion to catch the dark eye of a woman here and there and wink to her. The response was sometimes a drooping of eyelids and a sudden retreat, sometimes a coy glint and a giggle, sometimes a glare like promise of murder.

Hillier ran a halliard through block or pulley and the pole was elevated. While that work was in progress Chief Peguis arrived, slow of motion, benign, yet with an air, I thought, of giving the rule.

"What you do now?" he asked.

"Put up flag," replied Captain Macdonell.

"King George man flag?"

"Yes, King George man flag, and Hudson's Bay Company," the Governor told him.

"Hudson Bay. Good."

The time drew near for the ceremony—and for John Willis and other officers from Fort Gibraltar to be with us, if our invitation was to be accepted. Out through the mesh of bankside foliage of oak and elm we all looked hopefully. Yes, there came a canoe from the mouth of the Assiniboine. White men were in it.

During the winter at Nelson Encampment, Captain Macdonell had given us military drill, to which some had objected, but those who definitely refused to accept it he had left behind at York Factory as unsatisfactory, to return across the Atlantic. We at Red River with him could at least shoulder arms, present arms, form fours, form two deep, form fours, be as we were—and so forth. A smart little body of men we may perhaps have looked but I knew that many were amused at the rôle we played. There we stood by in readiness to give the ceremony the authentic military touch that our Governor desired.

"Now, men," said he, "we want this to be well done. Our friendly rivals of the North-West Company will be witnesses to our ceremony of taking seizen."

Already more Indians, accompanied by *métis* or half-breeds, had come along through the bush, realising that something out of the usual was afoot there, and were looking on wide-eyed. John McLeod had been given charge of the twelve-pounders with which a salute was to be fired. I was in the nature of a sergeant beside the saluting party.

Up the bank from the canoe came Willis, Frobisher, and Captain Macdonell's cousin, Alexander. The Governor and Hillier went down to meet them. Court Nez, I noticed, was not there. We were to see and hear more of him—much more—later, and through him I was to hear of my lost father (oh, more than that, indeed!) as in due course you shall hear. As he was not an officer of the North-West Company, Willis had not extended the invitation to him. On the farther side of Red River, the side from which they had come, the west side, upon the bluff, knots of people were visible, gathering there. We were told afterwards that the servants at Fort Gibraltar had been instructed not to come over.

As the visitors drew near I turned to the group that stood at ease, winked at them, and in the manner decreed by Captain Macdonell rasped, "At-tention!"

There was something as of observing ambassadors in the deportment of these North-Westers as they approached.

"Shoulder arms!" I rasped.

Captain Macdonell would have been depressed could he have got inside my head at that moment and known my thoughts. It was

pleasant enough to watch these evolutions being performed with
precision, but I perceived a touch of the ludicrous in them.

"Present arms!" I ordered.

The officers clustered there by the pole while we stood rigid, eyes
front. I was aware of the river flowing past and of high white clouds
sailing over, of some heedless half-breed children playing among the
bushes and of Sinclair and Heney (the local officers of the Hudson's
Bay Company) drawing near—with something of moodiness, thought
I, in their manner, due perhaps, I hazarded, to their clear knowledge
of what the Governor thought of the failure to have a store of
pemican—as ordered—awaiting his arrival. Chief Peguis, bowing
with dignity to all gathered there, joined the party.

I was impressed by the diversity of attire in that gathering. There
were long-tailed, high-collared blue coats, brass-buttoned, and coats
with capots, hooded coats. The capot, of course, at that season hung
down the back. The *métis* had a marked tendency to complete their
dress, whether of broadcloth or of buckskin, with a bright scarf round
the waist—with long ends, tasselled. Buffalo-hide leggings were worn
by many of the watching full-bloods, hip high, and long fringed skin
tunics. Some had a softly tanned buffalo robe over a shoulder and
under an arm, adding to the suggestion of toga and the Roman
aspect. Some had taken to wearing our calico shirts over the high
leggings in the same manner that they would have worn a deerskin
coat. One or two, I noticed, Peguis, for example, and Ouckidoat (a
chief who had come in from the prairie to see the new-comers) were
entirely dressed in white men's clothes which they had donned just
as we would, shirt-tails tucked in; but they kept their hair in braids,
did not discard ear-rings, and had refused the foot-constricting shoe,
retaining moccasins. One or two of the white men also wore
moccasins instead of shoes. The moccasin is the last thing an Indian,
imitating the invaders, discards and the first thing a white man,
imitating the aborigines, adopts.

"Well, gentlemen," said Hillier in that cheerful way of his, "it
was kind of you to come over to witness the ceremony," and he took
a crisp parchment roll from his pocket, opened it, glanced at John
McLeod who stood beside the twelve-pound swivel guns, and then
began to read: "*Between the Governor and Company of Adventurers of England Trading into Hudson Bay of the one part and the*

Right Honourable Thomas Douglas, Earl of Selkirk, on the other part WHEREAS . . ."

In the distance the voices of the half-breed children at play rose and fell. The hissing and gurgling of Red River threaded the day. Looking round on the faces of those who had arrived to see what was afoot, Hillier suddenly realised that some Frenchmen were there, either free-traders or voyageurs of the North-West Company—perhaps both—and that many of the half-breeds must be French half-breeds. From his explanation to me of the meaning of the word *métis* he no doubt knew French but instead of translating for himself he turned to Mr. Heney.

"Would you, sir," he requested, "be so kind as to translate as I go along?"

"With pleasure," replied Heney.

Ishman—he who had come from the Jack River post at the north end of Lake Winnipic as interpreter to the Indians—was there also but it did not occur to Hillier to ask him to translate to the few full-bloods present.

At the words come to anon : ". . . *absolute lords and proprietors of all these lands* . . ." I noticed Benjamin Frobisher glance at the flame-headed Alexander with, it seemed to me, a twinkle in his eyes. He appeared to be amused at the grim expression on Alexander's face.

Hillier came to the final sentences and, as Heney uttered them again in French, nodded to John McLeod who, stepping to the halliard, raised and broke the flag. As it fluttered on the wind——

"Present arms!" I ordered the men, who had again been at attention after saluting the North-West officers.

Smartly they presented arms before the flag, and as they did so those beside the twelve-pounders let loose their booming salute—causing one of the half-breed women to jump all of two feet from the ground and then to laugh at herself, clapping a hand to her mouth. The last boom sounded.

"At—ease! Dis-miss! Break—off!"

Round a ready keg of rum all gathered. Pannikins were produced and, with a roll of the eyes to the fluttering flag above, toasts were drunk. The onlookers drew closer and had their share. Then the North-Westers, having witnessed this ceremony of taking seizen, seemed not desirous to prolong their stay. Together hosts and guests went down under the flutter of oak and elm leaves to the riverside. Willis, Frobisher, and Alexander Macdonell stepped into their canoes. Our Governor and Hillier came slowly up the bank towards us, talking quietly together. The rum keg provided for the men and the onlookers was empty.

" What you do now?" asked Peguis.

" We build lodge now," said Captain Macdonell. " We build lodge for men. We go look good place."

Peguis realised that he, too, ought to go, that it might be a loss to his dignity to stay.

" I tell my people come trade you whitefish," he promised, and without a good-bye, accompanied by Ouckidoat, the other chief who had come to see the ceremony, departed.

The half-breeds and Indians who still remained, hopeful perhaps for the opening of another keg, understood that the show was over and drifted away.

" Whitefish—whitefish!" exclaimed Captain Macdonell. " A stopgap, that is all."

He looked after the Hudson's Bay Company's regional officers who were moving away a trifle sheepishly—and no wonder, I considered! Hillier read his expression.

" Thanks to them, no pemican," he said.

" Thanks to them. Oh, well, it simply means that we shall have to move most of the men sixty miles south to Pembina for the winter. For some reason the buffalo don't come and winter at all in the occasional bush-tracts near here, as one might expect them to, but prefer to be up on the plateau or along what is called the coteau. One would think it would be too bleak for them there, but there they are. I recall hearing once from my brother John that they have even been seen rubbing their backs against the logs of the trading post there. The majority of our lads will have to go to Pembina and turn buffalo hunters with the *métis*. Some of them will remain here to build and we must at once, while there is natural hay handy, gather fodder for the bull and cow."

" September, October," murmured Hillier, as though to himself.

" Yes," replied Captain Macdonell. " September, October, November, December: winter is not very far off." He looked up at the sky. " But this is a good land so long as one knows how to cope with its climatic changes. I wonder if the first settlers are coming in this year or are staying at Hudson Bay."

He stopped speaking. His gaze hardened as he looked over the river through the mesh of leaves, across to the mouth of Assiniboine. There was that in the puckering of his eyes that told us all not only thoughts of pemican lacking made his chin set grimly.

Where he looked we all looked—across the bronze flow of Red River—and saw a canoe, one of the long, light canoes, dart out of the Assiniboine and turn down Red River. The men who sat in it were digging in their paddles in swift unison. In the drift of the river they went quickly upon their way. Hillier, representing the Company in the recent ceremony, and Governor Miles Macdonell, who had taken seizen on behalf of Lord Selkirk, stood silent, watching. No one spoke till the canoe had disappeared round the first bend. Then——

"How far do you think they are going?" asked Hillier.

"To Fort William," replied Captain Macdonell.

"And their errand?" inquired Hillier, but only, thought I, for confirmation of his own suspicions.

"To send word to the Montreal partners of their Company that we have arrived," said our Governor in a hard voice.

CHAPTER THREE

I

ON the west side of the Red River, below Assiniboine, a prairie fire had recently run and burnt out the bush. On that triangle of land between these rivers, a triangle at the point of confluence, protected on both sides as it were by the deep moat of both streams, we started to build. There was a cabin already there belonging to the Hudson's Bay Company, and another building close to it that had been used as a smithy. Peter Fidler, I was told, had lived in the cabin when making his surveys for Lord Selkirk's purchase; but many more dwellings were required by Captain Macdonell.

Diverse were our duties. Some were felling and hauling trees, others building cabins with these; others again were ploughing, hoeing, sowing winter wheat, harrowing on the lands to be allotted to the settlers when they came.

On the 27th of October I accompanied the Governor some way down river from Point Douglas, in search of some of Peter Fidler's survey posts. That was the name he had given to the promontory on Assiniboine's north bank and Red River's west. It was his intention, autumn wearing on, to start the erection of individual small cabins on the farm allotments, cabins that would be at least temporary homes for the settlers.

Suddenly we stood still and raised our heads, listening.

" It sounds like sheep, sir," said I.

" Sheep! Well, it does, but how——"

The sound that had arrested us came again.

" That was the bleating of sheep," I declared.

" Sheep—AND—bagpipes!" exclaimed Miles Macdonell.

With his long stride he led the way to the bank; and there we saw them coming—the first settlers. In the leading boat a man was playing on the pipes.

" One—two—three——" I found myself counting the boats as they came round the bend, " four—five——"

" There are the sheep we heard," said the Governor, and sure

41

enough in two of the boats I saw the woolly backs, and the black mouths from which came the plaintive wavering cries. Eleven boats and three canoes made the total.

" Well, there they are!" said Captain Macdonell. " They are here, which is better for them than wintering by Hudson Bay even if we lack the needed staple of pemican for them."

Half an hour later, on that triangle of land, seventy-one men, women, and children were safely landed and seemed all to be raising their voices together in a hubbub of Gaelic and Erse (for a few were from Ireland), some in rejoicing, some in lamentation.

II

With the boats came a letter from my mother in which she told me they were greatly perturbed because of certain articles they had been reading in several journals about the folly of Lord Selkirk's scheme. Other news she gave me also: of the marriage of my brother James to Janet Lennox.

To Janet! My chief reason for leaving home I could not name for certain. Partly I had wished to be free of my elder brother's suzerainty; partly I had wished to emancipate myself from my own tantalising vacillation over the distracting Janet.

So brother James had married her! Well, it served him ri—no, even on the point of saying so, " served him right," a sense of blood being thicker than water made me stop, and—" Poor James," said I to myself. Would she in the end, I wondered, break him, or would he in the end break her? Or would they live the sort of cat and dog life that perhaps both enjoyed? For myself such a life would not be enjoyable but, recalling each of them, it seemed that perhaps they would find a harsh inexplicable pleasure in it. Poor James!

And then I laughed, laughed at myself. For some time before leaving home, so constantly was I called to account, haled to the domestic court, there had been growing in me a tendency to search my actions for possible censorable points. I had left just in time, I think, to be saved from settled self-distrust. Had I stayed longer I might have begun to recant my every statement, repent my every action, and become intimidated into a constant perching on the stool of repentance. But I laughed at myself then, thinking of how little

more than a year after having fled—and fled with a divided mind!—
from the infatuating Janet, my whole being had been shaken by the
mere glimpse of another girl as she passed through a room in which
I sat.

Often since that evening at Fort Gibraltar I had hoped to see the
half-breed girl again. In what spare time I had I frequently walked
across the plain and dallied past the gates of Fort Gibraltar, or rode
that way on a horse borrowed from some Indians after learning something of horsemanship, feeling sufficiently confident in the saddle.
The disturbance in me was always feverishly renewed on these expeditions, the object of which was to have at least another glisk, another
glimpse of her.

III

These were busy days not only for the labourers but for the clerks,
the writers. One of the new buildings had been turned into an
administrative office and there I spent great part of my time in
making entries regarding the allotments of land to the settlers and
the supplies advanced to them, but I had also to be out and about
frequently along the stretch of Settlement northward, assisting in
the verification of boundary lines with Mr. Fidler's maps and his pegs.
It had been Lord Selkirk's wish, on hearing of the topography there-
away, to have long and narrow allotments; the arable and larger
part of each was on the west bank, the clearer bank; the short strips
to east of the river, densely wooded, would provide fuel.

It was soon explained to those who had just come that, owing to
the lack of a supply of pemican, it would be necessary for most to go
to Pembina for the winter.

"That is sixty miles, you say! Why so far as that?" one asked.

"To be near the source of supply of buffalo meat," the Governor
replied, "on which we shall have to rely for sustenance till spring."

"Couldn't it be carted here to us while we go on with the
building?"

"Some of you will remain here," said Miles Macdonell, "but you
do not realise that the winters are sometimes hard. I cannot run the
risk of having everybody sixty miles from the food supply. Winter
transport is at times uncertain."

The Indians were very friendly to the settlers, would stand solemnly watching them at work on their houses and then begin to assist without any comment save occasional grunts and smiles and nods. Despite their friendliness many of the women-folk were adread of them. Before taking to the boats at York Factory, it appears, they had been served, for the fun of making them apprehensive, with terrifying stories of the natives by Red River. Some of them, therefore, were under the impression that all such acts of friendliness were but cunningly ingratiating to prepare the way for an easy massacre.

A mile from the new buildings on Point Douglas a family named Chisholm soon established themselves, and perhaps because they spoke English as well as Gaelic—which I did not understand—I often stopped to talk to them when commissions carried me along the new road. Hugh Chisholm was a man in his forties then who had been in the Lowlands in some sort of factory work and, hearing of the opportunity to own a piece of the earth, had emigrated with his dubious, questioning wife, and his two daughters: Mairi, eighteen, and Agnes, sixteen.

It was evident to me, practically from first contact with them, that Mrs. Chisholm was definitely assured that they had come to a sorry promised land. There was a look at times in her eyes as of dementia. Apprehension and anger lit them. Her husband, at least for the time being, had seemingly lost his Christian name and she could not find it. He was but " You!" or " Oh, you!" The girls had their own gaiety to sustain them; but it was clear to me that in their mother's estimation (whatever the cause) the elder, Mairi, could do little right and the younger, Agnes, could do no wrong. The two girls were not much alike in appearance. Mairi was slight and fair-skinned, Agnes was plump with roguish eyes and dark brown hair.

After the sea-voyage and inland-voyage, Mrs. Chisholm was ragged. She made no attempt to hide from strangers her belief that her husband was mentally deficient and had proved himself so by coming to such a place. Indeed there were moments, to judge by his face, when she won him to her view of him! The gaiety of the girls was then his only comfort.

These new-comers had been brought across the Atlantic and through the wooded and scented wilderness, where loons called across lonely lakes as I often remembered and the mosquitoes tormented, in the care of one Owen Keveny—under his despotic rule, said some whom he called unruly. With him came John Spencer, the secretary engaged in England for Captain Macdonell, of whom I had been told when appointed temporary secretary. But on the removal of the majority to Pembina, Mr. Spencer was to be left as deputy-governor, or sheriff, as he was styled, at Point Douglas, to look after the welfare of those who would be remaining there. The work of these people would be chiefly the building of houses on the allotments; but the bull and the cow would be tended by them during the winter, and they would also look after the imported Spanish sheep that they had brought with them across the Atlantic, up the rivers, across the portages, down Lake Winnipic, bleating through the wilderness: sixteen ewes and four rams. They would have to see, too, that neither wolves nor dogs got them.

These were busy days. Captain Macdonell had to make frequent visits to Pembina to arrange with those there—chiefly French half-breeds—for pemican to be supplied to him, and to have cabins built for the shelter of his charges. On these expeditions I accompanied him, bumping along beside him in my first efforts in horsemanship. Here and there on the way between Point Douglas and Pembina he saw to the erection of stages, platforms raised high on poles above the prairies on which food could be left beyond the reach of leaping wolves. He knew the possibility—or probability—of blizzard on the prairies. Those whose duty would be to sledge food from Pembina to the workmen at Point Douglas and on the allotments, must have *caches* of food along the route for themselves lest at any time they were storm-bound on the way.

During this period I was finding that the best way to have relief from the torment of not again seeing that lovely dark-eyed half-breed girl was to go along the new road to see the Chisholms who were living in the temporary shelters that Indians had helped them to build—wigwams of bark. The gentle gaiety of Mairi helped me, the badinage of hoydenish Agnes. Mairi's high spirits might sometimes, on my arrivals, be at low ebb if she had been recently unjustly reprimanded for this or that by her mother, but always, before my departures, it would be triumphant again. Flashes from her grey eyes, and laughter in Agnes's, somehow atoned to me for no further encounter with those dark eyes.

IV

Chief Peguis, when the time drew near for the great flitting, came to inquire anxiously of the Governor : " You go Pembina?"

" We come back," Miles Macdonell assured him, not understanding the cause of the anxiety in his voice.

" I not mean that," said Peguis. " I not like this thing. I think maybe good thing if you have some braves go along, some warriors. I think maybe all right, but I think also maybe trouble."

" Trouble? What kind of trouble?"

" Maybe other Indian," explained Peguis. " Not good too many woman and papoose all alone. Maybe other Indian," and with a gesture that was characteristic of his race he pointed off into the south-west. It was significant. It suggested that he was aware of the vastness of the land, aware of the curve of the world.

The Governor required no further elucidation of Peguis's anxiety, and neither did I. We knew of what tribes the chief warned us. Captain Macdonell's brother John had left a letter for him, on his way east that year, with one of the Hudson's Bay Company's men— they who should have had a store of pemican in readiness for us. That letter, which he showed to me, strongly advised adherence to the original plan of settlement, stated that not only did the best lands lie between " the forks or junction of the Red and Assinibouan Rivers and Lake Winnipick, a distance our canoe-men reckon twenty leagues," but also that it was a stretch of country fairly safe from the incursions of the Sioux Indians. It was from these Sioux, otherwise the Dakota Indians, to the south and south-west, that Peguis thought it possible that the settlers, on their way to Pembina, might have to be protected.

" I would give your warriors something," said the Governor.

" Oh, maybe some you give *régale*," suggested Peguis, " if you want," he added. " Some like *scoutaywaubo*."

That was the word, in the tongue of his tribe, for firewater. The *régale* was the tot of rum given to boatmen or paddlers after an arduous portage or an arduous day.

The half-breeds at Pembina we had found friendly on our visits. They seemed eager to provide buffalo meat during the winter for the settlers, and their terms were not unreasonable. Of the half-breeds westward on the prairie Captain Macdonell told me he was doubtful, from various remarks made by his cousin Alexander that he suspected were very possibly not merely dissuasive—wet-blankets to settlement ideas—without foundation. He was, in fact, he said, more doubtful of them than of the full-bloods farther west. Of the local tribes— the Crees of the district and the Saulteaux (Chippewa)—he had no doubts. Their friendliness to the King George men was manifest.

So it was that with a convoy of Indians the party for Pembina set out; and it was on that journey events occurred which served as a nucleus for stories to be disseminated in Scotland regarding the terrorisation of the Selkirk settlers by the natives.

The journey was undertaken in rough carts, those two-wheeled carts made by the half-breeds of the neighbourhood without aid of any nail, without iron in any part: the Red River carts. Some of the immigrants were philosophical over this new move, others melancholy. At first the way was westward, beyond the North-West Company's fort, to a ford of the Assiniboine. Thence it continued fairly direct south to Pembina. In the night camp on the way melancholy was apparently ousted. Beside twinkling fires the pipers strutted.

On the second day the caravan was strung out in a long line across the prairie. Despite the superficial aspect of flatness there, undulations existed. Carts far in advance disappeared, sank from sight, appeared again. The sound of their passage was deafening, a high, shrill squeal as the wooden axles revolved. As the long queue laboured on, the French half-breeds at Pembina must surely have heard us approaching before they had sight of us.

Long before we reached our destination, while we were thus strung out loosely, snaking across the plains, I noticed some Indians—or people that at the time I took for Indians because of hawk-feathers in their hair, paint on their faces—apparently agitating the occupants of one of the carts. I rode inquiringly closer and saw one of those in the painted and feathered group stretch a hand to a woman who sat beside the driver, pluck up the edge of her shawl, examine its pattern.

" You give me," I heard him say.

The driver, who was her husband, turned his head doubtfully.

" You give me," said the Indian again.

In the Gaelic, of which, as I say, I knew nothing save "Good-day," husband and wife exchanged some words and then——

"I suppose," said he to me, "it might be wise to let him have it, whatever?"

"I do not see it so," I replied. "The chief offered that his Indians should accompany us for our safety. I shall see Peguis. He is riding somewhere ahead with the Governor."

At the name *Peguis* these intimidating fellows wheeled away, laughing as over some private mirth, and then suddenly letting out wavering whoops put their horses to the gallop and went riding across the prairie with a dull drumming tattoo of hoofs. Their conduct puzzled me greatly.

After we arrived at Pembina I saw another woman weeping bitterly and the two Chisholm girls, Mairi and Agnes, among others, trying to comfort her. The Governor at that moment rode close to discover what was amiss. It seemed the woman had, fearfully, given her wedding ring to an Indian who admired and demanded it. Captain Macdonell requested details. Her husband answered him.

"What could we have done? What else could we have done?" he asked. "I did not want to bring trouble on the whole party. All might have been murdered. I am no coward," he added, because of the way Macdonell looked at him. "No, I am no coward, but I did not want to precipitate trouble. Besides, the cart in which we rode had fallen behind those in front a considerable distance. The one behind us was lagging so as to let others overtake it. These painted savages surrounded us."

"Could you not have shouted?" asked the Governor.

"The scream of these damned wheels," replied the man, protestingly, "would prevent any shout for help being heard."

They were in the midst of that discussion, the woebegone woman leaning against the side of the cart from which she had alighted, drying her eyes, when it was clear the Indian chief as well as the white chief had troubles. There was Peguis surrounded by several of his warriors and braves, all excitedly talking. Governor Macdonell looked at him reproachfully, disappointed in him. Peguis had offered to accompany us lest we were attacked by a prowling band of Sioux and it looked as though he lacked control over his own people.

Miles Macdonell was then afoot. He had given his horse into the care of one of his servants. He walked slowly towards Peguis. The chief, dismounting and leading his horse, walked towards Miles Macdonell. Without rancour—for he had no desire to allenate Peguis as I knew—the Governor told what had happened to the woman who stood there. Expressionless the chief listened. He waited for Captain Macdonell to finish. Then he shook his head.

"No, not my people," he said. "My people tell me now some white people"—to him half-breeds were evidently white people but next moment he realised they were not so to us and corrected himself—"some half-white people put feathers in head, paint face, make look like Indian, come and try to frighten your people."

As if to prove the truth of what he spoke there came then from the distance shrill yelping and wavering cries. We all looked round, out to the prairie, in the direction from which they came. There, on one of those low ridges of the superficially seeming flatness, was a line of mounted men. They were aware, no doubt, that at that place they would be seen against the sky. The wavering, yelping cries came shrilly on the wind. Then the riders all galloped out of sight.

"Not my people," said Peguis again.

"Dakota?" asked the Governor.

"No, no. White people—half-white people. Nor'-West Company half-white people."

The Governor turned to me.

"As far back as at Stornoway," said he, "we had evidence of the North-West Company instigating actions against us, and now——" he ended there.

"You do not think, sir, that Mr. Willis would incite the *métis* against us?" I asked.

"No, not Willis," said he, "nor Frobisher either, but——" and again he left a sentence unfinished.

I knew he was thinking of his cousin Alexander, strong partisan, as had been clear at that dinner-table in Fort Gibraltar, of the North-West Company. Alexander Macdonell's trading post was out on the prairies westward beside a considerable body of *métis* whom, no doubt, he could easily influence.

As for that wedding ring—lest any wish to know—it never came again to its owner. Captain Macdonell spoke to his cousin about it later, tactfully, when Yellowhead visited Pembina—spoke not as

D

though impeaching him of having any faintest responsibility for the affair but to have his opinion as to whether the woman might hope to have her ring again. Alexander expressed aloof sympathy with "the poor thing" and said that when he went out to Qu'Appelle again he would "speak to Cuthbert Grant out there." Grant, he explained, had "considerable influence" over the *bois-brûlés* and might be able to recover it. But no, it never came again to its owner; and one may fancifully invent what future history one will for that wedding ring.

CHAPTER FOUR

I

PEMBINA: a North-West Company fort, a collection of log cabins, leather tepees, bark wigwams, sixty miles south of the confluence of the Assiniboine and Red Rivers.

There, under the direction of John McLeod, with whom I had made friends on the sea-voyage, a post for the Hudson's Bay Company had been built called Fort Daer and, at the same time, more cabins, these to shelter the settlers close to the buffaloes' winter grounds. Some had no windows. Some had windows of parchment, pieces of skin scraped amazingly fine and stretched across the spaces left for them. When it was raining, or there was moisture in the air, they relaxed somewhat and on dry days tautened. Occasionally, when the sun had been warm on the outside, or the stove hot within, the parchment would emit a small *ting*! It reminded me in a way of the sound the river made before Nelson Encampment in the spring when the ice was cracking. It was as a faint, far echo of that.

McLeod and his party had worked well. I know that Captain Macdonell would have rejoiced to have him in the Colony service but he was a Company officer and soon after the installing of the settlers who were to winter there he went off, by orders of Heney (who in those days had the management of the Company's affairs in that district) with another Hudson's Bay man, Bostonois Pangman, as interpreter, he speaking the Cree tongue and the Assiniboine—which is the same as the Dakota—to establish a trading post by Turtle River.

I was glad that Mr. Spencer had been given the position of assistant-governor for thus, while he remained at Red River in charge of the winter activities there, I continued my secretarial work under Captain Macdonell at Fort Daer, Pembina. Often, when we were alone, the Governor would relax, suspend his authoritative manner. At the back of his mind all the time was anxiety regarding the supplies for his people—the supply of that staple of pemican. Not only those he had brought there, close to the hunting grounds, had to be

considered but those at " the forks." These *métis,* he said, seemed to
him too carefree. On the fringes of the village were tepees of Indians
and *thud-thud, thud-thud* went the drums out there night after night.
Always they were dancing. In Pembina itself the fiddles of the half-
breeds were playing, accompanied by other drums. The full-bloods
had not adopted the violin but the half-breeds had retained the
tom-tom.

The verve of these dances was extraordinary. In one of the larger
cabins the women sat round the walls while the men clustered in the
middle and violins began to play, drums to beat. Wrapped in their
shawls or blankets the women kept time to the rhythms where they
sat, shoulders swaying; and the men pirouetted, pranced about for
a time, tapped out the beat with moccasined feet, advanced to claim
a partner, gave her a little bow in the manner of white men, then
flinging out a hand snatched her up and away they would go in the
most vigorous jig imaginable. When, after watching them, I went
out from the heat into the prairie air I would hear the other music
from farther back in the history of the world, before fiddles, an
agitating pulse—the drums of the dancing full-bloods camped close by.

That music variously affected different hearers. To Miles Macdonell
I know it was as if the violins and drums joined together in a plaint
of *No pemican, no pemican, no pemican.* Would these people never
get out to the promised hunting? *No pemican! No pemican!* To
some of the young men who had complained of Owen Keveny
that he was despotic, those whom he had considered unruly, the
sounds of that music in the evenings was exciting. With proper
negotiation, they thought, they might have more than dancing, might
lure away a wild partner into the riverside brush. The *thud-thudding*
of the Indian hand drums sometimes caused a look of dread, I noticed,
to show on the face of a woman here and there. Assuredly they had
come into a new world, and they were not at ease in it, were apprehensive. *Thud-thud, thud-thud, thud-thud:* there was something in
that sound—especially when voices came with it, rising, rising, higher,
higher as more fervently the drums beat in the full-bloods' camp—that
was positively alarming to them.

For me there was more appeal in the drums and voices than in the
violins alone. Their rhythms moved me deeply, strangely. I felt that
they belonged to antiquity on these plains. They were very old. They

told of æons, æons of such nights and of the generations that had once danced to them and were gone. What an amazing response my throbbing heart gave to these throbbing drums, how poignantly the chanting voices moved me. I was on the edge of a world of which I would fain know more. Assuredly I, at any rate, had come into a new world.

II

It was by Captain Macdonell's desire that I went farther into that world. The Governor explained the situation to all, though to be sure few of us needed explanation again.

"We must have buffalo meat," he told us. "It is absolutely essential. I have no right to demand of any of you young men who were engaged as labourers or writers to do such work as buffalo hunting, but I should like as many as possible to go out with these half-breeds to the hunt. I simply ask for volunteers."

So it was that some days later I rode out of Pembina with a party going westwards to the buffalo hunting. A young *métis* of about my own age or a year or two older, whom I knew but by the name of Jules, had attached himself to me in a manner that seemed at one and the same time friendly and contemptuous. He would *learn* me this, that, and the other, he said. Miles Macdonell had arranged for all those who volunteered to go a-hunting to have horses. Jules gave me his bridle, explaining that he was so fine a horseman he did not need one. Some day possibly, he suggested, I might be able to ride as he did, with merely a piece of rawhide looped round the horse's lower jaw. The manner of that looping, as a matter of fact, made it as effective as a cruel curb, and the bit he gave me was but as an ordinary snaffle. There were moments when I swithered between gratitude and annoyance!

We moved off on to the prairies of the coteau, young men on horseback, women also on horseback but with tepee-poles affixed on each side of their mount and dragging on the ground behind. On shorter poles laid across these were the rolls of tenting, the pots and kettles. As well as the dragged poles, the *travois,* we had some Red River carts with us. I thought that these made noise sufficient to drive all the buffalo out of the country. Yet ever and again the scouts ahead signalled that they had espied a herd and the column would halt and away we went in chase.

Not once during the first two or three days did I get in a shot. The small groups, small herds we sighted were quickly slaughtered without my aid; the women made up on the hunters—half-breed wives and their daughters and those women from among the settlers who had volunteered to accompany them and learn, or be *learned,* as the half-French Jules would say, how to gralloch these beasts. Their fires at night they made of dried buffalo dung, " buffalo chips," with which the plains were strewn.

Then came a day when, out of the northward space, went lumbering right across our path a great herd. The carts and *travois* abruptly stopped and we rode ahead. It soon became clear because of the speed at which the buffalo moved that they were being pursued. There was herd panic there.

On that occasion I succeeded in getting within acting distance. Here, I realised, was a dangerous employ. Had the beasts been scattered out it would have been otherwise but they were already mobbed close. With the sudden arrival of these enemies on their flank they crowded against each other closer still in an attempt to veer westward. I recalled instructions regarding where to shoot—beside the shoulder—so that my shot would penetrate the heart. My aim was true, though less might it be called aim than a mere thrusting of my piece against the animal I selected—or rather that my horse selected, galloping alongside of it.

Down went the great bull upon his fore-knees, bowed on its head and succumbed. But I was not expert enough to reload with my horse at the gallop and found myself unable to slacken its pace. In attempts to reload I but spilt powder and came near to being spilt myself. I had killed a buffalo, one buffalo; I could kill no more. But my horse was accustomed to the game and it was obvious it was trying to keep level with another buffalo. The beasts with their heavily furred fore-parts and smoothed hinder-parts were soon all round me and their distracting lowing and bellowing was loud. I tried again to ride without rein, with but balance and leg-hold, and to reload my musket, but again in vain.

Then past me in the billowing dust went Jules.

"Watch me!" he shouted as he went by. "Like this! I learn you. Keep your bullets in your mouth, handy."

Suddenly his horse fell and he went over its head. A second later out of the dust cloud came a scream of agony. I tried to rein in but could not. My horse had its neck craned, its head up. The horn of a frantic cow to left grazed my thigh while the shrill bellowing rose on all sides and the smell of the herd was pungent in my nostrils. Grit was in my eyes and throat, the grit of the stampede. A veritable Indian rode past me. Another surged past. Both were armed with bows and arrows. I saw a forearm thrust out, an elbow drawn back, heard the twang of the release. As the buffalo fell the hunter's lean horse swung sidewise to avoid falling over it. For a moment the man's leg rubbed against mine, his pony's croup crushed my calf.

In that whirl of dust my horse was at last less anxious to continue. It was beginning to be blown with the chase and the excitement. Of its own will it slackened speed, loped, walked, permitted itself to be halted and in answer to a slap on the neck wheeled. The plain was strewn with buffalo I could dimly see in a slow subsiding of grit. By these Indians who had overtaken me I decided that the herd we had come upon had been started on its flight by a hunting party of full-bloods to north, and I wondered if they would consider that the half-breeds and we had no right to join the hunt, that the herd was theirs.

But Jules' scream was still as it were in my ears. What had happened to him? Where was he? When he fell the herd was dense, the beasts packed close in flight. As I turned back to look for him a riderless horse ran across the plain with the quick drumming rub-a-dub of a horse in panic. It was not Jules', and I began to speculate on how many accidents, or fatalities, there had been in that chase.

Through the falling dust I saw a group of men. There were several riders clustered together, both *métis* and Indians, but clearly not in a quarrel of any sort. One dismounted, then another. I drew closer. There lay Jules. There lay Jules, crumpled, trampled, torn.

One of those bending over him came erect and looking round saw me. In the act of dismounting, I immediately recognised him : that was Court Nez. Yes, that was the man so introduced by John Willis at Fort Gibraltar : "Court Nez, a free-trader—known by no other name on the prairies and desiring no other name." He also recognised me.

"So there you are, Baxter," he said. "Well, Baxter——" he repeated the name oddly; it seemed to me there was a note of derision in his way of saying it, "this is different from Renfrewshire, heh?"

I had nothing to say. There lay Jules' body, the blood in a thick pool beside it.

III

The Indians who had been looking on flicked their moccasined heels against the flanks of their horses and rode away, the incident evidently closed for them. The two half-breeds who remained were young. By reason of their youth and of Court Nez's superior years as well as his colour they awaited his instructions. From a swift dissatisfied examination of them he turned to me.

"These things have to be attended to," said he. "Are the people you are with far back?"

"They cannot be. We saw the herd crossing just ahead of us."

"Well, they will not want to bury him here. You will have to help me to lift him." He took the reins out of my hand and knotted them to the tail of his own horse, the long lines of which he had slipped over his shoulder. "Come along. Lend a hand before he stiffens."

As we lifted the body the head rolled back and the eyes opened. For a moment I thought Jules was alive, but his eyes were glassy, the spirit had gone out of them. We laid him across Court Nez's saddle.

"Do you steady him," cautioned Court Nez, "while I walk in front."

At my momentary hesitancy he gave me a backward frown of disapproval, then ahead he trudged, leading his horse, with uneven steps over the uneven ground. He went towards a ridge where some rocks showed, while I walked behind with one hand on the body to steady it.

"I can hear the squeal of their carts pretty near," he said over his shoulder to me, and then : "Here they come!"

Over a rise of the prairie came the Red River carts with the women.

"Are any of the corpse's family with them?" asked Court Nez.

"His mother," I replied.

"Well, you go and tell her."

"What have I to say?" I inquired, at a loss.

Court Nez frowned and tossed his head to one side as a man might do when evading the sudden lunge of a wasp.

"Tell her. That is all. Tell her. These things happen. That is life. Tell her. For God's sake, what can you tell her but that her son is dead?"

I left him and hurried on to meet the carts. In one of the first the mother sat, driving. She may not have been as old as she looked: to me she seemed then as old as a mummy. The dry air of the prairies perhaps had withered and creased her.

"What's wrong?" she asked, then with puckering eyes looked beyond me.

With tensity of expression she considered what she saw: a big white man trudging beside a horse over the back of which a body lay, and a led-horse behind. Her eyes narrowed.

"That Jules?" she inquired.

I could only nod my head at first. Then, "Yes," I said with difficulty.

"He dead?" she asked.

I inclined my head again.

Slowly she climbed over the cart's rail to the hub and came to the ground and with a tottering in her gait hurried to meet Court Nez. I followed her. She stood beside the horse, put one hand up, felt the body. She stroked the face. Tears coursed down her cheeks and made runnels in the dust on them.

"Plenty stone here," she muttered. "The wolves will not get him here."

By that time some of the young men who had been far in pursuit of the buffalo, unaware of what had happened, were returning. Several of them came riding at the gallop in a race to see which would be back first at the carts, emitting sharp yells as they rode. But others, the two who had been with the body when I found it among these, called to them warningly. They reined in. They looked left and right, questioning. Then they saw that group: the horse with the body lying over the saddle, the led-horse, the massive Court Nez, the old woman very small beside him. I heard them talking quietly together.

"Who is it?"

"Jules."

" I thought Jules."

" What does he say?"

" Jules—Jules Main-Gauche."

That was the first time I had heard him called by his name in full.

" So! That is his mother, then, as I thought when we rode up."

" What happened?"

" Fell."

" How?"

" I do not know."

" Who is it?"

" Jules—Jules Main-Gauche."

" Dead?"

" Yes."

Court Nez turned to them, spoke for the woman, called to them : " She says there are a lot of stones here to keep the wolves away. You could make a grave."

They looked one to another. They had the manner of each wishing that the other would do the work, though no arduous work it was, as I was to see. They scraped away a hollow, or rather they enlarged a hollow—a natural hollow—already there on the crest of the ridge. They slit the turf with their knives in the same manner as when gathering sods for the roofs of their houses; then with their hands they dug like badgers and made that hollow a little deeper. Their ancestors, upon one side, did not believe in putting the dead in the earth, wrapped them in deerskins and raised them up in the branches of trees or elevated them on scaffoldings over the prairie in lonely places. Most of them probably shared the doubt of full-blood Indians regarding interment, a doubt if the spirit would escape. To assist in that escape a shallow grave was desirable.

The body was placed in that shallow grave, the earth was kicked over it. Divots were dropped on the top and then they moved to and fro gathering stones and without exchange of a word piled them over that shallow grave. *Click, click, click* went the stones against each other, *click, click*, while the mother stood apart, sobbing. They seemed to be more embarrassed than grieving. Here was something that humanly had to be attended to on her behalf. At last they whispered among each other. Some said, " Enough." Others said, " Put some more." The first stones had been laid more or less circumspectly on the covering sods but the final ones were tossed there. They turned away. The sun had set. Immediately that it was hid below the horizon a thin wind that was blowing set me shaking with cold.

" You'd better come over with me," suggested Court Nez, " and I'll give you something to stop these tremors. My people are making camp close by, I see." He loosened the reins of my horse from the tail of his, handed them to me, swung to the saddle. " Come along, then."

I had the inclination to reply that I would remain with those from Pembina. But Court Nez read the refusal on my face.

" Our camp is already almost made," said he. " Better come with me."

So I mounted and we rode side by side over the rolling land. The sky still reflected the light of the sun. Westward were flecks of cloud from north to south, poised in space, their undersides as though molten. In the air was a suffusion of radiance. The horses' hoofs, as they passed through any slight indentation, trampled through twilight in the grass, and I had the feeling of sitting very high in the sunset glory. It was the exquisite hour, the melancholy hour, with its obvious hint of passing time. And on that wind was more than a suggestion of winter.

IV

" Odd," remarked Court Nez, " that we should meet here, us coming from Brandon and just going to make camp when we sighted the big herd and you coming from Pembina and sighting it dusting across in front of you. Yes, very odd our meeting—Baxter. Still shaking? Well, you'll get used to that kind of thing. Had you any special liking for the lad that was killed or was it just the sudden death that caught you that way?"

" I felt sorry for him rather than liked him," I confessed. " There was something childish about him."

" There is something childish about most of us."

Our horses were moving in unison, step for step, with flirting of dust from their hoofs and rhythmic swing of their long tails. At Fort Gibraltar I had felt strongly a revulsion against this man and as we rode side by side then I had also a feeling of being attracted to him.

Revulsion and attraction indeed I was then again aware of together.

We rode down into a shallow coulee through the centre of which a narrow stream ran, some tributary perhaps of the Pembina River. Indian women were busy pitching tepees there and by the length and weight of the poles it was arduous work. Two of them had just completed the erection of one by which Court Nez halted and were setting up the pole which held in place, as the wind ordered, a cowl-like triangle of hide that extended from the tapering top.

"My wife and concubine," explained Court Nez as the women walked away. "The Old Testament men had the right idea. I wouldn't want as many as Solomon but many hands make light labour, you know." He swung off his horse and commenced to unsaddle. "This is man's work," he said. "We do our own un-saddling. You'd better tie your horse. If you don't he'll go over to join his friends and you'll have to find your folks' camp afoot later."

There was a fringe of trees along each side of the twisting creek in the bottom of that coulee, cottonwoods and willows. To a cotton-wood nearby I tied my horse. One of the women began to carry bundles inside from a *travois* that lay upon the ground. The horse which had dragged it would be one of those then stepping and grazing, contentedly stepping and grazing, along the coulee slope. The other woman was tending a small fire in the open.

"Come in," said Court Nez, and led the way into the tepee. He sank down to a sitting position on the ground very much in the Indian manner. "We'll have tea presently. They know—soon as we camp—always."

The two women came and went, paying no attention to me.

"Different from Renfrewshire," remarked Court Nez as he watched them coming and going. Then he shot a quick glance at me.

I could not remember telling him that my home was in Renfrew-shire. Sitting there he gave me the impression of a man who held strange secrets, gave the impression, in fact, of a man brooding upon these. And it was as though coming out of a melancholy reverie he spoke again suddenly, looking round the tepee.

"Comfortable they make them," said he. "Buffalo robes to lie on and these wicker affairs behind you so that you can restfully recline. Sometimes I think even the Indians have too many possessions—possessions!—especially for a people who are on the move most of the time. But with more cows than bulls, of course," and he gave a laugh that reminded me of that evening at Fort Gibraltar, "one can have several housekeepers. Aye, aye! Well, here's our Soochow tea."

One of the women came in with a smoked kettle such as most of the tribes used, carrying it by a forked stick in which its brail was held. She set it down before Court Nez and opening a box made of bark and covered with hide, parfléched, she took out two tin cups and a small sack of sugar and placed them beside him. As she turned to go out she spoke a word or two and with but a word or two he replied. She did not drop the flap when leaving and I saw her bending over another parfléched box in front of the tent and taking out two long, gleaming knives. I saw her pass one of these to the other woman—wife to concubine or concubine to wife as might be—and they departed.

"I have just been telling them that I killed four, and whereabouts," said Court Nez. "I hope they have no trouble with the Pembina half-breeds in claiming them. I don't know if you noticed the arrows of my people in dead buffaloes."

"Not specially," I replied. "As I rode back I had been thinking of Jules and looked only for him."

"Otherwise employed, eh? Yes, you would be. I didn't use bow and arrows, of course, but I did, after getting my last one, mark it and the other three on the way back with a slit in the ears for sign. But if you had looked at the arrows on any carcase you would have seen different colours in the hefts. Every man has his own markings. That prevents wrangling over possession. Great people! Simple. Direct. One gets to like them."

"Some of them seem very dirty," I said—I know not why, considering his marked friendliness to the race.

"Usually clean dirt," he assured me, quaffing scalding hot tea with enjoyment. "And anyhow they are always trying to keep clean." He gave his thick laugh. "You can tell who is most deeply and sincerely courting among them when you see one of the girls sitting down with a lad's head on her lap and she going over it for him very carefully and affectionately with a small-tooth comb traded from the Hudson's Bay Company, or more likely the Nor'-Westers, eh? More likely the Nor'-Westers. The Hudson's Bay men have been content too long to sit in their forts and expect the Indians to come to them. These Nor'-Westers have pushed out to the ends of the land. Eh?" he snapped, as though prepared for argument, or inviting it.

What side, I considered, was this man on? Did he favour the Hudson's Bay Company or the North-West Company? I tried to recall if there had been any indication of his leanings when we met at Fort Gibraltar? What had he contributed to the talk when it touched on the ownership of lands or rival rights of occupancy? Nothing that I could remember save an interjection to the effect that the land had been parcelled out between allegedly civilised nations without by your leave of the Indians.

" Have some more tea," he suggested, and refilled my cup.

Twilight had been deepening in the coulee, in all the coulees, in all the creases of the plains, rising, brimming, running in the grass, and had given way to night while we talked. Outside I could hear voices of many people returning to the camp. There was a flicker of light at the entrance to the tent. One of the women came in. In her hand was a two-pronged stick, the prongs twisted so that it was a simple tongs, with which she carried flaming embers from the fire. She dropped them in the centre of the tepee, heaped them together, and up the leather wall behind Court Nez went his great shadow. He favoured the woman—wife or concubine—with a smile. She smiled back, went away, and returned with an armful of wood that, laid atop the small fire she had already put there, quickly ignited.

Suddenly there arose a sound extraordinary to me.

" What in heaven's name is that?" I exclaimed.

" It is the mother, I expect, of the boy we buried, wailing for the death of her son."

The sound rose and fell with utter melancholy. It accentuated in my mind that sense of the bigness of the land, gave me also a thought of its antiquity, of the ages long before the rivalry of Hudson's Bay Company and North-West Company, long before the Hudson's Bay Company's charter. Above all, in that wailing, was the sorrow of all humanity for the fact of death.

" What was I talking about?" asked Court Nez. " Yes, the Hudson's Bay Company and the Nor'-Westers. Here's Lord Selkirk, one of the chief shareholders of the Company, and he arranges for

Lord Selkirk of the Settlement Scheme to be sold an enormous tract of land for a mere song."

"Yes," I agreed. "And some of the Nor'-Westers, others besides Sir Alexander Mackenzie, I believe, bought shares in the Hudson's Bay Company with no other reason than to baulk him in that."

"Well, I don't blame them. He gets that all for a song."

"Conditionally," said I, on the defensive. "The Hudson's Bay Company retain justiciary rights over the territory."

"Oh, is that in the deed? I don't seem to have heard of that."

"Yes, that is in it. And a certain proportion of the lots have to be kept vacant for retiring Company employees. And if the earl does not settle a certain number of people on the others by a given time the land goes back to the Company."

"What, in that event, would become of those who had settled there?" asked Court Nez sharply.

"They would, of course, retain their property," said I. "That's in the contract."

"Well," said Court Nez, "as you know, the Nor'-Westers don't like it. They think it spells the beginning of the end of the fur trade."

"Captain Macdonell," said I, "thinks that the Nor'-Westers themselves may live to be grateful for a settled community there, between them and America."

"How blasted polite that Captain Macdonell is!" said Court Nez. "And he looked at me once, that night at Fort Gibraltar, as if he thought I was drunk! I can carry my liquor."

He threw his empty cup down beside the kettle in a gesture of annoyance and then, elbow on knee, grabbed hold of his chin and mouth with a plucking hand, and frowned, meditating.

"When one thinks of the size of all Rupert's Land," I observed, "the space that the earl has purchased, conditionally purchased, is next to nothing."

There was no reply. Court Nez might not have heard. His eyes, staring before him, had a blind aspect in them. But I continued:

"I wonder how many of the Hudson's Bay factors will want to retire in the land instead of going home."

The last words seemed to attract the attention of the brooding Court Nez.

"Going home?" he broke out, and then had the manner of a man trying to recall what has recently been said and only half heard. "Going home?" he said. "What would they want to go home for? Most of them, I should think, will want to stay in the country. A great country! I do not suppose you are homesick yet, are you?"

"No."

"No! What part do you come from? It is Renfrewshire, is it not?"

"Yes, it is. What made you——"

"Oh, it may just be that thy speech bewrayeth thee, or it may be that I made a good guess."

"Yes, from Renfrewshire—from Paisley."

"From Paisley. Mother alive? '

"Yes, she's alive."

"Any other relatives?"

"Just a brother."

"Just a brother. What does he do?"

"He is running a cartage, a haulage business. Our father had a cartage business."

"Did he take it over from your father?"

"Oh, no. He did all sorts of things first after leaving school but in the end he was a clerk in a haulage business. He eventually started up for himself. Mother said it was very interesting that he should do so because not only our father but her father had been in that business."

"Quite. I see. So your father—died—when you and your brother were both quite young?"

It was on the tip of my tongue to say, "Yes," but instead (out of my own uncertainty) I replied : "We do not know anything about our father."

"Oh!" said Court Nez.

"I've no recollection of him," I went on, "or only the very dimmest. I would not recognise him if I were to see him. I know that. He is just a sort of shape, faintly recalled. He went to one of the American colonies with the idea of setting up in business there." I paused.

"Yes. And?"

"The ship he voyaged on was not wrecked. My mother heard he had landed, but she has never had a word of him from that day."

"Phoo! He must have been killed by Indians. That is what happened to your dad."

"It is generally believed that he is dead," said I.

"Well, doesn't your mother consider he must be dead, seeing she does not hear from him?"

"I've never been able to make sure."

"Why did you leave your home?"

"To——" I paused. "To——" I began again and stuck.

Court Nez laughed.

"—make your way in the world," he suggested. "Make a fortune. Young man with the world at his foot, eh?"

"It is sometimes hard to give a reason for the thing one does," said I.

"That is so," agreed Court Nez, "and that is honest. A reason, says you. I would say reasons for our actions. There may be various reasons. Your brother? What sort of a fellow is he? What age?"

"He is three years older than I. He's the mainstay of the family, of the house. I did nothing much. He's an exemplary fine fellow. The largest sum of money I ever gave my mother was when I left home, from an advance of wages I got from Captain Roderick."

"Captain—Captain? Oh, what a hell of a lot of captains! Who the hell is Captain Roderick? Where is he? Do I know him?"

"He was recruiting for Lord Selkirk in Glasgow."

"Oh, yes, Lord Selkirk. Quite so." He had a gurgling fit of laughter. "Your brother ruled the roost and domineered over you."

It was as much a statement as an inquiry. I stared in amazement.

"Oh, I wouldn't say that," said I.

"Wouldn't say that? Quite so. Wouldn't say it. But you got away from that condition of affairs instead of putting him in his place. So what will happen? You'll take it out of somebody else. The chance will come for you, and because of the way your brother ruled it over you, you'll rule ruthlessly over whoever you get under you."

"Not at all, sir," said I. "I don't agree. Quite the reverse. All that has made me wish never to rule over anybody, or try to direct anybody, or act as if I thought I had the right to judge anybody."

Impulsively I had spoken, and having spoken I realised that I had admitted to Court Nez—practically a stranger—that the brother I

E

had called an "exemplary fine fellow" had been at least somewhat domineering.

"I see I was right," chuckled Court Nez, "about one reason for your leaving home. Well, here you are in the service of that damnably polite Captain Miles Macdonell and as loyal in your heart to him, I surmise, as he is to his crack-brained earl. Now I'm a free-trader. I'm not being traitor to any, though you met me, my lad, in a North-West fort, when I tell you that it might be well for you to suggest to your people at Pembina to go hunting more to the sou'-west than the west, for if you head on west you'll be meeting some of the Qu'Appelle half-breeds—whose chief occupation is supplying pemican to the Nor'-Westers. I know they are out there now. There might be trouble if you met. I don't say necessarily any killing, but they might collogue with these kind friends you've made at Pembina and affect them with their own view of you Selkirk settlers."

"Their own view of us?"

"Yes. As interlopers."

"I see."

"This is a warning, Baxter. I know what I'm talking about."

"I see," said I again. "Well, sir, it is very good of you to advise——"

"Don't be so damned polite!" Court Nez interrupted. "I have my reason. What did I say? My reason? Yes, yes. Blood's thicker than water. Or so to speak, so to speak. Two Lowlanders we are, two Lowlanders together, eh?"

The high keening lamenting cry of the Indian mother of Jules sounded again. He raised his head and listened.

"Indians," said he. "I like to have them round me, to be with them. I could talk to you by the hour of the Indians but that might give you an ennui. Many years ago I married an Indian woman. It was our daughter you saw, my lad, that evening at Fort Gibraltar."

Court Nez's daughter! Court Nez's daughter . . . That beautiful girl who had set my heart racing, made me haunt the fort in the hope of seeing her again! Court Nez's daughter! His eyes were keen, probing, sharp on me. I must not show on my face what my thoughts were.

"Where is she, sir?" I asked, and found my own voice strange to my ears.

" ' Where is she, sir?' " repeated Court Nez with mockery in his accent. " She is far from here. I have sent her to be educated at the Ursulines Nunnery at Quebec. Court Nez is this, Court Nez is that, Court Nez is the other, but he is devoted to that daughter of his. He would kill any one who did her harm. You understand me?"

" The man is mad," thought I, because of the expression in his eyes then; and yet, recalling well indeed how the girl had affected me when I saw her for but a moment at Fort Gibraltar, and how Court Nez had observed me observing her, I felt his question had a definitely personal significance.

" You understand me?" said he again,

" Quite so. Yes, sir, indeed," I replied, and thought: " This man is dangerous."

His manner suddenly changed. When he spoke again his voice had lost the challenging and harsh note.

" Yes," he said. " Berry Woman was the mother's name in translation. She wanted the child to have a white name, so I called her Christina."

" That is my mother's name!" I ejaculated, happily. This girl was far away, far from Red River, far from the coteau. I might never see her again. But her name was my mother's name. Wonderful! There was something I could look upon as a bond. There was something to ease my heart—at twenty-one.

" Indeed!" said Court Nez dryly. " A coincidence!"

The wailing voice came again.

" This business of dying is melancholy," he muttered. His manner changed. He might have been but talking to himself, or heedless whether I attended. " When Berry Woman died I got these other women. They are none too bad, but they are not as she was. She was *la belle suavage*."

He sat silent a while, looked this way and that, fidgeted. I had the impression that my host was weary of me, that I had overstayed my welcome.

" I must be going," said I, rising.

Court Nez made no response. I bowed to him and——

" Good-night, sir," I said.

Court Nez made no response.

Was he, I wondered, deep in meditation, so deeply that he was deaf for the moment, or had he lived so long among the Indians that he had fallen into their way of going without an adieu when he went, and had no ears for it when it was spoken to him by one who was departing? I stooped out of the tepee half-expecting a tardy " Goodnight " to follow me, but it did not.

The two women were still at work, dim shapes, moving between a *travois* and a tripod. A smell of fresh meat, a smell of blood was there. One of them, seeing me coming, walked towards where my horse stood dozing, hip-shot, his head hanging, faintly revealed in a flickering of firelight on the edge of the creek's aspen and cottonwood border; but I went past her, loosened the lines, mounted, rode aslant up the slope of the coulee to where I could see the twinkle of the camp-fires of the people from Pembina.

I had a sudden return of the shudderings which had caused Court Nez to take me to his tepee. Up and down my spine and over my loins ran the cold again because of the voice of Jules' mother rising and falling in lamentation. While daylight, or twilight, was still on the scene it had been sufficiently melancholy, I thought, for any human heart. In that domed night through which a bleak wind blew all the sorrow for the transience of life and the muteness of death was in it.

Then my thoughts went back to that man of mystery I had just left and I wondered why it was I felt both repelled and attracted by him. Of the Settlement I thought and was irked by the lack of pemican that delayed its fair founding. And, above all, of that half-breed girl I thought—Court Nez's daughter. What a father! I said to myself, and so was back again at marvelling why he should rouse in me such contradictory emotions. Not only of Red River Settlement but of myself is this narrative—and it is less lacking direction than perhaps, so far, to some it may seem to be.

CHAPTER FIVE

I

But I have no intention to give you an ennui by recounting in detail all that gave ennui to Captain Macdonell and us his officers during the next many months. Let me but tell briefly, as it were an inventory of mischance, that in the ship bringing immigrants in 1813 typhoid broke out and they were landed well up the coast from York Factory where they spent a dreadful winter. They had a surgeon aboard but the Governor sent our own, from the Settlement, to aid them. The crops planted at Red River in that year failed. Back to Pembina almost all had to go again. Those wintering, from " the fever ship," in huts at Hudson Bay would be coming on to join us when the rivers opened.

In desperation one day of January, in the year 1814, the Governor sat down in our quarters at Pembina. I knew by his tensity of manner he was near distraction. He took up a pen and commenced to write. There was no sound but the scratching of his quill and the hum of the Franklin stove. He was so engrossed that I had a feeling I must not stir. After a long while he turned in his chair and addressed me.

" Baxter," said he, " do you take a copy of this," and he handed to me the wet sheets.

At my table as I wrote my eyes widened in surprise, for this was my fair copy :

WHEREAS *the Right Honourable Thomas Earl of Selkirk is anxious to provide for the families at present forming settlements on his lands at Red River with those on the way to it, passing the winter at York Factory and Churchill Forts, in Hudson's Bay, as also those who are expected to arrive next autumn, renders it a necessity and indispensable part of my duty to provide for their support. In the yet uncultivated state of the country, the ordinary resources derived from the buffalo and other wild animals hunted within the territory, are not deemed more than adequate for the requisite supply.*

WHEREAS *it is hereby ordered, that no persons trading furs or provisions within the territory for the Honourable Hudson's Bay Company or the North-West Company, or any individual, shall take any provisions, either of flesh, fish, grain, or vegetable, procured or raised within the said territory, by water or land carriage, for one twelvemonth from the date hereof; save and except what may be judged necessary for the trading parties at this present time within the territory, to carry them to their respective destinations; and who may, on due application to me, obtain a licence for the same.*

The provisions procured and raised as above shall be taken for the use of the colony; and that no loss may accrue to the parties concerned they will be paid by British bills at the customary rates. And be it hereby further made known, that whosoever shall be detected in attempting to convey out, or shall aid or assist in carrying out, or attempting to carry out, any provisions prohibited as above, either by water or land, shall be taken into custody, and prosecuted as the laws in such cases direct, and the provisions so taken, as well as any goods and chattels, of what nature soever, which may be taken along with them, and also the craft, carriages, and cattle, instrumental in conveying away the same to any part but to the settlement on Red River, shall be forfeited.

Given under my hand at Fort Daer (Pembina) the 8th day of January, 1814.

There was a space left obviously for Captain Macdonell's signature for at the end of the line was scribbled the one word *Governor*, then followed " by order of the Governor "; and in the line below was another space for Mr. Spencer's signature, for at the end of it was the word *Secretary*. Mr. Spencer, as on the previous winter, was in charge at " the forks."

As I copied I felt a sense of dismay and even for a moment hoped there might be delay in delivery of this missive to those whom it concerned. It would cause trouble, perhaps serious trouble. And yet, what was the Governor to do? Court Nez, I recalled, had warned me that the North-Westers at Qu'Appelle regarded the settlers as interlopers and that they would probably influence the half-breeds at Pembina to the same view. Well, there was no doubt they were less friendly on this second year of having the colonists wintering beside them. Even the year before I thought Miles Macdonell had not been astonished when I repeated to him Court Nez's warning. But actually, I thought, it was the North-Westers who were the interlopers, Lord Selkirk who was the owner by his purchase from the Hudson's Bay Company who had the land by ancient charter.

I remembered the day we reached the forks when Captain Macdonell conferred with Mr. Heney, remembered his voice as, after that conference, once or twice he muttered, " No pemican, no pemican." The memory was so vivid that as I finished my fair copy it seemed to me he had actually spoken the words again. I turned my head. Perhaps he had said them, perhaps not. He was sitting back in his chair, his fingers beating out a quiet tattoo on the cover of a book that lay upon his table.

" It would be all to the good to have half a dozen copies of that," said he.

11

The storm did not immediately burst on our return to Red River in the spring. In fact there was a stony silence from the North-West Company forts and posts at which copies of that order had been delivered. There was no response of either *We shall obey* or *We shall refuse to admit your authority.*

The earlier and the later settlers alike were busy on their allotments of land. The Chisholms, during that last winter, had remained at Red River. Hugh had built a roomy house that, apart from the fact that it was of logs, took my mind back to Scotland, within and without. It was a strong building with attics that had dormer windows. " Haste ye back," was always the parting cry for me when I left there to go to the writers' quarters at Point Douglas under the stars in that high lift over the darkening and wind-whispering plain. I came to feel as one of the family there, to reckon Chisholm as a foster-father, Mrs. Chisholm as a second mother, Agnes, perhaps, as a tomboyish sister, but Mairi, somehow, not exactly as a sister though as one related—cousinly!

It irked me to hear her upbraided by her mother so often for faults that, in Agnes, would have been ignored or even looked upon with merriment as no faults at all. Mairi's patience when screeched at by Mrs. Chisholm I admired greatly. She seemed to forgive instanter. Chap-fallen for a moment, she would speedily recover; and by her expression I knew she was condoning, saying to herself: "Poor mother has her worries. It is all so new and strange to her here." And even if, as Mr. Chisholm occasionally protested, Mrs. Chisholm "made step-bairns" in the house, it had to be said for Agnes that she never showed any tendency to imitate her mother in carpings against Mairi. They were good friends these two girls so different in many ways, Mairie gentle and with a natural graciousness of manner, Agnes irrepressible, hoydenish.

Homing from the Chisholms under the stars I would still have the broad kitchen in my mind's eye, its crusie and its home-made candles, the bellows hanging to one side of the cobble chimney. Longest in my mind's eye would Mairi's face remain. I would find myself in the midst of a wordless pæan in her praise; and then, the farm left behind, I would think of Fort Gibraltar, where Assiniboine lapsed into Red River, and be back there again, in memory, on my visit with Captain Macdonell, Hillier, and McLeod, and see that girl who, later, I had discovered was Court Nez's daughter, Christina. On the remaining stretch of road from the farm to Point Douglas, the lights of Governor's House and the administrative building and the writers' quarters glinting like fallen stars, I would recall her dark eyes and the way she moved across the candle-lit room, and the night would seem utterly empty, she so far off in that convent at Quebec.

The next day I would be plunged again into the midst of the administrative affairs of the settlers and hear the Governor, over a survey of accounts brought in from the store by John Bourke to be viséd, remark once again that for all their sakes he looked forward to the day when the settlers would be self-supporting on their crops and herds. But whether the crops were that year to be profuse or scanty, we had not yet our own meal and flour nor a sufficiency of our own beef and mutton. *Pemican*: pemican had still to be the staple for the settlers.

The sole result of the embargo was that when messengers were sent to the posts of North-West Company and Hudson's Bay Company requesting consignments for the Colony, and offering payment according to the terms of the embargo, all the agents of the North-West Company and most of the factors of the Hudson's Bay Company protested either that they had none or but sufficient for their own needs.

News came to us of the war that had broken out between the colonists of the American sea-board who had won their independence and the old Mother Country, chiefly over the searching of American vessels on the high seas for British seamen by press-gangs from His Majesty's warships. At first I think Captain Macdonell saw himself commanding a force of allied Hudson's Bay men and North-Westers, our Colony men and troops of *métis* and local Indians, against invaders at what he called the back door. But we were farther off than even a back door, remote from that strife and with our own troubles that even then, indeed, were preliminary—though of course we could not know that—to bloodshed.

III

In May Captain Macdonell decided that he must act. Some of our people had seen heavy-laden canoes going down Red River in the night very quietly and suspiciously. They were probably, we decided, North-West canoes on their way to Winnipic for the Saskatchewan country with pemican. He sent an armed party some way up the Assiniboine to watch for North-Westers coming down; but they discovered nothing save that their movements were being watched by spies from Fort Gibraltar.

Only from Peguis's band could we obtain any of the much needed pemican. A watch was kept day and night for more canoes going down river, running the contraband out of our territory, but none appeared. It was conceivable that, knowing they were being watched, the North-Westers were sending pemican to their northern posts across country from Qu'Appelle instead of following the water routes of Red River, Winnipic, Saskatchewan.

So the Governor sent Sheriff Spencer and a Mr. Howse for his lieutenant with some men up river again to make further investigations, see what they might see. In but a few days they returned, Spencer very cheerful, pleased with himself.

" Well, Captain," he chanted, coming breezily into the accounting-room, " good news! "

Captain Macdonell put down his pen and awaited it.

" We have four hundred bags of pemican," Spencer announced.

"Four hundred! Purchased from whom—North-West Company, Hudson's Bay Company, or both?"

"We had them from the North-West Company," replied Spencer after a second's hesitation.

"And were you able to obtain them without discord?" asked the Governor.

"Discord!" Spencer laughed. "We took them."

"Took them! They refused to sell?"

"We went up to the Souris River and waiting there saw that supplies of pemican were coming to the North-West fort both down the main Assiniboine and down the Souris. One day we saw a laden batteau arrive. After the boatmen had unloaded it and gone I went with our men to Fort la Souris. They would not open. There is a man called John Pritchard in charge there. I showed him a copy of the embargo through a grill in the gate which was fast shut. He told us that he could not give us entrance and that he must also refuse to recognise your order."

"What did you say to him?" asked Macdonell.

"There was no more to say. It was incumbent upon me then to act. I had to do so, Captain. I told him I must have the pemican. He said it was being held there, was not being shipped out. So I left him at the gate and bade my men remove three pickets from the stockade to allow us to get through. We went in and took the pemican from the storehouse."

"Was the storehouse locked?"

"Yes. It was locked."

Miles Macdonell nodded.

"We broke the lock," explained Spencer. "We took the four hundred bags and carried them on to the Hudson's Bay post, Brandon House, and gave half to Mr. Fidler there to hold for us. He has none, truly none to spare. He tells me that all the local hunters have been influenced by the Nor'-Westers to trade entirely with them. The other half we brought down here—two hundred bags, Captain. At Fort Gibraltar they were evidently watching for us. These Nor'-Westers, I feel convinced, are able to get Indian runners to carry messages speedily for them. They were watching for us. But we were very fierce and prepared of aspect, muskets in hand, as we came by. So they just watched us come and returned to their fort."

" Tell me this," said Macdonell : " When you took the stakes from the stockade at la Souris, and when you broke the lock of the store-house, was no resistance offered at all?"

" None. They offered no resistance. They went into their quarters and stared at us from the doors—that was all. They were afraid to engage us."

I could see the Governor doubted it was fear that restrained them, and was of opinion they were thus inactive by an arranged policy. He did in fact later on remark to me that these enemies of the Settlement might be hoping for us to take such action as would be definitely against us in a court of law.

" You did offer to buy it from them?" he inquired.

" I did," said Spencer.

" I am glad of that," said the Governor.

" But they refused. So what was I to do but what I did?" Spencer went on, as in self-defence, perhaps reading doubt of the wisdom of his action on Macdonell's face.

The Governor made no reply to that. He was meditating, I felt sure, from that remark he made to me afterwards, on what a court of law—despite the claims of Lord Selkirk—might have to say to the Sheriff's well-intentioned action of the picket drawing and the lock breaking, and thinking, also, of word we had had of a new agent at Fort Gibraltar. We had been told he was a person both plausible and strategic. He had come to take the place of Mr. Willis who was retiring from the service of the North-West Company by reason of ill-health, though not leaving the country.

The agents at Fort Gibraltar had not only control there but were the advisory heads for all their Company's proceedings in the farther Indian Countries westward. This new man, Duncan Cameron his name, had probably received minute instructions regarding procedure from the Montreal partners. Beyond doubt they had been kept aware of all that was happening by Red River since our arrival and the ceremony of taking seizen.

" They offered no resistance at all," repeated Spencer. " It was all as easy as kiss my hand!" and he laughed.

Captain Macdonell nodded, and almost in a whisper :

" Too easy," said he.

CHAPTER SIX

I

Captain Macdonell, in reminiscent mood, was telling me of the last talk he had with Lord Selkirk in London.

". . . and ever and again it comes back into my mind," he ended, "how the sun drifted off the map that lay on the table and the earl remarked, 'There is a shadow on my Red River Settlement.' We have had shadow enough, Baxter. This new agent at Fort Gibraltar, this man Duncan Cameron: I hear he lays claim to the rank of captain. I am told that his commission was in the Voyageurs' Corps, and is a recent one. I do not know how it can be recent, for the corps was actually disbanded about two years ago. I cannot help but surmise some stratagem with intent to impress the settlers that he has equal rank with their governor!"

"He is already visiting a great deal among them," said I. "My friends the Chisholms have a feeling of doubt in him. He is too ingratiating. Or at least that is Mr. Chisholm's view. He has been inviting many of our people to Fort Gibraltar and giving them great banquets there by all accounts, with birds and venison and the best wines."

"Yes, and talking the Gaelic to them, I am told," remarked the Governor. "He is a cunning gentleman, I gather, with a commission I should like to examine, sent hither to undermine me."

There the conversation was interrupted by the entrance of John Spencer, on that occasion with no chant of "Good news." Captain Macdonell, at sight of his serious face, awaited the ill news.

"That man Howse," began Spencer, "who assisted me in getting the pemican at la Souris, has been set on, Captain, set on and carried away into Fort Gibraltar. I could not think what the stir was. I saw the commotion from a distance. One of the half-breeds who hang around the North-West fort told Tipotem" [Tipotem was the name of an Indian whom the Governor had brought with him from Oxford House in 1812] "that Cameron is going to send him to Montreal to be tried for burglary."

76

"A high-handed gentleman!" ejaculated Macdonell, though probably recalling his own qualms on hearing of palisade pickets drawn and lock broken by his representatives at la Souris. "Well, he has taken the law into his own hands. We can make our response. There are canoes coming up all the time now to them from Fort William. We will mount some of our swivels on the bank here and stop the next canoe and take the men prisoners. Fort Gibraltar, indeed!"

Next day he had his desire. A sentry announced canoes coming up river and he hurried to the bank with several of us. The guns had been placed on its edge where there was a gap in the ribband of trees. They were thus plainly visible, at a bend, trained on the river. Beside each were men clearly ready to fire at a signal.

At our shout of "Halt!" the paddlers, who had already seen the guns, poised their paddles. At Miles Macdonell's order, "Come ashore here!" they held speedy conference and obeyed. Wide-eyed, amazed, they drew in. That there might be trouble on Red River they most likely knew, but none had expected such a reception as that. Some of them, we heard later, thought that those who halted them must be their enemies of the war then being waged eastward, Americans who had raided hither possibly by way of the Ouisconsin country.

They were promptly unarmed by our men who were carrying muskets with fixed bayonets, and short but deadly bayonets they were. In one of the canoes was a chest of firearms which was appropriated. And then they were told (they numbered, by the way, one clerk and twenty voyageurs) that they might proceed to Fort Gibraltar and give information that until Mr. Howse was set free all canoes would be stopped and those in them held prisoners.

II

The response to that from the enemy fort of Gibraltar was the departure down river of a swift canoe. Its coming was reported to the Governor who went out to look at it. I was with him, and as he saw it flashing round the lower bend he must have recalled, as I did, that other one we had seen passing as swiftly down river after the ceremony of taking seizen.

The next canoes to reach Red River were crowded with men. At the command to come into the bank they promptly obeyed. But they were clearly not taken by surprise. By their deportment it might be hazarded that they were prepared to land there uninvited, and fight.

A grim-faced man rose in the first one, leapt out and confronting Captain Macdonell inquired : " Were you signalling for us to come ashore, sir?"

" We were," replied the Governor. " Macdonell is my name. Captain Miles Mac——"

" You'll be the man they call the Governor," said the new-comer. " My name is McDonald—capital M, small c, capital D, o-n-a-l-d : John McDonald of Garth."

A powerfully built man was this McDonald of Garth but with one arm hanging loose at his side. It was the arm that gave the Governor a hint of his identity. He had heard of a McDonald with a broken arm who had been in the fur trade in the west from the days even of old feuds between the North-West Company and a rival one called the X.Y.

" Yes, I am the Governor," replied Macdonell. " And you will be he whom they call Bras Croché?"

" Indeed I am so," answered McDonald in a manner as of one pleased.

This Bras Croché, McDonald of Garth, was brother-in-law of William McGillivray, one of the " kings " as they used to say of the North-West Company.

" I am just on my way," he said, " from the Pacific coast through New Caledonia and by the Athabasca Pass and our Prairie Fort, and down Saskatchewan, for Fort William and Montreal. At Bas de la Rivière " [foot of the Winnipic River] " I heard strange stories of affairs here and turned aside to see if I could be of any assistance." He gave a low laugh. " A wee bit conference between us might be better than training these guns on the river and stopping the traffic."

" There is one of our men held prisoner at present in Fort Gibraltar," Miles Macdonell told him, " and I would be glad to have him released. It is high-handed to attack and hold people in that way. I am merely demonstrating that if I were so minded I could institute reprisal."

" I am astonished at Duncan Cameron doing a thing like that," admitted McDonald. " But I dare say we can come to terms. From what I heard at Bas de la Rivière I presume it is your pemican embargo that is at the root of the trouble."

"Or the refusal to obey it, sir. As Governor of the territory of Assiniboia on behalf of the owner, Lord Selkirk, I am forced to establish it for a year."

"I believe they are looking into all that—about the ownership of Assiniboia—at Montreal," observed McDonald. "Well, I have no doubt I can speak Cameron fair for you and get that man released if you let us go on now. And maybe we might arrange for a discussion at an early date on the pemican and provisions question."

"I shall be very happy to discuss the matter with you," said our Governor.

McDonald, with the ease of one long accustomed to such river voyaging, slipped lightly, despite his bulk, into his canoe, saluted Miles Macdonell—who graciously saluted in return—and off went that small and far-voyaged fleet.

Macdonell of Scothouse looked after McDonald of Garth with interest.

"There is a man," he remarked, "with whom affairs can be discussed."

And by what followed it seemed he had rightly appraised him, for Howse was released and returned bearing a letter from Bras Croché requesting an appointment to discuss the pemican embargo.

III

The conference, by our Governor's plan, was to begin with dignity, and, if all went well, end with a dram. The sentry had orders to announce the visitors smartly. It was I, however, as it happened, who announced them first.

"This must be they coming now, sir," said I, "for I see a man in a red coat."

"So he has donned it to call on me! It may have impressed some of our settlers, Baxter, but all it arouses in me is suspicion. Well, here they are."

The sentry stepped in at the door.

"Mr. McDonald of Garth," said he, "and Captain Duncan Cameron."

"How do you do, gentlemen? How do you do, Mr. McDonald? We have met before but I have not so far had the pleasure of a visit from—er—Captain Cameron."

Cameron was a man very large, and very self-important of carriage I thought him as I stood at attention to one side, self-important to the point of being ludicrous. I preferred the other man, he with the broken arm. Cameron was so grand that he must surely, thought I, have no sense of proportion. My own captain, the Governor, Miles Macdonell, was punctiliously bowing to them, Spencer with him.

"I have been busy since my arrival," said Cameron, consequential of manner.

"Let me introduce Sheriff Spencer," said Miles, "and Mr. Baxter."

McDonald gave a genial nod of his head to both of us but Cameron raised his, closed his eyes, and bowed with them shut. His companion looked at him as though half-astonished, half-amused and, if he did not suffer from a facial twitch, then he winked to me—or thus at least I decided.

"Sheriff?" inquired Cameron. "Sheriff? I did not know you had any with civil or forensic titles here, did not know you had a sheriff."

Macdonell raised his brows.

"Much as I was unaware, sir," he retorted, "of your military rank. Might I ask the regiment, Captain?" for there was no regimental insignia on Cameron's coat.

"The Voyageurs' Corps."

"The Voyageurs' Corps. Let me see : I have heard of it. It was a short-lived regiment, was it not? It was disbanded, in fact, a year or two ago, I think."

Cameron evaded him.

"By order of the officer in command at Michilimackinac," he explained, "I received my commission. Alexander Macdonell, a cousin of yours, I understand, is by the same order commissioned a lieutenant, and Seraphim Lamar of my staff at Fort Gibraltar an ensign."

"Well, well," murmured the Governor and determined then, I imagine, to make full inquiries regarding these military titles. There were, however, the courtesies of a host to remember, so though he was dubious of the red coat and the commission he seemed to be ready to let the subject rest for the nonce.

"Might I respond by asking *What regiment?* of you?" said Cameron.

"Surely. There is nothing to hide—explain," answered Macdonell. "I have spent many years in actual service. Back in 1782 I received my commission as ensign in the King's Royal Regiment of New York, and served in that regiment till its reduction in 1784. Ten years later I was appointed lieutenant in the second battalion of the Royal Canadian Volunteers to which my father, the Speaker of the Assembly in Upper Canada, had been gazetted as captain. In 1796 I received from Lord Dorchester my commission as captain. My father was then lieutenant-colonel of the regiment."

"Well, well," murmured Cameron.

"But why are we standing?" asked the Governor. "Pray be seated, gentlemen," and he glanced at me.

I moved chairs forward for them. They looked one to another as they sat down. Cameron cleared his throat violently several times.

"Let us get straight to business," he began. "And first let me say this : The sentiment of the natives here—who are not ignorant of the state of things—will show you, if rightly represented, how far it is necessary for the existence of your infant colony that a perfect understanding and an intercourse of mutual good offices should exist between us."

Here was a preliminary speech to consider and all considered it; and all heard it, McDonald of Garth included to judge by a frown he gave, as a threat thinly veiled—a threat that the Indians might be raised against our Colony. The Governor, I knew, was disappointed that McDonald of Garth was not the spokesman but, glancing at him then and noting the frown and, afterwards, his relaxed and patient posture, hoped he was just allowing the grandiose Cameron to fire off his artillery and that later he would speak to better purpose. Miles Macdonell was not a man to be threatened. McDonald, looking at him, probably so considered. He seemed to have a sudden itching in his face by the way he rubbed it over.

Cameron opened his eyes wide to stare fixedly at the Governor, at Spencer, and then at his companion as though for evidence of the effect on them of that volley. He ignored me. And he saw blank faces.

"I have two charges to make against the Colony," he said. "First

F

of all it would appear, Captain Macdonell, that you are not yet conversant with the usages of this country. Do you know the French word *cache*?"

" Surely."

" A private cache is looked upon as sacred," said Cameron. " Men have been killed——"

He hesitated because McDonald of Garth impatiently moved, turned in his chair as if for a more direct scrutiny of him.

" I am not threatening—I am explaining," Cameron went on. " Men have been killed for robbing a cache. It is a highly serious offence among the natives. A party of our voyageurs in the farther Indian Countries had occasion to do more than cache some provisions, to leave them in a storehouse, and I have information that the store was robbed by your people."

" I think I know to what you refer," replied Captain Macdonell. " The officer I sent in command of that party had sufficient evidence that pemican was being held there for later export contrary to my orders. The gentleman in charge at the place did not deny the assumption."

" Nor admit it," said Cameron.

" Quite," said the Governor. " Therefore, as purchase was refused, my men—being within the confines of the territory over which I have authority—took a certain quantity for which payment will be made according to the terms of my embargo."

" We do not want your payment in British bills at the customary rates—to quote the words of that absurd and arrogant embargo," said Cameron, and raised his head, closed his eyes. The whiteness of the lids on his sunburnt face gave a repellant effect to me, bending over my table, quill in hand, but observing all under lowered brows. " That party, under orders from you, sir, broke into the storeroom of our fort at la Souris and carried away four hundred packages of pemican. They drew three stakes to get into the fort from the palisade. Mr. Spencer here, whom you call Sheriff Spencer, we were unable to arrest on hearing of the affair. But Mr. Howse, who assisted him actively, was arrested because of that on a charge of burglary."

" I cannot think on what authority," said Miles Macdonell.

Swiftly I saw him look side-long at the Sheriff, expressionless himself but curious perhaps to see if Spencer showed any sign of regret

for the manner in which he had conducted affairs that day. It was not
that the Governor was going to blame him for his methods. There
was, indeed, a part of him that had been amused over the whole thing
though he had seen the possibility of the North-Westers making precisely the charge that Duncan Cameron voiced then.

"You forget, Captain Cameron," he pointed out, "that I had issued
an order and that it was being flagrantly flouted. You cannot deny,"
he added, "that your Company continues, in face of it, to export all
the provisions on which I put an embargo. The most important to
me is the pemican. My order is flouted."

"You question my authority to make the arrest of your Mr.
Howse," said Cameron, "and I question your authority to issue—
or at least to compel—such an edict as you put your hand to with
Mr. Secretary Sheriff Spencer witnessing."

He then settled himself more solidly in his chair, sat large and mute,
head back, eyelids superciliously lowered. McDonald of Garth beside
him tossed one leg over the other, at ease.

"I think we might be able to come to some arrangement," he
suggested, and cupped a hand over his mouth and plucked his lips.

"Before we go further, gentlemen," said Miles Macdonell, "would
you care to have a dram?"

Cameron opened his eyes and looked seriously at him.

"Eh? A dram? Oh, yes, Captain Macdonell. A dram would go
down well!" he exclaimed, much less pompous.

The Governor turned and nodded to me and I stepped to the door
to bid his servant, who awaited instructions there, to attend to that.

"This matter," McDonald of Garth persisted, "can surely be
settled amicably. We don't need to be at each other's throats. You
see, Captain Macdonell, the North-West Company needs pemican
too as well as your colonists. It is needed for the voyageurs. Whitefish and geese by the lakes, moose meat in Athabasca, poor rabbits by
the lakes and fat rabbits in Athabasca, salmon and wild sheep on the
Pacific side of the Stone Mountains—these are part of the bill of fare.
Everywhere pemican is needed. It is the staple. Could we not come
to an agreement?"

The servant entered with a tray of goblets and bottles. There was
a pause in the discussion till all four were served and then, after the

formal elevation of the glasses and the "Slainté!" of these Highlanders——

"Where was I?" said McDonald of Garth. "Yes—take this very
seizure you have made : four hundred bags of pemican. Couldn't
we make, on these, a basis for an understanding? You have two
hundred down here in your storeroom now. The other two hundred
you have at Brandon House. Could you not give instructions to Mr.
Fidler to let us have those at Brandon House back again and you
settle with us for the two hundred you have here? We need pemican
as well as you, and that was a considerable seizure," and he chuckled
as though amused at it, and drank, smacking his lips.

Duncan Cameron leant forward and very heavily he spoke.

"We have somewhere about double the number of men at Fort
Gibraltar that you have here," he said.

It was another threat to the ears of all, McDonald of Garth included
again, rather than a suggestion for a greater need for provisioning,
because it took no account of the settlers, was spoken only as in
comparison of the numbers of the staff at Gibraltar with the men
visible at the administrative quarters at Point Douglas.

"Yes, yes," said McDonald hastily. "We have lots of mouths to
fill too. But, my dear Cameron, we must not forget that Captain
Macdonell has all his settlers to think of along the riverside as well
as the people under your nose here." He turned to our Governor. "I
want to discuss other aspects of provisioning with you, Captain
Macdonell. Oatmeal is a thing that the North-West Company lacks
badly. I understand that the Hudson's Bay Company has shipped in
a larger supply than usual, enough not only for its own people but for
sale to the settlers till they can become their own millers. I was
wondering if we could have, as well as a certain limiting of your
embargo, a kind of trade agreement. For instance : Let us say on our
side we promise to supply such and such a number of bags of pemican
to you on condition that you use your influence with the Hudson's
Bay Company to let us have such and such a number of stone of
oatmeal."

Here was a new aspect of the commissariat question. Would that
the Colony, I thought, was further advanced, with flourishing crops
and grist mills. Would that we could ourselves supply that meal!

"I believe, sir," replied Miles Macdonell, "that we could arrange something of that sort."

"And something else: I heard at Bas de la Rivière that, because of the American army occupying Detroit, our Company is anxious regarding transportation of furs and provisions. I suppose because of the Royal Charter of the Hudson's Bay Company that His Majesty's ministers, as well as the Company, would have to be consulted regarding permission for us to use the York Fort, or York Factory, route. Should this war with America bring more fleets of theirs on the lakes, should they get up as far as Lake Superior, we might have serious trouble in the shipping of our furs to Montreal. A concession from the Hudson's Bay Company to use their fort would be welcome. With all else amicably arranged perhaps you could pen a word to Lord Selkirk anent that, he being their chief shareholder. But we can leave that in abeyance. All that remains is for us to agree to meet and discuss the details of give and take in the pemican problem now that we have got this far towards an understanding."

He rose then and Cameron, looking at him gloomily, rose also.

"A *deoch-an doruis*," suggested the Governor as he and Spencer stood up, Spencer watching him thoughtfully.

"Yes, yes, indeed," said Cameron, less gloomy. "I see nothing against it."

The doch-an-doris being duly elevated and drunk, that conference was at end.

IV

When that meeting ended a weight was assuredly off the Governor's mind and the ex-soldier could tell himself, I thought, that as a statesman, a diplomat, he had done none too badly. After one or two more amicable discussions he put his signature to a reciprocal agreement, much on the lines that Bras Croché suggested that day, beside those of McDonald of Garth and Duncan Cameron who subscribed himself, "Captain, Voyageur Corps, Commanding Officer, Red River."

Then a little while and Captain Macdonell realised how a statesman or politician may be criticised. He had to suffer the rebukes, the contumely of Hudson's Bay officers from Red River to Hudson Bay.

It was balm to him to hear that neither Hillier nor John McLeod in their distant and far-severed posts had turned against him but defended his decision instead of scoffing that he had given an order and weakened in its enforcement, as many did. At York Factory, Superintendent Auld was disgusted when he heard of the terms agreed upon, declared that no oatmeal could be spared, and added that if Captain Macdonell wished to have a treaty with the North-Westers by which, in return for sales to him of pemican, they might have meal he had better make haste and have it to provide from the Settlement. The Governor was even criticised by some Hudson's Bay men for allowing a surgeon of the Settlement to go to Fort Gibraltar to attend to the dying John Willis there.

Macdonell was well able, indeed, to sympathise with John Pritchard, who had been in charge at la Souris, over the attacks made upon him by his own Company. Many of us believed that Duncan Cameron had advised those in charge of North-West posts to act much as Pritchard had acted when Spencer took the pemican, towards adding to the impression of the North-West as injured party should these affairs be brought to a law court. Be that as it may, when the matter was thus apparently settled through the diplomacy of Bras Croché, John Pritchard was so painfully censored by the Montreal and Fort William partners of his Company, and by Cameron and cousin Alexander also, for permitting the taking of the pemican without fight, that he retired from the service and purchased a parcel of land at the Red River Colony. He was far from being a coward, as coming events were to show, and their innuendos of cowardice made him wish to be done with them as associates.

And McDonald of Garth, Bras Croché, though he was brother-in-law of McGillivray, was set upon violently for what he had done by the chiefs in Montreal on his return to the east. He should have crushed the Governor of Selkirk's Settlement, they told him there. His action, they declared, had been tantamount to admission of Macdonell's right to establish an embargo. His record, already made, prevented any calling him a coward but they called him, jeeringly, the peace-maker.

Depression came upon Miles Macdonell. He seemed to me to be a sick man. Under all the criticism to which he was subjected his mental power of resistance flagged. He even wrote to Auld that, with so much hostility against him, he felt it advisable to tender his resignation to Lord Selkirk and explain that there were too many different interests to reconcile.

Promptly came a reply from the inspector that he read with a deepening frown: *You may be assured I will use my utmost endeavours to satisfy the Noble Earl of the Propriety and Necessity of his accepting cheerfully your resignation by which you thus give a most feeling mark of your devotion to his interests while you follow the only road to your own true happiness.*

He gave me that letter and as I read it said he: " Mr. Auld is too eager to aid me to depart; but I have had enough of it."

He had made up his mind. His resignation was written. But I consoled myself with the thought of the great distances between him and his employer and the realisation that he would have to remain with us until he received acknowledgment of his resignation and the appointment of a successor—with a sort of rider of a hope that the earl would prevail upon him to reconsider his decision and stay where he was.

CHAPTER SEVEN

I

THE time of year had come when the sultriness of day frequently lingered after sunset. The moon was adrift in a cloudless night. On my way to the Chisholm home I heard, with pleasure and a sense of relief, faint ruffling in the top of a clump of cottonwoods. From distance came the sound of bagpipes. That made me consider anew how far this place was from the land from which I had come. Yet it seemed suddenly to my mind like a small outpost of that land, surely its farthest outpost. Beyond, in the west where the last of daylight had gone from the highest cloud, were only the Indian Countries.

I passed the MacBeath place. They were at family worship there. I could hear the voice of MacBeath and knew the tone, the tone of reading out of the Scriptures. I continued on my way, passed another clump of cottonwoods, and arrived at the Chisholms'. Because of the sultriness of the night, and for admission of those occasional refreshing airs that fanned it, the door stood open. Drawing near I saw the small flicks of silver—of moths—poising and twinkling inwards.

I heard voices not of the family only and then, close, saw that there were visitors within and was about to turn away when Mairi, bending her head to shield her eyes from the crusie light, saw me and beckoned. I stepped inside. There were several people seated with the family and evidently what they talked of was engrossing. Mrs. Chisholm turned her head on my entrance, looked at me as though without recognition or even as if aware of me, her mind elsewhere. Hugh gave me no more than a glance but that he uttered no word of welcome did not mean that I was not welcome.

Mairi signalled to me to come to her side of the room and to sit down there. As I found a way past the visitors two of them looked up and not knowing me paid no attention to me. An elderly man was speaking, in English.

"Yes, that was worse than anything so far," he was saying. "I cannot understand our Duchess. Even sick folk had to get out. They fired the thatch over the houses of the bedridden and these had to be carried out with the embers falling on them."

Here, I realised, were some of the settlers who had recently come from distressed Sutherlandshire. Those to whom this was a new story sat round listening, and those who had seen that heartbreaking eviction gazed before them with eyes that, in memory, saw it all again.

"Did none offer resistance?" asked Mrs. Chisholm.

"Most of the able-bodied men were away at the time. But at any rate it was God's will, sad though it may seem—God's will."

I was amazed that any could think there was God's will. Mairi turned to me.

"He's just been saying," she explained, "that almost all the clergy told them that. The clergy," she went on in a lower voice, "would lose their livings, you see, if they spoke otherwise."

"It is very sad indeed," said Chisholm, "but here you are in a new land where you will never be turned out."

"Oh me!" sighed a woman. "But it's far from home and the graves of our folks, and it's sad to think of those that died of fever in the ship on the way in their wandering graves, buried at sea there. Ah, that was sad, seeing them weighted down and glimmering away from sight in their wandering graves."

One of the younger women looked anxiously at her and, leaning to one side, spoke quietly in the Gaelic what sounded like a warning.

"What does she say?" I whispered to Mairi who, though she had been some time in the Lowlands had retained her Gaelic.

She shook her head as though to silence me, then whispered back: "She says better not to talk of it all. I think she doesn't want to upset——" her voice was too low for me to catch the rest.

"Doesn't want what?" I asked.

"To affect that other old lady there," Mairi whispered, "to have her upset."

But the warning had come too late. The old woman suddenly bowed her head and began to sob. It was a strange sobbing. It rose louder, it had a sound of abandon in it, and then from sobbing her voice changed and she called out words in the Gaelic, words that required no interpretation. Clearly they were of lamentation.

There was sympathy in the room but there was also, certainly among the Lowlanders, embarrassment. Ecstasy of lamentation was in that voice, something primitive, uncontrolled as it rose higher and she wailed. No one spoke. The moths ricochetted from wall to wall, whirled in circles under the low ceiling, dashed into the lamp flame, nearly extinguishing it. As the woman wailed I was reminded vividly of the buffalo hunt on the plains to west of Fort Daer, of the charging herd, of Jules gored, of the shallow grave, of the *click-click* of stones laid over it, thrown over it, to prevent disinterment by the prairie wolves, of sitting in the tepee with Court Nez, and of the wailing cry that came into the midst of our talk in that tepee, the lamentation of Jules's mother.

A man rose—I presume the old woman's son—and bending to her spoke at first quietly and gently, then more vigorously, then harshly. At the harshness some of the women protested but others, turning to them, nodded their heads reassuringly. The more stern, more commanding tone penetrated better. She allowed herself to be led out, her son looking over his shoulder and bidding good-night to the Chisholms. The other guests, save a lad called Robert Wallace who was there, after a brief space of silence with words of adieu followed.

The sound of their feet passed away on the Settlement road. The Chisholms, Wallace and I, moved to the door and watched in the moonlight the shadowy forms disappear towards where other lights twinkled northwards.

Robert Wallace, from Ayrshire, had come out with the 1812 party, the party Owen Keveny conducted. Apparently Agnes had cast some sort of spell on him. Mr. and Mrs. Chisholm turned indoors, Wallace and Agnes followed, but Mairi and I stayed outside, sharing the night. There was no sound at all but the occasional stirring of wind in the cottonwood tips. There was not a cloud then in the sky. Its blueness was manifest, almost as though it were day. The moon had put out the stars.

"It's hard to understand," said Mairi, "hard to understand cruel things like what they were talking about when everything is so beautiful. But she should not break down. We can't break down, David, ever. I shouldn't say that, perhaps. She's old. We're young."

Often when I was with her some simple enough speech of hers would cause me to tell myself that all girls were not like Janet from whose power I had torn myself away, that a very different spirit inhabited Mairi's quiet body, looked out at the windows of her eyes. No, I thought again, standing there, I must not judge all girls by

Janet who had loved to tantalise and to create occasions that gave proof of her power. Even Agnes, though she did not attract me in the same way as did her sister, would never be cruel, invite specially to rebuff. Agnes was far too genial and kind to seek proof of the devotion of admirers in their acceptance of testing affronts.

And then, even with Mairi at my side, I remembered the half-breed girl, Christina, who to my consternation had been revealed as Court Nez's daughter—and in the mere remembering of her I felt again that emotion I had experienced, and that had never truly left me, on seeing her pass through a candle-lit room in Fort Gibraltar.

Agnes's laughter came out to us and her inquiry : " What's keeping you two? Can't you come in and be happy and forget that old woman?"

We passed back into the house again.

II

That evening I heard criticisms of the Governor. Agnes broached the subject. She loved light banter and a subject that her mother had been discussing that day struck her as an excellent one with which merrily to assail me whose devotion to Miles Macdonell, I knew, had always been obvious to all.

" Have you heard the latest?" she asked me, with a roguish glint. " Have you heard they are saying our Governor is not competent?"

" Not competent!" I exclaimed.

Laughter bubbled from her.

" You tell him, mother," she suggested.

" Oh, hoots!" said Hugh Chisholm.

" Ah, but there is something in what they say," Mrs. Chisholm declared.

" Hoots!" said Chisholm again.

" You can hoot," said his wife, " but they say rightly that he is a soldier and not an agricultural man."

" Indeed he might be both," Chisholm pointed out.

" He had a farm of his own," said I. " I know, for he has mentioned it once or twice to me. Lord Selkirk, years ago, when visiting in the Canadas, went to see him there. Yes, he had a farm at a place called Osnabruck, I think, in Upper Canada. If I had known the subject was ever going to be brought up I would have taken special note of it at the time!"

"Don't be so serious, David," begged Agnes; and suddenly realising her game, and that she knew I was devoted to the Governor, I laughed. "But you can bear me out," she added, "that he is drilling you every day over there at Point Douglas, all those of you that he can get to drill."

Chisholm remained serious. These repeated aspersions on Captain Macdonell disgusted him.

"As for that," he said, "it is clear enough to all except these folks deluded by Cameron's smooth talk that the North-Westers are not friendly to us and I think our Governor does right and wisely to prepare some of the lads for defence in case protection is needed."

"Protection from the North-Westers!" scoffed Mrs. Chisholm. "It is the Indians we've got to dread, Captain Cameron says. He is afraid that the Indians may come along and attack the Settlement. That is why he's offering, for any or all that would care for him to do it, to make arrangements on their behalf to get good safe locations of farm land free for them in the Canadas instead of here. There would be no risk there, he says, of a pack of savages coming down like the wolf on the fold."

"Very well, then, very well!" said Chisholm. "Let us say it is sensible of Captain Macdonell to think of protecting his people from the savages that Mr. Cameron fears may come down like wolves upon us—or that Mr. Cameron hopes may come down like wolves upon us."

"Captain Cameron is the name," his wife corrected him.

"The soldiering, as you call it," said I, roused again and delighting Agnes thereby, "is just because he is thinking of the farmers," and into my mind came a sentence from one of the letters of Captain Macdonell to Lord Selkirk that I had copied. I raised my head in a manner that amused Agnes and added, really quoting from that letter: "Seeing people well prepared often prevents mischievous consequences."

Hugh Chisholm, unconsciously, aided and abetted his daughter then.

"That may be so," he agreed, "but it may make the others get prepared too. However! We're getting away from the point, as usual. Or I am—maybe I am. All this criticism of the Governor we have been hearing is being fostered by that man Mr. Duncan Cameron."

"Captain Cameron is the name," corrected his wife again. "And he says that the earl has sent us all here and left us in the lurch. I was hearing to-day that Macdonell just thinks of himself. I was hearing that he got the Earl of Selkirk to use his influence to get one of his sons a commission in the army."

"And why shouldn't he?" shouted Chisholm. "Might it not be a pleasure to the earl to do it for the man he has made governor of this place? Oh, my God, the way people try to belittle——"

"Captain Cameron," interrupted Mrs. Chisholm, "is thinking for the good of the settlers here. You needn't belittle him! He speaks the Gaelic and——"

"Yes, and that helps him to get around them for his own ends. Captain Macdonell can speak the Gaelic too, so far as that goes, and the French——"

"And Spanish also," said I, ready to offer a word in praise of him, though neither Chisholm's remark nor mine was much to the point. I had seen the Governor reading a copy of *Don Quixote* by Cervantes in the original. His father had been in the wars in Spain (was called Spanish John thereby) and perhaps had interested his son in that foreign tongue.

"To get back to our subject," said Chisholm, "it is amazing how gullible some people are. That man Cameron—him and his Gaelic!—wants to get quit of us all to the Canadas. That's his design."

"Or to Scotland again for that part!" said Mairi.

"What are you interrupting your father for?" snapped Mrs. Chisholm, her eyes flashing. "Can't you hold your tongue and keep your peace and not interrupt?"

"Yes, you're right, Mairi," said Chisholm, nodding to her. "He'd have us go to the Canadas, to Scotland—or to Hell! And they don't see through him. Him and his red coat! He only got that coat, and calls himself captain, so as to be upsides with our Governor. I know which is the better man."

"Well, what has our Governor done for us?" demanded Mrs. Chisholm. "Taken us up to Fort Daer for the sake of the buffalo.

Doesn't get enough of farming implements for all. And look at the winter we had! Look at the bad summer!"

"It's too bad he neglects his duty regarding the weather," observed Chisholm. "Even the weather he doesn't manage right."

Agnes giggled but no one else dared to show sign of amusement or relish of that riposte.

"I," said Mrs. Chisholm, "think it entirely natural that those poor Sutherland folk especially should be pleased to have Captain Cameron taking an interest in them and being sympathetic with them. If you had had the thatch burnt over your head, and then had had fever on a ship in mid-ocean, and then had been buried at sea, you might have some sympathy."

Chisholm chuckled. Mairi's eyes danced. Wallace and I became most excessively solemn. But Agnes unrestrainedly, boisterously, laughed, throwing back her head.

"If you had been buried at sea, dad!" she shouted.

"Oh, you, laughing at your mother!" said Mrs. Chisholm with doting gaze upon her second-born.

Chisholm rose, felt his biceps, felt his sides, clapped his hips, and "Och, aye!" he sighed, stepping towards the door. His wife's favouritism towards Agnes irked him, I think, as an injustice.

I rose then to go and with a " good-night " to the others we walked together to the gate. On the Settlement road someone was riding slowly past.

"Good-night to you, Mr. Chisholm," he hailed.

"Oh—oh, it's you. Good-night to you, Mr. Cameron," Chisholm responded. When Cameron was out of earshot he turned to me. "There he goes," he said, "from his visiting and his smooth talk—aye, with the Gaelic too—doing his best to get the people to leave here. I wonder now, I wonder now, if he can't get enough to please him to go away if he will try rough methods instead? I wouldn't put it past him."

III

The summer went on with " grand growing weather." North-West Company brigades and Hudson's Bay Company brigades from the interior—la Souris and Brandon, Portage la Prairie and Qu'Appelle—

came down Assiniboine, paused at Fort Gibraltar or Point Douglas, and went on their way, the North-West ones bound for the south end of Lake Winnipic and the first turning to the right (as shown on Arrowsmith's map that hung on the wall in the Colony store) on their long trip to Montreal, the Hudson's Bay ones for Lake Winnipic, Hayes River, York Factory.

Near the summer's end word came from Benjamin Frobisher at Fort Gibraltar of the death of Mr. Willis. Though retired from the service he had remained there. The funeral was attended by many Hudson's Bay and Colony officers—both commissioned as it were and non-commissioned. Hillier, who was then at Red River from the far Churchill River country on a visit to our Governor, attended. The flag of the North-West hung at half-mast all day at their fort and of the Hudson's Bay Company on the pole of its trading post built at Point Douglas. And we all walked or staggered home after the funeral, according to capacity, feeling very sorry that Willis had gone—for he had been not unfriendly to us—though glad for his sake that he was free of pain; and all, whether drunk, or betwixt and between, or full sober, were somewhat subdued with thoughts of mortality, the knowledge that it was no longer possible to go over to the fort and find John Willis there despite all the talk we might hear of life eternal. There might be life eternal, but not here. The prairie flowers that bloomed that year died that year; the flags that had been at the mast-head fluttered of his friends' regrets at half-mast only for a day in the little eddies of wind.

Duncan Cameron had apparently lost interest in what he called the welfare of the Selkirk settlers, and for whose sake he had suggested, visiting them formally, that he would do all in his power to have them happily installed eastward in Upper Canada. Because of the reigning tranquillity Miles Macdonell considered he might safely absent himself long enough to go to Hudson Bay to meet the additional immigrants who would reach there that summer.

And during his absence the deceptiveness of that tranquillity was revealed. His absence was Cameron's opportunity. He left Sheriff Spencer in charge with one Archibald McDonald as assistant—usually spoken of as Mr. Archibald to avoid confusion, there being many bearing his surname variously spelt and in some instances pronounced similarly, in others with but slight difference. There was the

Governor himself, Captain Miles Macdonell; there was his cousin, Alexander Macdonell; there was a young writer for the Hudson's Bay Company, Michael McDonnell from Killala; there was McDonald of Garth, still spoken of; and there were others also of the same patronymic in the vicinity. Archibald had but recently come to Red River. Though a young man, the care of the immigrants of 1813—they of " the fever ship "—had been entrusted to him by Lord Selkirk.

On September 5th there was a sudden converging upon Governor's House of people not connected either with the Colony or with the Hudson's Bay Company. Some rode out of the thickets to west, some appeared from the riverside's fringe of trees eastward. One or two, who had ridden past the door as though on a visit to the farms, came riding back to join these. Others galloped from the direction of Fort Gibraltar. Governor's House was surrounded. There they all were, all armed. The foray had clearly been carefully arranged beforehand. There was no discussion regarding procedure when they ringed the place. The posts were assigned. The reins of the horses of those who alighted were promptly held by others and into the office the dismounted men swiftly trod.

At the central table, facing the door, Spencer sat. Archibald was out in the Settlement. I was at my desk, or table, to one side, busy over some accounts with Michael McDonnell, the Hudson's Bay clerk. We had heard the sudden drumming of horses' hoofs and given ear inquiringly. This abrupt belligerent entry, following upon that, startled us.

" John Spencer," said a man in advance, " I have a warrant here for your arrest on a charge of burglary at the North-West Company's fort of la Souris." And then, with a half-turn to those behind, " Take him, men ! " he ordered. " Take him ! "

Round both sides of the table the invaders hurried as if expecting Spencer to snatch a pistol from the drawer and make some resistance. But he merely sat back, looked left and right at them as they encircled him, and then across at the man who had spoken.

Michael and I leapt to our feet, seeming, no doubt, like two trapped animals, or at bay. I glanced quickly back and forth from Spencer to the crowd closing in on him. At the moment's urge I felt ready for any desperate chance, to fight a way out and shout for a rescue party, or madly to attempt a tussle with these people. But pistols and muskets menaced us and, more gruesomely intimidating than the muskets, the horrid bayonets fixed to some of them.

Spencer, without rising, stretched a hand, took the proffered missive from the warrant-bearer and read it.

"'*Archibald Norman MacLeod, Major, Voyageurs' Corps, justice of the peace in the Indian Countries,*'" he read aloud in a voice steady but harsher than usual. "Now I wonder!" he said, pausing in his reading. "This is Assiniboia."

"That document is all in order," exclaimed the man who had presented it, a stoutish, lumpish fellow in an attire part of the eastern cities, part of the Indian Countries, an elegant stock at his throat, beaded moccasins on his feet.

John Spencer scanned the warrant, sat back, pondered, and for the time-being at least had the manner of master of the situation.

"Take him, men!" said the leader again.

But at that Spencer stood up, dabbing the palms of his hands in air on either side as a sign to them to let him alone, not to touch him.

"Very good," said he. "I shall come with you but I will require to write a letter and leave it here—a letter of explanation to Governor Macdonell and another to my Lord Selkirk."

"You need not trouble to do that."

"I cannot leave here unless I do," replied Spencer firmly.

Sitting down determinedly he took up his pen. Those who had gathered round the table then returned to join the group before it. Spencer paused in his writing, considering a word or a phrase, perhaps, his head up. He glanced at me and I took that glance for one of appeal. What was he trying to convey? To suggest a rescue? Perhaps so. I strode to the door.

"Stop there, you! You can't go out," said the leader.

"All right, Baxter," said Spencer. "The game that Mr. Pritchard played of no resistance is, I think, the game for me now—best for all," and he began to write again.

There was talk, sudden and urgent by the sound, among the men outside and those inside hurried to the door. Spencer halted once more and stepping closer to the table I whispered: "Shall I shout for help, sir, or try to dash through?"

"No, no," he replied, urgently. "They'd shoot you."

G

His letters finished he rose and handed them to me. Then he addressed the warrant-server who had turned back from the door.

"I presume," said Spencer, "I may be allowed to give orders for a servant to pack my things and accompany me to Fort Gibraltar?"

"Certainly," said the man. "Captain Cameron said you would expect that, but you must have him bestir himself and follow you promptly. We have a light canoe ready to start at once. You can give orders to one of these lads what servant you want to accompany you and what apparel you will need."

"A light canoe! How far do I go?"

"To Montreal."

"So!" said Spencer.

He gave the necessary instructions to me, surrendered to my keeping a ring of Colony keys, shook hands with me, shook hands with Michael. With sullen eyes for those who arrested him we watched him go. My own helplessness infuriated me. There was a led-horse for him—all had indeed been carefully arranged—and surrounded by the armed group he rode away.

IV

Immediately Michael and I hurried out to give information of what had happened. I dashed to the store, that being the nearest building, to tell John Bourke, babbled all out with scarce pause for breath.

"Well," said Bourke, "I heard a galloping of horses and thought it was just some of our own Indians riding by, or one of their herds grazing on the plain cavorting near. I was busy and did not come out. If I had they would likely just have rushed on me and bidden me tarry with them at the pistol's end till they were ready to go. Quick work it was. It seems to me, from what you say, that Mr. Spencer did all he could. But what should we do now?"

"Go tell the settlers," said I. "The Hudson's Bay men here must also know. Everybody must know. I would that Mr. Hillier were still here. John McLeod is back again from one of his trips to prairie posts. He'll be at the Company's Indian Hall, I expect, with the factor—Mr. Sutherland."

Michael, who had followed me, stood close behind me.

"We could both carry the news," he suggested, "one to Indian Hall and the other to the farms."

Indian Hall and the old cabin known as Fidler's house were near, but the first settler was about a mile away. Nearly two hours had passed before there were a sufficient number of men gathered at Governor's House to confer or act. I went to call the settlers and Archibald, hearing the news while he was engaged on some duty in the Colony, hastened back with me to Governor's House. Into his keeping I gave the letters Spencer had written to Lord Selkirk and Captain Macdonell, also the ring of keys.

That was a stormy gathering. Duncan Cameron had made many friends among the settlers and some of these came to the conference. To all suggestion of a rescue by force of arms they shouted No. One or two of these even said that Spencer had but got his desserts. Others of the Colony, who had never been beguiled by Cameron's advances, were very differently minded. A Murray, a Bannerman, and a Sutherland (not related to James of the Hudson's Bay Company, William Sutherland, a farmer) demanded muskets and ammunition for rescue. But Archibald refused to give them the hangard and armoury keys.

"I would," he cried out, "that the Governor were here!"

They pointed out that the North-Westers had taken advantage of Captain Macdonell's absence to make the arrest and that the Governor would expect him to act.

"There would be bloodshed," he said. "I would not take the responsibility."

Several rushed away then to Indian Hall to see if they could get muskets there. James Sutherland was in the store alone. John McLeod, though recently returned from a distant post, was out that day visiting in an Indian camp on Company's business. Most of us thought that if he had been there we would have had a different reception. McLeod, we believed, would have lent us a stand of arms. Factor Sutherland, however, refused. We pled with him, then went back disgruntled, some even saying that we should have taken by force what we were refused, and joined the crowd round Archibald to make one more plea of him for firearms.

Hugh Chisholm was there but he was not one of the voluble. He had no advice to offer, no suggestion to make. I knew quite well what he was thinking: if we could get arms, and if a decision was made by a reasonable number to go over to Fort Gibraltar and demand the return of Mr. Spencer, he would be with them; but with a wife and two daughters behind him he was not eager to urge such action. As a corpse he would be of no service to his family.

"I was right," he remarked in my ear. "It's not the Indians we have to dread coming down on us like a wolf on the fold. It's the Nor'-Westers."

"They said they had a canoe ready to take him away at once," I told the crowd.

That information roused those that were all for rescue to new fury. Several posted off at once to the river bank and on arrival there all, turning, shouted and beckoned together.

"Come!" cried Bannerman, who had stayed behind. "Let us break down the hangard doors and take the muskets we need from the armoury!"

Those by the river were waving frantically. The others rushed away in response to the excited summons. Archibald and I followed them and found it was a summons to chagrin. We came to the bank just in time to see two canoes going downstream at great speed, the paddlers digging in violently.

"Impotent! Impotent!" ejaculated Murray.

"Have we to admit that they have the law on their side?" I asked bitterly of Archibald.

"Probably not in the last resort," he replied. "I do sincerely trust not in the last resort. But the warrant for arrest, you say, was issued by a justice of the peace in the Indian Countries, and if we attempt an armed rescue we would, as I see it, make ourselves amenable to law."

CHAPTER EIGHT

I

It was not till the 19th of October that the Governor returned with the new immigrants.

The change of air, the inland voyaging again by Hayes River and Lake Winnipic, seemed to have helped him, restored his health. Mentally he was better. I thought he was by no means as depressed as he had been when he considered it advisable—in view of that difficulty "of reconciling so many different interests," as he had expressed it in the letter to Lord Selkirk—to tender his resignation. He was sustained by the knowledge that there would be no more "tripping" to the vicinity of the buffalo wintering-grounds that year, no marking time at Fort Daer, but a winter at last, after a summer of splendid crops, at Red River Settlement.

When I told him the news of the arrest of John Spencer he felt such sudden fury that he shook. Here was a quandary for him. Where now was the reciprocal agreement he had signed with the North-West representatives, with McDonald of Garth and Duncan Cameron? While away he had been fondly imagining that the Colony and the North-Westers were on amicable terms. He had tried while at York Factory, on behalf of those at Fort Gibraltar, to arrange for supplies of oatmeal, as he had promised them he would, but Mr. Auld continued to affirm that he was unable to provide any. On his way back the Governor had thought that one of his first duties would be to make apology to Duncan Cameron for his inability to make the arrangements. But that became a small matter compared with the arrest of John Spencer.

When at York Factory he had received various communications from Lord Selkirk. His resignation, of course, had not reached the earl. It was, indeed, only by then on its way out of Hudson Bay, in the Atlantic somewhere. It went on the ship that had brought these new immigrants. Many were the reminders of distance between them, both for Lord Selkirk and for his governor at Red River. Several letters, however, had come to him from the earl by that ship.

One of them he had perused with doubt. He spoke of it to me when he had calmed himself sufficiently to discuss affairs.

"Lord Selkirk," said he, "writes me that he has been advised by his lawyers in England that his Governor here should give those who have built in the territory of Assiniboia orders to quit. It is a mere formality or legality to prevent them, as he explains, from claiming what the lawyers call a prescriptive right. I have to order them off: that is all. Conceive the result, Baxter. The North-Westers will of course refuse to move. I hope they will understand it is but a formality for, if they do not, my failure to take steps to enforce it will win their contempt—and not only their contempt but also that of the Hudson's Bay men and settlers who charged me with pusillanimity because, after ordering an embargo on pemican, I was willing to temporise and make some compliances."

"It could be explained to them," said I, "that the order is a legal formality."

"I could not do that, Baxter," replied the Governor. "I could not go about explaining to them, to get their approval. As for Mr. Spencer: it is too late to bring him back. I will make out a report of the affair and send it to his lordship, and he will take it up at head-quarters."

A few days later he handed me the draft of a letter, requesting that two fair copies be made, one for his signature and another to be placed on the Colony file:

District of   *To Mr. Duncan Cameron, acting*
Assiniboia.   *for the North-West Company at*
                       the Forks of the Red River.

Take notice, That by the authority and on the behalf of your land-lord, the Right Honourable Thomas Douglas, Earl of Selkirk, I do hereby warn you, and your associates of the North-West Company, to quit the post and premises you now occupy at the Forks of the Red River within six calendar months from the date hereof.

Given under my hand at Red River Settlement this 21st day of October, 1814.

Despite his belief regarding the possible results of that notice, I am inclined to think that Captain Macdonell felt a certain pleasure, some satisfaction, in putting his signature to it. It was, in a way, a retort for the arrest of Spencer during his absence. And——

"Well, there it is for him!" he said, and despatched me to Fort Gibraltar to serve it.

II

It was a clear day. Along the top of the bank of Red River, the leaves having fallen from the oaks and elms, there was a web of twigs. The air carried sound clearly. I could hear the shouts of children at play over towards the river. Far off, out of sight, my ears could not decide from which direction it came, a Red River cart was squealing and complaining on its way.

The gate of Fort Gibraltar was on the southern side, the side that faced the Assiniboine. As I came round the corner from a tepee pitched nearby a string of dogs rushed at me but when only two or three feet off they whirled away, circled behind me, snakily followed me, then left me.

The gate was shut. Odd, thought I, for the gate to be shut. A placard was on it, a placard explaining why, I supposed; but coming closer I found, half-astonished, half-amused, that it was an important-looking form setting forth that Duncan Cameron bore a captain's commission in the Voyageurs' Corps and—what else I did not read for I was interrupted by a sentry looking at me between the gate-stakes, a half-Indian by his appearance, *bois-brûlé*. From the red sash he wore I noticed a pistol-butt protruding.

"Good-day to you," said I. *"Bon jour."*

"Good-day to you. Where do you come from?"

"From Red River Settlement."

"You can't come in, then. What do you want here?"

"I want to see the officer in command, Mr. Duncan Cameron."

"Captain Duncan Cameron. State your business with him."

"I have a message from the Governor."

"What governor?"

"Governor Macdonell of Red River Settlement."

"Governor!" scoffed the sentry. "As much governor as I am, they tell me."

In my rage at that remark I would have knocked him down had the closed gate not separated us.

"And captain!" said I. "A genuine captain!"

The sentry, with a twist of his neck, leered awry at me.

"What is your message?" he demanded.

"I have to deliver it to Mr. Cameron."

"Captain Cameron I told you!" he rasped.

He moved away and spoke into a small log cabin by the gate. Another *métis* came out then, took stock of me between the stakes, and sat down with his back against the cabin wall. He who had been on duty went smartly enough to the officers' house.

"There he comes!" I ejaculated to myself a minute or two later.

There indeed came Duncan Cameron, not in his red coat but very important of bearing. When he reached the gate he clearly recognised me, recalled me from the day of his visit to the Governor with McDonald of Garth. But though recognising me he gave no salutation, just raised his head high and looked with condescension on me.

"Yes?" he said with a note of haughty inquiry.

"I have a message from the Governor for you," said I.

"What governor?"

"The Governor of Assiniboia, sir," I told him, speaking definitely, firmly.

I held out the missive but the sentry, who had returned by then on Cameron's heels, took it from me and passed it to his chief. The other man who had come out of the cabin to sit on guard while the sentry went away, dawdled back into it, looking over his shoulder curiously.

Duncan Cameron read the order slowly. As he read his face was suffused with scarlet through its tan. There was a gleam of rage in his eye. His aspect of arrogance was accentuated then.

"Well, well, well," said he, controlling himself with difficulty. "Too bad! But I presume he was ordered to send me this and 'tis but a formality. Too bad nevertheless. By the way, young man, you can tell your Governor—for yours he is though none of mine—that Bras Croché McDonald of Garth had no knowledge of how the Fort William and Montreal partners were looking upon this Selkirk scheme of settlement. He had been on the Pacific coast. To them his agreement with your Governor is nonsense. They cannot abide it—nor abide by it. Your Governor might as well commit his copy to the flames. I too have had advice from my headquarters as he has had from his, I take it, to send me this."

He was holding the order to quit in his left hand and at these words flicked it contemptuously with the back of his right.

"The advice I have received," he said, "applies not only to the Settlement but to the Hudson's Bay Company, seeing they have befriended the settlers. Mr. McGillivray at Fort William cannot stand the insult of that pemican embargo, the assumption of authority in it. So I have an order to make also. Pray convey it to your Governor, pray acquaint him with the latest order affecting him and his friends. It is no formality, you may assure him. It will soon be at all the forts of our Company. This is it: From now on, resolved that no one connected with the Settlement organisation and no Hudson's Bay employees be allowed within the walls of our forts unless in the event of starvation—absolute starvation. Tell that to your Governor!"

Duncan Cameron cleared his throat, wheeled, and walked grandly away.

III

I looked at his back with resentment against the final impression it conveyed of contemptuous dismissal.

"And that is the man," I thought, furious, "who can make himself utterly engaging to the settlers when he wishes to! In my case there is no occasion for him to be ingratiating."

I looked at the sentry as if for some human sympathy even from one in the enemy camp, but the sentry had done with me also. So I turned away, annoyed at the feeling of ignominy that this errand had brought me. The dogs rushed at me again from that tepee, when two or three feet off wheeled round me, slunk at my heels a little way and then left me.

But as I walked quickly across the plain the feeling as of having been dishonoured ebbed. I pictured myself at the gate demanding to see Cameron, handing him the order, replying to his rough inquiry of, "What governor?" with, "The Governor of Assiniboia, sir," very definitely enunciated. After all that Mr. Duncan Cameron had been irksomely pompous towards me, and at the end had left me with more than a suggestion of contemptuous dismissal, did not mean that I was contemptible! I squared my shoulders, breathed deep of the clear air, slowed down in my walk. Rightly considered my mission that day had been an important one and instead of feeling insignificant— just because of that insulting reception—I should feel honoured that my Governor had sent me with it.

Within an hour of my departure to Fort Gibraltar I returned to Point Douglas. I walked smartly into the administration room, very much on duty, and stood before Captain Macdonell's table.

" Well, Baxter?" said he.

" The sentry would not give me entrance, sir," I told him, " but went to inform Mr. Cameron I was there. Mr. Cameron came back with him and turned violent red over the order, bridled up like a bubblyjock and then said he supposed you had your orders to send it and that it was a formality."

" He said that!"

" Yes, sir, he said that. Then he told me that he had an order also. I was to inform you that Bras Croché McDonald of Garth, coming from the Pacific coast to the east, had no knowledge of how the Montreal and Fort William partners look on affairs here. That agreement come to betwixt Mr. McDonald and you was nonsense to them, he said, and you might as well destroy your copy. And he went on to ask me to convey to my Governor the latest resolve regarding not only the Colony but the Hudson's Bay Company's employees: None of them are to be allowed within the gates of North-West forts unless in case of absolute starvation—absolute starvation. ' Tell that to your Governor,' he said, and turned on his heel."

Miles Macdonell, listening, relaxed and nodded his head slowly once or twice.

" I wonder," said he, " what will be the next move?"

CHAPTER NINE

I

THE winter evenings came, lit indoors with crusies the settlers had brought from Scotland or the candles of their own making. A gregarious instinct brought us together despite the cold. With woollen mittens and large fur-lined gloves that were traded from the Indians, and skin caps traded from the Indians also, we crunched over the frozen snow on nights when, going out, there was a feeling as though particles of steel were in the air. To north the Aurora Borealis would be active. Tall pale green columns moved to and fro in space, reached up to the zenith. Occasional whirls of radiance would dash over the dome of the night like the lash of a whip. Indoors, by Franklin stoves such as were used in the Canadas, and that the Governor advised for all, the outer cold could be forgotten.

What a diversity of people were in the country by that winter of 1814! Sometimes the talk at their forgatherings was about the lack of any spiritual adviser. The Earl of Selkirk had promised them that they would have these advisers according to their creeds, the Settlement to be unsectarian, but so far they had none. There had been hitches in all his attempts to have shepherds of souls among them. So they elected a God's Good Man, one who had been an elder of the kirk at home, to officiate at the two great moments in human life—marriage and death—and to baptise when the surgeons and midwives had successfully brought another life into the world. Court Nez, it struck me, hearing the douce talk on these matters, would have given his thick laugh of amusement over expressions of disappointment that they had no spiritual adviser. But on New Year's Day even some of the douce ones seemed to recant their usual views regarding strong waters. There were peregrinations from house to house, not empty-handed. At " first footing " one must not be empty-handed. Court Nez I had not seen for some time.

During that winter it seemed to many of the settlers that all they had heard regarding the animosity of the North-West Company towards Lord Selkirk and his scheme was calumny. Even from as far as Qu'Appelle, away up the west fork (the Assiniboine) of Red River, came visitors to Fort Gibraltar, and Duncan Cameron invited the farmers to merry gatherings there and banquets at which those who still accepted his hospitality reported there were such wines served as they had never tasted before, wines such as their former landlords, who had cast them out of their homes in Scotland, drank. That no officers of the Hudson's Bay Company and no officers from the Settlement were called to these feasts did not make them suspicious of the hospitality. They well remembered that their Governor had had trouble with their hosts over the pemican embargo and they knew of the more recent order to quit that he had served on them as well as of the arrest of Mr. Spencer. It was not to be expected that Duncan Cameron would invite Miles Macdonell or his officers to these convivial gatherings.

Only a few of the young men had gone to Pembina that autumn, young men to whom " the tripping " was no boredom by any means but an adventure. They were to send buffalo meat down to the forks for the making of pemican. The lament of some of the elders that these lads were becoming like wandering Indians in their ways made them only laugh.

" After all," Captain Macdonell pointed out to these critics, content that but a few, and they only young men, had still to go to the hunting, " 'tis only a generation ago that the Highland clans were very much like the Indian tribes. The men were all for the chase and war."

But that year there was trouble at Pembina, the half-breeds there as little friendly, in these days, as those out on the western plains by Qu'Appelle. Cousin Alexander had had his way with most of them, turning them against the settlers. Our young men went hunting alone that autumn and often, when they came upon a herd and began their stalking afoot, as they had few horses for the work, a mounted party of half-breeds would appear, stampede the beasts away and leave them with hardly a kill. Protests led to strife. John McLeod, at Fort Daer again, going to a half-breed camp to make complaint, was held prisoner for a week.

News of that being swiftly carried to Captain Macdonell he advised his young men to raid the other camp and retaliate by taking hostages to hold till McLeod should be released and—angered over the whole business—sent an order, as Governor of Assiniboia, that the buffalo were not to be *run* on the coteau, not hunted, that is, on horseback. His young men being afoot, they would have little chance of getting meat if the half-breeds continued to spy on them, follow them and, when they found them drawing near a herd, charged in on it mounted.

An Indian runner a few days later brought a note to inform the Governor that Peter Pangman (Bostonois Pangman he was usually called) was held prisoner. He had formerly been with the Hudson's Bay Company but left it after a tiff with Mr. Fidler and joined the North-Westers. Tit for tat became the game. Cuthbert Grant, leader of the half-breeds at Qu'Appelle, came down and seized four Hudson's Bay men at Fort Daer—and with a warrant as well as by force of arms, a warrant signed by A. N. Macleod, as had been the one for Spencer's arrest. Cuthbert Grant, a sturdy youth, was the son of a Scot and had been sent to Montreal to be educated, I discovered.

That series of incidents took our Governor away from the Settlement again. He did not wish to leave it, remembering well, of course, that when he had gone to York Factory to meet the immigrants of the last summer his absence had been taken advantage of and Spencer had been arrested. He consoled himself with the reflection that Pembina was not as far off as York Factory and that he could travel even at that time of year to Fort Daer in two days. The half-breeds there would probably as little acknowledge him as law-giver in Assiniboia as would the half-breeds of the west. They had not recovered from their indignation at the pemican embargo; the order he had sent, because only some of our fellows were mounted, not to *run* the buffalo had definitely added to their hostility; but at last he succeeded in arranging an exchange of prisoners.

II

On a Sunday in April, while Captain Macdonell was away, I was at the Chisholm house in the evening. Spring was in the air. Long whizzing cracks sounded from the splintering river ice and muffled belchings beneath it. Young Wallace was there: he seemed to be always visiting the Chisholms. Two other lads were there also, struggling with their shyness, laughing hilariously at nothing. More boys than girls, as a matter of fact, visited that home. Their presence always made Mrs. Chisholm pleasantly excited. She listened with delight to Agnes's sallies of badinage.

On that evening, however, her mind was occupied with more than the joking and daffing of Agnes and her swains. Mr. Cameron (she had ceased to call him Captain because of annoyance at him) had been telling lies to the people, she said.

"I have come to doubt if he is sincerely interested in the welfare of the settlers after all," she announced. "It has come to my ears that he has been telling folks that they have really been lucky so far and that easily some year—perhaps this year—they might be visited by a hail-storm in midsummer that would ruin their crops. I can't believe that! That's a lie. I've lost confidence in him."

"Well," said Hugh, "there might be some truth in it. An Indian I spoke to said he had seen it. There might be such a thing as a summer hail-storm."

"No, I can't believe that!" declared Mrs. Chisholm. "You are credulous! The Indian didn't understand you, or you did not understand the Indian. I'm done with Mr. Cameron."

"Captain Cameron is the name," said Agnes, slyly.

"Captain, indeed!" snorted her mother. "I hear he has sent a written message to one of our neighbours down the road here with whom he is hob-nob, advising to take the swivel guns away from the store and cart them over to Fort Gibraltar for safe keeping."

Listening to that I decided that here, at any rate, was surely garbled news. No one should attach great importance, I decided, to anything Mrs. Chisholm repeated. Chisholm, by his placid manner as she spoke, was evidently of the same opinion.

But on the Monday morning I had reason to amend that view.

Archibald was in the office. Michael was there, leaving some invoices from Indian Hall. I was at my desk over the account books when suddenly the room was filled with people, with settlers. They came in as abruptly as the North-West party that had arrested Spencer. There was Campbell in the forefront, in his hand a letter.

"I have something to read to you here," he began brusquely. "It is a letter addressed to you from Duncan Cameron in command at Fort Gibraltar."

"From him to me? Then let me have it. How does it come that you have it to read to me?" asked Archibald.

"It was sent to me first so that I could acquaint the people with its contents. There was a covering note to that effect."

"Extraordinary manners!" exclaimed Archibald. I thought he looked very youthful facing these grown men.

"Well, I'll read it to you: '*Mr. Archibald McDonald. Sir, As your field pieces have already been employed to disturb the peace of His Majesty's loyal subjects in this quarter and even to stop up the King's highway, I have authorised the settlers to take possession of them and to bring them over here, not with a view to making any hostile use of them, but merely to put them out of harm's way. Therefore I expect that you will not be so wanting to yourselves as to attempt any useless resistance, as no one wishes you, or any of your people, any harm. I am, sir, Your obedient servant, D. Cameron, Captain Voyageurs' Corps, Commanding Officer, Red River. To Mr. Archibald McDonald, Red River Settlement.*'"

"Good God!" ejaculated Archibald when Campbell had finished. "He takes a lot upon himself! I would that our Governor was here. I feel sure he would not tolerate this."

"Well," said Campbell, "you are going to tolerate it in his absence. And neither you nor these writers here will move till we permit."

As he spoke the men beside him, bringing their hands forward, showed that they carried cudgels. From outside came a new sound as of clips of an axe and loud talk of many gathered together. In the rear wall of the office was a glazed window. Campbell and his followers looked towards it then. Archibald rose, turned to the window for a view, and was followed by Michael and me.

With our heads all close there we saw a party of settlers busy at work heaving the swivel guns and then a howitzer into carts. Two or three men who were strangers to me were directing them. They had broken open the hangard. When the last of the pieces were shouldered into a cart one of these strangers raised a musket and fired it in air. That was evidently a signal, for as soon as the report rang out there came Duncan Cameron leading a horse from a clump of bush. He swung to the saddle and advanced to the carts. He was in his military clothes and very proudly he bore himself.

What he said none of us in that room could hear but obviously he

was praising the men for their work. His little speech being ended
he wheeled his horse while they were cheering themselves, or him, or
both. Away all went, the carts with the guns, the mob, Cameron,
in the direction of Fort Gibraltar and, after a further five or ten
minutes, Campbell and those who had come in to prevent any one
in the office from going for assistance, left the building.

Archibald stepped back to his table. His face was white. Campbell,
before going, had tossed down the letter so discourteously, so oddly,
sent. Archibald picked it up and read it for himself, though already
it had been read to him, read it slowly aloud, then looked at us.

" I suppose," he said, " when he writes of stopping the King's
highway with the field pieces he is referring to the time when Captain
Macdonell had some trained on the river to halt their brigades after
they had taken Mr. Howse prisoner. The effrontery of the man! *I
have authorised the settlers,'* says he. That is on the strength of his
red coat. And that's a threat at the end : *' I expect you will not be so
wanting to yourselves as to attempt any useless resistance . . .'* I would
to God the Governor had been here. But you can bear me out that I
could do nothing."

As he was speaking John Bourke, the Colony storekeeper, came in
with a bandage round his head and a hand bandaged. He reported
the affair from his side.

" I refused to give up the keys of the hangard where the swivels and
howitzer were kept," he said. " Some of them attacked me. Much
good I did myself! A broken head and a cut hand are all I got—and
being without the keys they used an axe to break their way in."

III

Campbell did not return to the Settlement and it was common
knowledge throughout it—known alike to those who were under
the spell of Cameron and those who saw him merely as a plotter
against them and no true friend—that he received one hundred pounds
from the North-West Company, both for his assistance, no doubt, in
fomenting discontent among his fellow settlers and for taking a
leading part in the removal of the guns.

But another who had also taken an active part in the seizure, whom
we had observed at his work from the office window, was arrested

by Mr. Archibald's orders. John Bourke, with bandaged head, was very willing officer in charge of the men who went to apprehend him. He was brought into Governor's House and stood, sullen, awaiting sentence.

"I am confining you," said Archibald, "till the return of the Governor. You will be kept in one of the storerooms and a sentry will be placed at the door to attend to your legitimate needs, but with orders that, should you try to escape before Captain Macdonell comes back to deal with you, he is to shoot."

The man laughed in his face.

"You do not know," he sneered, "what awaits you people who think you own this land. Captain Cameron has told us, and told us truly, that the worst friends we ever had are Lord Selkirk and Mr. Miles Macdonell. I am leaving here as soon as the ice is out of the waterways. I am going to the Canadas."

"Well, it will be a good riddance," replied Archibald, "but for the nonce I shall keep you in custody—till the Governor is here."

The prisoner decided to shout for help, and vigorously he shouted. He was dragged away by Bourke, still shouting.

"Are you wanting to be silenced by a crack on the head?" Archibald asked him.

"I dare you to!" he called back. "Some of us, most of us, are leaving here when the ice goes. I'm not the only one. Captain Cameron says he believes that those who stay will be massacred by the Indians."

"Is that so?" said Archibald. "By whose orders?"

No answer came. The man was increasingly sullen as he was hustled away.

"I have the impression," said Archibald, very serious, turning to me, "that the fellow is divulging a plan of campaign of the enemy."

It cannot have been more than half an hour later that we heard many voices drawing near. Archibald dashed to the door and I was at his heels. There along the Settlement road came a body of men. Again, as when they had accompanied Campbell with Cameron's letter, and to take away the guns, they were carrying oak cudgels. One or two were armed with pistols. Seeing the two at the door they began to run towards us.

"They will kill the sentry on guard!" I exclaimed. "They are

H

come to release that man. We can do nothing unless you let us have arms, Mr. Archibald, we are so much outnumbered."

"We can't shoot at our own settlers!" said Archibald. "Why, man, they are in our care! They have us in a cleft stick!"

"They will kill the sentry! They may assault Bourke also," I said. "He will fight."

"He will see their numbers," said Archibald, "and——"

"It will make no difference to him. You do not know John Bourke," said I.

Out I rushed, Archibald after me.

Bourke had seen these people coming and guessing their intention had hurried out from the Colony store to aid the sentry who was on guard at the adjacent shed in which the prisoner was held. He had his back against its door and in his hand was an axe-handle he had snatched up on hurrying out. His jaws were clenched so tightly that his mouth was puckered down at each corner. His brows were lowered. That was the grimmest face I had ever seen. Beside him the sentry stood, musket ready, glaring, at bay.

"All right, Bourke," called Archibald. "It is no use. Let them have their way. They are too many for us."

With that the mob was close. Archibald and I ran to place ourselves with Bourke and the sentry but we were all speedily surrounded, hustled to one side, pistols thrust against us. With a great cheering and din the door was broken down. With hubbub and shouting they released the prisoner and took him away with them.

"I wonder who the strangers were who were leading them," said Archibald. "Three I saw."

"Yes, three," said Bourke and I together.

"One of them I know," said I.

"Oh? And who——"

"He is a man who used to be in the Hudson's Bay service at Pembina. I saw him there frequently. He left the Company after an altercation with Mr. Fidler and went over to the North-Westers. His name is Pangman, and he is usually called Bostonois Pangman. I understood he was being held prisoner at Fort Daer. The Governor had word he was being held there in return for the making prisoner of John McLeod by the North-Westers. Perhaps this means that

Captain Macdonell has settled the trouble there, got McLeod out, released Pangman, and will be here again soon."

"He cannot come too soon," said Archibald McDonald.

He came next day, accompanied by John McLeod. His rage at hearing what had happened—of the advantage taken by the North-Westers of this his second absence—reminded me of his return from York Factory to the news of the arrest of John Spencer.

"I think by the signs," said he, "that we are now definitely at war!"

CHAPTER TEN

I

THE Governor decided to go among the settlers on a personal inquiry into the cause for what had happened. To Archibald and me he remarked, sitting at his table with his long legs out-thrust, his brows puckered : " If they were soldiers I had in my care here there would be occasion sufficient for a court-martial of mutineers—and the cat! These are civilians. Well, before considering action for the recovery of these guns they carried off to Fort Gibraltar at the instigation of the North-Westers, I shall go among them to discuss the matter, instead of giving an order to bring the rebels here. I shall at least know the sheep from the goats."

The ice, I recall, had been breaking in the river while he was away, behaving variously in different stretches. In some places drifting plates, atilt together, had made dams against which the water rose to a final overwhelming pressure till the dams burst, shattered, scattered, and the river poured on over further ice, honeycombing it, rotting it. From the distant headwaters, thawed before these lower northern stretches, swirling freshets of melted snow had come down, raising the river's level, broadening it daily up the sloping banks. The clash of ice islands jostled and jostling—another manifestation of Nature in this vast land—had been awesome in my ears. On the day Captain Macdonell went to confer with the people in the Settlement flights of ducks were passing overhead, above their hurrying shadows, passenger pigeons were again on the wing.

My work in the administration-room finished for the day, I procured a horse from an Indian who was camped in the vicinity and went for a ride. The ground was still sufficiently moist from the thaws and when riding by the prairie's edge round Point Douglas, following the swervings of the river, I heard the wet pit-a-pat of hoofs at a lope behind me and then a hail of : " Well, young man?"

The rider was Court Nez.

"Good-day, sir," said I, and had to restrain my mount. As if with the spirit of a racer it leapt ahead; but in a moment or two both horses were loping in step. "I have not seen you for some time."

"No, you have not had the pleasure of seeing me for some time," replied Court Nez, laughing.

He was astride a big horse to carry his weight and he sat back in the saddle with an expression that I could not put a name on. Was it derisive? Was it mocking? It reminded me of our first meeting; it reminded me of the expression on his face when he rallied me on showing myself stricken by the sight of the half-breed girl, his daughter Christina, as she passed by.

"Not all this winter have you seen me," he said. "I have been hibernating. I have been hibernating more or less, but I am at last clean again, bodily clean, I mean. I've been having sweat-baths."

"Sweat-baths?" I asked.

"You must have seen the Indians at it," said he.

"Oh, yes, yes. Or at least I remember seeing half-breeds at Pembina having them."

"Yes, there are various usages among the Indians that the half-breeds do well to retain and that the white folks might imitate. You should try a sweat-bath some day. The polite name for them is sudatories. The first time I had one . . ."

I was not listening. I was thinking of this man's daughter, recalling again her movements as she passed through the candle-lit room at Fort Gibraltar, recalling the turn of her head towards the guests, a motion as swift as the swerve of a swallow and yet in my mind vividly retained.

". . . keep your head down low," Court Nez was saying. "Remember that, if ever you have one. The heat up above makes you think your skull will burst. And pour water from the bowl over your head. Yes, remember what I say if ever you have one—keep your head down, and keep it wet. You sweat yourself clean." His gaze met mine and he frowned. "Not interested!" he ejaculated. "Not interested in Indians. Think them an inferior race, eh?"

"Oh, no, sir!"

"Oh, yes, sir! Not interested in that bit of advice the old man has given you. Well, how does all go with you?"

"Very well."

Rub-a-dub, rub-a-dub went the horses' hoofs in time.

" Keeping off booze and the women?" he asked, then at the look on my face, I suppose, bellowed his laughter. " Keeping in touch with your people?"

" Yes. I write."

" Hear from them?"

" Yes, I heard from them by the last year's ship."

" Both well?"

" Yes, very well."

" Last year's ship! God, what a large country this is and how far away from the old home, the old life, eh? Feel a sense of freedom here?"

" Oh, yes."

" Sufficient to make the hardships of the land not too hard?" and he looked shrewdly at me.

I merely nodded.

" Queer man this," I mused.

The horses of their own accord slowed from the lope to a quick step, their heads rising and falling in unison and the legs of the two riders, as we sat easy in the saddle, lightly swayed with the motion under them.

" My horse always thinks of turning back when he gets near the Settlement," remarked Court Nez. " But I'm not a Nor'-Wester. I'll trade my pemican or my furs to Hudson's Bay or North-West with equal pleasure. In fact there are times I don't care whether I trade or not. I'm one of these white men, as they say, who has gone into the Indian Countries and God knows why, they say, but he's stayed there. I'm not the only one. Why do we stay there?" he inquired, but when I glanced at him it did not seem he expected a reply. " Why do we stay here?" he inquired again and answered himself : " For me, at least, because it is better so. For most of them too, I suspect. I'm not satisfied, I've never been satisfied with my own people. Even as a boy at parties I had to pretend an interest, force an interest. I didn't belong. I tried to fit in but—oh, hell!"

He was suddenly resolved to say no more, just when I became curious regarding him. But instead of talking of himself he swerved off to talk of Indians again.

" He's Indian daft," thought I; and wondered how—without being derisively laughed at—I could ask when, if ever, his daughter was coming back from Quebec.

On he talked about Indians, about some tribes on the Missouri who lived in fixed habitations of clay-covered timber and grew maize and pumpkins, and of a young chief called Ma-to-to-pah who was the most perfect host that he had ever known.

"Well, damn you!" he suddenly exclaimed. "You are not interested in the Mandans, or the Aricarees, the Minitarees, or the Ahnahaways."

"Indeed I am, sir."

"Liar! But I am interested in you. And so before my horse stops and turns I have a word for you. The Nor'-Westers are honing their knives for you people. Little, so far, is committed to writing. It's been all by word of mouth—here to Fort William, Fort William to Montreal, back to Fort William, and on to here. The distances of this enormous country have made the progress of the business slow. That pemican seizure at la Souris gave them a *casus belli*, a sufficient excuse to make to onlookers for objecting to you. The more your people can make themselves amenable to law the happier they will be. But I've something else to tell you. Yellowhead Macdonell, your Governor's relative, arrived at Fort Gibraltar a few days after me. I've been there a week now. He brought a bunch of Crees with him from out on the plains, full bloods, and he has kept them drunk ever since he got here, trying to whip them up to come yelling down on your people. Don't worry! I've seen to that. I've passed on a private word or two to them. Yellowhead is beginning to be annoyed at the waste of good liquor. They drink it and listen to him saying that these white men, in the little wooden lodges along the riverside, breaking up the prairie and sowing seed, should be driven out or killed. They drink and listen, and nothing happens."

He laughed over that until he had a fit of coughing. I waited for more, without speaking.

"But I've something else more serious to tell you," said Court Nez. "A message for your Governor. They are going to arrest him."

"Arrest Captain Macdonell! They can't. This is Selkirk's territory and he is Governor for Selkirk and——"

"My boy," said Court Nez gravely, "Duncan Cameron waved the arrest-warrant at us at the fort the other night: it is signed for the arrest of your Governor. This is no blabbing of a secret of my Company. I'm a free-trader, I'm no Nor'-Wester. I'm one of these men that I told you of—out in the Indian Countries, God knows why, as people say. And we both come from Renfrewshire as it happens." He laughed thickly. "You might care to warn Captain Macdonell so that he is not taken by surprise and can have time, as the elders would say, to mak' it a matter of prayer."

He turned his horse then and mine wheeled after it.

"This horse I have borrowed to-day must surely be a racer!" thought I.

II

As Court Nez put his to the gallop, mine tried to follow, was determined to follow. I had to wrestle with it. There was much pivoting and then at last it gave me my way, tossed its head, and went loping on northward to the Settlement. As soon as I had returned it to the Indian from whom I had borrowed it, I hurried to Governor's House to inform Captain Macdonell of what I had just heard. I reached the door as he came out.

"I must tell you, sir," I began.

He did not hear.

"I must tell you, sir," I began again.

He turned in that lithe way of his and raising one hand slightly gave it two small dabs in air.

"Presently, presently, Baxter," said he.

"But, sir——"

"Presently, Baxter, presently," he repeated, and went off with long strides to the storehouse, evidently intent upon a duty he felt to be immediate.

As I waited I saw several men approaching, none of whom I knew. Immediately I felt suspicious of them, then told myself that I was so only because of what I had learnt from Court Nez. They clustered close to Governor's House and spoke quietly to one another.

Back came Miles Macdonell in long strides from the store.

"Captain Miles Macdonell?" said one of the men, stepping forward to halt him.

"That is my name," replied the Governor.

The man then tapped him with one hand on the shoulder, as in a formality or ritual.

"I have a warrant here for your arrest," said he, producing it from a pocket like a conjuring trick.

"A warrant for my arrest! Who the devil from?" demanded Macdonell.

"From Captain Duncan Cameron."

"From Mr. Cameron," said Captain Macdonell. "Does he lay claim to be a justice as well?"

"It is signed by Major A. N. MacLeod who is a justice of the peace," said the man. "I must warn you not to resist arrest, and I have witnesses here with me," and he nodded towards his companions.

"What, might I ask," said the Governor, "merely out of curiosity, are the whereases of it?"

"I have to order you to come peaceably. The charge against you is of complicity in illegal entry."

"I have to order you to go back to your master and order him to go to the devil," said the Governor and he swung on upon his way.

The men looked one to another with a smugness that gave me a sudden fury against them all. I recalled what Court Nez had said of the North-Westers welcoming a *casus belli* that might make the officers of the Settlement amenable to law.

The group turned away, apparently sufficiently satisfied with the result of their attempt to serve the warrant. And then, just at the door, Captain Macdonell bethought him that I had tried to stop him on his way out. He turned round.

"There was something you wanted to say to me, Baxter?" he asked.

"It is too late now, sir. I had information regarding the warrant coming and wished to prepare you."

He showed astonishment.

"You had information?"

"Yes, sir. When I was out riding this afternoon that man Court Nez made up on me and told me of it, advised me to warn you. He had been at Fort Gibraltar and saw the warrant there. Duncan Cameron showed it to him. And your cousin Alexander is there also, he said, with some Crees from the plains. He is making them drunk and trying to whet them up to come and drive out the settlers or kill them, but he cannot rouse them to it. Court Nez has used his influence with them, advised them to let us be. He is very much amused that the Indians have been drunk for days at North-West expense and yet have failed Yellowhead in his design in bringing them here."

"So!" said the Governor. "Queer man, that Court Nez."

"Queer man indeed," I replied. "He both attracts and repels me. He said he was one of those that go out into the Indian Countries and live with the Indians, and people say God knows why."

"He's not the only one. They are dotted here and there, running away from some past, no doubt." He paused. "Well," he said, "I must write my report of this latest move in the game while it is fresh in my mind, as well as the result of my inquiries among the settlers," and he dismissed me with a nod and went indoors again.

Then, as he had recently mused, I mused: "I wonder what will be the next move." And even, thought I, had I arrived long before these men who brought the warrant, and found opportunity to inform Miles Macdonell of its existence, there would have been no change of any consequence. Prepared he would, no doubt, have acted just as he did unprepared.

An emotion of fatalism was in me at that moment.

CHAPTER ELEVEN

I

It was the first Sunday in June. I had been visiting Mr. Pritchard—he who had retired from the North-West service because of the way he had been reviled by his Company's officers over his inaction at la Souris when Spencer broke in there and carried off some pemican. Pritchard loved the west and for that reason had taken up a parcel of land in the Settlement. After a chat and a dish of Soochow with him I strolled by the riverside and then went to the Chisholm farm, having been invited there for supper.

After supper I was sitting with the family outside and the talk was naturally of recent events.

"To my mind," Mr. Chisholm remarked, "some people round here are sadly simple. It is by their simplicity that Duncan Cameron has won over so many to the notion of leaving the place. I wish they would give more loyalty to a man that is doing the best he can for them in the face of many set-backs—our Governor. Can't they see that the Nor'-Westers just want to get quit of them?"

Suddenly there came a high shrill wavering series of cries and along the Settlement road in the dusk went a string of horsemen. It was they who let loose these sounds into the night.

"Isn't that fearsome!" ejaculated Mrs. Chisholm. "What does it mean, do you think?"

"It means that the North-Westers are trying to alarm you," said her husband. "And we'll get more of it, I'm thinking. There are somewhere about two hundred people in this Settlement now and somewhere about a hundred and fifty of them are getting ready to leave in a week, I understand. That yelling you heard just now is to keep them from changing their minds and biding here. That's not Indians—it's half-breeds playing at Indians to frighten folk, at Cameron's bidding if you ask me. The first time we went to Pembina we had the same kind of thing by the design of Yellowhead. It will go on——"

He was interrupted by a renewal of the shrill shouting. It made us all raise our heads, inquiringly.

"—it will go on," he repeated, "in the hope of getting the balance of us to quit too."

Along the road to south came sounds again of galloping and other shrill wavering yells.

"Here are some more wild Indians!" said Mrs. Chisholm. "It is fearsome."

"These are not Indians," declared Chisholm again. "I don't believe it. I hear Yellowhead is back at Fort Gibraltar."

"Yes, he is," said I. "He brought a lot of Crees with him, full-bloods, and has been filling them with rum to get them into fighting mood, and inciting them to come down on the Settlement and attack it."

"Attack us!" Mrs. Chisholm cried out.

"Don't worry," I said. "They won't do it. Some of them came to see the Governor yesterday. We could not think what they wanted. Strange people! They were very drunk but they knew what they were talking about. They said they were not going to attack us; they were going home. One of them gave him a fine pipe and then they all lurched away, dodging the doorposts, and got on their horses and went off."

"I'd have been terror-struck!" exclaimed Mrs. Chisholm.

Down the road went another rub-a-dub of hoofs and another group of men passed giving shrill cries. Then silence fell. A peace that might be called Sabbath peace was in the evening. There was something very precious in the tranquillity of the night then. I rose.

"Let's daunder," I suggested.

"You can daunder yourself," answered Mrs. Chisholm.

Mairi moved slowly after me.

"Where are you going?" demanded her mother.

"With David," she replied easily, unruffled.

"I don't like it," said Mrs. Chisholm.

"It's only a lot of half-breeds riding down the road yelling," Mairi assured her. "There's nothing to be afraid of."

"David's with her," said Chisholm in soothing tone.

Our eyes, as we had been sitting outside by the door, were accustomed to the deepening darkness. With the brightening of the stars the fields and the road were clear enough to us. We walked leisurely to the gate.

"There's nothing wrong with this place," said Mairi, suddenly. "Father says it is a good rich soil—and although midsummer is hot and midwinter you need bodily protection, it kind of takes hold of one, this land does, this river does."

We leant on the gate. Here and there we could see a light in a house like a low star. We passed on to the road and daundered a little way. Then I raised my head and listened. There was a fluttering in the bushes nearby. It accompanied us, kept pace with us. I glanced at Mairi, saw the gleam of her face in the starlight. There was a tensity on it, I thought, but was not sure if she had heard the sounds.

"I think we'll turn," I said, lightly.

We turned and walked slowly back. As we did so the ruffling in the bushes across the road again kept pace with us. I halted.

"There is something scuttling about here," I said in a high voice. "I wonder if it is any kind of a wild creature. If it's a skulking wolf we should shoot it."

We moved on and heard no more the stealthy sounds in the scrub.

"That frightened him off, whoever he was," Mairi whispered.

At the admission that she too had heard I laughed.

"I'd say nothing about this to your mother," I advised.

"Oh, no, of course not."

But when we returned Mrs. Chisholm was in a tremor, had gone indoors with her husband and Agnes.

"What a time you've been away!" she exclaimed. "I wonder at you going for a daunder on a night like this. You can feel it in the air that anything might happen."

"We only went a wee bit along the road," said Mairi.

"Well, the night's wearing on. I think I'll get back," said I.

"I'd be feart if I was you," said Agnes. "Better wait and see if there are no other visitors here to go over with you, or watch for some returning to headquarters at the Point who have maybe been visiting farther along the Settlement."

"There is nothing to be afraid of," I vowed though, I admit, with a definite element of dread within me.

I stepped to the door again, giving my good-nights, but Chisholm accompanied me and Mairi also. They walked as far as to the gate.

"You'll be all right?" asked Mairi in a low voice, she who had said earlier that there was nothing to be afraid of.

"There is nothing to be afraid of," I then told her, and feeling for her hand gave it a reassuring pressure.

But she was alarmed for my sake. She linked her fingers round mine as if she did not wish to let me go. Suddenly, taken by shyness, she released her hold.

"You've plenty of courage," she said. "I think you're brave to go alone."

"Haste ye back, lad," said Chisholm.

"Thank you, sir," I answered, setting out.

She thought I was brave! It was a stimulus to me. I felt vigorous and powerful trudging along the dim track, thudding down my heels. Wonderful the effect that a woman can have on a man, thought I, as though inducted into some great mystery.

On I trudged—and suddenly leapt from the ground, for there was the crack of a piece and the whizz of a bullet, instantaneously, it seemed, past my head. Should I walk on? With an emotion half-way between fear and bravery I halted and shouted.

"What the hell are you doing?" I cried out. "Who fired that piece?"

Silence. Just the stars overhead and the dim road. For a moment I wondered if I was asleep and dreaming. I stood still, listening. That musket had been fired very close, and fired deliberately at me. Anger was then dominant, anger at my helplessness. I was unarmed—and I could not see who shot at me.

I was glad to get on along the half-mile of road between the Settlement and the houses on Point Douglas. Lights in the window of Fidler's old cabin and Bourke's home (Bourke had married a lass who came out with the party two years earlier, and he had built a new cabin near the store), lights in the trading post, Governor's House, and the writers' quarters were very cheering.

When I arrived at the writers' quarters I found Michael, Wallace, and some others gathered there.

"A peaceful Sabbath night," I remarked caustically as I entered.

Michael looked at me sharply.

"You seem to me as if——" he began.

"As if what?"

"You have a strained expression."

"Have I? Well, somebody shot at me just after I left the last farm coming south."

"Is that so!" several ejaculated.

"That is so," said I.

"There has been a lot of whooping round about," said Michael. "The Governor says we may have to defend ourselves against attack but he does not expect it at once. He thinks they are trying to intimidate the folks who don't want to take Cameron's offer of other lands in the Canadas, in the hope of getting all to go. There was a man in to see him this afternoon while you were out at your courting—or whatever takes you out. He's a free-trader who lives with the Indians. He was in to tell the Governor that they tried to get the Red Lake Chippewas to come up and wipe out the Colony but they wouldn't do it, any more than the Crees. But he warned that there will likely be trouble from the half-breeds. A wild-looking man he was himself. What's this they call him—some French name?"

"Court Nez?" I suggested.

"Yes, that's it."

II

The oblique organised intimidation of the settlers continued during the next days and nights, and at night was especially active. Parties of half-breeds from Qu'Appelle, well primed with rum to aid their fervour, rode whooping through the bush close to the Settlement road, firing off muskets in air. At night their cries rose here, there, yonder, closer, and to go out on the road after dark was dangerous because of the shooting which was not up in the air then. The Governor had muskets loaded and stacked ready for action in the Colony offices and in the writers' house.

Chief Peguis, aware of course of all that was going on, came to offer the services of some of his men to drive off the threatening parties but it was not Captain Macdonell's desire to begin a war. To Peguis's regret all the service he could do us was to have bands of his young men camped near the road, ready to ride to Governor's House and report if the half-breeds made any definite assault. A mounted patrol of our own people was established the length of the Settlement.

On the following Sunday, as I was going from the dormitory to the mess-room, I heard a shot outside and next minute there was a quick step in the doorway.

"That was a close shave!" exclaimed a voice I knew, the voice of Surgeon White who had come to the Colony with the last settlers.

Immediately there was another report. Surgeon White came into the mess-room.

"Someone shot at me from the bushes back there to west between here and Governor's House," he said; "and there's a crack at somebody else."

At that moment John Bourke entered.

"A North-West barbarian," he remarked, "has evidently gone mad. Are we to stand all this. I was shot at just now when walking past the house. Where are the muskets? Ah, there they are!"

He went to the corner where they stood in readiness. Two of the Hudson's Bay Company clerks were also there, early risers—James McIntosh and Archibald Currie.

"If we steal round the end of the house here," suggested Currie, "we can get cover in bushes and have a crack at them if they fire again."

There was another shot outside and two of the labourers a moment later ran into the room asking where the muskets were, by no means intimidated by the whizz of a bullet past their heads but in great rage. And rage was in me also. I thought of that shot in the dark of the last Sunday evening as I was coming home alone from the Chisholms. Here was opportunity for revenge if not on the one who had fired, then on one of his side.

The two labourers, the two Hudson's Bay clerks, Bourke and I, with muskets loaded and reserves of ammunition, went smartly from the house and not too precipitately—lest the enemy might think us afraid—into the thicket mentioned by Currie as good shelter from which to retaliate. There was not only one mad North-West barbarian, in Bourke's phrase, in that scrub to east. As we took cover there were several reports and the buzz of bullets about our ears.

Then from Governor's House came a shot. We glanced that way and realised that either Captain Macdonell had himself opened fire from the small rear window or Mr. Archibald was firing at the attackers. There was another report from the rear of Governor's House and it was followed by a long scream in the thicket—a scream very different from those wavering yells designed to alarm the settlers.

One of the labourers beside me fired, reloaded, fired again, and then gave a gasp, a grunt as from the depths of his being. I put out a hand to support him as he was collapsing and in doing so my palm was at once warmly and stickily wet. The weight of the man made my attempt to stay his fall utterly in vain. All I did was to save him from smiting the back of his head against the ground. In his cheek was a small round gash from which came a trickle of blood but it was from the back of his head that the blood poured. I withdrew my hand in horror at the flow.

"Oh my, my!" he said in a swooning voice. "Oh my, my!" he sighed again in a tone of utter melancholy, and drew a long sigh and was dead.

His voice remained in my ears. I seem to hear it still, across the years. The tone of it could best be described as one of utter disappointment—and then he was no more. Along with my rage against the enemy was a feeling of misery over fate, over life, over an existence in which such things could be. I aimed in fury and misery at the thicket from which the shooting continued to come.

From Governor's House firing also continued, speedily. Both Captain Macdonell and the Sheriff (as Archibald was called since taking the place of Spencer) were apparently shooting there, and to purpose. After a few minutes of these volleys several figures rose out of the bush and ran away, veering as they ran, dodging to left, dodging to right, to left, running straight a little way, then veering again. Content to see them go, the party that I was with ceased firing, let them retreat without pursuing shots, and there was no more firing from Governor's House.

Then it looked as though those who had risen and withdrawn so had been making an experiment, anxious to find out if in retiring they would be aimed at; for immediately up from that thicket rose others who moved away eastward, carrying with them either dead or wounded. They had evidently secreted horses in a clump of oak trees a little farther east and had crept to that bush to take aim at the people passing among the administrative houses. Beyond the

I

wood we could see some riding away, some walking beside horses over the saddles of which hung bodies which they supported as they walked, of wounded or dead.

Miles Macdonell and the Sheriff came hurrying to see how we fared. They found that as well as one being dead (the labourer whose blood reddened my hand), the second labourer and the three Hudson's Bay clerks—Currie, McIntosh, and Michael—were wounded. Here was work for Surgeon White. In the midst of all that my old friend John McLeod appeared.

" Do you know who attacked you?" he asked.

" What do you mean?" inquired the Governor. " The North-Westers surely attacked us."

" I mean their identity. The young fellow I had a glimpse of, he in the red coat, is Seraphim Lamar, a clerk at Gibraltar. The big fellow is Cuthbert Grant, and I think William Shaw was there too. I was watching from Indian Hall. Pangman, of course, you recognised."

" I thought that was he!" exclaimed the Governor.

" Yes. He was there. He is none too bad. I would to God there had never been that altercation that sent him to the enemy!"

White was calling for help to carry the wounded labourer indoors as he had fainted while being probed for the bullet that was in him. Bourke and I carried him in. Then I had to go to the cook-house for hot water and after that assist the surgeon, feeling all the while (to my vexation) that only by assisting did I keep myself from going off in a faint like the patient and that I might do so later, when the calls on me to hold basin and lint were over.

When the duties were finished, and the wounded patched and stitched by Mr. White, some words that the Governor had spoken recently came back to my mind and rang on and on: " I think, by the signs, that we are now definitely at war." And a dead man's voice continued to sigh in my ears as in a poignant and final disappointment in the moment of going: " Oh my, my!" My faintness I had mastered but I was sunk in melancholy. The body lay on a form in the room, a handkerchief over the face and a haze of flies over the handkerchief. On the floor was a pool of blood and flies hovered there. I felt sick and woebegone.

I heard the Sheriff's voice outside : " Yes, you know, men, where to get the spades." And then : " What in hell is this now?"

There came a volley of sharp, shrill yelps such as, during the recent nights, had terrorised many of the settlers. Captain Macdonell was evidently there with Archibald.

" That's Cameron leading them," I heard the Governor remark. " And in his red coat!"

III

I stepped to the door to look out. Much of that day has remained near the surface of my mind, easy to recall, returning at the slightest jog, at a jog so slight I might be unaware of it. I was often to think of the Governor's face as I saw it then. It had an expression of bitter amusement. His mouth was twisted up at one side.

As the horsemen with the red-coated Cameron at their head came from south, a party of settlers was tramping from north obviously, by every tread and swing, in determined agreement over what brought them there. The horsemen drew closer. They and the settlers, thought I, would arrive together. Was there to be more fighting? I wondered.

" Ha! There he is also!" Captain Macdonell exclaimed. " There is cousin Alexander. And he in a scarlet coat too!"

Alexander had been riding a little to rear and was eclipsed by Cameron's bulk. Side by side they came then.

The advancing settlers swerved from the road that ran north and south and came directly to where they saw the Governor and the Sheriff beside the mess-house. Then, because of the riders from the direction of Fort Gibraltar being close, and turning our way also, they moved to one side. Had it been prearranged, the joint arrival could not have been more neatly accomplished.

Miles Macdonell waved a hand.

" I have not pasted my commission on my house, Mr. Cameron," said he. " Pardon if I have failed in a formality. And there you are, cousin," he added. " I must congratulate you on your epaulette."

" I will congratulate you if you get out of this alive," threatened Alexander.

" I have come on your behalf," said Duncan Cameron.

" On my behalf?" inquired our Governor.

" Yes. To advise you to obey the warrant that a few days ago you refused," said Cameron, loftily. " It will be the worse for you if you do not—and for your settlers : for your settlers. You have had plenty of hints of what may befall. There are women and children for you to think of."

" Hints!" thought I. " He as good as admits that all these yells and shots in the dark were of his ordering!"

From behind me came McLeod's voice : " He is a big man on horseback, David."

" Might you not think of them yourself instead of instigating the half-breeds to violence?" suggested Macdonell.

" I instigating, sir? I am doing my best to restrain," replied Cameron. " Ask your people. Ask these settlers here, who look to me as though they are here to protest to you. They know. I have been telling them of my efforts to restrain first the Indians and then the half-breeds. But both full-bloods and half-breeds look upon you as interlopers here. I have even arranged to convoy one hundred and forty of your unfortunate colonists to a safe country." He paused. " And you charge me with instigating violence against them!"

" Yes. You have won over one hundred and forty. When they are gone what are your intentions regarding those who will remain?" asked the Governor.

" They have had their chance," Alexander interjected, answering for Cameron.

" That is so," Cameron agreed. " I have done my best."

" So if those who remain are attacked by half-breeds you will feel conscience-clear in the matter?" asked Captain Macdonell.

" There will be no more trouble if you obey that warrant," responded Cameron.

" You mean you will restrain the half-breeds from trying to intimidate further?"

" I have nothing to do with the objection of both full-bloods and half-breeds to your Settlement," said Cameron.

One of the settlers stepped forward from the group that stood listening.

" I would have a word with you, sir," he said to the Governor. " We feel that it might be for the good of all for you to go. You see what has happened already."

"Will you men come indoors to discuss this?" requested Miles Macdonell.

He did not lead them over to Governor's House. He signed to them to enter the building by which he had been standing when they arrived.

"You will pardon me, Mr. Cameron, if I keep you waiting," he said with ironic accent and (as Cameron and Alexander exchanged a glance) turned to follow the deputation of his people.

As they clustered in the room I noticed they all looked with the same expression at the dead man lying on the form with the kerchief on his face—the silent witness, the heedless witness, the man who was no witness, who had died with a sad "Oh my, my!" They saw also Michael, the Hudson's Bay Company writer, sitting there, his head bandaged, and the other labourer, his left forearm bandaged, Surgeon White handing him a bowl of Soochow to revive him. The other clerks who had been wounded—McIntosh in a shoulder and Currie in the head—they did not see for Mr. White had made them lie down in the dormitory. But there was sufficient evidence of the seriousness of the shooting they had heard when on their way to put some resolution or proposal before the Governor.

Captain Macdonell spoke to the man who had addressed him outside.

"Am I to understand," he inquired, "that it is your wish for me to leave you to his tender mercies," he gave his head a sidewise inclination towards the door, "their tender mercies—undefended?"

"It is you they want, sir. If you surrendered, those who do not go to the Canadas but remain here will not be molested."

"Was this what you were coming to say when the unprovoked assault was being made on us here?"

"We did not know of an assault to be made, sir, but that is what we were coming to say."

"What makes you believe that if I surrendered those who remain here would not be molested?" asked the Governor.

"Well, we have been talking to Captain Cameron and Mr. Grant and Mr.——"

"Oh, yes, and talking to the devil it might as well be said, gentlemen. If I go you will have no one here to protect you, or those of you who stay I should say, for I think most of you here," he glanced round the crowd, "have decided to leave. You remember what happened on the two occasions when I was away."

"Yes," admitted the spokesman in a slow voice. And then, after a pause, as in slight discomfiture, said he : "These last nights have been more than any could stand, sir. The half-breeds have ridden to and fro close to the farms and when any one went out after dark bullets whistled—all because you refused to acknowledge the warrant of arrest, they say. They assure us that if you go all will be well."

Some of the Hudson's Bay Company officers had followed John McLeod. The obvious deputation of settlers, the group of waiting North-Westers at the door with Cameron and Alexander, made them curious. James Sutherland and Peter Fidler, who had recently come from Brandon House, were there.

The Governor turned and looked at them . . . Fidler nodded his head.

"They may be right," he said. "The Nor'-Westers are determined for you to go."

"I think so too," agreed Sutherland. "I feel that Mr. White is with me."

The surgeon looked up from his recovering patient and nodded his head.

Miles Macdonell waited for John McLeod to speak, but McLeod did not speak. The Governor waited for him even to nod his head, as the surgeon had done, hoped, I believe, that he would shake his head; but McLeod made no sign.

"What is your view, McLeod?" Macdonell asked.

"I would rather not express an opinion," said McLeod.

"If you were in my place——" began the Governor, but one of the settlers interrupted.

"They say that all will be well with us if you accept the warrant of arrest," he declared very firmly.

"A hundred and forty are going with them to the Canadas," the Governor remarked in a voice much as of one speaking to himself in meditation. "I cannot stop them apparently. They are thrawnly determined. That leaves about sixty—some valiant men among them. They will have to be protected until our numbers are increased, beyond their daring to attack us, by the large party of immigrants due to come out this year from Ross and Cromarty. We cannot trust their word that those who decide to stay here will not be molested. I do not need to be reminded that there are women and children."

"There will be no further trouble if you go," he was told once more by the leader of the deputation.

"You are more trusting than I," said Miles Macdonell. He turned again with pleading in his expression to the officers.

"I fear you will have to give in," said Sutherland.

The Governor then looked again at John McLeod, looked long in his eyes. They did not evade his but he could read no advice in them. He addressed the deputation of settlers.

"Very well," he said quietly. "I shall accept the warrant as if it was authoritative as I see among you some who told me, when I visited you recently, that you had no intention of leaving the Settlement."

"A few of us have been inclined to change our minds since then," one of them said. "We feel we can only remain if you go—as we understand it is to you the North-West Company object because of your pemican embargo and your high-handed order to them to quit."

The Governor looked at him with steady gaze. Truly, as he had written to Lord Selkirk, there were too many of different interests. That was a long look, unblinking, direct. Then he turned and swiftly strode outside to where the North-Westers waited.

Dejected I watched him pass through the doorway. I saw the group of horsemen, the horses fidgeting a little this way, that way, some hoofing in impatience and tossing their heads, restless. I heard Miles Macdonell's voice, heard him say clearly, deliberately: "Very good. I shall accept that warrant." I saw the light of triumph in Cameron's eyes and was eased by John McLeod's voice behind me.

"He might have the courtesy to get off his horse to talk to the Governor—above all when he is getting the submission."

I saw the look of triumph on the face of cousin Alexander and hated him for it.

"We will wait for you," said Cameron.

"Be damned if you do!" blazed my Governor. "I shall come to your fort when I have had my servant pack for me and am ready. I may not come till to-morrow or the next day. I shall have a vast amount of correspondence to attend to."

"You had better come now," advised Cameron.

"You do not understand, sir," Miles Macdonell replied. "I shall come later, to-morrow perhaps, more probably the day after. If that does not suit you I think I have still a few behind me who would fight it out with you."

"All right. So be it," said Cameron.

He spoke a word or two to his men and they rode away with him.

The Governor stood there a moment or two, watching them go, then turned towards the administrative building and as he did so almost collided with Surgeon White who held out an arm to him, showing the sleeve.

"See that?" said White.

"Your sleeve is slit," said the Governor. "How did that happen?"

"When I was shot at. It was a closer shave than I realised."

I noticed the Governor's eyes suddenly lose their intentness. He had other matters to think of. The deputation of settlers began to move away but he wheeled and called them back. They came, wondering what he had to say. He but wanted them to send the elder they had chosen to officiate at religious observances to read the burial service at the funeral of the labourer who had been killed.

That labourer was a man unattached, a bachelor, and Captain Macdonell, having made that request to the departing deputation, turned to me and bade me look up the man's enlistment record and supply him with information regarding next of kin as entered in it; and to that next of kin he wrote a letter of a sort he had learnt how to write no doubt when in the war of Independence. As I copied it for the Colony files I could hear again in my ears that melancholy "Oh my, my!"

Late in the afternoon the interment took place and during the best of that day the Governor was engaged in lengthy correspondence.

IV

On the day following he had a long conference with Sheriff Archibald on affairs of the Colony, and with Surgeon White. By the warrant he would be taken to Montreal. As soon as he arrived there, said he, he would write again to Lord Selkirk acquainting him more fully with what had happened. Other letters he left to go to the earl by way of York Factory with the summer brigades.

I thought he had markedly aged in the night, in a day and a night. There was a gauntness about his jaws to my eyes. I was devoted to this man and dreaded the approaching separation. I was glad to see he had the manner not of one beaten but of one baffled, though ready to fight.

A servant he had appointed to pack for him came to announce that all was ready.

He went over to the Hudson's Bay Company's trading-room then and asked me to accompany him. We found James Sutherland, the factor, and Michael McDonnell, the young writer, there; but John McLeod had gone out to a prairie post that day, so to him the Governor could but leave a "good-bye."

"I feel you are acting rightly and wisely, Captain," said Sutherland as they shook hands, "for the sake of those who are staying in the Settlement."

"I would I were as certain of that," said Miles Macdonell, and as we returned to the administration house he remarked to me: "I wish that John McLeod had given his opinion the other day when I asked the officers of the Colony and the Company whether I should submit or no. He is a good man, a brave man."

His servant, who was to take his belongings to Fort Gibraltar, stood ready, awaiting him, at the door of Governor's House, holding the reins of a pack-horse laden with portmanteaux and his old military kit-sack. But there he delayed, anxious regarding the safety of those he was leaving. There were to be some changes in the governance by the Hudson's Bay Company in Rupert's Land he knew. Inspector Auld had left the Company's service and gone back to the Old Country with the ships that sailed out of the Bay in 1814; but even before his retirement, it appears, there had been intention—because of the Company's desire to engage in keener competition with the North-Westers—to send out a governor to investigate and direct from York Factory to Pembina, from Winnipic to Athabasca.

"Such an one will be out this year," said Miles, "and he should be of great help to you. Captain Robert Semple is his name. He will probably accompany the new settlers. I would suggest that you confer with him."

He stood silent then, thinking, right elbow cupped in left hand, right hand holding his chin. All in the room were standing, his moment of departure being apparently close.

"Huh!" he muttered. "There it is. You will have to carry on as best you can." Another meditative pause. "Well, perhaps they are right who think my surrender will end the intimidation for the settlers who remain. I devoutly hope so." Then he looked at me. "I must thank you, Baxter, for all your loyal service. Aye, well!" Still he tarried. "I feel," he added, "that if, before Captain Semple arrives, you are in difficulties and require advice, you could not do better than confer with Mr. McLeod." Then—"Adieu, adieu!" said he, stepped to the door, to which Mr. Archibald and Surgeon White accompanied him, and went out in long swift strides.

CHAPTER TWELVE

I

" So we have lost the Governor," said Hugh Chisholm for first remark when I called on him a day or two later. " He's gone and can't be brought back. He has left Fort Gibraltar by now, I suppose?"

" Oh, yes. He was taken away at once. Duncan Cameron went with him himself. That's a relief. He's going properly; and he has a servant with him too, put at his service by Cameron."

" You seem to know what goes on at Fort Gibraltar."

" We get all their news and they get all ours. The half-breeds and the free-traders that move about from one place to the other keep their eyes and ears open. When they sit smoking in Indian Hall we get the gossip. Two of the chiefs heard of Captain Macdonell surrendering and went over to ask Cameron to release him. Cameron was very angry and stormed at them—which did not make them any more inclined to be friendly with him. Then they came to see Sheriff Archibald and offered to gather their braves together to fight the Nor'-Westers."

" They would be a good match for the half-breeds, I should think," observed Chisholm.

" Yes, but the Sheriff was against it. So Peguis and Ouckidoat went off very despondent."

" Well, it would have meant bloodshed and that is always regrettable."

" I think we should fight," said I. " I know it is distressing to have to fight but at the same time I get furious over these constant intimidations, all this yelling of war cries of the *métis*, all this riding up and down the road and firing off their muskets. It is not right that such threatening methods should accomplish victory."

" Tell me about that fight last Sunday," said Chisholm.

So I told him all and when I was done——

" You might not feel so eager to take up arms against the Nor'-Westers and their *métis* helpers," Chisholm suggested, " if you knew that you had killed any of these men. You were just firing into the

139

bush where they were secreted. You don't even know if you wounded any."

"I don't think it would make any difference," said I, "if I knew I had wounded all who were wounded, and killed all of those who may be dead. I'm angry, angry at our Governor having to go—and that way. Those who try to establish a reign of terror should not be submitted to. They should be challenged."

"Are we fit to challenge them?"

"We would have the Indians on our side," I pointed out. "He's sly that man Cameron. I agree with you, from what he let out in the talk with Captain Macdonell despite his protestations, that he has been inciting the half-breeds to the singing of their songs up and down and the firing off of their guns, in the neighbourhood of the farms."

"Oh, well, we'll see what we'll see," said Chisholm. "And here is the day for the departure of those that accepted Cameron's kind offer—kind offer!—of lands in Upper Canada. It's time now that we went down to the river. I've been hearing the stir and hum of the folks for some time and there are the pipers now. Though what I want to see them off for I don't know, unless it is to span my nose at them!"

We all went down to see the departure—Chisholm, Mrs. Chisholm, Agnes, Mairi and I. The air trembled with the sound of the bagpipes. They were being played in various parts of the Settlement.

"If we could only have the one tune!" Chisholm complained. "I suppose each of the pipers canna hear the others playing for his own music at his ear. Ah, that's better—one of them has stopped. My people are Highland and have been for centuries but I do say that the pipes are for the open air—and one tune at a time."

He laughed. So gaily he laughed that his wife, ahead, looked over her shoulder with a blend of reproach and astonishment. That was a sad day for her, a day of farewells. She had friends among those that her husband called the runagates.

We came to the riverside and, looking on, marvelled at the service being put at disposal of those who had decided to go. They had packed their effects for themselves but did not have to carry them to the boats. Labourers from Fort Gibraltar were doing everything for them.

"Don't you wish you was coming with us?" said one woman to

Mrs. Chisholm as she passed down the bank. "See how we go, all like grand and noble ladies and gentlemen attended by our servants. We are having marked attention."

Mrs. Chisholm at that inclined her head stiffly and felt the bows of the ribbons that tied her mutch.

"Aye, you are," said she. "So I see. The Nor'-Westers have had their way with you. You've accepted their offer for land somewhere in the Canadas, and you're having your free transportation, food provided on the way, and all given to you—given to you," she repeated, "like a charity. You do not understand. You say it is better than the Earl of Selkirk did for us. You don't realise that the Nor' Westers have simply set their faces against having an agricultural settlement here, and that that is why you have to go."

It was Chisholm's turn to stare. Here was his wife, voicing as from the heart at last, views he had expressed and she had questioned, doubted, contradicted. Not only he stared at her but the girls also. Actually she was being, simply, Mrs. Chisholm, but somehow they never became accustomed to her capacity for sudden changes. Constantly she was unexpected to them, constantly she astonished them.

"Indeed I expect you will wish you had come with us before another Sabbath passes," prophesied the woman who had drawn from her all that.

To this parting remark Mrs. Chisholm made no reply.

There was a web of shouting up and down the banks. Children who did not seem to realise that they were going jinked at play among the trees and had to be collected and shepherded away. Indians stalked by, looking on. A woman with a cradle on her back halted beside Mrs. Chisholm.

"You not go?" she asked.

"No."

"Good! Sorry so many go."

She passed on and Mrs. Chisholm turned to her husband.

"There!" she said triumphantly. "It's not the Indians that are a menace."

Loudly the pipers began again, close at hand, playing in unison. The boats were leaving. We moved along the top of the bank with others who were remaining, watching the departure. Out into the stream went boats and canoes. In the voices of those who left us there was heard no emotion save of satisfaction. Snatches of final hails came to our ears. From bank to boat a voice shouted, "You will be back again!" and from boat to bank came promptly the reply, "Never, never, never!"

"You will be coming after us," called a man from a canoe.

"Never, never, never!" from shore came the vehement protestation.

The drooping branch of an elm, low on the bank, touched the water and from its dragged tip there was a spreading of ripples on the surface. It claimed my attention. It divided me in twain by some occult influence. David Baxter, a young writer, a clerk of the Colony, gave supremacy to another David Baxter who, watching that spread of ripples, for a few moments lived not in time but in eternity—or thus, remembering these moments later, would be my fancy: at least my fancy. My reverie was that the Red River would go flowing on for ever and ever; drooped branches touching the surface would drag their fans of ripples so, for ever and ever, while people came—and went.

Then the other David Baxter, the Colony writer, took over control from that meditating one, and—"I'll have to be going back to the counting-house," I said.

Mairi's voice had something for me then though she was speaking apparently to her father or to Agnes. What they had been discussing I did not know, but I heard her say: "Well, we must be brave in the face of it. To sit down and girn won't help!"

"What did you say?" Chisholm asked of me.

"Say? Oh, just that I had better be getting back to work. The Sheriff let me out to see these people go but I must not stay too long."

I had no friends among those who were leaving. The Chisholms were my most intimate friends—and they had not gone. The Murrays, the Bannermans, one of the Sutherland families I also visited occasionally, and they were staying. John Pritchard, of course, was remaining.

"What is that smoke?" somebody asked.

"Look at that smoke!" said somebody else.

"Where is that smoke coming from?" Mrs. Chisholm cried out.

All along the bankside many were at the same time talking of smoke, smoke.

I looked northward and saw several columns rising. In that still afternoon they ascended straight, trembling as they rose, quaking pillars of coiling tones, dun and dusky blue. Each at about the same height could rise no more, toppled, and was thinly dissipated. The effect was of unstable smoke mushrooms with amazingly long stalks, standing up, slightly trembling, on the plain.

There was an immediate movement of many persons northward. They went like a flock of sheep suddenly started in a run; they went like a wave; they did not seem to be individuals; they seemed, each, but as part of a whole, cohering, an agitated whole. Away they went, atilt, running north, their eyes on the columns of smoke.

I I

With a parting salute to the Chisholms, who were turning back towards their home, I hastened off at a tangent from the river towards the Settlement road and had just got a little way beyond the Murray farm when I heard the sound of the bleating of sheep and a yelp-yelping not of dogs but of men, presumably driving them.

I had a glimpse of the oscillating shoulders of several riders. Left and right they moved—yes, obviously herding before them the sheep that raised the bleating of fright and trouble. By their seats in the saddle I knew they were half-breeds. Any one who had lived in the Settlement a few months could tell, with a mere glimpse of a rider, were he a mile away, if he were white man or Indian though he might find it hard to explain what to him was the distinguishing difference in seat, carriage, gait. The half-breeds somehow partook more of full-bloods than of white men in their saddle seats.

I climbed the roadside fence for a better view over the expanse.

"Yes—half-breeds," said I to myself, "and driving sheep before them."

Then the tall columns of quaking and ascending smoke had my attention again. I was balanced so on the snake-fence that zigzagged along the road, when I saw another group of mounted men, a hundred yards or so away, dismount and begin to pull the bars down. I could see the coloured scarves round their waists that told me they also were half-breeds. As I watched they got into the saddles again and went back the way they had come.

I climbed down and instead of going on towards Point Douglas passed northward along the road to discover what they had been about. By the time I reached the gap they had made I had full explanation, for they came riding back urging before them a bull that I knew well by sight. I had had its markings fixed in my mind when coming to Red River. That was the first bull of the Settlement. That was the bull that Captain Macdonell had bought from the factor at Oxford House. That was the Settlement's pride. That was the bull that had weathered through these winters and tossed a wolf or two in its valiant life.

The half-breeds evidently intended to drive it out on to the prairie at the place where they had made a gap in the fence, but it ran along the road. They came galloping after it, whooping with laughter. It halted. It turned.

Then on the road came another rider. He wore a scarlet coat and paid no heed to me, gave me only a glance and looked away. He may have recognised me but he was not going to acknowledge me if he did. Very arrogant indeed did cousin Alexander look on that occasion.

" Shoot him there," he ordered the men. " Shoot him there if you cannot drive him to your camp. You are going to have him roasted this evening at any rate. It was only for convenience I told you to drive him to your camp."

Suddenly the bull turned again, turned back to the gap, dashed through bellowing and with its tail waving high. After him went the half-breeds. Alexander, looking again at me, assuredly recognised me.

" Ha, Mr. Bently!" he exclaimed. " So you have not gone."

" No, Mr. Macdiarmid," I replied. " I am still here."

Alexander's eyelids narrowed. He peered at me.

" Did I name you wrongly?" he inquired.

" Baxter is the name," said I.

" Well, then, Mr. Baxter, you have not gone with your Governor."

" I may be of more service to him here," said I, and looked at my hand and plucked from the palm a splinter that had stuck in it when I was climbing the fence.

" I cannot but think it would have been better for you to go with these people to-day," he remarked.

" Time will tell," said I.

"Yes—and sooner than perhaps you imagine," said Alexander.

He rode off in the direction from which he had come, back along the Settlement road towards the smoke columns. I watched him go and——

"Well, he can ride, he can ride," I thought. "I must say that for him."

Horse and rider dwindled in size down the straight rutted track. There was no breath of air. The smoke columns rose steadily, toppled and were dispelled. I turned south and began my trudge homeward. At the last farms were no people. I knew that those who lived in them were remaining, were not with the majority, not with those who had accepted Cameron's offer of transportation to the Canadas. Where were they? I wondered, and then presumed they had gone, like the Chisholms and myself, to watch the embarkations and after the boats and canoes had put off had hurried on to discover what caused these pillars of smoke.

I swung upon my way. For a little while—such always was the illusion there—Governor's House and Fidler's old cabin across the plain, the house that John Bourke had built when he got married, Indian Hall and all the buildings clustered together on Point Douglas, seemed to move away from me. There was a tantalising feeling of just keeping up with them. Then suddenly they stayed motionless and anon began, in the gratifying completion of the illusion, to come towards me.

Thus far had I gone when I heard a horse approaching behind me. The rider was in no haste. It might be Sheriff Archibald, I thought. Archibald, I knew, had gone on horseback to see the exodus of Chisholm's "runagates." I looked round. Yes—the Sheriff. Some people said he was too young to take over the guidance of the Colony. The earl, to be sure, had entrusted him with the care of a shipload of emigrants out of Scotland, but to be deputy for the Governor was a more onerous task.

I was within five hundred yards of Governor's House when he made up on me.

"Well, Baxter," he said, "they have begun quickly."

"Begun what?"

"The smoke!" he ejaculated. "Have you not seen it?"

K

"I have been at the riverside. I saw the columns of smoke but did not——"

"They have set fire to the houses of all those who went away," he interrupted, explanatory. "The remaining settlers were watching these go and by the time they saw the smoke and got to the deserted farms it was too late to do anything. I rode on all the way when I saw the smoke. The houses are ablaze beyond saving."

"I suppose," said I, rage at the way of our enemies surging in me again, "that to those who are left you will be serving out muskets and ammunition."

"According to Duncan Cameron," answered the Sheriff, "there will be no trouble for the ones who are left," but his bitter ironic tone made clear what he thought.

"Yellowhead is here now," said I. "I saw him. He has told the half-breeds they can have our bull, the one we called our first settler, for a feast. I have little doubt he ordered the burnings. And that man Grant, who has the Qu'Appelle half-breeds at his call, is doubtless hereaway also."

"You are saying what I have been dreading," confessed the Sheriff, "but fighting men cannot help us. They could go on bringing in their fellows from the plains. We are desperately outnumbered now——"

"We could have the Indians with us at a word," said I, striding along beside him while he rode his horse at a walk. "It is the intimidation that infuriates me. It is their view that all they have to do is to threaten, and that——"

"Yes, that is exasperating. But I have to think of the women and children even as Captain Macdonell had to think of them."

"Couldn't we get up a party and go out and attack them where they have their own settlement," suggested I, "at Qu'Appelle?"

"We might, but others would attack here while we were away," said Archibald. We had come to the cluster of houses by Point Douglas and he dismounted.

"The Indians are eager to fight for us," I said. "Peguis and Ouckidoat both are, and the other one—I cannot pronounce his Indian name—who is called le Sonnant. You could, just by saying the word, have a war here that would let these *métis* realise that they made a mistake when they allowed themselves to become the tools of the North-West Company."

"I shall confer with Mr. White and Mr. Sutherland on the matter," he said.

"And John McLeod," said I.

By the lift of his head and the lowering of his brows he gave me to understand that I was presuming beyond my position. He was not at all like brother James but at that juncture reminded me of him. But I would not be put in my place by a frown. No, I would not be subdued by that facial expression. I persisted. I had more to say.

"The Governor, you remember," said I, "advised that if you needed help you might well confer with John McLeod."

"I believe he is off at Turtle River again, or Swan River, or somewhere," said Archibald, answering me abruptly, as one may make answer to a speaker when engrossed on his own train of thought.

A servant came to take his horse from him. He turned away with no final manner as of snubbing me. The suggestion of frowning on presumption had been momentary and perhaps, thought I, that frown had been less deliberate than accidental and but at annoyance at interruption of anxious cogitations.

From thoughtfully watching him go into Governor's House I looked northward again. The sun was setting. Shadows lay over the land. In all the small creases of the seeming flatness dusk was forming in segments that later would brim and overflow and make unanimous night. But high clouds were golden and pink, and the columns of smoke were lit with delight for the eye on their western sides.

I listened. From far off I could hear the yelping cries of the half-breeds as they rode to and fro in the fields of those who had gone, trampling down the good growing grain, returned again to the Settlement after driving off the sheep, some kine, and our "first settler," the historic bull. For that was what they were about then as Bob Wallace and Michael, coming in later, wrathfully reported.

PART TWO

CHAPTER ONE

I

AN end had come apparently to the attempts to terrorise by shots in the dark. Ten days had passed since the departure of the hundred and forty. Their houses were but ash heaps and the crops in the forsaken fields were hoofed under, but the sixty who remained that was all, men, women and children : just sixty—were evidently to be tolerated. It looked as though with submission of our Governor to arrest the promise was going to be kept that there would be no further intimidation.

It was Sunday, June 25th. (The year was 1815.) I walked from the administration quarters on Point Douglas to the Chisholm farm. When I reached there I looked in at a rapt and rigid family group. Chisholm was seated with a sheet of foolscap in his hand; Mrs. Chisholm, stunned of aspect, sat beside him; in the background, looking over their father's shoulder, frowning intent on the sheet he held, were Mairi and Agnes. They did not hear me. I saw Mr. Chisholm run the back of a hand across the missive as though by doing so he could obliterate its message.

"What is wrong now?" was my salutation at the open door, and——

"Oh, what a *fleg* you gave me!" Mrs. Chisholm ejaculated.

Only the eyes of the others moved. The writing on that sheet of foolscap held them as in a trance. Chisholm again stroked it several times before he spoke.

"Are you people at the administration office aware of this?" he asked.

"Aware of what?"

Chisholm was for once petulant.

"This, this, this!" he said.

I took the sheet from him and read :

Article of Agreement entered into between the Half-Breed Indians

151

of the Indian Territory on the one part and the Honorable Hudson's Bay Company on the other, viz:

   1. *All settlers to retire immediately from this river and no appearance of a colony to remain.*

   2. *Peace and amity to subsist between all parties, traders, Indians, and freemen in future throughout these two rivers, and on no account is any person to be molested in his lawful pursuits.*

"I must tell you," Mr. Chisholm interrupted my reading, "that to every occupied house in the Settlement, every house still standing, a copy of that has been delivered—and here were we fondly imagining that we were going to be left in peace, we who refused the offers of other lands!"

I merely raised my eyes and looked at him. Otherwise I think I did not move. The document was holding me as surely as it had been holding them.

   3. *The Honorable Hudson's Bay Company will as customary enter this river with if they think proper three to four of the former trading boats and from four to five men per boat as usual.*

   4. *Whatever former disturbance has taken place between both parties, that is to say the Honorable Hudson's Bay Company and the Half-Breeds of the Indian Territory, to be totally forgot and not to be recalled by either party.*

   5. *Every person retiring peaceably from the river immediately shall not be molested in their passage out.*

   6. *The people passing the summer for the Honorable Hudson's Bay Company shall not remain in the buildings of the colony but shall retire to some other spot where they will establish for the purpose of trade.*

I came to the end and looked at Mr. Chisholm.

"Aye," he said. "It stuns you, does it not? It takes some study too. We have been studying it since it was delivered by a half-breed this morning. 'Everybody is getting one of these,' he says. You will observe it is an agreement not between the Colony and the half-breeds but between the Hudson's Bay Company and the half-breeds. And you will notice," he pointed out, his brows knit over the memorised clauses, "that all settlers have to retire—immediately. There's no offer to us of free lands in the east. We had the offer and we did not take it; and when we go the Nor'-Westers, the Hudson's Bay factors, and the free-traders at Pembina and on the plains will all be brothers again. It's the settlers that are responsible for all the discord between them by that."

"I see a threat in Clause Five," said I.

"And the one that follows it," said he, "the last one. It shows their intention to wipe out all the Colony buildings. If we go our farms will be burnt like the ones of the folks who have already gone. Aye, it's a grim document."

"And everybody in the Settlement has had a copy of it," said I, "everybody, that is, except Mr. Archibald. Evidently he has not to know about it yet. This is being done at his back. Their idea seems to be for him not to know of it till a deputation of settlers comes to tell him they are going."

"But are we?" demanded Hugh Chisholm.

"Are you?" I inquired.

"God knows," said Chsholm. "I suppose again it will be at the decision of the majority."

"May I have this?" I asked.

"Indeed you may. I have it all in my head. If you want to show it to that poor young man on whom all the burdens are devolving you are welcome to it."

"I'll take it and go, then," said I. "He must know at once"; and at once I set off.

11

"Sabbath peace": Yes, there was Sabbath peace by the riverside. The wild events of the day when the settlers went away were hard to credit under that quiet sky—the driving off of the sheep to slaughter, of the bull for a feast to the half-breeds from Qu'Appelle. Sheriff Archibald had sent a Note, a Protest, against these events to the Officer in Command at Fort Gibraltar, and had received a verbal message in reply that the officer in command there had nothing to do with these things, that he had heard of them and understood they had been the work of Indians, or perhaps of half-breeds.

As I hurried back to Point Douglas that was in my mind as firmly as in my clenched fist the missive, the smooth ultimatum, that I carried. The officers of the North-West Company, thought I, were acting astutely. Duncan Cameron, before he left with Miles Macdonell, had no doubt advised them to these methods. The North-West Company was not mentioned in that paper. Presuming that all these machinations came to be aired in a law court some day, where would there be evidence that North-Westers had done harm to any? On I trudged. There was the usual effect of being in pursuit of the houses across the open plain, of a halt in their flight, of their coming to meet me, looming larger.

And then, as I had felt something amiss when looking in at the grouped Chisholm family, I felt something amiss there. The movements of men about the houses were not normal. What, I asked myself, were they doing? One I could see running from Indian Hall to Governor's House. He disappeared there, appeared again, and hurried on to Bourke's place. From Fidler's cabin several others went more than smartly, went urgently to the smithy. All boded something amiss.

I cut across the open, intent on showing the paper of ultimatum to the Sheriff, when a shout halted me. John McLeod was beckoning from the door of the trading post. There was the man, I considered, who had been named by the Governor on the moment of his troubled departure as the one to consult in any difficulty that might arise, fortunately back again. More to the purpose might it be to show the missive first to him instead of to Archibald.

" We'll need you, David!" he called. " We'll need you. We're to be ready for an attack being made on us."

" An attack! Has it anything to do with this?" and I held the sheet to him.

" What's this?" He took it and—" So this is the paper," he muttered as he read. " I haven't seen it before but I've heard of it. Peguis came to see me just when I returned and told me that he knew the Nor'-Westers were going to order the last of you to get out. Well, my lad, the latest is that they are going to attack Point Douglas." He pointed towards Gibraltar. " Over on a little knoll there they have put some field-pieces—field-pieces they stole from you. No, they were too clever for that, weren't they? Field-pieces that some of the settlers themselves took by force out of the Colony storehouse and carried off and asked them to take care of. I believe Captain Macdonell was planning an expedition to bring them back again just before he was plunged into all the events that ended in him leaving here. Yes, they are smooth. They realise that the law may some day inquire into it all and they want to have good cases."

" They won't have a good case if they continue to attack us!" said I.

I was full of excitement but had no fear, which pleased me greatly. If they attack, thought I, there will be opportunity to have revenge on them for having arrested our Governor.

" Well," said McLeod, " go get your musket and ammunition. I am having everybody warned. We've got the wives of the few men that are married here into Bourke's cabin, to shelter there with Mrs. Bourke. It is built of stout logs on which stray bullets will but dunt; and it is on the main buildings they will use the field-pieces, if they're planted on that knoll for more than just to try to intimidate us. All that Peguis heard was that they planned to rush in on us armed."

He looked again at the paper in his hand and smoothed it somewhat as Chisholm had, as though smoothing would help; and then he flicked it with a finger in a gesture reminiscent of that with which Cameron flicked the formal order to quit that I had delivered.

" The Sheriff should see this," he said, handing it to me. " Obviously we of the Hudson's Bay Company are to have our copies later— perhaps after due pressure." He looked along the plain to southward. " And here, if I mistake not, is the pressure coming now."

A haze of dust was moving rapidly towards us—such a haze of dust as is raised by many horses at the trot or the gallop. I dashed away to Governor's House and as I entered nearly collided with Archibald who was coming out.

" Oh, here is a document that has been delivered to all the settlers," said I. " You will remember that when Cameron sent a letter demanding surrender of the guns he did not send it direct to you but sent it for the people to read first and act upon. Now here's this: Every house has a copy before one comes here. This I had from Mr. Chisholm. Take it, though there is no time to read it now. They are riding this way and——"

" John McLeod told me to expect them," replied the Sheriff, and brushed past me, the document in hand. He had belted on a sword,

I noticed, as though prepared to come to close quarters, and had a pistol in his belt.

I hurried into the accounting-room in a corner of which muskets had been ready for many days. And there I was when Bourke came in.

"You and I," he remarked, "have shared one or two excitements together. I've just wrote to my mother in Sligo to tell her that I am now going for a soldier."

"That's the way to take it," came McLeod's voice in the doorway. "It's too serious to take any other way. Come, now. All will be needed."

We had just stepped to the door when very high and shrill came the yelping that we had not heard since the day when the settlers who had accepted Cameron's offer of lands in Upper Canada went away. They had a fervour that was new. Past the house went a galloping stream of feathered and painted riders. I knew they were not local Indians and because of my knowledge that the Crees, brought from the prairies by cousin Alexander in the hope they would attack the settlers, had all gone home again, the paint and feathers did not mislead me. Full-blood Indians they were not. As they rode with a fierce drumming of hoofs they fired to left and right at the houses, at windows, at doors.

Excitement possessed me. For a moment or two I was as one looking on at a spectacle in which he has not to participate. The sullen impact at my ear of a bullet in a log of the wall made me act. I raised my musket and taking aim at a rider pivoted on a heel as he surged by, touched the trigger and saw him fall forward suddenly, desperately clasping his horse's neck.

"I got him, I got him! I got one!" I found myself shouting.

Bourke, by my side, stared at me as if in surprise. McLeod, who had been standing outside close to the door, out of cover and shooting, looked round with the same inquiry in his eyes as was in Bourke's.

"Nervous?" he asked.

"Oh, no!" I ejaculated.

"Good! For here they come again."

They were indeed coming back again, returning at a swift gallop, and firing as they rode. McLeod stepped inside.

"One of you go to a window," said he.

I dashed to a window and knelt by it with my forearm on the sill so that I could take better aim. Excitement made me tremble. I had to hold the musket-butt very tight to my shoulder to steady it. I shot and missed, loaded and shot again and missed, and then there was a searing pain in my left wrist. I dropped the musket. Blood from my arm ran on the floor.

I was wearing that day a neckerchief that I had bought at the Colony store. I pulled it off and with one end in my teeth tried to bind up my arm to stop the bleeding, but could not. The ragged wound went higher than at first I thought. I pulled off my coat and rolled up my shirt-sleeve. Not only was my forearm torn but from under the arm came a trickle of blood.

Outside was the high shrill *Yi-yi-yi* of the riders. I heard the report of fire-arms. Eddies of dust and powder-smoke came in at the window. Then I heard a voice moaning and I came to myself, still in that room, near the window, with Surgeon White bending over me. Beside him stood Bourke, a basin in his hands, a basin that was full, it seemed, of blood.

"Yes," said White, "it is a good thing the bullet struck the barrel as it did. Close call for you, young man. It hit the barrel just below your hand, I'd judge, ripped your forearm, nipped a bit off your upper arm, and went over your left shoulder. Well, that's better than a direct hit bang in the eye! You're still here. Going off again? No. Staying this time, eh? There that's the forearm done. Now let's plaster this nick higher up."

"I'm all right," I said, sitting up, but feeling dwaumy.

The Sheriff entered.

"This will help you," he said, and handed me a noggin of whisky.

McLeod appeared in the doorway, asking for help.

"We've got to get that cannon over to the smithy," he announced. "They may use the field-pieces now."

"Cannon!" ejaculated Archibald. "We have no cannon. They stole all our cannon, and refused to give them back save to those they said had put them in their care. Just before he went the Governor was planning——"

"I know, I know," interrupted McLeod. "But there is an old one that wasn't with the others. It was here before Captain Macdonell came. Peter Fidler had it but never mounted it. It's in the shed behind his cabin. McLean is fetching it to the smiddy in a cart while this lull is on. We hadn't time before. And he's taking over all the lengths of chain he can find to make shot from. You'd all better get over there now. We'll make a fort of the old smiddy!"

I rose, drained my glass, set it down. I was ready to fight again. I wanted to pay back for the ache in that arm. Out all went and, following them, as I reached the door I had to step aside to make way for a man who was backing in, carrying one end of a load. The load was a dead man. The sudden sight of him was shocking. I knew him only slightly. He was not a Colony employee but one of the Hudson's Bay Company's staff, a man called Warren. The other man who helped to carry the body in was Bob Wallace. He had evidently been wounded in the hand for there was a bandage round it.

Soon all those on Point Douglas were gathered in the smithy, their faces glowing intermittently as the fuffing bellows decreed. Swiftly McLeod and McLean worked, preparing shot for that four-pounder from the chains. None too soon was their task accomplished.

"They are going to try a rush on us again. Here they come!" warned Archie Currie, on the look-out.

On a makeshift carriage the gun was run out. The riders approached in a close body. They realised that the Colony and Hudson's Bay employees had gathered there, all in the one house, and they were, apparently, ready to scatter out in single file so as to sweep round in a half-circle in the manner of attacking Indians, when the cannon was touched off. It tossed up its nose and leapt back, smoking, was pounced upon by McLeod and his helpers and reloaded.

Several of the enemy fell at the first spray of shot, and two horses also. Men and horses spasmodically twitched, kicked, lay still. Other riders swept past in consternation, without shooting; but those within the smithy took aim at them to some purpose through the crannies. As it was not a dwelling-house the interstices between the logs were not caulked. They swept on well beyond the smithy and did not come back.

"Thank God," exclaimed Bourke, "we got all the women here into my house. We can keep an eye on it through our chinks. They are safe there behind its stout logs though they'll be worrying about us."

"The *métis* have ridden well past it," said someone.

" Where have they gone to?"

" Where are they?"

" Perhaps they have had their bellyful!"

" Perhaps they are leaving us and going on to attack the settlers instead."

That suggestion brought immediate anxiety to all.

" Surely they would not do that," said Bourke, alarmed. " That would be an attack on separate homes—with women and children."

" I would not put it past them," declared McLeod. " I think some of us should make a sortie along the road and find out."

" Who will come?" asked Archibald.

There must have been somewhere about thirty-five men gathered there, Hudson's Bay employees and Colony employees together. Only thirteen of them were unwounded. When Mr. Archibald asked who would volunteer to go along the Settlement road, lest the *métis* were up to mischief there, all responded as ready, both wounded and hale responded. I was among those finally selected to go. I was specially eager to be of the party because of my anxiety regarding the Chisholms.

" He'll never be able to hold a musket with that hand and arm," objected the surgeon.

" I can use a pistol," said I. I was in considerable pain. At every throb of my heart there was a throb of pain in the arm and the insistence of it was sickening. I was squeamish all the while.

" Come along, then," said the Sheriff followed by twelve of us he had hastily selected.

The smithy door faced southward by east, towards the river. Archibald suddenly halted.

" What's all this?" he inquired.

All looked out at that exclamation and saw coming towards us a great number of men, women, and children, on either side of them riders.

" They are bringing the settlers along here," said Archibald.

" No—not the half-breeds," said McLeod. " These are full-bloods, these are Indians."

" I believe you are right," said Archibald. " I wonder what does this mean! And where are the *métis* who rode past last time?"

McLeod pointed over the plain to west.

"There's a dust-cloud rising there. They are possibly under that," he suggested.

Soon we knew, soon we heard all. While the attack had been in progress at Point Douglas another party of *métis* had gone down among the farms evidently intending to terrorise there; but Peguis, who had failed in his plea to be allowed to bring his warriors and braves to fight against the North-Westers, had been in the neighbourhood with some of his men; and now here came a deputation to see the Sheriff, to put their case before him, protected by these friendly natives.

They had made up their minds. They were going away. Some were for returning to Scotland; some were for going only to Jack River post (that before long, by the way, was to give place to Norway House, built by a party of Norwegian labourers for the Company), to wait there till the settlers expected that summer arrived. They knew that Captain Semple, the new officer for the Hudson's Bay Company, was expected that year, empowered with much authority over all Rupert's Land. As the Hudson's Bay Company had retained judiciary rights in the territory of the Selkirk purchase he would have a say there. The general belief was that he would be bringing a considerable body of men as a protective force with him.

These settlers had elected no speakers. Many spoke at once; but despite the babel it was clear that they were all determined to leave Red River—a few for ever, the majority in hope of a return.

Elated by the rout of the half-breeds in that last attack and, because of the throbbing pain in my arm in a state of belligerence, I suddenly broke out with: "Stay and fight! Stay and fight! We were fighting here. Stay and fight!"

"All very well for the young, hot-headed, unmarried lads to talk of staying and fighting," answered one who had several children, "but we are outnumbered by these half-breeds, and there are our families to think of."

"Don't the women want you to fight?" I demanded.

No one heeded that. I had the impression of all backs being turned on me, of being dismissed from attention.

It was at that juncture that four men came riding from the south, one of them carrying a white cloth atop a twig, a flag of truce.

"It must be the *métis* you will have to deal with," said McLeod
to Archibald, "for here come Cuthbert Grant and William Shaw,
Bonhomme Montour and Bostonois Pangman. If it was the Nor'-
Westers you had to discuss with we might expect to see your
Governor's cousin, Yellowhead Macdonell, or Ben Frobisher, or at
least that cherub called Seraphim Lamar in his ensign's livery, whatever."

His insouciant manner at that moment was encouraging to every
one. The four riders drew closer. Cuthbert Grant it was who spoke
first, and to McLeod he addressed himself. He was a young man,
dark-skinned, big and fleshy.

"Well, John," said he. "I have a missive here for you to read,"
and he touched his horse with his heels and came ahead of his
companions.

"Your father," remarked McLeod, "by all we hear of him, would
have had the courtesy to dismount."

"I was about to do so," replied Grant, but by the shadow on his
face he had not been and was ashamed by that rebuff. He dismounted
and with the lines of his horse in one hand stepped forward to give
the document to McLeod, who read it through while all remained
silent.

When he had finished reading said McLeod:

"Yes, it is the same you delivered to the settlers. But it is only of
partial interest to me. The first clause does not concern me for I have
no authority to bid the settlers retire from the river. I am in the
service of the Hudson's Bay Company, not in the service of Lord
Selkirk. Clause two interests me in its desire for peace and amity
between the Companies: I shall be glad to have that—it will be a
pleasant change from recent behaviour of the North-Westers. Clause
three is fair enough; it simply means a *status quo ante* in the trading
here. Clause four being in the nature of Forgive and Forget I am
also happy to read. Clause five—as it again appertains to the settlers—
has nothing to do with me, though if I were a settler I would be
rendered combative by the threat in it."

"The threat in it!" exclaimed Grant.

"Yes. It might have been written, to judge by its smoothness, by

L

Duncan Cameron. Is there any chance that he prepared this precious agreement for you before he went away?"

Grant made no reply to that.

"I see by the sixth and final clause," McLeod continued, "that even the buildings of the colonists are objectionable to those who drafted the thing. I am amazed, Grant, that you allow yourself to be made what they call a cat's paw, or otherwise the one to take the chestnuts from the fire."

There seemed to be a simplicity or naïveté about that large and strong-built man, Cuthbert Grant, standing there with his horse's reins in hand. His expression announced as much of shame as anger. One of the settlers helped him to recover his aplomb by stepping forward then.

"As for these clauses, Mr. McLeod," said he, "that are nothing to you—they are much to us. We are going."

McLeod passed the paper to the Sheriff.

"It does not appear to be addressed to you," he said as he did so, "but there it is, Archibald. You will notice also that the North-West Company is not mentioned in it. It is betwixt the half-breeds of the Indian Territory and the Hudson's Bay Company. So far as I can see, the Hudson's Bay Company, if its officers sign this along with the half-breed officers, will share with them the guilt of driving Lord Selkirk's people out. Oh, yes, surely," he broke out in a new voice, turning again to Cuthbert Grant, "here is the hand of Duncan Cameron. Behind all, of course, is William McGillivray, the Montreal king, and behind him is Sir Alexander Mackenzie; but if there is to be any question at law over it all I see the half-breeds and the Hudson's Bay Company sharing the guilt and the North-Westers wiping their clever hands of the whole thing."

Grant just bit meditatively on his upper lip, his under jaw a little out-thrust.

"Too bad, Pangman," said McLeod, "to see you on that side."

"Well," responded Pangman, and laughed, "I shall have the pleasure of seeing Peter Fidler put his signature to that, in accord with me."

"No you will not. He is absent from here at present."

A group of settlers had gathered round the Sheriff and drawn to them also James Sutherland of the Hudson's Bay Company. They were conferring eagerly, head to head, with waggings and mutterings and occasional oblique glances at McLeod.

"Who is in charge of your Company's trading post here?" asked Grant. "Is it you, McLeod?"

"I seem to have a number of charges in the neighbourhood," McLeod told him. "I go down to Bas de la Rivière to recover furs stolen by the North-Westers from one of our parties in transit." That was a recent expedition of his. With only two men to support him he had daringly gone there and brought back the stolen bales. "I go to Manitou Baa to trade. I go to Turtle River," he laughed in his chest, "and am taken prisoner and held for four days till the Governor of Assiniboia takes some of your people as hostages. By various signs I am looked upon as having some standing here."

His manner made all four men before him laugh loudly. It would appear they admired him, or his way of taking them.

"Then you can sign that on behalf of the Hudson's Bay Company," said Grant; and Pangman, dismounting, simultaneously remarked : "You can sign and we can sign and have the whole thing settled."

McLeod shook his head.

"I have not the authority," he replied, "to sign such a document, though all the authority needed to go to a North-West fort and recover stolen property."

They laughed again at that instead of being angered.

James Sutherland had stepped out from the group in which he and the Sheriff were the centre.

"The majority of those remaining here," said he, "apparently wish to go—in fact I might say all, for a small minority would hardly stay on when the great majority left. That being so, and as I am the senior here and on the books as the local chief factor, I shall take the responsibility to sign. And," he stretched a hand to put it on the surgeon's shoulder, "Mr. White here will sign with me, I think."

There followed the interchange of a word or two that sounded quaint to me for no other reason than that two men had the same Christian name and by their Christian names then addressed each other.

"You agree that it is the wisest procedure, James?" asked James Sutherland.

"I do, James," replied James White.

"And now, John McLeod, you will sign also," said Pangman.

"I will not!" said McLeod definitely.

"Well, the two signatures will serve," said Grant.   "You, Mr. Sutherland, will subscribe yourself, I presume, as you stated yourself just now—chief factor?"

"Yes, yes."

Bonhomme Montour and William Shaw then alighted.

"Shall we go into your office to sign this?" suggested Sutherland to Archibald, who stood by silently looking on.

"I have to provide the ink for what I am not invited to sign," said the Sheriff, "or given the opportunity to refuse to attest. I represent Lord Selkirk's Settlement, but the whole affair is arranged between the half-breeds and the Hudson's Bay Company."

"You see it as I do," said McLeod.

"Well, well, well, we can go over to Indian Hall to avoid whatever is to be avoided," exclaimed Sutherland, a faint look of disgust on his face, followed by a shrug carrying the suggestion that he was willing to humour a trivial stickler.

Thus it was that the document was signed, in duplicate, opposite the words *Chiefs of the Half-breeds: Cuthbert Grant, Bostonois Pangman, William Shaw, Bonhomme Montour*; and opposite the words *For Hudson's Bay Company: James Sutherland, chief factor, James White, surgeon.*

As they departed towards Indian Hall, McLeod turned to the Sheriff.

"There they go," he said, "with the intention to sign the Colony's death warrant. Be content that your signature is lacking." Then his considering gaze fell on me. "What happens to you now?" he asked. "Do you think you will go all the way back to Scotland or will you wait at Jack River to see if the people arriving this year are sufficient in numbers to——"

I did not let him finish. Every throb of blood in my arm was a throb of pain. Suppressed rage was in me. I was irascible with disappointment over this seeming end to all our hopes.

"I'm not going at all!" I interrupted. "I am going to stay here."

"The surgeon will be leaving," McLeod pointed out, deliberately, blank of expression. "Who will there be to dress your wounded arm?"

"Some Indian, if no one else?" I replied. "No, I will not go!"

"I wonder have you a fever on you, or are you merely exceedingly annoyed?" said McLeod.

"I am so greatly annoyed I feel, at this moment, I could bite through the steel of a bayonet," I answered.

McLeod laughed.

"Well," said he, "whether this be just passing excitement speaking in you or no, I may tell you I am stopping."

"And me too," said MacLean—he whom McLeod wrote down later in his diary of those days as *noble Hugh MacLean*.

CHAPTER TWO

I

THERE was much that was melancholy then in my mind and not easy
to expel. I had attended the funeral of Mr. Warren; I had seen the
half-breeds carry away their dead. As John McLeod noted, writing
in his diary after that fight, both Hudson's Bay Company's men and
Colony men involved in it had " shot to kill " and there were casual-
ties on the other side. The elder who had been appointed, in lack
of a clergyman, to conduct religious services, had gone with those
who had been coaxed away by Cameron; but a book of religious
offices was found in Fidler's cabin and one of the settlers read the
burial service over John Warren. The dead horses, by order of the
Sheriff, were removed at the end of ropes, out beyond Frog Plain,
where the wolves could have them instead of being a prowling
nuisance close at hand.

Depressed and yet excited—with an excitement that accelerated my
heart-beats and at times gave me a sensation as of choking—I went
to witness the departure of the colonists. They were going at once,
for their minds were made up beyond changing. Here was not a
case, after all, as James Sutherland had prophesied, of a majority
being followed by a minority. The attack on the administrative houses
at Point Douglas created unanimity : All would be gone, and without
delay.

They were carrying their belongings down to the river to boats
and rafts. That was a busy scene. For the youngest, those to whom
the " trippings " to Pembina had been enjoyable, there was some
piquancy just in moving again, but the anxiety regarding the future
that subdued those of mature years, as they went about their final
tasks, affected even the most carefree. What laughter sounded along
the bank came chiefly from the groups of half-breeds who rode past.
Many full-bloods of the neighbourhood were there. They moved
dejectedly about among those with whom they had traded ducks and
gold-eyes and venison for sugar and tobacco; and it was obvious that
between them and the exulting *bois-brûlés* there was enmity.

"If these Indians were not here," Sheriff Archibald remarked, "I think the half-Indians might become troublesome with rejoicing over the fact that they are having their way."

Losing touch with him in one of his transits, I went where most I desired to go: I went to the Chisholm farm. The last bundles were ready at the door and with heavy heart I helped to carry them down to the waterside. There was no laughter even from impetuous Agnes that morning, but she walked about with a frequent indignant hoydenish toss of her head. Mairi, at first, had apparently nothing to say; at last impulsively she spoke out of her heart.

"It's all so bonnie," she said. "I cannot understand folk behaving this way. We are doing nobody any harm. The Indians don't object to us being here."

A sound of sobbing caused us to turn. An Indian woman stood on the threshold, weeping, looking in at the emptiness. It was she who, at the earlier exodus of settlers, had remarked she was glad that the Chisholms were remaining.

"You go now?" she plaintively inquired.

As I have already indicated it had been for long difficult to assure Mrs. Chisholm that the Indians were truly friendly. And in vain it had been for her husband to seek to assure her that their proffers of friendship were sincere. Latterly she had learnt to realise the truth of these assurances; and at that moment of going, of separation, she had no doubt at all. So there stood these two women weeping at each other. Looking at them the thought came to me that here were not two people of different race so much as simply two women heart-broken.

Mairi and Agnes then shared a thought: Was there anything they could give her, for memento, at parting? In the packing they had forgotten a kettle.

"Give her that?" inquiringly whispered Agnes to Mairi.

"Give her this?" inquired Mairi simultaneously, in a whisper, of Agnes.

"Oh, the kettle!" exclaimed Mrs. Chisholm. "I forgot the kettle." Then, the intensity of the feeling of that moment gathering them together, she took it from Mairi and handed it to the weeping Indian. "You take this," she said.

The woman accepted it like a mute child.

"Well," said Chisholm, returning from the river, "there is plenty of evidence now for you that the Indians were not our enemies."

"Yes, indeed. I have always said that," declared Mrs. Chisholm. "I have always known and said they were our friends."

Her husband stared at her, his mouth open in astonishment. Mairi and Agnes heard as though doubting their ears. Suddenly Agnes threw herself back and loudly laughed.

"What are you laughing at?" demanded her mother. And that ended that.

I was aware of Mairi, her head slightly lowered, pensive, considering me.

"With whom will you be making the voyage?" she asked.

"I have not decided yet," I answered evasively. "I am supposed to be attending on the Sheriff this morning but we have lost each other."

Three half-breeds riding neck and neck along the road suddenly emitted wavering screams and thrashed past at a gallop.

"I'm thinking," said Chisholm, "that as soon as we have gone our homes will share the fate of those who accepted the Nor'-Westers' offer in Upper Canada. Oh, they're cunning. They got two-thirds of us away—peaceable and friendly. Now it is the half-breeds that give the lave of us notice to quit."

I looked along the road. There was Court Nez, riding a spirited piebald horse, coming our way, two feathered Indians with him. He caught sight of me, turned aside—the gate stood open—and riding close reined in. The full-bloods, following him, halted a length behind, lean expressionless men whose mouths were lipless slits, whose eyes glittered between puckered eyelids.

"So there you are, David Baxter," said Court Nez.

By his utterance I realised that he had taken sufficient drams for the morning, though he was not what could, by a general vote, be called drunk. He surveyed the group—father, mother, daughters, the Indian woman. Then from me to Mairi he looked, from Mairi to me, back and forth, and gave a knowing nod, a grimace that might be taken to convey comprehension of something—though of what, who could say? Mrs. Chisholm's bearing suggested, as definitely as though she spoke the words, "And who may you be?" This presuming air of shrewdness in a stranger made her part puzzled, part indignant.

"So there you are," he repeated. "And you're off and away?"

I made no reply.

"All the way down Lake Winnipic," Court Nez continued, "and on to Hudson Bay, and then the ship home. Home!" He drew a deep breath and straightened himself in the saddle. "To see if you can sustain the old life, eh?"

"No, sir, not that," I replied, promptly. "Certainly not that. I shall be back," said I, and added, "if I go."

Mairi, I observed, gave me a quick look.

"Oh, not that, eh?" said Court Nez.

In response to the slightest pressure of a leg, the slightest motion of thumb and forefinger on the reins, his horse pivoted round, leapt lightly to a lope. Off he went, followed by his Indian companions.

"Who's he?" asked Mairi.

"Who's he?" echoed Mrs. Chisholm.

"Who's he?" cried out Agnes.

"They call him Court Nez," said I, "just Court Nez, nothing else. He's a free-trader. A queer man. I would like to know his story. He told me once he was one of these men of whom people say, 'They are out in the Indian Countries—God knows why.'"

I looked after the riders, their three backs lightly swaying, fuzzed in the dust from the horses' hoofs. The Indian woman, carrying her kettle, moved away baggily to a clump of bushes and there sat down.

"We'd better get on our way to the boats," suggested Chisholm.

"What have you done with your cows?" I inquired.

"Slaughtered them," he said over his shoulder, "those that weren't driven off when the others left. Divided the meat with those who had no cows. We offered some to the Indians for various services they had done us but they don't like cow meat. 'No good, make sick,' they say. Well, I've got to like pemican myself."

Mrs. Chisholm began to be flurried.

"I think everybody's down at the river," said she. "We mustn't be left."

At these words excitement surged anew in me.

"I must go and find the Sheriff," I said.

I turned to Mairi. I wanted to take her in my arms for I might never see her again. " She's a darling, she's a dear," I told myself. I looked on her as a very close friend. Had we been alone I would have dared to hug her, but with father and mother there I refrained.

" In case——" I began, and tried again : " In case I get in a boat a bit away from you I had better——" I looked from Mr. Chisholm to Mrs. Chisholm, from Mrs. Chisholm to Agnes.

Agnes rescued me.

" Kiss us all good-bye for the now, anyway," she advised, and flung an arm round me, kissing me on the cheek.

She wet my face with sudden tears, then laughed shrilly. From all the work when going up and down the river bank she was heated. I was enveloped in her wildness. There was an odour of sweat in my nostrils. My cheek was wet with her weeping. Her laughter was loud in my ears. She pushed me violently against her sister.

I held Mairi's shoulders and she looked in my eyes with a question in hers, having surmised by then, as I heard later, my intention to remain. *Are you leaving here?* she asked—as one can ask without speech. I shook my head in reply to that wordless inquiry and kissed her frankly.

Mrs. Chisholm was blind with weeping. She embraced me as if I had been a son.

" Well, well, we may be back," said Chisholm, high and shrill, as though his voice had its pitch from shouting into the wind over distances. " We're going no farther than Jack River to begin with. There's another party of settlers due this summer and with things passing from bad to worse, with the antipathy of the Nor'-Westers, there is no saying but that Lord Selkirk may have arranged for what Governor Macdonell—as once you told me, David, thought that there ought to be here—may have arranged for a more or less military body of men to enforce his rights and ours. But for the now we're away. We're away!" he chanted, picking up a last bundle and slapping me on the shoulder. " We'll see you even if you don't get in our boat. I suppose you'll be with the young Sheriff?"

He had not seen the question in Mairi's eyes. The shaking of my head at her had not signified to him that I was staying behind.

Off they went along the field's edge to the riverside and passed under the bank's fringe of trees. A ripple of light and shade from the branches of oak and elm ran over their backs. They went down, par://

down. They did not look round at the home they had built or at me. They disappeared.

I stared at the fringe of trees. They had been; they had gone. I had a sickness at the heart. Here they all had come expecting to have homes from which they would never be evicted. They were gone. Combatively I confronted the sense of desolation and emptiness which, felt by Mrs. Chisholm, had caused her to be suddenly flustered with anxiety to join the others at the river.

A shadow slipped over the fields, the Settlement, over the riverside's fringe of trees. There was a sudden gloom and then a pattering of great drops of rain, wide apart, great drops that made a loud noise in the corn, on the roofs of the barns, the roofs over the empty houses. How quickly they went! All the people were down in the gash of the river. The Bourkes were there and Michael McDonnell who, like Bourke, had come out on the *Edward and Anne* with me. Mr. Pritchard accompanied them but was very taciturn over the expulsion, the withdrawal.

No pipes played for that departure. What sounds they made did not reach me. I was suddenly aware of the Indian woman sitting there in a thicket, motionless as an effigy, the brass kettle in her lap.

11

The Selkirk Settlement was apparently left to her and to me alone. Out of sight were the colonists, the half-breeds who had come to watch them go, the Indians who had come for the same reason and also to protect them if there was any attempt to molest them.

The excitement of uncertainty possessed me. To abolish an intruding impulse to go away with the rest I decided to put space between myself and the river, passed back to the deserted road, turned south, and then thought I: "I am mad!" There was pain in my arm. Looking back I could see—yonder and yonder, northward—empty farmhouses, the sun-bleached roofs from which rose no smoke. From the administrative houses also no smoke rose. To go or stay? Thus I swithered.

McLeod, I reminded myself, was not going away. Mr. MacLean was not going. I tried to recall the last clause of the agreement that the half-breed chiefs and Sutherland and White had signed. It was to the effect that the Hudson's Bay employees, passing the summer by Red River, would not remain in the Colony buildings but retire elsewhere to trade. McLeod must be somewhere there despite the feeling of utter emptiness under that dome across which the snow clouds were sailing. The trill, the roulade, the one short bar of a song of a prairie lark sounded and for some reason hurt me, perplexingly hurt me. I remembered Mairi's remark of that day—and a similar one of another day—to the effect that it seemed all wrong there should be inhumanity in so beautiful a world. Again came the lark's bar of song, part of the beauty of that day.

There was someone ahead of me—a man whose build, whose gait, I knew: There went John McLeod walking from riverwards on a path between two of the most southerly farms. Powerfully he strode along. The easy swing of his arms betokened his great physical strength and carried a suggestion of much reserve. Chancing to turn his head and look behind him on reaching the road he saw me legging it there, and delayed for me.

"Well, David," he said, "you seem to be in a hurry. What have you forgotten?"

"I'm not going," said I.

"So it wasn't just from fever after your wound, or out of a passing excitement you said you would stay. You're not going."

"Not if you are staying—not if anybody is staying."

"Of course I'm staying," replied McLeod. "I'm in the service of the Hudson's Bay Company, whether we retire to some other spot—in the words of that impudent document—in the vicinity or no. And three good men are staying with me: Archie Currie and James McIntosh, both Company men, and Hugh MacLean, a settler who like you has decided not to go."

"Yes, I heard him say he would stay."

"Well, well," remarked McLeod and walked on. I fell in step at his side. "Maybe even with one working arm you can help. We're going in here. We've got to save some seed-grain," he explained, and turned aside into a farmyard.

He led the way into the barn and there I saw Currie and McIntosh busily filling sacks in a haze of grain dust.

"Oh, look who's here!" exclaimed Currie, and laughed.

"Yes," said McLeod. "The Red River Settlement is not really

at an end. Other settlers are coming. You see what we are doing, David, taking as much seed as we can to store in Peter Fidler's old place. That's surely Hudson's Bay property, having been built for a trading post before the Settlement was planned, before Peter went back to his surveying profession on behalf of it. According to the terms of that agreement, goodwill and amity are to be in the land between Hudson's Bay men and all these others: traders, Indians, freemen. No free-trader was asked to sign it, I notice—and there are many handy, forby that strange man Court Nez. If he was invited to sign, which I doubt, he did not. Well, I hope no one objects to us saving a pickle of seed in case any settlers should wish to settle here in the future. The way I feel just now it would be a bad business for any if they did object! I just took a run down to see these folks go and I am exasperated for their sakes."

He turned away.

" Come over to the next farm," he suggested. " I think we can add to our store from there."

In the doorway we halted. Again there were columns of smoke rising here, there, yonder, through the Settlement.

" So—so—so!" hissed McLeod. " While their Indian friends were down at the river to see that they were not molested as they went, there were half-Indians along there setting fire to the houses."

" And that black cloud going up there," said I, pointing, " that's from the grist-mill."

" That's what it is! They will be working along this way soon. They will certainly burn the administrative buildings. They are seeing to the terms of that document. What were the words again? ' The people,' " he quoted from memory, " " passing the summer for the Hudson's Bay Company shall not remain in the buildings of the Colony.' Well, we're going to pass the summer here, in our own buildings, anyhow. You'd better carry this sack over to Fidler's house."

" Here are some riders coming now," said I.

" No. It's Hugh MacLean with the pack-horses I asked him to get. Seed-grain—seed-grain—that's what we have to think of now. We'll store as much as we can. But I think that maybe we will be smelling sulphur again in the process, whatever."

III

It was perhaps only because of the promptitude of our action that we did not smell more powder than we did. Downstream, with their Indian friends convoying them—some of these in canoes, others on horseback along the west bank—went the settlers. If the *métis* who watched them go had sinister intentions, if they were there not only to watch the departure but to speed it, should opportunity offer, with violence, that intention was frustrated by the presence of the full-bloods.

When the boats went off in the current the enemy had not followed. Up over the bank they came and split into many parties, riding through the deserted Settlement. These did not stay on the road that ran from Point Douglas to the last farm northward. Where fences impeded them they tore them down. Home after home they turned into bon-fire. The settlers, going down river and looking back, would see the pillars of cloud and to many they may have signified that all was indeed over for the Red River Settlement.

But McLeod had a different view.

" This is not the end," he vowed.

By the late afternoon we had stored in Fidler's cabin not only the seed grain but various agricultural implements that had been left behind. From north we could hear the *Yip-yip-yip* raised in an ecstasy of triumph by the incendiarists.

" We've saved all we can," said McLeod. " We had better get to our quarters."

We went to the smithy, having let the pack-horses go. McLeod chose it because it was not chinked, or if it had been the chinking had fallen out. All round it, between the logs, were slits of daylight. It commanded, through these slits, the four quarters. From one side of it a marksman could pick off any one who went to meddle at Fidler's place; from another side any one approaching the Hudson's Bay Company's trading-house, Indian Hall. There we remained while party after party of " the breeds," as McIntosh called them, rode by.

" They do not know we are here," said he and Currie together.

The next party, however, turned aside and dismounted at Governor's House, entered it, came out and went over to the cabin that Bourke had built when he married. While they were in it smoke rose from Governor's House and as they emerged from Bourke's a blue haze ascended behind them there. They passed then into the Colony store.

"They are firing all the Colony houses," said McLeod. "If they go across to Indian Hall I think we shall let them know we are here and that we have our cannon still."

"They are leaving it alone," said MacLean.

"That trading-house was built for the Company after Governor Macdonell came here," McLeod remarked, "but they are going to recognise it as a Hudson's Bay building as well as Fidler's old house and this shell of a smiddy."

"There is something fascinating in watching a fire," said McIntosh.

"And we have been seen watching!" I exclaimed, for eager to know what was being done we had gone to the door instead of being content to observe between the logs.

"Get your muskets ready, boys, in case it is to be fight," said McLeod.

The half-breeds rode closer but at a walk which suggested rather inquiry than attack; and although we had thought ourselves observed it was to Fidler's house they went first. As several dismounted and passed indoors McLeod, who had been peering between the logs, stepped outside and when he spoke it was to give an order.

"Do not set fire to that place," he hailed. "These are stores I have left there."

It was clear enough then that the half-breeds had seen us. His appearance and his hail took none by surprise.

"What stores?" asked one.

"Stores! Stores!" snapped McLeod. "Is that not enough? Do you expect an inventory?"

"Settlement stores!" the man shouted back to him. "You are a Hudson's Bay officer, but these are Settlement stores."

"Do you want me to tell my men to shoot? We have you all at the ends of our sights from here. I have just to tell them to fire and you are dead men. It would be wisdom for you to move off."

Speedily they conferred together at the threshold of Fidler's house. Then all mounted and rode away.

Smoke haze made the twilight dusky blue. Governor's House was a crackling bonfire. The small cabin in which Bourke and his wife had lived tottered, the roof fell in between the flaming walls. A volley of sparks rose up, trembled, wavered down, light as feathers. I thought of Miles Macdonell. Where would he be then? Well on his way, under arrest on a warrant possibly spurious, illegal, to Montreal, up Winnipic River by then, on the Lake of the Woods or Lac la Pluie. The Chisholms in their boat would be well down Red River as far as the mouth, no doubt, where Peguis had his most settled village. The Indians would leave them there and they would go on, out on to the great ocean-like expanse of Lake Winnipic, headed for Jack River post.

I came back from the reverie hearing the others talking of having a meal. McLeod had seen to the storing of sufficient food to keep us for a time. The blaze of Governor's House died down; the mess-quarters sent up a shower of sparks and caved in. A peace immune from our troubles was in the grass. Tranquillity was in the fading light as we ate supper.

Then suddenly we heard once more a rising series of war-whoops, the rub-a-dub of hoofs. The *métis* were back again and sweeping in a semi-circle round the cabin, not a complete circle but a semi-circle so that, as they rode, they could fire without risk of shooting any of their own number. None of us in the smithy, leaping to our feet and snatching up the muskets, required the example of McLeod's composure: Currie, his head bandaged from the earlier siege in that place, McIntosh, Hugh MacLean (" noble Hugh MacLean "), I with my disabled left arm.

" They must have bullets to spare," said McLeod as the *plunk, plunk, plunk* of them sounded in the log walls. " We may as well let them have it. Let them have the musket-balls, boys, till I get the cannon loaded."

Because of my wounded arm it was hard for me to hold a musket. The closing of my hand round it to aim caused excruciating pain and my difficulty was so obvious that McLeod called me to help with the cannon.

" Give me a third hand here, David," he requested.

But the cannon was not required. The half-breeds drew off with three wounded. That night a watch was kept. My perceptions seemed especially acute when I was on guard duty. Long after I would remember my watch, the midnight watch, when I moved round and round the cabin, ears alert, and looking up at the sky saw the glittering scarf of the Milky Way flung round the world, picked out the Plough with its pointers, the North Star to which they pointed, Cassiopeia climbing up the eastern curve of the sky. Looking at the uncounted stars I recalled Mairi's words on the pity of all the strife in a world so beautiful. "What a night!" said I, gazing at that mystery of lights.

McLeod had heard that Indians were wont to launch attacks in the last hours of night, and of this he warned us: "So late that it is almost morning they often charge. It is supposed that watchers by then will not only be tired but off guard." We were prepared for these half-Indians to follow the Indians' tactics, but the glory of the dawn was undisturbed. Breakfast was being cooked when we heard high eerie shouts coming our way.

"Ha, ha!" ejaculated McLeod. "Now we are to see something. There is rum at the back of this, by the sound of it. They have been celebrating all night, I expect."

We went to the door and looked out. There were about a score of horsemen approaching, all raising wavering yells as they rode.

"Put any of them afoot and I doubt if he could stand, whatever," said McLeod.

"Let 'em have the cannon, John," urged Hugh MacLean.

"And give the first blow?" asked McLeod.

"Oh, perhaps we might wait to see what they are about," said MacLean, and began to laugh. He seemed to be enjoying himself, to be finding life at that moment amusing.

The riders turned from group formation to single file and once again round the cabin went a rub-a-dub of hoofs. In the old logs sounded that *plunk, plunk, plunk* of imbedded bullets but also sounds of splintering. Here and there came marks on the more sun-dried logs as of scratched designs of starfish but through the chinks no bullets, so far, buzzed.

Again I lent a third hand to McLeod in getting the little cannon into the doorway with a feeling of extreme goose-flesh all over my body. At any moment a bullet, instead of hitting the walls, might come between the logs—hence my tingling flesh.

M

"We'll let them come in close before we touch off," said McLeod, and we two hunkered down beside the cannon and waited.

The half-breeds were riding round the cabin more in an elipse or oval than a circle and several as they took the bend lurched in the saddles, recovering poise.

"Aye, truly they are drunk!" observed McLeod with a laugh.

One of them fell, rolled, got to his feet, staggered along in an attempt to catch his horse. The rider behind stooped and caught him round the shoulders; and in long, swinging strides the dismounted man was helped away beyond reach of a shot. He went staggering after his horse but our attention was diverted from him by the rising yells of the others.

"If they come closer this time we'll touch off this little fellow," muttered McLeod, and he blew on the smoking tinder in his hand till it glowed bright and flared.

But "the breeds" did not come again. They rode off, yelping— back to Fort Gibraltar to crack another few bottles, Hugh MacLean suggested.

We agreed that for some little time at least it would be advisable to stay fast in our makeshift fort, and so that all need not be on the alert together guard was kept and changed just as during the night. It must have been two hours later that I, on duty again, announced two men coming from the direction of Fort Gibraltar.

I V

The riders were Cuthbert Grant and Bonhommie Montour. Grant dismounted, leaving the lines of his horse in Montour's hand, and walked to the smithy. In the doorway awaiting him stood McLeod and MacLean, the rest of us clustering close behind them.

"Well, John?" said Grant.

"Well, Cuthbert?" said McLeod.

"Well—John!"

"Well—Cuthbert!"

Each laughed lightly then. Cuthbert Grant had a great admiration for John McLeod by reason of all he had both seen and heard of him; and John McLeod had come by the opinion that Cuthbert Grant was being used by the Nor'-Westers and might possibly become the scapegoat were an inquiry into the intimidation of the Selkirk Settlers instituted.

"I'm taking the Qu'Appelle half-Indians off," said Grant, "and came to let you know. I want you to realise that all we objected to here was the Settlement. You saw that deed we signed with the Hudson's Bay men."

"I saw the deed you signed on behalf of the half-breeds with James Sutherland and James White," replied McLeod.

"Well, it is all there, direct enough. We are back where we were. All's well."

"Then why are your people attacking us here?" demanded McLeod.

"They have an excuse, you see. They say you have stored Colony implements and seed in a Hudson's Bay Company's building."

"I have. But my signature is not on that deed. I have promised them nothing," said McLeod.

"That's true too. We'll let it go. Otherwise all is as it was—*status quo ante*. And a damned good job. That accursed Settlement made those who were only rivals in trade deadly enemies. After all, if it amuses you to store these things——" he shrugged his great shoulders. "You can rest in peace now, John McLeod. I'm getting those fellows back to Qu'Appelle."

"Very good," said McLeod. "And I may tell you that I think you are the least to blame of all."

"Least to blame of all! What do you mean?"

"You know what I mean. Or if you don't know now, by meditating on it as you ride back you may find out. Yellowhead and Duncan Cameron are at the back of all this trouble—and they by advice from east. Yes, you've been the chestnut picker and may yet be the scapegoat."

Grant looked moodily at him, heavy of countenance. Without another word he turned on his heel, mounted, and rode away with Montour who had contributed not a word, had been merely a silent witness.

McLeod, MacLean, McIntosh, Currie, and I—the five in the smithy fort—watched them as they departed, watched these two horsemen dwindle in size, riding south. Occasionally it seemed that we had seen the last of them. Down they went, down, down to the shoulders, then up they came again, all of their bodies visible. The flat plain

had its creases. There went the two figures, jig-jogging, and across
the great expanse light chased shadow, or shadow chased light as one
might see it: light and shadow alternated as the clouds passed across
the vast dome.

With the half-breeds gone and the officers at Fort Gibraltar attending to their own affairs there was peace again by Red River. Local
métis and French Canadians—free-traders—cabined in the neighbourhood, were happy enough to assist McLeod in a task to which he had
set himself. Rumours of it going to Fort Gibraltar may have caused
annoyance. He had his trading post, that had not been burnt, Fidler's
old house, and the cabin that had been used as a smithy: Why, no
doubt they asked themselves, was he getting us to build for him
another much larger place? A fine house it was too, by all accounts
they would hear, a strong building of two stories; and when it was
completed he set a party of French Canadians to work erecting a
strong palisade all round a wide parcel of land, a strong palisade to
match the one at Fort Gibraltar. Of old the Hudson's Bay Company
had been content with what the traders called a post there, just a
cabin or two, sufficient to store the trade goods and the furs, and to
lodge the few employees for the district. But this was not a mere
post; this was a fort that McLeod was building for his Company.

For his Company? The Nor'-Westers knew that he had stored
much seed-grain as if in hope that another Settlement would rise
from the ashes of the old. Was he thinking of possible new farmers as
the men built Fort Douglas? For that was what he called the building on Point Douglas. They heard that the people he had gathered
round him were ploughing in some of the trampled fields and
resowing, but they let him be. Yellowhead, we were told, was enraged
at the news, pondered plans for putting an end to these activities but
could not interest the chiefs of the half-breeds, least of all the head-
chief, Cuthbert Grant. We heard that Grant had said to him: "The
settlers have gone. That is enough."

And then, when autumn was in the air by day and chill hints of
winter at night, the Indians from whom we had been trading for fish
and fowl arrived eagerly at the fort with news.

"Canoe come! Many canoe come! Many white man come in
canoes!"

"Who are they?" asked McLeod.

" I think Hudson Bay man."

Up the bank came a young man, as massive of build as Grant, with something of the importance of bearing of Cameron, about as physically robust as McLeod—a young man with keen eyes. Into the fort he was followed by several bronzed men of his own type.

" Mr. McLeod?" he inquired.

" Yes, sir."

" Robertson is my name—Colin Robertson."

The two shook hands, gripped hands, crushed hands. Each let the other know he had a grip.

We had all heard of this man and knew that he had been for a few years in the service of the North-West Company but had resigned some while back to join their rivals the Hudson's Bay Company.

" Where have you come from, Mr. Robertson?" asked McLeod. " From York Factory?"

" No, sir—from Montreal. I have the honour to lead the first Hudson's Bay Company's brigade that has come over the Nor'-Westers' route."

" Indeed!" exclaimed McLeod, a look of triumph in his face. " And whose idea was that?"

" It was on the advice, I understand, of Lord Selkirk," replied Colin Robertson, " who feels that the Company is being too greatly put upon by the Nor'-Westers. He thinks that the time has come for them to understand that we are not asleep. At Bas de la Rivière I heard that the settlers had been driven out so went after them to Jack River and have brought some back. I came on ahead with a few of my men but left others to accompany them in case of trouble on the way. They are not far behind us. They will be here in a few days."

" Well, not only did we save seed-grain but we sowed some of it for them," said McLeod, and a great bellow of laughter broke from him.

CHAPTER THREE

I

"It is essential," said Colin Robertson, sitting next day in a room upstairs in that grand new two-story house we had built, where he had been listening to a full account from McLeod of recent affairs, "that we send word to the Earl of Selkirk of the latest developments here."

"With an ocean between us——" began McLeod.

"No, no—no ocean between. He may be in Montreal by now."

"In Montreal!"

"Yes, in Montreal. He has been planning to come out for the last years. Just before I left Montreal I had a letter from him in which he stated that this Fall he will be able to have his wish fulfilled. So he may be there by now. We must get some man who knows the way east and would be willing to take it at this time of year. The snow will be flying on the winds and ice forming on the waterways before any one leaving now could get there. I would ask some of my voyageurs to go but we may need them here."

"I believe I know the very man for the task," said McLeod. "A French Canadian——"

"Like most of my canoe-men."

"A French Canadian, Jean Baptiste Lagimoniere. He knows the Indian Countries as few do, from Fond du Lac to Fort de la Prairie."

"He is at hand?"

"He is. He is a free-trader. When I wanted men to help in the sowing and rebuilding here, he was one who found me many assistants." Then McLeod shook his head. "The expenses pile up for Lord Selkirk, I'm afraid. A pretty sum he must have spent so far on his settlers without a penny in return. He had need to be a philanthropist to continue with his scheme in face of all the thwartings."

"A philanthropist—or a fighter," said Colin Robertson. "He may be something of both. If he be no natural fighter the treatment he has received may make him one."

"I hear he is a good deal of a scholar," remarked McLeod, "so he may be philosophic over the affronts his hopes have suffered."

"I do not know if he be a scholar," replied Robertson, "but I hear he is an amateur in painting. He may have various sides. This man Robert Semple, who has been appointed Governor of Rupert's Land by the Company, had his appointment chiefly on Lord Selkirk's recommendation, and he is both a soldier and a contributor to the quarterlies. Well, Selkirk is coming out this year for certain and I must get a letter to him in Montreal, somehow, to acquaint him with all that has recently occurred here. On the strength of such information he may be able to obtain military protection for his settlers from Sir Gordon Drummond, the Canadian Governor."

"To be sure. He will learn a good deal from Captain Macdonell, now in Montreal. He may have heard enough already from Howse and Spencer, who were haled off there before Macdonell. Cameron, who only went as far as Fort William with his prisoner, came back to Fort Gibraltar a day or two ago."

"He did? Had I, westward-bound," remarked Robertson, "met those Nor'-Westers, eastward-bound with their prisoner, there might have been another story to tell. Unfortunately we did not meet. We must have passed each other somewhere, with a lake-island between or a mist on the water or while one party shot down some rapids that were being avoided by the other in a portage. Anyhow—we did not meet."

"They are artful," said McLeod. "The gossip is out already that the trials will be postponed in Montreal, or even that the prisoners may be released. I suppose they don't want to air their games in a law court, even in their stronghold. Obviously they only wanted to get Macdonell away from Red River to aid them in breaking up the Colony.

"Well, before we interview this Lagimoniere—it was Lagimoniere you said?"

"Yes—Jean Baptiste Lagimoniere. And what a man!"

"First, then, before that," said Colin Robertson, "I am going to call upon Mr. Duncan Cameron to recover lost property, seeing that he is back from taking Governor Macdonell as far as Fort William. I am going over to Fort Gibraltar to get the cannon that you told me, in our first little chat yesterday, had been stolen by the North-Westers."

"They were carried away," McLeod reminded him, "by some of the colonists. I only mention this," he added with a nod, "because they will say they did not steal them."

"Quite," agreed Robertson. "I catch the quibble. There has been a great deal of thought, especially by Mr. Cameron, on legalities. The diplomatic service would have suited that gentleman!"

He looked round the room. Along a wall he had ordered his men, the day before, to erect a rack for their muskets so that it had something of the appearance of an armoury. The pieces had all been set in place with bayonets fixed, and standing near was a chest of ammunition.

"A dozen of us will suffice," he said. "I have already ordered as many to fall in. I think here they come now," and he looked out of the window. "Yes, here they come. So, Baxter, do you take down these muskets and serve them out. The bayonets might be sharper but——"

My mouth twisted as I looked at the short steel weapons. Colin observed the grimace.

"Yes," he admitted, "they are ugly. They would hurt. A jab with one of them would make a sore." He eyed me thoughtfully and then laughed. He did not think me a coward. He knew of how I had fought beside McLeod, for McLeod had told him about all that had happened during that troubled summer. "I expect you would like to accompany us?" he added.

There came a sound of men talking together, occasional laughter as they mounted the stairs.

"Come in, men!" Robertson shouted. "Come up and take your weapons. Do you serve out the ammunition, Baxter."

My heart fluttered. All very well to say that the mere show of force might suffice. The affair would be carried off with success I did not doubt, but there might be, to begin with, some resistance. I remembered the cry of utter disappointment in that labourer's throat as he fell, how he had sadly complained and died. I remembered the body of John Warren being carried past me in a doorway. Into my head, after those swift pictures of the dying labourer and the dead John Warren, came suddenly a memory of the beautiful half-breed girl I had seen at Fort Gibraltar, Court Nez's daughter, and with it a poignant desire to see her again.

Colin Robertson had evidently already discussed his plans with his men as with cronies, but they would have pleased Captain Macdonell in that they had an idea of discipline and recognised the necessity for obeying a leader whether or not he fraternised with them.

Well armed, we all descended the steep stairs and clustered together outside in the square.

"Fall in!" said Robertson—and with them I fell in. "Number off!"

"One . . . two . . . three . . . four . . ."

"Two deep! Form fours! Shoulder arms! Right turn!"

He carried a pistol in his belt, and a sword in its scabbard was against his left hip. He stepped to the front of the squad.

"Quick—march!"

The men whom McLeod had engaged as carpenters, still at work on buildings within the palisade under construction, ceased their hammering to watch us go. The sentry at the gate came smartly to attention. Robertson took the salute with swagger—perhaps, I suspected, also with amusement. There was often a look of amusement in his eyes, I was to discover when I knew him better, as though he saw this or that seemingly solemn occasion on which he was engaged as not without its whimsical aspect.

Across the plain we marched in good order, came alongside the east wall of Fort Gibraltar.

"Right—wheel!" rasped Robertson. The end man pivoted, marking time. "Well done—a fine body of men," said Colin as they wheeled there, a laugh in his voice.

The men laughed also, accustomed to his ways.

"Silence in the ranks!" he ordered.

We came to the gates. In the deep wedge in the bank below the fort a water-cart was mounting. The gates were open. A sentry was there and at sight of us he stared. With a glance to one side I noticed that Cameron's commission was no longer in evidence. It had served its purpose, thought I, had not merely been seared by the sun till it was an eyesore to be removed. It had influenced those among the settlers who had been invited to Fort Gibraltar to partake of Cameron's designing hospitality. Well, these were gone—they were gone: they were off in the Canadas somewhere, Red River days all past in their chequered lives.

"Why don't you come to attention?" Colin Robertson demanded of the sentry as we swaggered inside the gates.

The man continued to stare. This quick-stepping body of men, with arms at the shoulder and fixed bayonets gleaming, astounded him. On to the officers' house we marched.

"Right turn! Halt!"

The door opened and there in the entrance was Duncan Cameron— whom Robertson recognised at once, having met him when himself in the service of the North-West Company.

"Good-day, Mr. Cameron," he said. "Or is it Captain?"

"Good-day," said Cameron and drew back his head, closed his eyes in a manner of loftiness that clearly amused his caller.

"I have come," Robertson explained, "to take back some cannon belonging to the Red River Settlement that you have kindly been holding in storage." ·

"Cannon, sir?"

"Cannon, sir."

"Well, go get them, sir," said Cameron. "Have you a search-warrant and authority?"

"To take back cannon kindly stored!" ejaculated Robertson. "A search-warrant for that! Oh, surely not!"

"I know nothing of them," said Cameron. "If they are here, and you can find them, you are welcome to them I assure you," and he closed the door.

"Well, we'll begin," said Robertson, taking that rebuff lightly. "They have not mounted them, I take it. All right, men. Those we can glimpse from here are of another calibre by what Mr. McLeod told me—not ours. You can fall out now and we'll start the search. There's a storehouse over there. We'll try it first."

Robertson appeared to know the interior of the fort. I presumed that he had visited it when he was in the service of its Company.

No cannon were visible within that storehouse. We passed on, watched at a distance from a doorway here, a doorway there, and halted before another house that seemed also for storage. That door was padlocked.

Colin Robertson considered it.

"Now, Mr. Cameron," he said, addressing the lock, "I suppose you would say that to burst that would constitute burglary—but you have retired into your den, after having told us we could search."

He nodded to me. I prised the padlock apart with my bayonet and we all peered into the dusky interior. A gleam of brass showed to rear beyond some corded bales. Colin Robertson climbed and thrust a way across.

"Here they are, or two of them," he said. "Get them out."

In all our searching we found no more.

"We need not ask where the rest are," said Robertson. "They have been scattered long since, I expect, to other forts."

"Well, sir, we can shoulder these back then," said I.

"You do not need to. In expectation of getting all I ordered that a cart should follow us—and here it is."

He raised his hand, waved, signing to the driver at the gate to enter. The two guns were loaded into it and slowly it moved away. There was a pucker of anger between Colin Robertson's brows. His chin was tilted. Well he knew that our movements were being observed. From the officers' quarters, which had windows of glass, we saw that we were being watched. From those smaller houses that had windows of parchment we were also being watched, no doubt, from doors that stood ajar, though no one appeared in the open.

"Fall in, two deep, attention!"

The men fell in as ordered.

"Right wheel . . . left wheel . . . quick march! In step—left, left, left. Halt!"

We were at the door of Cameron's quarters again. Robertson stepped forward and rapped smartly. Cameron instantly appeared on the threshold.

"Well, Mr. Cameron," said Colin Robertson. He stepped closer but Cameron remained rigid. Behind him several men rose and walked forward, challenging of aspect.

"Well?" said Cameron.

"We've got two of the pieces," announced Robertson. "The rest may have been sent to other North-West forts to be stored for the settlers. We shall find them perhaps. These two we are taking with us now."

"I remember," said Cameron, still lofty, his head back, his eyelids drooped, "that some of your unhappy colonists were disturbed about Macdonell having so many. They wanted to leave the abortive Settlement and were afraid that he might turn the guns on them if they prepared to do so."

"Who gave them that impression of him?"

"It seemed to be their own. They were naturally greatly dissatisfied with the Colony. Few promises have been kept. I did the best I could for them when I took over command here after Mr. Willis's retirement. The Hudson's Bay factors had no pemican, even, ready for them when they reached here, and things did not improve. Many wanted to go back to Scotland. I managed to get an offer for them of free lands in Upper Canada—and when Miles Macdonell heard of that he was greatly exasperated. They were afraid he might get them to stay by force, so they seized the cannon and brought them over here."

"I see. And you and some half-breeds, I'm told, drew near just to back them up. And when the settlers had gotten the guns you said to them, ' Well done, my hearties!' You made a mistake in showing yourself then and bestowing your praise, Mr. Cameron, a mistake if you would have any one believe your assertion that the idea of taking the guns was entirely theirs."

"I was sorry for them," replied Cameron, superficially bland. "You know yourself that those who did not accept the offer I managed to obtain for them of lands in the Canadas wanted to go home to Scotland—those you turned back after they had gotten as far as Jack River."

So gossip not only of Robertson's arrival but of the settlers on their way back had come to Fort Gibraltar, thought I.

Colin Robertson stood, head on side, studying him.

"Smooth, smooth!" he exclaimed. "Some did talk of going home to Scotland—after you had terrorised them out of the country."

"After I had terrorised them! I deny it! Prove it! I wasn't even here. I understand that the Indians affrighted them by riding and whooping and shouting."

"No, not Indians but half-Indians. You got Cuthbert Grant to see to all that for you. You used that boy. You got Yellowhead Macdonell to use him while you kept in the background."

"Nonsense! I was away with Miles Macdonell before these poor deluded people left. I expect if truth were known you had to wheedle or order them to return."

I saw Robertson's back stiffen. There was an element of truth in that, as a matter of fact, for when he reached Jack River there had been several whom he had had to assure of continued protection before they would embark for the voyage along Winnipic back to Red River. But the remark struck all of us, I am sure, as unfair.

"I've a damned good mind to horsewhip you for a trickish schemer!" he blazed, which was perhaps an unfortunate remark as it may have been from it that there blossomed a story that Colin Robertson, on that visit to Fort Gibraltar, had thrashed Duncan Cameron.

He looked into the room. By their attire he could tell at once which were the officers and which the servants who had come, presumably, from an adjoining room lest they were required for support.

" You have three officers to assist you," said he.

"Indeed yes, though I cannot understand how it concerns you."

"Only," answered Robertson, " that I intend to leave you in sole charge here, under my eye."

" You can't do that!"

"Can I not? I think I shall leave you in charge, as I said, and send these others down to your fort at Bas de la Rivière where I can have them on the other side of me."

" You can't do that!" exclaimed Cameron again.

Robertson turned and called: " First file there, come in and take these men."

They promptly stepped forward, their muskets with fixed bayonets in hand. They pushed Cameron aside as they tramped into the room.

" Take these men away," Robertson ordered.

One of the North-West servants had a pistol in hand.

" Drop that, or put it in the rack," said Robertson.

The man hesitated but when one of our voyageurs walked towards him with bayonet warningly pointed he stepped to a rack and put it in place. The three officers then, at bayonet's point, came out. I did not know them. Their faces were all new to me. Frobisher, who had been there with Mr. Willis and Miles Macdonell's cousin Alexander on the visit of three years past, was not among them. As they marched into the open the cart with the cannon was squealing out at the gate.

"There are rumours already by Red River," said Colin Robertson, "that you are again attempting to rouse the full-bloods and half-breeds on the plains to come in and destroy the Settlement. Well, I leave you here, Mr. Cameron, sole in command. If anything happens you cannot say it was by error of your officers. You are alone now with your Jacks." That was the name for the ordinary labourers at any post or fort.

One of the three officers thus taken spoke then.

"May we not get our things together?" he demanded. "Have we to go as we are—in what we stand up in?"

"That is how you are to go," replied Colin Robertson. "It is not far to Bas de la Rivière. Mr. Cameron can send after you what wardrobes you have here." He strode away from the door. "Quick march!" he rasped at us.

Off we went, back to Fort Douglas, our three prisoners sullenly with us.

II

The three officers were taken down to Bas de la Rivière in charge of John McLeod who found there, and brought back with him, some more of the stolen cannon. By the time that he returned Colin Robertson had completed his account of affairs at Red River, as he found them.

"I have completed my report," said he to McLeod, "and Baxter here has made a copy for Mr. Archibald to put on his files; so do you, Mr. McLeod, produce that man you said would be likely willing to go to Montreal as messenger."

A lean man he was: Jean Baptiste Lagimoniere. His eyes had laughter in them and at times a dreamy absent look, but every now and then those who talked with him would see, at a passing thought, or some suggestion from the conversation, a Jean Baptiste look out at these windows who was clearly dauntless—a Jean Baptiste of the Last Ditch. Colin Robertson knew his breed. He had some of the same type in the crew he had captained all the way from Terrebonne, near Montreal.

"If the North-Westers suspect that you are on a mission for us," said he, "they will try to have you intercepted. I must warn you of that."

"Yes, I suppose they will," said Lagimoniere.

"And they will stick at nothing."

"I can make friends with Indians as well as they," replied Lagimoniere. "If I am uncertain anywhere on the way I can get guidance from the Indians." A distant gaze came into his eyes. He was looking, no doubt, at known and imagined wilderness. "I think I shall travel alone," he added.

As he said so I recalled a map that had been in the old Colony store and wondered by what routes he would go. Would he go by the Winnipic River, slipping past North-West forts there and Lake of the Woods and Lac la Pluie; or would he go up Red River and by Red Lake and the St. Louis River to Fond du Lac; or would he pass from Red River at the Traverse to those southern flowing waters that ran into Mississippi and at Prairie du Chien turn east through the Ouisconsin country to the other, more southerly, Fond du Lac and so to Michillimackinac? Or would he go east by none of these known arteries of travel? Soon all the waters would be frozen, snow on the wilderness. "If I am uncertain anywhere on the way I can get guidance from the Indians," suggested that he might be planning a straight, though unknown, course across country.

"When I leave here," said he, "I shall "—he waved a hand in air—"disappear. Or such is my ambition. I shall endeavour not to be seen by anybody till I am in the streets of Montreal."

"It is a service for which I feel sure Lord Selkirk will pay considerably beyond the ordinary voyageur's wages," said Robertson, "realising what it means."

"It does not mean so much!" scoffed Lagimoniere. "It is only to go on, to move. There will be no mosquitoes now as in summer."

"What of Madame Lagimoniere and the children?" Colin asked. "There are houses here. There are more houses being built. I suggest that she should be within the fort with us till you return."

"That would be good," Lagimoniere agreed. "She would not be nervous in her cabin, if that is what you are thinking, but at the same time here would be good."

"Then that will be arranged. The children and she will have every care and attention while you are away."

" *Très bien*. Is this the packet?"

" That is the packet."

Lagimoniere took it up, thrust it inside his buckskin tunic, voiced neither heart nor touching *adieu*, merely repeated, " *Très bien,*" gave a nod and an inclusive roll of his eyes to all in the room and went out with springy steps.

CHAPTER FOUR

I

HERE was change again by Red River.

None of the outcast settlers any longer entertained an intention to return to Scotland, though some of those who formerly had that intention had gone on even beyond Jack River to York Factory. The landing there of the new immigrants from Ross and Cromarty, however, made them change their plans, partly because these were numerous and determined and partly because they brought with them sad tales of the treatment from whence they had come. To go back to Scotland would be, as one said, out of the frying-pan into the fire and back into the frying-pan again! A few had remained at Jack River, after Robertson left there, resolved to come back to the Settlement with that year's party of new-comers but the majority under protection of his men had arrived.

Along the riverside they erected temporary abodes of tree-branch and bark beside the ruins of their former homes. Seeing the palisade round the new buildings their confidence was renewed. They too, they considered, they as well as the North-Westers, had a fort—a strong fort within the walls of which they could go for shelter should they again be molested; and the force of men Colin Robertson had with him, ready to fight if called upon, dispelled all fears. Robertson had been on his way to the much more distant Athabasca country, with an advance party of a score of voyageurs, to organise more intensive competition in trade against the rival agents there. But affairs at Red River, being the manner of man he was, caused him to remain there with these hard-bitten, picked voyageurs, to protect those he had convoyed from Jack River. To John Clarke, who had been following him with a larger brigade, he left control of the Athabasca adventure. His duty, he felt, was to this Settlement of one of the Company's chief shareholders.

" I knew you were going to bide here," Mairi said when again we met.

" I knew you knew," I answered.

I was intensely glad to have the Chisholms there again but noticed, with regret, a difference, a change, in both girls. Mairi was brooding. Agnes was more highly-strung than ever, excitable. But my visits to their farm for a while were few, so much I had to do in preparation for the arrival of the new immigrants and the residue of the evicted settlers.

These new immigrants reached York Factory in August but with a mass of farming impedimenta it took them two months to get to Red River. Captain Robert Semple, who was in charge of them on that inland voyage, had a new title as Colin Robertson had told us: Governor of Rupert's Land. Recent manifestation of enmity of the North-Westers demanded one in such a position who would move through all Indian Territory, report conditions and advise procedure.

It seemed to the newly appointed Governor of Rupert's Land, installed at Red River, that Colin Robertson was an excellent man to whom to give temporary care of the Settlement. As for me, once more at a table fulfilling the duties of a secretary, I preferred to have my orders from Robertson. He had his own arrogance of manner, perhaps, but he also had merriment, a wild gaiety. Semple—twenty years or more his senior—was more distant. He had been born in Boston seven years before the Revolution, had travelled widely in Europe, Africa, and both Americas, and had written accounts of his journeys. He was not by any means ingratiating of manner, had no turn for conciliation, was direct, downright, and a martinet.

Robertson, acting as Semple's lieutenant there, might ask me how this or that had been done under Governor Macdonell and, hearing, give a nod and say it was well enough and to continue so; but Semple frowned disapproval at the suggestion that instructions on how a matter should be dealt with were required, and never conceivably could he ask how anything had been done by Captain Macdonell. His view was that he had arrived almost too late to retrieve that Governor's blunders and mismanagement. When he was told details of the arrest (during Macdonell's absence at York Factory) of Sheriff Spencer, and of how the settlers had wished to rescue him, he was as adversely critical of James Sutherland refusing to give them arms as of young Mr. Archibald MacDonald for advising non-interference and not allowing them entrance to the Colony's armoury.

When Colin was in the service of the North-West Company he

had been under Bras Croché, McDonald of Garth, and had been very much in the wilderness. He could call his men (a mixed crew they were, many of them seasoned French voyageurs) by their Christian names and yet rule them. Somewhat pompous though no doubt he was at times—even I, who admire him tremendously, have to admit there was that likeness to Cameron in him—he talked as man to man with all: immigrants, labourers, writers. We were all as human beings to him, but to Semple we were mere cogs of the machine—and by his manner there was a suggestion that he doubted if we were satisfactory cogs!

"Ploughs!" I heard him exclaim once, looking on by the riverside where I was taking tally of the unloading of some boats. "Ploughs! The people will be able to get their land tilled now instead of eternally living on pemican."

I felt annoyance at the remark. I wished to turn upon this auto-cratic ruler and inform him that there had been ploughs and harrows earlier, to inform him also that even some who in the old land had had to be content with hoes, had ploughs here. I was touchy regard-ing any possible hint of disparagement of the earlier governance of Miles Macdonell. He had had much against him. No pemican had awaited him on his arrival, although it had been ordered—so what could he do but lead his people to Pembina to be near the buffalo pastures for the winter? He had been blamed for that, but I knew that Semple was already proposing to do the same. Once again, this time because of the havoc of the *métis* in the Settlement fields, and the late arrival of this last party, there would have to be, willy-nilly, a "tripping" which, thought I, would have depressed Miles Macdonell. There had been good crops, thanks to John McLeod's forethought and organisation, but there was this additional influx of settlers, and here was winter coming.

I looked up at the Governor of Rupert's Land there on the river bank, and wondered how he managed, by his posture as he watched the unloading, to convey arbitrary power. He was inclined to stout-ness and in stature was not near such men as Cameron and Grant, the dashing, swaggering Yellowhead, the departed Miles Macdonell, or the recently arrived Colin Robertson. At that moment Robertson appeared at the top of the slope, large, easy, vigorous, and engaged the Governor of Rupert's Land in conversation, Semple measuring him from toes to merry eyes, then lowering his head to listen.

Both moved away and I was suddenly intent upon the flow of the river under the bare trees—the face of it, the snatch of small ripples where a leafless branch touched the water. I had to remind myself that I was there to take tally of the unloadings, order my mind to the moment's duty out of timelessness.

11

That night Captain Semple was giving a dance to celebrate the new beginning.

Sounds of the occupancy must have carried to those over at the North-West fort of Gibraltar, convincing them that the Selkirk scheme had not yet failed. Before the new two-story house pipers strutted and played.

Robert Semple dined formally with the officers of the Settlement and of the Hudson's Bay Company : Archibald MacDonald, whom he thought incompetent but excused because of his youth; Surgeon White, whom he suspected of being a toper (on hearing that he had been in one of His Majesty's ships—the *Beagle*, by the way—he commented that in the navy there was too much addiction to rum); James Sutherland who might, he thought, be a sensible man although he had refused a few muskets and some ammunition towards rescuing Sheriff Spencer. Sutherland, he understood, engaged in correspondence with Lord Selkirk, had advised him that Colin Robertson would be a good man for the Hudson's Bay Company to employ in special duties. Colin Robertson, of course, was at that table, of whom he thought more highly than of any there; and John McLeod, who came next, and closely next, in his esteem. Outside as they dined a piper played. No, there was no depression there.

Downriver thin threads of smoke rose from the cooking fires of those who had encamped, in tents and wigwams, bark and brush shelters, beside their properties and whose new homes were not ready for occupation. Between the cook-house in the fort and other tents and brush shelters within the palisade, people came and went, carrying pots and pans that steamed, savoury and appetising.

Supper over at the fort and throughout the Settlement, crowds

began to gather for the promised evening's entertainment. The long
large room in the two-story house, with which all were greatly pleased,
had been cleared for dancing. In one of the lesser rooms a table was
being loaded by Semple's orders with refreshments in preparation for
the festivities. There had, of course, been no invitation to the officers
at Fort Gibraltar to join in the rejoicing. After all that had recently
transpired, to send such an invitation would have been more like a
taunt than a signal of forgiveness. But many free-traders had been
invited and were there with their families; and half-breeds who had
taken no part in the recent terrorisations were there, arrayed in their
best buckskin coats, wearing red sashes and the most gaily beaded
moccasins; their women in attire that was a blend of city and wilderness—of stuffs and pelts, fabrics and furs. Indians were also there,
pleased that those for whom they had offered to fight had come back
again. Some of the new-comers turned to stare at these as they strolled
past. Wild-looking folk they thought them. Gaelic and English—
both the new English and the older English that the Lowland Scots
spoke—French, Cree, Ojibway were being spoken there.

My duties over for the day, I looked in at the door of the long room,
thinking it would not be large enough for the concourse. Whoops of
laughter sounded and when they subsided I heard a fiddle being
played. There was one of the new-comers, a Mr. Sinclair, entertain-
ing the first arrivals before the festivities had formally commenced.
He was giving them his own great composition which he delighted to
call the *Blue-Bottom Fly* so as to be shocking in the esteem of those
who would prefer *Blue-Bottle*. When he had a dram or two in him
he would enter into argument regarding blue-bottle and proclaim it
was an evasion of blue-bottom. He had on a Glengarry bonnet and
was dashing to and fro playing his violin as he jigged, imitating the
movements of the fly in a confined space, dashing from window to
wall. Still with elbow violently working, bow sawing, he made a
leap to a stool, from stool to table, and bumping himself against the
wall by which it stood made buzzing sounds between his teeth in
accompaniment to the strings.

As I stood there watching him, a delighted grin no doubt on my
face, I saw a woman in the doorway observing the excitement with
love and regret.

"There's his wife—that's Mrs. Sinclair," I heard someone remark.

When laughter of a certain type rose from any gathering, if her husband was not by her side, Mrs. Sinclair had to find out if he was the cause of it and how he was causing it, whether in genteel fashion or in a fashion that required the catching of his eye by her and a little headshake of warning not to go too far. As she entered he was leaping down again from table to stool, from stool to floor. He flourished the bow in air and made a deep obeisance to all. The laughter, to his wife's mind, was evidently not too greatly of amusement at him for making a fool of himself, was sufficiently of appreciation of his whimsicality. So she joined in it but still with a little anxious peering in his direction, desirous to discover if he had been moved to presenting the *Blue-Bottom*, or *Blue-Bottle Fly* by natural spirits or by those from a jorum. The night had not really begun; it seemed early for him to give that composition to the assemblage.

Other violinists then came out from the refreshment room, wiping their mouths, and way was made for them to a platform at the chamber's end. As I stepped outside again to see whom I could see I had to stand aside to let Governor Robert Semple and his odorous attendants pass. They had all wined well, thought I. Semple was smiling left and right but was very much the Governor of Rupert's Land as he went into the room.

There was a jostling in the doorway, many crowding in to hear him make an expected opening speech. I caught a word or two, sufficient to get the drift. ". . . to celebrate the safe arrival of the newcomers and the return of those who have suffered various vicissitudes . . . hope . . . a happy evening . . . celebrate . . ." There was applause within; and at the door, without, the piper who had followed the officers and listened there, as with an ear cocked for the applause proclaiming the speech's end, began again to play.

III

A burst of laughter in a voice I knew drew my attention. There was Agnes Chisholm with several young men round her. There was a touch of hysteria in that laughter and she threw back her head in a way that suggested abandon. The lads with her, I noticed, glanced round with looks of embarrassment, or stared shrewdly at her. I noted also that she had attracted attention elsewhere. Mrs. Sinclair, going by with her husband (he with his violin under his arm), looked censoriously at the girl and turned to make some remark to Sinclair who was also, though otherwise, considering her.

Suddenly my gaze alighted on Mairi. She was solemnly considering me as she walked slowly towards the young people. She had been watching me watching Agnes, thought I. Even after my eyes had met hers she continued so to study me, with no smile of greeting. That was a look I could not fathom, long and serious, serious and inquiring. I smiled, and at my smile the considering expression passed from her face like the passing of a cloud shadow. I stepped closer to her.

" Well, Mairi," I said, " it is like a fair here this evening."

" Yes, like a fair," she agreed.

She continued to walk on and I fell in step with her, and so we joined the group in the midst of which Agnes stood. There appeared to be no cause in all that was being said there for such hilarity. They were merely exchanging the nonsense of young people embarrassed when mute.

Halting beside her sister and these others, Mairi paid no further attention to me. I was seemingly dismissed. I did not suspect that she might have reason to be engrossed on something secret, to the temporary extinction of small talk, or any talk, with me. She stood beside her sister with eyes roving over the throng. I had to ask her twice to come and dance before she heard that I was speaking to her.

" What did you say?" she asked, abstraction in her eyes.

" I hear them playing reels over there in the big room now," I said. " I hear the violins. Will you come?"

She shook her head.

" No," she said. " I must look for mother and father. We were to follow them here. Are you coming, Agnes?"

" Coming for what?" demanded Agnes.

" To find mother and father."

" Oh, let them look for us," said Agnes, and let loose a peal of laughter again. Then she linked an arm in Mairi's. " Och, we might as well," she said.

They turned away together.

" Now what have I done?" I asked myself. " Of what am I guilty?"

IV

I strolled over to the river bank in the deepening dusk. It did not there go down abruptly to the water. From the prairie-rim it sloped to a lower bank and thence dipped again. Along the upper edge a trail wound, and there was another lower down. Despite the time of year it was a mild night. There was no snow on the ground. On both trails guests had been arriving. Some came in canoes across the river, not yet frozen, not, by the temperature, likely to be for some time; others came from the direction of the North-West fort, preferring to walk that way, by the windings of the stream, instead of directly across the plain.

As I reached the edge of the plain I saw, just below me, a man advancing. Behind him were three women.

"*Bon soir*. Good-evening," he said.

"Good-evening," said I.

"Those bagpipes carry far," he remarked, very friendly of manner. "They tell us of merry-making and now—close—we hear the violins. We must show them how the old voyageurs dance the jigs."

"It is a good occasion," I agreed.

"Oh, yes. *Belle occasion, mais oui.*"

With that exchange of speech he passed on, followed by a lady of uncertain age. A bright bandana was round her head, as I could see in the moonlight. By her rustling she was apparently wearing a satin dress. She went on discreetly with downcast eyes. The moonlight drifted in among the tangle of branch and twig. The two other women were coming at a tangent up the bank.

"No, I don't think I will go after all," I heard a girl say. "I'll turn back here."

That voice moved me much as at Fort Gibraltar I had been moved by a glimpse of a half-breed girl.

"Oh, come and dance, Christina!" the man called coaxingly. "It will do you good. We are friends of the settlers, have always been, and they will welcome us."

Christina! That was the name of Court Nez's daughter.

Then the woman with her spoke, in a French accent like the man's: "She does not want to be too far if Court Nez comes back to-night."

The man's voice had sounded familiar to me but I had remained uncertain of his identity. The voice of a Frenchman speaking English might be, to my ears, that of almost any Frenchman. Yet I had thought he was one of the free-traders called Lapointe. Whether it was he or not, I had to speak to him then because of the sudden realisation that the girl below was Court Nez's Christina, returned from Quebec to Red River again.

" Is that you, Monsieur Lapointe?" I inquired.

" Yes, *c'est moi*. And it is the young man, David Baxter—is it not?—one of those who stayed with Mr. McLeod when those who would not go by guile, as they say, and soft words, went away at threat of death."

" I would rather go back," the girl protested.

" I understand, my dear," answered the woman beside her. " *Très bien*, you go back. You do not want me to go with you?"

I looked beyond her at Christina whose grace caught my heart as when first I saw her on the evening that I accompanied Miles Macdonell to Fort Gibraltar. And again, as then when our eyes met, I had that inexplicable feeling as of having known her of old. On the earlier occasion there had been candle light in her eyes; on this there was the moonlight on her face.

" This is Mr. Baxter, Mr. David Baxter, Madame Lagimoniere," said Lapointe, turning back a step or two while the woman who had passed with him strolled slowly on. " Your husband and he must often have met at Fort Douglas."

I bowed and Marie Anne Gaboury Lagimoniere bowed. I realised that this must be the wife of the Lagimoniere who had helped McLeod and MacLean in getting workers for the sowing and the building after the half-breeds drew off—the Lagimoniere who had gone away with a message from Colin Robertson to Lord Selkirk in Montreal. Of her I had been told that she was the first white woman to come west into the Indian Countries.

" And this," Lapointe continued, " is a young lady, part *Ecossaise*, just come here from Quebec, whose father it is possible you have met. He is known as Court Nez and——"

I bowed again, and had impulsively to interrupt :

" I only know you as Christina," I said.

" You have met before!" exclaimed Lapointe.

" Court Nez has spoken of her—of you," I replied, looking from him to Christina. "And we have met though we were not introduced. Perhaps you do not remember——"

"I remember," she said, and——

"O God," was the silent cry within me, "how I love this girl!" Madame Lagimoniere clambered up the bank, Christina remaining a step or two below. In her own language the French woman began to explain that Christina did not want to go on and then reverted to English : "She wants to be back in case her father happens this very night to come in."

Here, thought I, agitated, and controlling agitation, is most admirable chance, like a gift of God.

"If you will allow me," I offered, "I will be your convoy back to Fort Gibraltar."

"I am only going back to the Lagimonieres' cabin," said Christina, "but I would not take you away."

"You would take me away from nothing. I came here for a walk by the river. At any rate the night is young. It has only just begun over there. I could be back here before—oh, before the late-comers."

"She would not be afraid to go alone," said Madame Lagimoniere.

"What is there to be afraid of?" asked Lapointe.

"I shall go with her," said I.

"It is very gracious of you, m'sieur," murmured Lapointe.

"It is nothing to thank me for," said I, and went down the bank to Christina.

CHAPTER FIVE

I

" May I come with you?" I asked.

' If you wish."

" Do you want me to come with you?" I demanded, as though eager for more than mere permission.

" Yes," and then she added : " You are sure you would not rather be dancing?"

" I would not," I answered definitely. " I would rather be with you. Shall I go first?"

" Oh, no; I can see the trail well."

" It is not too dark down here for you?"

" It is not too dark, even down here."

Walking behind her I had then a feeling that I was taking part in something more than of the moment. I could not tell how, I could not tell why, but all we said seemed to have meanings beyond the superficial subject of exchange of speech. It was as if she led me into mystery. Here was one of those occasions that took me out of time into eternity.

" Am I going too quickly for you?" she asked

" No. But you are in no hurry, are you?"

" I do not want to be long away."

The trail broadened and I walked by her side. She had on no hat and wore a shawl over her shoulders. By her soundless step I decided she had on moccasins. Silks and satins with moccasins were not ludicrous combination by Red River. Settlers who had been there but a few months learnt to prefer the pliant moccasin, even on dress occasions, to constricting shoes.

" I was not here when these poor people were driven out," she said, stepping slower when we walked side by side.

I wondered if she had gone quickly at first so as to come to the place where we could walk together; and then I heard voices—men's voices, women's voices. I fell behind Christina to give them passage-

203

way. Mutual sidelong scrutinies in what moonlight there was down there showed us strangers to each other.

"Pardon, m'sieur."

"Bon soir, m'sieur."

"Good-night."

They went on their way.

"I heard that you had stayed," Christina continued when I moved level with her again.

"Yes, I stayed," said I. "You have been in Quebec all the time?" I asked.

"In Quebec. I have been there almost ever since I saw you."

"I remember that time well," said I.

She laughed joyously.

"My father was funny to you about looking at me," she said.

"What is your father's name? I know him only as Court Nez."

"I know him only as Court Nez also," she replied. "When I was at school in Quebec some girls jested at my name—Christina Court Nez—just as they would at Indian names. It is funny to them that a man should be called Duck—but not that he should be called Swan. The name of Buffalo made them laugh but not the name of Fox!"

"You were not happy there?" I suggested.

"Oh, yes, I was happy there!" she exclaimed. "I was at the Ursulines convent. I was very happy. But I am happier here. Everywhere, of course, there is something to make one sad and something to make one happy."

"What makes you sad?"

She did not answer. I presumed, as we walked on without speech, that she was considering a reply, but if she was she dismissed the intention. I did not repeat the question, respected her silence. We came to a place where another trail from the upper level led down to the one on which we were. She stepped on to it and as it was narrow I lagged behind again; but I was glad she mounted there to the prairie, for it was becoming too dark where the trees were close, even leafless though they were, to see her as I would.

Just as we came to the top we met a man and woman walking on the level towards Fort Douglas.

"Is that you, Christina?" asked the man.

"Yes, it is I. Has my father come?"

"No, not yet. They know at Fort Gibraltar to tell him that you are at the Lagimonieres'. But he will not come to-night. Some men are in from the Souris River and they say he will not come yet. I thought you were going to the Selkirk dance with Madame Lagimoniere and the Lapointes."

"I was, but I turned back. I was adread he might come as soon as I left."

"You are too greatly devoted to him," remarked the woman over her shoulder, passing on.

"If your father is not expected to-night," I suggested, "perhaps you would care to join the settlers at the dance. We can go straight across here instead of by the river paths, for a change, if you like. You and I could run the distance in five minutes."

She looked across the dim level of the prairie to where, between bosses of deeper darkness, the bosses of scattered clusters of trees, Fort Douglas was revealed in the wavering radiance of festive bonfires.

"Would you not like to dance?" I begged. I wanted her to dance with me for the sake of the contact—that I might touch her, hold her.

"Not unless you want to," she replied shyly.

I felt a choking in my throat.

"I am glad just to be with you," I said.

"Let us walk on this trail by the edge of the prairie, then," she said, accepting me as if she had known me all her life.

There was a tattling, a rattling, a thin piping of a breeze in the leafless trees along the twisting cleft of the river.

"I feel as if I had known you long before I met you," said I.

She stopped. She stood still.

"You are not just saying that?" she asked.

"Just saying it?"

"You are telling me the truth? You do feel so?"

I began to tremble and trembling drew her to me. For a moment I feared she was going to thrust me away but it was not so. She was only leaning back to raise her head and look into my eyes.

"Christina," I whispered. "Christina Court Nez!"

"David, David, David!"

"How can I see you better?" I demanded, and looked up at the sky as if craving for more light.

With a little laugh she turned about.

"There, can you see me now? Can you see me as I can see you?" she asked.

I held her closer.

"All Rupert's Land round us," I said, and then: "How foolish of me, Christina!"

"No, I understand," she said. She withdrew herself, glancing in the direction in which we were going. "There is something moving there."

"Where?"

"Over there."

We walked on but soon discovered the movement was not of any one coming towards us, only of grazing horses. We heard them tearing the grass and blowing through their nostrils.

"Can you still see the trail?" I asked wonderingly, for the moon had gone behind clouds and I could not see a path.

"Yes, I can see the trail," she assured me. "We keep along here near the top of the bank. I am staying with Madame Lagimoniere till my father comes, and she is living in a cabin on the edge of the belt of woods here until another one in the fort is ready for her. There is the light. We'll go quietly. The children will all be asleep, I expect. We left an old Cree woman to look after them." As we drew nearer she remarked: "This is a little place but a palace compared with what they have been living in. You must get Madame to tell you of their life one day. For the last months they were away up the Assiniboine in a hut without so much as a window. When they came here he said he thought they should stay for a while for her to have a taste of civilisation," and she laughed. "I expect she will stay here until he comes back from the East."

She tapped at the door very gently. It was opened by an old Indian woman in a print gown and with a bandana round her head. In Cree they greeted each other. Inquiringly the old woman looked at me and in Cree Christina spoke a few more words to her. She nodded, smiled, and held out her hand. I took it lightly, in the Indian fashion. No hearty grips such as were intended to convey amity by our folks did the Indians indulge in; they just touch hands lightly or, to show special friendliness, gave a gentle pressure.

II

Along the floor to one side, on layers of buffalo robes that served as mattresses, with Hudson's Bay blankets cast over them, three children slept. I looked round the place—the "palace" compared with what Madame Lagimoniere had been living in of late. Well, it was comfortable enough. The interior was much like that of a tepee. There were even, in place of chairs, the back-rests upheld by tripods such as Indians used. A stack of saddles was in one corner. On the walls hung deerskin bundles of their possessions just as, in tepees, such bundles hung from the poles. On the table was neither lamp nor candle but a crusie of iron, a wick alight at the spout end. An odour of melting grease was in the place. I noticed that there was a room to one end with a door and to the other end another, a blanket hanging at its entrance for curtain.

"I have often heard of Madame Lagimoniere," I said, "but I have never seen her till to-night."

"She was at Fort Gibraltar in the spring of the year you arrived but I think they were out on the prairies when you came over with Governor Macdonell."

She looked at the sleeping children again and then back to me.

"Well, I hope to hear her stories some day," I said, and moved to the door.

The Cree woman had seated herself solid and apparently stolid and heedless of us. At the door I turned and smiled at her. Her eyes moved in my direction but as if sightless. I stepped outside and Christina stood on the threshold. A distant sound of cheering came to our ears. I did not want to go. I dreaded the closing of that door.

"They will probably be cheering after a final speech by Governor Semple," I said listening. "He will likely retire at a good hour and leave it to them." Then I looked up at the stars and tried to think of something more to say, wishing she would not stand where the Cree woman within could see her. "May I come soon to hear Madame's stories?" I asked. I was annoyed with myself for that! It was not to hear Madame Lagimoniere's stories I wanted to come back soon.

"Yes, come and hear her stories," said Christina.

"And to see you," I added, my voice husky.

She came outside then.

"To see you," I said again, deliberately, clearly. "Did you hear, Christina?"

"Yes."

Aside from the doorway, the Cree woman could not see us. I bent and kissed Christina then with a surge of utter gratitude. I kissed her again and again until she drew away from me with a small cry as of astonishment. Had I been too vehement? She moved backward to the doorway and I turned away but, looking round at her and seeing her there against the faint inner light, I had a sense of gratitude again when she raised a hand and waved it before going inside and closing the door.

I marched northward along the edge of the riverside woods, my eyes blinded. I could not see the ground at my feet, to say nothing of the trail, but I trudged on lithely, taking the inequalities of the way with pliant steps. And as I strode on I found myself saying, "Yes, I can see the trail—I can see the trail," recalling her guiding voice.

After I left her she was still with me. A part of her strangely accompanied me, and I wondered if there in the cabin, while she talked to the Indian woman, she talked with but half a mind, thinking of me as I of her. Where we had climbed to the prairie level I descended to the lower trail on which we had walked, simply because we had walked on it. Below was deep darkness, but in an ecstasy of desire to be still with her I must needs go fumbling down the bank and retrace my steps by the way I had come with her.

The river, glimpsed between the tree-stems, was more clear than the trail, and reflected stars. I stumbled on slowly, there, thinking, "A little while ago we walked here," and suddenly felt utterly alone. She had gone. She was not there. In another few minutes I would climb to the prairie again and go over to Fort Douglas, and the river would be flowing on in the night as for ages it had flowed there.

My eyes became more accustomed to the dark. I too could see the trail. Ahead I heard a ripple of laughter, a girl's voice, a giggling. I was coming near to the place where I should mount up the bank to cross the level to the fort. I could hear movements in the bushes on the slope. Peering down I found the track that led to the top and as I stepped on to it I saw against the spangle of stars a man and a girl fumbling their way down. Hearing my approach they went farther along the slope. That I could distinguish them against the stars no doubt did not occur to them. I saw the man suddenly grip the girl, upsetting her balance, and as she fell catch her and break the force of her fall. She did not resist.

" She wants him," thought I, " but she is not averse to the appearance of being forced."

Up the bank I climbed and from the edge of the plain saw a fire in the open sending up sparks, and dancing figures round it. Across the plain I went, passed those who danced to the playing of one fiddle and one drum by that bonfire, and entered the gate. Another bonfire, within the palisade, was dwindling, untended. As I walked to the house where the people had been gathering when I left there, John Bourke and his wife went by with a " Good-night, David." I looked into the long room. On forms round the walls were mostly young people sitting, but also a few older ones who looked tired, waiting for the young ones to tire also and to think of going home. I could not see any of the Chisholms. On the platform the fiddlers were resting and refreshing themselves with a dram. None of my friends could I see there. From the next room came loud talk, thick talk, that suggested that those there were taking full advantage of the Governor's hospitality in the way of refreshment.

I did not want that night to end, but knowing it would end I did not wish it to end there but where, with less distraction, I could think of Christina. I wanted to be alone with the memory of her, thoughts of her, to hold as long as I might that sense, or fancy, of her being still with me. I went out of the fort again and walked on the Settlement road.

As I walked, thinking of Christina, Christina, I recalled how I used to go along that same road in the evenings to the Chisholm farm, chiefly for the happiness I had in seeing Mairi there. That had been a different pleasure from the pleasure of this night. There had been no terms of endearment, no kisses, though often I had been loath to leave that house because of Mairi there. Yet I could not feel that I was being untrue to her in what had befallen. How could I be untrue, never having so much as told her that it was for her more than all that I liked to visit the farm? I was in an ecstasy made up of the star glow and the winds and Christina, Christina.

o

I came to where, a stone's throw from the road, was the tent in which the Chisholms were camping till their new home could be built, saw the gleam of the canvas. Beyond it was a bark shelter. On I went and though I walked there, as I imagined, slower, I must have been walking fairly quickly for I found myself making up on a couple ahead. I heard Mrs. Sinclair's voice.

"Well, we'll say no more," she was saying. "The head you will have in the morning will say it all for me!"

"Never, never!" Sinclair chanted. "Why, woman, we live but once. We have been through a lot of troubles these last years and a little exeralation—or ciralation or——" his voice tailed away, "will do no harm. They turned aside to their shelter.

Suddenly I halted. From another shelter by the roadside came the singing of settlers closing their evening with a hymn. I stood listening and when they ended turned about, still thinking of Christina, and returned to the writers' quarters at Fort Douglas, a line from that hymn—"A thousand ages in Thy sight are like an evening gone"—chiming in my mind with thoughts of time and eternity, an evening gone.

CHAPTER SIX

I

IN the morning I had the impression that Governor Robert Semple's temper was on edge.

He was not going to remain in the Settlement, having had instructions to make a tour of inspection of the Hudson's Bay posts far into the Indian Countries. But before departing on that duty he wanted to organise a system of accountancy and record-keeping for the Colony. He had also reports for Lord Selkirk regarding the trip from York Factory, the finding of the evicted families there and at Jack River, the meeting with Colin Robertson, the new occupancy at Red River, with item this, item that, item the other affixed. In the burning of the old Governor's House many papers had gone up in smoke; and files that would surely have shown him that Captain Miles Macdonell had a good system no longer existed.

He had already announced to Colin Robertson, in my hearing, that he had " a pretty mess " to clear up. Regarding recent events at Red River he seemed to attach more importance to the views of those who were disparaging in their opinion of Macdonell than to those who extolled him. He had apparently no suspicion that the disparaging hints came from those who envied him his position. He continued, obviously, to be dubious of the competency of those who had worked under the direction of the former Governor. There were moments when I wanted to inform him that I was one who had remained there in an attempt to prevent utter wrecking of the Colony, though when any one spoke to me of that with admiration I was embarrassed and had nothing to say for myself save " Oh, that was nothing. Mr. McLeod and Mr. MacLean were the heroes of that, McIntosh and Currie too."

In the afternoon of that day, late afternoon, Colin Robertson, who had been at work outside, came in and sat down. He was not over-awed by Semple, was courteous enough to him but with a manner as of one considering that he was himself of considerable importance.

" A pretty mess!" Semple broke out.

"Yes," said Robertson, "as you have remarked before. These Nor'-Westers played hell here, or influenced the half-Indians to do so. But things might be worse. Thanks to John McLeod everybody won't have to go tripping, as they call it, to Pembina."

"Tripping to Pembina!" exclaimed Semple. "That man Macdonell came out with the first party in 1811 and here's '15 and still there's this *tripping to Pembina* for them to be fed through the winter."

I looked up from my table. I wanted to give him a list of all the set-backs with which Miles Macdonell had had to contend. I wished that Robertson would speak up. Why did he remain silent? Then Colin spoke.

"Macdonell," said he, "had devilish hard luck. And just when things were beginning to show signs of real progress the Nor'-Westers——"

"Yes, yes, I know—got a warrant for his arrest. I hear some fine speeches about this late Governor Miles Macdonell," said Semple, "but they irk me. By acknowledging that warrant he sealed the destruction of the Settlement. It was really his fault that the settlers were driven out."

I rose from my table and walked heavily to the desk at which Captain Semple sat.

"You will pardon me, sir," I began very quietly, "I cannot but hear what you are saying and——"

"What the devil!"

"—and I must speak, to affirm that Captain Macdonell did not acknowledge the legality of the warrant for his arrest at first"—I hurried on, the words telescoping because it seemed that he was on the point of interrupting me—"and would not have acknowledged it in the end were it not that most of the officers, and a deputation from the majority of the people, urged him to."

"Ho! Very condescending of you, young man, to rise in his defence," said Semple, tucking his chin back in his neck and glaring. "But was he so weak that he had to take their advice?"

"The Nor'-Westers," I replied, "had informed the settlers that if he did not acknowledge the warrant worse would befall."

"You seem to be taking upon yourself the task of *advocatus diaboli*," remarked Semple. "Pray continue."

Colin Robertson tossed one leg over the other and sat back, tilting his chair and smiling. Astonished at myself I halted, halted despite that fleering request to proceed. The Governor put the flat of his hands on the table before him and stared up at me. So I squared my shoulders—and continued.

" If that means a devil's advocate, sir," said I, " I do not think the words are appropriate."

" Your place," said Semple, " is at that table over there, doing the work given you."

I inclined my head. I was about to turn away when he spoke again.

" A minute, young man," he rasped. " Your action just now savours of insubordination and insolence. But I will say this for you—and for the man you defend. I will say this: It is possible that within his capacity he did his best. Within his capacity he was at least loyal to his employer: he was loyal to Lord Selkirk."

" Indeed he was," said I. " I have often heard Captain Macdonell defend his lordship when people criticised him."

" Well, I will say this: He was, in my opinion, incompetent, but he was loyal. You, young man, within your capacity, I realise, are loyal to Miles Macdonell. That is your excuse for this breach of discipline—that and your youth. Perhaps Captain Macdonell permitted his staff to enter into argument with him?"

" Captain Macdonell used to say, sir," I replied, " that much would be different in army or navy—that he was dealing with civilians."

" And that is right too," interjected Colin Robertson, bringing down his chair from the tilt and sitting forward with elbows on knees, looking from me to Semple and back again with appraisement and some amusement.

" All right," said Semple to me, dismissing me again.

I slammed one heel against the other in the military manner and turned away. Well, I had spoken. I had spoken! And I was glad I had spoken! At least I had got Robert Semple to admit that Miles Macdonell was loyal to Lord Selkirk. I was young enough to feel elated that the new Governor of all Rupert's Land had acknowledged my loyalty to the Settlement's Governor who was gone. As I sat down at my table again——

" Eh gad, Robertson," said Semple, " I hope I may have as vigorous an advocate if ever I need defending."

But I was not, as they say, " supposed to hear that." I buried my face in my letters and accounts, glad the ordeal I had given myself was over, glad that I had spoken.

II

Sunday afternoon : I set off across the prairie to the Lagimoniere cabin. It was a tranquil day, crisp and sunny. On wall and roof of the cabin before the bend below Assiniboine River was a shadowy tracing of branch and twig.

Christina, seeing me approaching, ran out to meet me and behind her appeared Madame Lagimoniere. How beautiful, thought I, was my Christina, and because of what had already been between us my blood pulsed as to the tune of " I am my beloved's and my beloved is mine."

" I would have come before to-day," I said, " but Governor Semple has kept us working both day and night in the counting-house as he wishes to get away on a tour of inspection before the snow comes. When I was free it was always too late to come over. I doubt if he would recognise this day as one of freedom were it not for the religious among the settlers who would be shocked at Sabbath labour."

I looked beyond at the house. Christina, turning her head, saw Madame Lagimoniere at the door and laughed.

" I think she knows," she said.

" You have spoken of me to her and——"

" No, I have not spoken. Perhaps that is why she knows. She has looked at me sometimes and laughed, and stroked my cheek and laughed again."

Madame Lagimoniere welcomed me with a wise look and a merry twinkle. There was frost in the day but in nooks out of the wind, because of the cloudless sun, there was sufficient warmth to permit of sitting down outside; so that Madame could watch the children at their play—the youngest was only five years of age—we sat on a fallen tree by the top of the bank, the women wrapped in shawls, I in my warm coat, and soon Christina drew Madame into talking of her life on the prairies. Yes, she said, she was supposed to be the first white woman to cross the plains. From Maskinoge, in the diocese of Three Rivers, Quebec, she had come. Lagimoniere, who had spent five years in the west, came home and won her heart there. She had thought he was going to remain, settle down, when they were married. " But you know how it is," she said, " or if you do not yet you will know in time. The Indian Countries have a way of bringing people back——" and with an occasional prompting from Christina, or an inquiry from me, she talked of her adventurous life.

In one of the pauses I asked : " Would you like to go back to Maskinoge?"

She looked before her as if picturing the old home.

" This is my life," she answered. " I am here now. I have my children, my husband."

Christina then moved. She turned slightly and looked at me. Our eyes met. I smiled and in her dark eyes a smile came in response. Madame Lagimoniere rose with a " Pardon me. I must see what the children are doing." A tangle of riverside bushes, though leafless, hid them from sight. As Madame went down the bank Christina held a hand out to me. I drew closer and as I did so, thrilled at her touch, her fingers closed round mine.

" Your father has not yet come back?" I asked.

" No, not yet."

" When he comes," said I, " I am going to tell him at once."

She just nodded, looking very solemn, but with a radiance on her face.

" Captain Semple, as I said just now, is going away soon," I went on. " He is leaving the charge with Mr. Robertson. I am to continue as secretary. We can get married immediately."

She sat trance-like, in meditation, and I studied her—the contours of her dear face, the curve of eyebrows, the curve of cheek bones, the shape of her mouth. I wondered what she was thinking. As I had felt on the night of our walk by the trails that had been dim to me I felt again : I had a sense of time flying and of desire to hold the passing moment, to keep it for ever. Thinking so, I considered that there was not much time for living. I looked again at her face, saw its smooth tones and thought of these as being over a base of bones, small delicate bones. O dear God, within a hundred years there would be only that base of bones—and Red River would still be twisting past as on that day!

" Don't," she said without looking at me.

" Don't what, Christina?"

" You know, my dearest. Let us sit quiet a little while together, sit happily here till she comes back."

" I love you," I said. " I love you so dearly, Christina. I was thinking of how time flies and——"

She turned and raised her face to me. I put a hand behind her neck and, holding her head so, kissed her. Then we both started abruptly. There, close by, was Court Nez walking towards us in that ponderous way of his.

III

We both rose and as we did so any doubt whether or not the embrace had been observed was dispelled by his greeting: " Ah, *les amoureux, les amoureux!* "

His eyes were bloodshot and his hue announced a very recent drinking bout.

" Well?" he rumbled. " Well, well!" and held out his arms to Christina, clasped her to him for a moment and then stepped to me. " Well, Baxter?" he said, his eyelids narrowing.

He took my hand and crushed it in his enormous one till my knuckles cracked. That was not a greeting. It was a declaration of relentlessness or a warning. I permitted no sign on my face that I felt pain.

" How do you do, sir?" I said.

He gave my hand another vice-like grip at that.

" I do very well," he replied.

I felt a great rage against him then. " The hulking, drunken brute!" I thought. " He may be strong, he may be massive, but he cannot terrorise me—if that is what he is attempting."

The Lagimoniere children then came scurrying and scrambling up the bank, their mother with them. At first glance at Court Nez she showed what was simply revulsion. He could not but be aware of that look. He bowed low. He held out his hand and took hers very lightly, bending over it almost as though he were going to kiss it, then drew erect and noticed how she put it to her side and, in doing so, instinctively rubbed it against her dress.

"So you are back again, m'sieur," said she. "We have been expecting you for several days."

"Detained, Madame, I was detained," he replied.

"Soochow," she said. "We will now have a cup of Soochow—and I have some oatcakes," she turned to me, a small light kindling in her eyes, "that I have made because I thought you would be with us to-day."

She went indoors and Christina followed her, saying, "Let me help you."

"Well, Baxter," said Court Nez, "we have not met for some time."

"Not for some time," I agreed.

"Some time, yes," said he. "I heard that you could not run away, you could not be driven out. You stayed with that handful of die-hards. Come, let us stroll a bit and while we stroll you can tell me about it. First-hand I would like to hear of that. You could not run away, heh?" His voice was jeering. He jeered at what others had praised!

"There is not much to tell," I replied. "Mr. McLeod and Mr. MacLean are the ones who deserve chief praise, and then Currie and McIntosh."

"But you deserve some too, heh?"

"I wouldn't say that," I replied, pacing by his side. "I just did not like to turn tail and run."

"No, you couldn't turn tail and run. Well, that is good. I am glad to hear that you cannot turn tail and run."

Court Nez drew himself up as though to make himself as tall as he could. He seems even, thought I, to be trying to puff himself out, humping his shoulders, crooking his arms—a toad of a man! But it was not to hear of the affair of the smithy that he led me away. When we came to another fallen tree by the top of the bank——

"Let us sit down," said he, and subsided.

I seated myself, but not close. I disliked even proximity to the man that day. Court Nez measured the space between us with a narrowed gaze, under puckered eyelids, then laughed and bumped himself along the fallen tree till he was so near to me that his great haunch pressed against my leg. He raised a hand in air and brought it down suddenly and heavily on my thigh. The pain that impact caused was extreme, for by the way I was seated I could not let my leg yield to it. Not only my thigh on which the hand smote was hurt. I thought for a moment that my knee was dislocated. But as I made no sign of pain when my hand was crushed, I made no sign of pain then.

"Intentions!" exclaimed Court Nez. "It's a word in all polite families in the old land. *Intentions.* You must have heard it. What are your *intentions*?"

"Intentions?"

"Yes."

"What exactly do you mean?" I demanded.

"You know what I mean," and down came the great cupped hand again.

"What are you doing this for?" I asked, rage in me, and added: "Do you want a coward for a son-in-law?"

"Now I ask you—what exactly do you mean?" said he.

"You know what I mean," I replied. "You know what I mean as well as I know what you mean. You saw us. You saw us when you arrived just now. I may tell you that you cannot terrorise me."

"Oh, can't I?" and he gave me a red glare. "I can tell you that you cannot behave lightly with my daughter."

"And I tell you, sir, that you go the wrong way about it—as probably," I added, infuriated, "you go about everything. Everything!"

"I do, do I?" said Court Nez, the wild remark having apparently cut him. "Everything, eh? Well, there is one thing I have gone the right way about—and that is regarding my daughter. I have done my best for her and——" his jaws clenched grimly.

He raised his hand in air again and just as he was bringing it down, even more violently than before, I moved my leg quickly sidewise. Down on the tree-trunk came Court Nez's hand. It was nearly closed that time and he not only bruised the finger-tips but, by the force of its descent, skinned his knuckles. Beads of blood showed on them.

"Damn you, you whipper-snapper!" he growled. "What do you mean by trying to get away from the point? I saw you: and I ask what are your intentions regarding my daughter. I am not going to have any lad thinking that because she is a half-breed——"

I met his eyes.

"My intentions," I said, "are to get her away from you."

"Oh, to get her away from me?" He raised his other hand and clenched it as though about to whirl and hit me.

"Put that hand down," said I. "You insult her and you insult me. I care for her so much that even though she is your daughter I am going to marry her."

"Ha!" shouted Court Nez with exaltation, as if he had won a victory.

I was infuriated anew. My fists clenched.

"You can't terrorise me," I told him again.

"Can't I? Why, I would kill you if you played fast and loose with her."

"Damn you!" I cried out. "If you were not her father——" There I stopped, controlled myself. "I want you to know," I said, "that you are not forcing me to do anything I had no intention of doing. While you have been bousing out on the prairies somewhere, by the sodden look of you, I have been waiting for you to come here to tell you I am going to marry your daughter."

He sat back and considered me. Then a cunning look came on his face.

"You mean that you were waiting to ask me if you might?" he suggested.

"I did not mean that," I answered. "I shall marry her whether you give permission or not."

Court Nez continued to study me. Then he gave a chuckling laugh. Slowly on his face came a smile that seemed to me idiotic. "The dipsomaniac's smile," I meditated. "This man will crash some day."

"O God, O God!" exclaimed Court Nez, and lowered his head. He sidled close to me again. He nudged me with an elbow. "So you couldn't run away, eh?" he asked. "And you think I go the wrong way about everything, eh? Well, perhaps I do. And as you are going to marry my daughter you might like to know a little more about me. You might like to know, for instance, how I came to this country." He laughed again, thickly, as if about to embark on a highly humorous anecdote. "There was a girl. And that's all you need to know. I ran away. I—ran—away!"

I stared at him.

"I—ran—away!" he repeated, again shaking with laughter as if at an excellent joke.

"The man is mad!" thought I.

"Yes," said Court Nez, "and I went out to Georgia to try and forget her, and then came on to the Indian Countries hereaway. I've been back only once to the Atlantic seaboard."

La Reine—the eldest Lagimoniere child—suddenly appeared running round the bend of the bank.

"Soochow!" she called. "Soochow and oatcakes!"

Court Nez sighed and rose. And—"Coming!" he shouted in reply.

The child ran back ahead of us.

"There is neither priest nor clergyman here," said Court Nez as we turned towards the cabin.

"No, not yet," I answered. "Some people blame Lord Selkirk for that but I had it from Captain Macdonell himself that the earl has been doing his best. There have been hitches."

"Quite so, but that is not the point. There is no need for you to defend your late Governor to me—no, nor your blasted earl either!" he ejaculated. "What I was thinking was that you and Christina can go to a chief factor of the Company and have him enter your union in the books, and he will give you a paper signed and witnessed. It is valid, or at any rate it is sufficiently valid. There was a man out here did as most of us do—took an Indian woman. He had a large family by her, then left them all and went to Montreal. There he married a white woman. When he died she got all his money, but a half-breed son went east and claimed part of it for his mother. The white wife refused anything, so he engaged lawyers, but the case never went to court—for her legal advisers urged her to settle out of court and let the Indian family have half. They would never have done that if they had not believed that in the courts she would have lost everything. They evidently considered that she was not his legal wife and that witnessing before a Company's factor was valid."

We were in sight of the cabin again. At the door Madame Lagimoniere and Christina looked towards us and on their faces, it seemed to me, was expression of relief. Court Nez held out both hands to his daughter.

"Well, Christina," he said, "Baxter has been telling me. You have

a good man, my girl. Oh, a good man! He would never run away."
He beamed down on her, and then the smile vanished. "The only
trouble," he muttered, as if at some new thought, "the only trouble
is that streak. Oh, well, you both have it, no doubt. You both have
it and so you can make the best of it."

I think we must all have shown puzzlement. I know I felt it. But
by a sudden change on Madame Lagimoniere's face I think she
promptly decided that he talked so, incomprehensively, by reason
of being deranged by a recent bout. Then——

"Your hand!" she exclaimed. "Look at your hand!"

He raised it and examined the skinned knuckles, the drops of
blood.

"Now, how did I do that?" he asked.

"I think," said I, "that you knocked it on the tree we were sitting
on."

He was still considering his knuckles.

"That was a foolish thing to do," he said. "Quite unnecessary,
eh?" and he laughed.

Madame Lagimoniere, hurriedly, as if to create a diversion, passed
into the cabin and took up from the table a platter of oatcakes.

"This smell," said she, holding it to me, "it makes you think of
home, *hein*? It makes you want to go back, *hein*?"

The diversion was successfully created and during the remainder
of my visit of that day all was normal, at least on the surface.

As for Court Nez's remark about a "streak" that no doubt
Christina and I had in common, which had puzzled us and that
Madame, if I read her aright, had looked upon as evidence of mental
derangement, I may as well say here that a day was to come when,
with a sense of shock, I was to recall it, made fully aware at last of
its significance.

CHAPTER SEVEN

I

ON the following day I was sent down river by Captain Semple with a message for Lieutenant Holte, formerly of the Swedish navy. Miles Macdonell, when first he came to Lake Winnipic, had considered that stronger and larger craft than canoes or boats should be built for service there. The earl agreed and eventually this ex-naval officer had come out to superintend the building of a schooner and to take charge of transport on the lake. With the outcast settlers Holte had gone to the Jack River post, and after assisting them in their return he had been busy on the conveyance of the many effects of those who had come out in Captain Semple's charge. That being over he was superintending the building of another schooner for future and possibly increased lake traffic.

Returning to Fort Douglas from that absent duty (which had taken four days) I saw Hugh Chisholm a stone's cast from the road and turned aside to talk to him. The welcome he accorded me was as friendly as ever. There was no suggestion of restraint or coldness such as I had felt from the girls on the evening of the celebration, but trouble showed in his eyes. Clearly something was wrong, something worried him.

"Well, lad," he said, "I had a glisk of you going north two-three days ago, but you didn't see me. Come in. Will your horse stand there or has he to be tied?"

"I'd better tie him."

Together we walked towards the tent, past a pile of logs. At the pile Mr. Chisholm stopped.

"These are for the new biggin," he announced. "I should have finished it by now but there have been many things to attend to. But we'll be housed before the snow comes, we hope."

"Good logs," I commented.

"Aye, good logs," said Mr. Chisholm. He remained staring at them. "You mustn't mind if the wife seems kind of odd with you," he added. "We've had our troubles. She's had her vexations."

222

" Indeed you all have," said I, " all here."

" This one is private. It's domestic. If she's odd with you, take no hurt. She's not outs with you. It's not you she'll be objecting to."

" I'm sorry, Mr. Chisholm. What is the matter? But if it's private I should not ask."

" Well—never heed, never heed. Every cloud has its silver lining. We've just found the silver lining to this one. Aye, they are good poles," and he waved his hand to them as we walked on to the tent.

Before it stood a wide-spraddled tripod of green boughs over a cooking-fire. From the centre a chain depended and as we drew near Mrs. Chisholm came out carrying a pot which she hung there. She looked at me with a face of gloom.

" Well, there you are," she said. " Just in time for a bite to eat." She spoke without a smile.

" I can't stay for that," said I, " much though I should like to. I must be getting on to the fort."

" Just as you please," she answered with a shrug.

Chisholm took up a stick with a charred end and began to stir the fire into a blaze.

" You'll give the food the taste of smoke!" snapped his wife.

" I'm just making——"

" Making what? A blaze, I suppose you were going to say. Making smoke is more like it."

Mairi emerged at that moment from the bark shelter that stood near the tent and at sight of me she looked quickly and inquiringly from father to mother. It took no keen reading of an expression, especially after the hints from her father, to see her look as of one questioning, " Have you told him?" Definitely something was amiss with all these friends of mine—and might be told to me, or withheld from me.

" Well, Mairi," I said.

" Well, David?"

Mrs. Chisholm turned and went quickly back to the tent just as Agnes appeared, bending low at the entrance to the bark shelter. She saw me, seemed on the point of retreating inside again, then stepped out with a toss of her head. Immediately I realised what the trouble was in the house of Chisholm. On the return from Jack River, I recalled, Agnes appeared to have put on flesh. I recalled also her strained manner, her shrill, almost brazen laughter. Yes: she was in the family way.

Out from the tent came Mrs. Chisholm again.

"What are you standing there for, Mairi?" she demanded. "Has your mother to do all? Has your mother to do all the cooking and your father all the fire tending? Can't you see if there's no' a kettle to be filled and put on the fire?"

Mairi hurried away and Agnes, with another toss of her head and a pout, met my eyes.

"Well, Agnes," I said. "I've been down with a message to below the rapids and just looked in for a minute on my way back."

"That's like old times," she remarked, and her air of indignation or annoyance at my tactless stare at her midriff went. "I suppose I should be helping too, and see what's to be done."

Mairi reappeared with a kettle. She filled it from a barrel of water standing by and was making a place for it by the fire when her mother followed her.

"What are you at there?" screamed Mrs. Chisholm. "See what you're doing. Raising all the ash into the pot! Oh, we are all turning into Indians here. Wood-smoke and wood-ash, and syne we'll be off across the plains to that haunt o' the *métis*, the half-breeds. Half-breeds! They're worse than the Indians."

I felt a stab at my heart.

"The Indians are no' so bad," declared Chisholm. "They have been good friends to us. If ever it comes to it—and some of them have been suggesting it—that we send a petition direct to the Prince Regent for military protection here, it will have to be told that it is not the full-bloods we need protection from, that they have been good friends to us."

"They are not so bad," admitted his wife, "apart from some of them being lousy."

Agnes exploded laughter and then suddenly checked herself.

"What are you laughing at?" Mrs. Chisholm asked—but not of Agnes, of Mairi.

My mouth must have opened, I think, because of my astonishment. I could see no harm in anybody laughing over her vehemence—but did the woman not know it was Agnes, not Mairi, who had laughed?

Aware of how I stared at her, and thinking myself rude to do so, I felt flustered and spoke the first thought in my head.

"No," I said, "Indians are none too bad."

"You are not going to marry an Indian woman like some of the lads, I hope," Mrs. Chisholm said, violently.

"Not a full-blood," I replied in a level voice.

My accent made all look at me curiously.

"A half-breed," I added. "A Scots half-breed."

"A half—och, you're joking!" exclaimed Mrs. Chisholm, tossing her head.

Agnes laughed loudly again. Mairi and Mr. Chisholm considered me steadily.

"No, I'm not joking," I said.

Unaware of what he did, Chisholm turned his head and looked at Mairi. He seemed to be studying her.

"Well, there are some fine half-breeds in the country," he said at last, "as well as fine and kindly full-bloods. Even that man Grant has his good points. He's a tool of Alexander Macdonell, him they call Yellowhead. Whose daughter is she, David, might I ask?"

"The daughter of Court Nez."

"The free-trader?"

"Yes."

"I remember him. Yes, a free-trader—not in the service of either Company."

"No. She's been in Quebec for some years. Court Nez sent her to a convent there."

"A Catholic!" ejaculated Mrs. Chisholm.

"I don't know."

"Well, what was she at the convent for?" she demanded.

"Oh, they give good educations at the convents," her husband said in consoling tone.

"Huh!" She frowned at the pot on the fire. "Well, you'd better stay and have a bite to eat." She turned again to Mairi. "Bestir yourself," she said. "Why do you stand there like an Indian or an effigy in a dwaum? Get out the bowls and spoons."

"I must be going," said I. "Captain Semple will be expecting me. Good-bye, Agnes."

"Good-bye."

P

" Good-bye, Mairi."

She looked directly at me, then past me, as if in long farewell.

" Good-bye," she said.

" Good-bye, Mrs. Chisholm."

" Aye, aye. Oh, well," she said, " if any one but yourself had told me that——" she did not finish the sentence. " When's the marriage to be?" she asked.

" Very soon."

" I'll come to the gate with you," said Mr. Chisholm.

We walked in silence till we came to the stack of logs and there he halted. He waved a hand at it.

" Grand logs," he said. " Grand logs for the new biggin. Isn't it extraordinary? You see how she takes it. If it had been Mairi instead of Agnes I don't know what would have happened." He waved a hand again over the logs, stooped and felt the surface of one. " You could hardly believe it, but when she found out how Agnes was she blamed Mairi. Had she known? Yes, she had known. How long had she known? And why hadn't she told her mother? And then she raved and ranted at Mairi for not telling her sooner. Well, I've had it out with the lad and I'm thankful to say he's willing to marry her. One of the old kirk elders can take the service. That's how you'll be getting married, I suppose, in the lack of a minister?"

" More likely before the Hudson's Bay Company's factor," said I.

" Oh, aye."

We moved on to the gate. I took the reins of my waiting horse from the post. Chisholm held out a hand.

" Good-bye, lad," he said. " I've no doubt you are doing the wise and right thing. Forget what she said about Indians and half-breeds. I've no doubt you'll have a real nice wife."

I swung into the saddle and as I rode away looked round. I waved to Mrs. Chisholm and the girls but only Mairi saw. A hand went up, she waved in reply and, as she did so from her other hand, by a moment's negligence, she let fall a bowl that she had been carrying. It was shattered. Mrs. Chisholm stood up from the fire, a spurtle in hand with which she had been stirring the broth. She flourished it in the air as she reprimanded her elder daughter on her carelessness. The words I could not hear, only the harsh rasping voice as I rode away.

"I shouldn't have waved," I said to myself. "If I had not waved, Mairi would not have waved and dropped that bowl. It's a shame—the way Mrs. Chisholm treats her, and she such a fine lass."

II

It had always been a puzzle to me why Mr. Sutherland, a Hudson's Bay officer, had left Red River with the settlers. True he had been one of the signatories of the agreement for their departure, that document forced upon the Company's officers there by the half-breeds who were exploited by the Nor'-Westers. But by that agreement it was only the settlers who were to retire; "no appearance of a colony" was to remain. The Hudson's Bay Company was free to continue in the vicinity in trade. Sutherland had, however, gone with them—and returned with them. Before him it was that Christina and I presented ourselves a day or two later to announce our desire to have entry made of our union in the Company's records.

Court Nez was there, sober, and with great pride in his sobriety. Colin Robertson was there, his genial best for the occasion. John McLeod, who showed a fraternal interest in me since the fight in the smithy against the *métis*, was there. Christina was dressed not in the way of Indian camps but of Montreal and Quebec and fashion, but she showed the native blood in her, in the curve of her lips and in her eyes, dark limpid eyes.

"You are a lucky man," Colin Robertson said to me as all gathered for the declaration and the witnessing.

In the books an entry was made of the marriage of David Baxter of Renfrewshire in Scotland to Christina Courtney, daughter of Mr. Courtney, free-trader. The ceremony over (if making that entry in the Company's books and the presentation to us of a paper signed by James Sutherland, witnessed by all present, can be called a ceremony) we all went to the Lagimoniere cabin where Madame had prepared a feast in our honour.

Court Nez, who visited both Companies, traded with both Companies, rode over from Fort Gibraltar near where he was camped. He followed afoot behind the bridal party, leading his horse. He could not, I think, forget the marvel of his sobriety on the occasion. He had told Madame Lagimoniere (and she had whispered it to me) that he had made a resolve of sobriety for that day as a sign of respect for his daughter, and was apparently all puffed up over his abstinence as only one who knew no half-measures could be puffed up. When Madame produced a bottle of wine—not rum, or whisky, or brandy, merely a bottle of wine!—at the wedding feast, he put his great hand over his glass and——

"No, thank you," said he. "I never touch the stuff. I've stopped taking the stuff in any form."

The feast was not long over when John McLeod announced that he must be going. Since the return of the settlers, and the removal of the stored hoes and harrows out of the old cabin known as Fidler's house, he had been living there. It was outside the palisade, a stone's throw beyond some sown plots called Colony Garden, and when he left it, it would be unoccupied. So he had suggested we might there take up house on our marriage. No one would object. The place would be empty after he went. He was immediately setting out on to the prairie to another of his adventurous duties.

"I have a two or three hundred miles journey before me," he told us, "all the way out to Thieves River to found a post there."

Court Nez rose with him. He seemed suddenly nervous, strained.

"You to Thieves River," he said, "and I out into the Indian Countries somewhere. I may go to the Cypress Hills and collogue with the Blackfeet a while, or down to the Missouri to my Mandan friends. A little of white people goes a long way with me," and he laughed, a laugh that might mean what one would, enigmatic.

He turned, went out. There was something in his manner that made Christina and me look after him anxiously, questioning. Madame Lagimoniere had the appearance as of one listening, head on side. The muffled thud of hoofs sounded. Court Nez was back, the reins over a forearm. He held up both hands, palms open, lowered his arms slowly towards us.

"This is the Indian sign of blessing," said he.

We all noticed that he was trembling and that his face twitched. Then suddenly he put foot to stirrup, swung up, settled in the saddle and was away. Christina and I ran to the door but he did not look round. Across the prairie he rode at a lope, as easy as in an armchair, one hand raised fairly high before him in the Indian manner when riding. The earth was hard with frost that day and the horse's hoofs rang sharp.

McLeod cleared his throat.

"Well," he suggested, "you two might as well come over with me. I'm going to your home, you know, to get the last of my things— and then I'm off too, I'm off. That's the way of life, Madame: meetings and partings."

Christina glanced at me.

"Perhaps we should go with Mr. McLeod, then," I said. "Madame Lagimoniere, you have been very good and kind to us."

"It has been a pleasure," she replied, smiling. "You two, I think, are made for each other." She put an arm round Christina and kissed her, then kissed me on the cheek.

"I may not see you again, Madame, for some time," said McLeod. "After building the post at Thieves River the Governor wants me to report to him at Fort Daer in the winter, where he will be when he comes back from his first tour. Colin Robertson will be here. You will remember, Madame, that Mr. Robertson hoped that in your husband's absence you would come in to Fort Douglas where you would have every consideration and attention. A cabin is waiting you there, at your service."

"I shall be going to occupy it very soon now," she replied. "By the look of the sky the snows will soon be here."

"Well, *adieu*, Madame," he said.

"*Au revoir et Dieu vous benisse.*"

III

Those were happy days in Fidler's old house. In the evenings I worked on the recaulking.

"To-morrow night," I said, when that work was completed, "we must go along and visit my friends the Chisholms of whom I have spoken to you."

But on the next day preparations began for the departure to Pembina. The first snowfall, a wet snowfall, had melted. The earth showed clear again, though by the colour of the sky a more wintry fall would come soon. The tents of those who had been quartered at the fort were being taken down and rolled. A row of bullock-carts, driven by free-traders hired to assist the flitting—more expense to the Earl of Selkirk!—came screaming in at the gate, wheeled in a semi-circle and stood there waiting. The other settlers, those who had returned from Jack River under Robertson's care and had been at work on their old lots, were also packing. More hired carts creaked along from free-traders' camps by the Assiniboine and passed down the Settlement road to their assistance. At noon I hurried off to my new home beyond the Colony Garden for the midday meal with Christina. As we ate we heard the screaming of these carts returning from north.

" What a din they make! " said I.

" Yes. One of my earliest memories is of a brigade coming over the prairie, out at Qu'Appelle," replied Christina.

" All wood," said I. " Not a nail anywhere. All pegs. And I suppose if one put grease in the hubs it would just make a paste of the grit that gets in and grind the wood down quicker than it is ground down anyhow."

We went outside and there, along the road, came the slow-moving string.

" They've Indians riding with them," Christina commented.

" Peguis, as usual, is determined to see them safely to Pembina," I told her.

The carts came nearer. In one of them I saw Mr. and Mrs. Chisholm and Mairi. The Chisholms, I knew, had been uncertain whether they should go to Pembina or remain at the Settlement that winter; but, after Agnes's marriage to Bob Wallace, large buffalo herds being reported south, they unanimously decided to go and help in the preparation of pemican there.

" Come," said I, " here are the Chisholms."

We stepped to the roadside. At sight of Christina, Mrs. Chisholm stared. How tactless she could be! She could not even give a greeting to me. Instead she stared at the girl who stood beside me.

" But this is not your wife! " she exclaimed.

" This is my wife," I assured her. " We intended every night to call on you but——"

" So this is your wife! " she interrupted. " Well, I must say I am maist agreeably surprised."

The cart did not stop. Had it done so the ones behind would have been forced to halt also. Christina and I walked along level with it.

"How do you do, Mistress Baxter?" said Chisholm, and executed a fine bow.

Mairi leaned forward, holding out her hand.

"I'm Mairi," she said. "David told us he was going to be married."

She smiled down at Christina and Christina up at her. I saw Mr. Chisholm glance from one to the other.

We had to talk loudly to be heard above the persistent squeal of those Red River carts. Mrs. Chisholm opened her mouth to speak again but the noise was too much for her.

"Agnes is there," Chisholm shouted, "in that third cart back there."

I looked round. Agnes had evidently been waiting for recognition. I had not to search for her. She rose and waved wildly at me, her condition obvious as she did so. Then she sat down laughing and talking to young Wallace who was driving. Apparently all was well. If she felt any shame at her premarital haste it was gone. Or perhaps she knew that there were many who gossiped of it and in defiance of them she was thus cheerful of manner.

At the fort the string came to a standstill. Colin Robertson was talking to a man in the lead. He gave him a wave and turned away. Immediately the line of carts moved on. They were off. The accompanying Indians, who had drawn aside in milling groups, reined their horses into single file again on either side.

"We'll see you in the spring," I called.

"What did you say?" cried Mrs. Chisholm.

"We'll see you in the spring!"

"I hope so."

"Good-bye, Mr. Chisholm."

"Good-bye, lad. And good-bye to your pretty wife." He waved to Christina and she waved back.

"Good-bye, Mairi," I shouted.

She leant over the side of the moving cart and gave me her hand.

"Good-bye, David," she replied. "I like her."

"What did you say?"

"I like her, I said—I like her." Then, to my surprise, tears suddenly dimmed her eyes and she bit her lip.

Christina hurried alongside.

"In the spring you'll come and see me, Mairi," she called.

"I beg your pardon? I cannot hear."

"In the spring you'll——"

"Oh, yes, yes, I will that. I'll come and see you."

Mrs. Chisholm gave a regal bow. The cart in which Agnes sat came level.

"See you both in the spring!" she shouted. "See you in the spring, Mistress Baxter," and she laughed.

There was a babel of talk everywhere. It gave a sense of confusion to what was orderly enough. Suddenly there was a sound of humming and then a rising of voices. An inspiration of music went from cart to cart. Everybody began to sing, men and women.

Christina stood listening, entranced. There was no knowing where it started, in front, at the end, or from someone in the middle. There was first just a humming, like a warning, like a tuning, then came the singing, rising, rising. She put out a hand to me, felt for mine, held it. We stood still, listening and watching. There went the grating of wheels, the squealing of wheels, and that surge of voices, heading off to the south-west for the ford of Assiniboine River.

CHAPTER EIGHT

I

SITTING in Fidler's old house it was hard for me to believe that not long since it had been used as a storehouse for seed-grain sacks and hoes and harrows, and that in the smithy walls, not a stone's cast away, the bullets fired by the circling half-breeds had sounded their *plunk, plunk, plunk.*

There were books to read in the evening, books sent out to Rupert's Land by the Hudson's Bay Company. While playing our part in the history of Red River, but not thinking of ourselves then as doing so, we read a volume of Rollin's *Ancient History of the Egyptians, Carthaginians, Assyrians, Babylonians, Medes and Persians, Macedonians and Grecians*, that someone, by evidence of the inscription in it, had brought down from the library at York Factory and that in the spring would be returned there, an odd volume of an eight volume set, the one with an engraving of the death of Socrates, as I recall, for a frontispiece. With the snow of Assiniboia scudding against our parchment window we read of Brazil in a book by Robert Southey, and in another of his, in the light of home-made candles, Christina was lost in the story of Joan of Arc while I read in *Quarterly Reviews* of a year past and more.

From Pembina came news of the settlers wintering there, in a letter from McLeod. He had established the new post at Thieves River and then gone to Fort Daer, Pembina, to report to Governor Semple. On the way he had halted at a camp of Saulteaux Indians and passed the night with them, and a few days after his arrival at Pembina a free-trader came in there with the grim news that the night after McLeod left a band of Sioux from Dakota had made a night attack and killed thirty-three out of the thirty-six . He had tried to keep the grim news quiet but the free-trader repeated it to his womenfolk and they passed it on to the settlers' womenfolk visiting among their cabins. Some of the settlers, he wrote, were out with the Pembina *métis* and there was great anxiety among many regarding them. Mrs. Chisholm it had been hard to console. Her husband was out at one of the hunting camps and their daughter Mairi with him. Wallace was out there also, his wife and newly-born baby remaining with Mrs. Chisholm, who was sure that all would be killed.

I handed the letter to Christina and she paused to meditate over the pages. Glancing up she found me watching her.

" What is it?" I asked.

" Nothing," she said, and then: " I was just thinking," she confessed, " that Mairi Chisholm loves you."

" Loves me!" I exclaimed, startled.

" Yes. The more I remember her the more I feel so. She looked at me and searched me to see if I loved you that day when we met, when they were going to Pembina, and she knew I did love you, and was grateful to me. She's a sweet girl, David."

" She is indeed," I agreed, thinking of many evidences I had of that.

" You love her too," said Christina.

" I think I love them all," I answered, " even Mrs. Chisholm, in spite of her uncertain temper."

" Do you love the other girl too, the married one?"

" Agnes?" I laughed. " Oh, yes. She's a hoyden and has had an easy time because of being the mother's pet, but she has splendid character. She never takes her mother's side against Mairi, for instance. The two sisters are really devoted."

" David——"

" What?"

" If—if anything happened to me I know Mairi Chisholm would be a good friend to you."

" Happened to you!" I exclaimed. " Oh, Christina, my darling, you are too much alone here. We'll leave this house—we'll get one that they are finishing inside the new fort."

She laughed at that suggestion.

" No, no, I don't want to leave here, David. We're so happy. I have never been so happy," and she returned to her reading of the letter from John McLeod.

11

At Christmas time and New Year there were the usual festivities at the fort. For us both the time fled. The new year was on us as with a pounce. The thermometer dropped and there came a spell of extreme cold when, if one ran and heated a horse that was drawing a sledge, making it breathe violently, an icicle a yard long would depend from its nostrils. But so long as there was no wind cutting over the expanse the cold was endurable and in our cabin the stove at night hummed its hymn of sanctuary.

Christina by then knew she was with child. While I read she was making baby-clothes with fine needlework, richly embroidered, the sort of work she had learned with the Ursulines at Quebec.

Crisp snow was pattering against the parchment windows of the accounting-room towards the end of an overcast day in March when there was a sound downstairs as of the smiting of a coat against the outer wall to free it of snow. The door opened and instead of Sheriff Archibald entering, as I had expected, there was John McLeod and behind him another man.

Colin Robertson looked up from his table.

" It's McLeod!" he said. " Hold-the-fort McLeod and—and Bostonois Pangman." He rose and shook hands with them. " So you've come back to the service of the Company of Adventurers of England Trading into Hudson's Bay," he said to Pangman.

" As a prisoner," replied Pangman.

" As a what?"

" That's right," McLeod assured him.

" Sit down," Robertson begged. " Sit down. Explain. Have a drink. Where do you come from?"

" Pembina."

" Rode?"

" Yes. Two days. A snell day this too, in the snow," remarked McLeod.

" Well, sit down," said Colin again. " Have a drink."

He strode to the door, opened it, and shouted for his servant to bring in glasses and a bottle.

Here, thought I, as they drank and talked, is a quaint incident: The temporary governor, the prisoner and his guard taking their dram together and discussing the rights and wrongs of the arrest. John Bourke was in the room to see me regarding some Colony store accounts and though he and I continued our examination of books and invoices we heard, and heeded, the talk.

"How came the arrest?" asked Robertson after the three had toasted each other.

Pangman looked at McLeod and McLeod at Pangman.

"The reason for it can no doubt be defended," responded McLeod. "I'd rather express no opinion on the matter. I have been sent here with the prisoners."

"Prisoners? More than one?"

"Yes. The others—clerks and labourers—are in the Jocks' mess-room now, getting warmed."

Colin Robertson laughed.

"Amusing situation," he remarked. "Anybody killed?"

"Oh, no. Nobody offered any resistance. Governor Semple just ordered it to be done : Seize the North-West fort and take the people prisoners."

"On what charge?"

Again Pangman looked at McLeod and McLeod looked at Pangman.

"Conspiracy, I believe," said McLeod. "We got fresh news of what is still going on out on the plains. Yellowhead is trying again to raise the Crees to join the *métis* and come down and drive out the settlers when they return here from Pembina and the rivers are open— keep them moving."

Pangman said nothing.

"It's all by word of mouth, I understand," McLeod continued. "That's the trouble—for Semple."

"If it goes to the courts," said Robertson, "you mean there will be lack of evidence?"

"Yes."

"Semple may alter his opinion of the governorship of Miles Macdonell yet," said Robertson. "It is a pity you went over to the Nor'-Westers," he added to Pangman.

"They think it is a pity you went over to the Hudson's Bay Company," said Pangman, and laughed. "I went because Mr. Fidler would not allow me a refund of expenses I had incurred. He told me I had incurred them needlessly. He and I did not pull well. So I resigned and went over to them."

" I remember when that happened," said McLeod.

" I have heard of it," said Colin Robertson.

McLeod was fumbling in a pocket. Taking out a letter he handed it to Robertson who read it, as he did so elevating his brows.

" Well, Bostonois," he said at last, giving Pangman his other name, " we'll see you are comfortable here till it is time to send you off. You won't try to run away?"

" No. I won't do that."

" Have another dram on it, then."

The glasses were refilled. They raised them, nodded to each other across the brims and quaffed while the parchment windows dulled in the darkening day.

McLeod moved over to my table and sat on it, swinging a leg.

" Well, lad," he said, " I saw your father-in-law when I was out building that new post on the prairie."

" Oh, you did. And——?"

" He was just as usual. A queer man, your father-in-law. He was on his way to visit the Mandans down on the Missouri River. What's his real name?"

" I don't know. Christina doesn't know."

" No, I suppose not—I remember at your marriage that Court Nez was all he offered for the record. I admit the shortness of his nose. I noticed the name was entered in the books in its English form, Courtney—which probably comes from the French. Queer man, David! Queer man! He's a mystery, and there are one or two mysteries like him out in these spaces. I've often wondered what first sent them there. He's a strange man, is Court Nez—but maybe it is a breach of manners for me to talk so of your father-in-law."

" Not at all. Frankly, he both attracts and repels me."

" Attracts and repels, eh?"

" Yes. And I'm sorry for him and can't tell why. I'm drawn to him against my will."

" Of course you have a sense of pity," McLeod pointed out. " It's not every one who has. Pity is near akin to love with you, lad. I don't know that many would feel sorry for him, but I understand what you mean. There's an impression that he has some gnawing demon in him, whiles. He sent his remembrances to you and his daughter."

"Was that all?"

"That was all."

"Was he sober?"

"When I saw him he was."

There was a suggestion in McLeod's voice that Court Nez had not the appearance of having been sober long, but I asked no more questions. Robertson was on his feet, obviously waiting for McLeod to end his talk with me, and both, with Pangman, went out of the room together.

When they had gone John Bourke and I looked one to the other.

"What do you think was in that letter from Semple?" inquired Bourke.

"I should imagine it was an explanation as to why he seized the Nor'-West fort at Pembina," I replied.

"Perhaps more than that," said Bourke. "If he had reason to seize Pembina and take Pangman prisoner he may want Cameron for prisoner also. I take it he considers he has a case against Pangman that he can put forward in the law courts."

"In Montreal or in England?" said I, recalling some talk I had heard between Hillier and Macdonell of the Canada Act, which stated that those guilty of crimes in the Indian Countries, save certain major ones, must be tried in Canada and not taken to England.

"What was that you told me once—something that Captain Macdonell used to repeat?" asked Bourke.

"I don't know what you mean. Do you mean about the Canada Act?"

"No. Something he recalled now and then from his last interview in London with Lord Selkirk, something about a shadow——"

"Oh, yes: 'There is a shadow on my Red River Settlement.'"

"That's it. Well, I think there is a shadow on it and I expect that before long—but let us have a light in the room first. Candles, candles!"

Bourke was lighting the candles when Colin Robertson returned, so what we might expect before long Bourke did not say. Colin was laughing to himself.

"Do you remember that day," he said to me, "when you got up from your place and made your defence of Miles Macdonell?"

"Yes."

"Well, I'm thinking Robert Semple by now has more sympathy with your point of view." In the candle-light his eyes danced. "We're going to see some fun here yet," he declared, but what manner of fun he did not prophesy and apparently decided to say no more, at the moment, on that head. "You need not stay any longer when you have finished your checking of these accounts with Bourke," he went on. "It looks like blowing up a blizzard. When you finish that job you had better go home to that bonny wife of yours, David Baxter."

"We have just finished," said I.

Through the drive of snow I hurried home to tell Christina all—of the message from her father, of McLeod there in the fort, of Pangman and the arrested clerks and labourers, of Colin Robertson's comment that Captain Semple might yet realise the difficulties of Miles Macdonell and disesteem him less.

"I love your loyalty to Captain Macdonell," said Christina.

"I could never be otherwise than loyal," said I, "feeling as I do regarding him."

"No, I know," she said, "but I often think of what you told me Semple said to you—about Miles Macdonell's loyalty to the earl and yours to Miles Macdonell. What do you think would be in that letter Mr. McLeod brought to Mr. Robertson?"

"Probably just an explanation of why he had arrested the Nor'-Westers at Pembina."

She shook her head.

"Governor Semple is not the sort of man to write an explanation to his lieutenant here," she said.

"Possibly," I suggested, "it contained just an order regarding holding the prisoners. It is March now. They will be held here till the rivers open."

We were silent then and heard, from far off or near, hard to tell, the melancholy call of a prairie wolf.

"It gives me a shiver down the spine and over the hips," said I.

"Always it does that to me too," she answered, "and yet it fascinates me."

"I like it too."

" I wonder why?" she asked.

" Perhaps because it tells us there is space in the world. It tells me I am in a freer world here, away from the narrow life I used to have with censuring and fault-finding and being watched for anything I could be corrected for."

The call came again. She went to the door and opened it in order to hear better. It came again, with others.

" How I love this country!" I exclaimed. " I feel that it is ours."

" Something of that sort was perhaps what father meant we had in common," she said, unsuspicious as I, then, of what was in his mind when he made the remark to which she referred.

At the same moment I was saying : " It is going to be a cold night."

An eddy of wind sent the snow sifting in. It jammed the door with an icy crunch as I tried to close it. I had to scrape the snow away from the sill to shut it and, that done, beat my hands on my chest to warm them after the scraping. Hardly had I closed the door again when I had to turn down the draught of the stove as it roared to a rising wind that drew the heat up the chimney.

" How happy we are here," I said, " happy and secluded. I wonder where your father will be now."

" Where father will be now?" She gazed before her. " I often think, I often wonder. As I grow older, David, I feel it more and more : my father is a very mysterious man."

CHAPTER NINE

I

WITH his otter skin cap rakishly on his head and his short hip-length buffalo skin coat open, Colin Robertson came into the accounting-room early next day.

" Ha, alone!" said he. " Mr. Archibald not arrived yet."

I had a glimpse behind him of some of his men ascending, and by their bearing was reminded of the expedition we made to the North-West fort to retrieve the cannon.

" Serve out the muskets, David, and the bayonets," said he and then, as I stepped to the racks he explained : " We are making another visit to Fort Gibraltar, by orders of Captain Semple."

" Do I go too, sir?" I asked.

" Yes, if you care."

Colin Robertson was less, that morning, the big boy playing a grand part with a sense of humour over himself than on some occasions. The muskets, the bayonets, the ammunition having been served out to them again, the men passed downstairs. I fell in line with them and we numbered off at an order from our leader.

Again we marched across the plain. A keen wind stung our faces. There was a sense of bleakness in the whistling expanse. There was frost in the air so that our breaths were like smoke. Our footsteps (snowshoes were not needed, the snow being hard) sounded shrill. The sound of our marching was *Chirp-chirp, chirp-chirp.*

Since the seizure, or recovery, of the cannon and the despatch to Bas de la Rivière of Cameron's lieutenants, there had been a party of Hudson's Bay men in residence at Fort Gibraltar. He could not expect help from Bas de la Rivière, indignant though they might be there over the news brought to them by his three ousted officers. There were only about a dozen men there.

The North-Westers, for the time being, were outnumbered by Robertson's men. Further, some of the returned settlers, with a little assistance, would be ready to fight and among the last to arrive, as no doubt Cameron had heard, were many very resolute fellows. He could not hope, and indeed made no endeavour, to wheedle them away. He was practically a prisoner in his own fort. Robertson had at least a temporary mastery. Here was a downcome from the days when the order had arrived from east, and been duly proclaimed, that no Hudson's Bay Company's employee might, unless in the event of absolute starvation, enter a North-West fort.

At the gate one of our own men stood on sentry-duty. He had taken off his fur mittens—they hung from cords at his wrist—and was blowing into his hands, marking time with his heavily mocassined feet for the sake of warmth, when the party swung round the east wall. He drew his mittens on promptly and, ceasing to mark time, came to attention. Colin Robertson made acknowledgment and on we went to the officers' house.

Again Duncan Cameron came out to meet us.

"Good-day, Mr. Cameron," said Robertson without a smile.

"Good-day to you," replied Cameron, his manner very grand. I could not but feel then a certain admiration for his poise.

"I regret to say," began Colin, "that I have orders from Governor Semple to take you over to our fort and hold you there."

The slightest movement of his eyebrows showed Cameron astonished.

"Have you a warrant?" he asked.

"Only the warrant of the Governor's order."

"Governor!" scoffed Cameron, taking hold of himself and the situation. "Another governor! From whom does he have his appointment? From your Earl Selkirk?"

"No. From the Hudson's Bay Company."

"You think that gives him greater authority? Oh, yes, yes," said Cameron, his jaws moving up and down. Apparently he had been disturbed at a late breakfast. "I've heard it all before: This fort is on the Assiniboine River, and the Assiniboine flows into Red River, Red River into Lake Winnipic, Lake Winnipic drains into the Hudson Bay. We have heard it all before, all about the Hudson's Bay Company's unquestionable charter over all lands thus drained."

"Then I need not repeat it," replied Robertson, pleasantly. "Do you be so good as to order your servant to pack what you may require and bring it over to Fort Douglas."

"Fort Douglas? And where is that?"

"Strange that you should not know!" remarked Colin. "It is the name we have given our new fort."

"Named after the head of the Settlement," said Cameron. "That is noteworthy. I thought it was built for the Hudson's Bay Company."

"Named after a shareholder of the Company," said Robertson, "Thomas Douglas, Earl of Selkirk, as Fort Daer at Pembina was named by Governor Macdonell after another title of the earl, and as Fort Wedderburn in the Athabasca country is named after a brother-in-law of the earl, another shareholder. Quite so! Yes, it was named Douglas—this new fort built on the site of the houses burnt by the North-West Company."

"The North-West Company!" exclaimed Cameron. "You speak wildly, sir. You speak without proof. I know of that burning. The Indians of the plains——"

"Oh, enough of this dirty attempt to lay the blame on the full-blood natives."

"I would point out to you," said Cameron, "that it is in writing that the last of the settlers went out by agreement with the half-breeds. But we have discussed all this before : I have told you the North-West Company had nothing to do with that."

"Except to word the paper of agreement for the half-breeds."

Cameron shrugged his shoulders.

"Well," he said, "I shall come with you. I shall come under protest. I can see that your so-called governors one by one are merely strengthening the rope for their hanging." He turned away, then turned back and inquired : "To satisfy my curiosity—what does this Governor Semple give you as a reason for this behaviour?"

"Reasons," corrected Colin. "There are several. After your—perhaps I had better say *presumed*—complicity in recent attempts, of which we have had information, to rouse the half-Indians again to hostility, I would mention a seizure of furs, a theft of furs belonging to the Hudson's Bay Company that were being carried from one of Mr. McLeod's farther posts to——"

"So far as that goes," Cameron interrupted, "the same Mr. McLeod went to Bas de la Rivière and seized furs there."

"No, not seized, Mr. Cameron. He went there to look for these stolen bales of peltries—and found them. And some of our cannon he also found there, by the way, when he went thither with the officers

I removed from here. You scattered them to various forts of your Company, instead of very kindly storing them all here."

Cameron took the opportunity offered to evade talk of stolen furs, at that additional mention of the cannon.

"The cannon," he shouted, "were brought here by colonists of Lord Selkirk. How many times must I tell you that? I mislike the word *stolen* in reference to them."

"Let us stick to talk of furs, then," said Robertson. "You give me an ennui with your childish evasions. The furs were, beyond any quibble, stolen by the North-West Company and held at Bas de la Rivière. Mr. McLeod recovered them—and with but two men," he added, "and there was a garrison of over a dozen there." The admiration of Colin Robertson for John McLeod and of John McLeod for Colin Robertson was marked. "Another item, another reason for——"

But there he stopped for just then came a jingling of bells at the gate.

II

Colin Robertson turned and looked in that direction. Into the square came a string of dog-sleds. The drivers ran behind, then stepped up on the sled-tails and bearing down hard gave the order to halt. Out from one of the houses came two or three labourers.

"Get back, you!" shouted Robertson to them. Then to his own men: "Don't let these fellows get near the sledges," he ordered.

At once we ran between the sledges and those who had come from the houses. The new arrivals were clearly nonplussed, wondering what they had come to.

"Let me have the mail-sacks," ordered Robertson, walking up to the leader.

"*Sacre-bleu!* Be damned if I do!"

"Let me have the mail-sacks!"

The other drivers came closer.

"Not to you! They are for delivery to Mr. Cameron," said the one to whom Colin spoke.

"He is my prisoner," answered Robertson.

The man pushed against him suddenly, thrust him violently aside so that he stumbled. Recovering himself Colin shot out a fist that caught his assailant under the chin and sent him reeling over the sled on his head. He lay there, stunned. The second driver gave a snarl and loosening his sash felt at his belt and him also, before he could draw his knife, Robertson felled.

"*Au secours! Au secours!*" shouted that one as he scrambled to his feet.

The labourers who had come out to meet the winter mail-carriers from west massed closer but they were unarmed. We stood between them and the sleds with fixed bayonets at the ready. Then back to the house they ran. Cameron's voice boomed high and commanding.

"Stay where you are, you men!" he shouted.

They halted in their angry charge to the cabins, presumably for weapons. They looked round at him.

"I want you all as witnesses," he explained.

The voyageur who had been knocked unconscious rose and stared round, regaining knowledge of the actual world. He saw Robertson and whipping open his coat drew a knife and leapt like a wild animal on him. Colin at that moment had turned towards Cameron, wondering what he was about, but I sprang forward and thrusting out a foot before the voyageur brought him down. Robertson wheeled instantly and seeing what had happened placed his foot on the man's back and, stooping, took his wrist in a vice-like grip.

"Let it drop," he commanded.

The man would not loosen hold of the knife and bit hard on Colin's wrist.

"Oh, that's it!" exclaimed Robertson. "The voyageurs bite—bite, scratch, gouge, eh?"

Colin wrenched the man round on to his back and, holding the arm rigid, crouched and once, twice, thrice, knelt smartly in his midriff. He gasped as a fish out of water, but still he held the knife. Robertson knelt on his midriff again till the man's face was purple and as he lay there, gasping, he relaxed his hold on the knife.

Colin took it. Raising his hand he flung it past Cameron and, despite the frost over all, with a blend of *ting* and a *thud* it stuck in one of the logs of the officers' house. Then he gave his attention to the other driver who had offered fight. They looked each other in the eyes for a few minutes till a foolish grin showed on the voyageur's face. He closed his coat. He knotted his sash again. Colin laughed and as he did so the driver laughed also.

" Now for the mail," said Colin, and signed to one of our men who began to unfasten the covers. A sack was lifted out. " Open it," said Colin.

" Interception of mails," remarked Cameron. It happened that at the moment there was extreme quiet in the square. No one was speaking. His voice sounded amazingly clear. " I want you as witnesses to this," he said to the labourers he had called back.

Colin Robertson sat down on the first sled and commenced to riffle through the contents of the sack. He opened one letter and read. Nobody spoke, nobody moved. There was no sound save the panting of the dogs, all lying down in the snow before their loads with lolling tongues. He finished that letter and opened another, whistling softly as he read, whistling *En roulant ma boule* and I was never to hear the tune again without recalling that silent square, these waiting men—all watching for a signal, all prepared for anything. He looked at the addresses of other packets and laid them aside. Still whistling softly he opened another. He became the centre of that gathering. There he sat with his otter skin cap askew on his head, largely humped on the sled as if lost to his surroundings, reading, and whistling softly.

At last he looked up—without sitting erect. Under his eyebrows he considered Cameron, ceased whistling and laughed low in his chest; then, opening his short buffalo coat he put that apparently amusing letter in the breast pocket of his under coat. He began to whistle again, higher, not in a mere whisper as formerly. The sound sharpened as he continued to look through the budget, set some more packets aside, opened others. One of the labourers beat his hands against his sides, swinging them out and back, *thud, thud, thud.* Colin did not seem to hear but to many of the others, I noticed, intent on watching him, that thudding was annoying to judge by the frowns they gave. He read on, still whistling, then sat back with another letter in his hand, held it up, exhibiting it to Cameron.

" Ha!" he said. He made a jab in air with it before putting it in his pocket. He rose. " Well, men," he said, " you can all have your mail now. I was only acting on behalf of Mr. Duncan Cameron."

A chorus of snorts followed that. One might hear them as one would. Some were no doubt of indignation or disgust at his effrontery, some expressive of admiration for him.

"Interception of mails," repeated Cameron.

"Oh, I shall provide copies," Colin assured him. "Mr. Baxter here will attend to that for me. And when you come over with me to Fort Douglas I shall have pleasure—yes, I shall have pleasure!—in reading all that I have intercepted to you." He buttoned the frogs of his coat. "No," he said, "you need worry no more, Mr. Cameron, whether Governor Semple acted wisely in taking your Company's fort at Pembina—and I need worry no more about his order to entertain you, or about my inspiration to go through the mails. Are you ready, sir?"

"Yes, I'll come with you," Cameron answered. "But I consider you merely implicate yourself deeper and deeper. I'll come to your Fort Douglas with you."

He turned and went into the house. A murmur arose among the labourers. They talked furtively one to another, with eyes aslant at Colin Robertson and at us, standing by with muskets and fixed bayonets in hand round the sledges.

Suddenly Robertson looked up at the chimney of the officers' quarters. A great volume of smoke rose from it. An acrid odour filled the air.

"Paper!" he said.

It was indeed paper that was being burnt. Every one looked up at that smoke. It volleyed from the cobble chimney and in the midst of it charred fragments, dusky cinders with glowing spots, quaked away. The North-West employees smiled knowingly. The Hudson's Bay men frowned one to another and then looked at Robertson while he watched the smoke.

Cameron came from the house, an otter skin cap on his head to match Colin's, also wearing a short buffalo hide coat, frogged. Robertson nodded to him and then to the decreasing volume of smoke.

"I've enough evidence here," said he, tapping his chest. "What you had on files in there and have burnt would no doubt have been helpful, but I have enough. Well, shall we move? Fall in, men."

He gave a mocking bow to his prisoner. The two walked together to the gate. We marched after them, the North-West labourers and the Hudson's Bay men on guard there watching us go. The sentry came to attention and both Robertson and Cameron responded, but I thought there was something of ridicule in Cameron's salute.

We wheeled after them round the fort walls. There lay the plain before us towards Fort Douglas. The twiggy tops of the riverside trees were a frosted white lace-work. The wind had fallen and so the cold was not as greatly felt as earlier. It had blown the clouds away and the sky was dazzling bright. Out of the trees came two screaming jays, of a darker blue than the shadows of the snow.

I saw both Robertson and Cameron turn their heads to look at the birds, and the men I marched with looked at them too. I had a feeling of love for this land, its sights and colours and sounds. These men ahead of us, Colin Robertson and Duncan Cameron, were enemies and yet, thought I, as they both looked at these brilliant birds with similar expressions, but for the fact that they were then in rival companies they might be friends, although Cameron would be, perhaps, doubtful of Colin's impetuosity, Colin doubtful of Cameron's plausibility.

Left-right, left-right they went in step, and there came to me a sense of there being much in life that is a waste of time and worse. How often a man, I considered, may be implicated, involved, entangled in feuds that are not his! What had I, I asked myself, to do with this discord? Behind me I heard the screaming chatter of the blue jays as I crunched on, in step with the others.

III

In the accounting-room upstairs at Fort Douglas, Colin Robertson signed to Duncan Cameron to take a chair.

" Be seated, Mr. Cameron," he said. " You will pardon me if I give you *Mr.* instead of *Captain.* I think it is about time." He opened the drawer of his table and took out some papers. " Captain Miles Macdonell," he went on, " was a stickler for courtesy and on your first arrival here, in one of his letters to Lord Selkirk, he asked for information—if you get my meaning—regarding how properly to address you. Lord Selkirk made inquiries for him and had a reply in time to acquaint Captain Semple of the result before he sailed. I have here, from Captain Semple, a copy of the letter that his lordship had in answer to that inquiry he made of Sir Gordon Drummond."

"Sir Gordon Drummond has nothing to do with it," interjected Cameron.

"Quite so. But he was administering the government of Canada when Lord Selkirk approached him, so could institute inquiries. Sir Gordon very obligingly looked into the matter regarding appointments made by his forerunner, Sir George Prevost, with the result that he discovered Sir George had given no authority for the issue of commissions to persons in the Upper Country as officers in the Voyageurs' Corps, but that a general order," he glanced at the sheet in his hand, "of 10th May, 1814, gave to Norman Macleod the rank of Major and by an order of 25th May the rank of Lieutenant Colonel to Mr. McGillivray, and by the general order of 7th September the rank of Major to Pierre Rochblane, Esquire, in the Indian and conquered countries. That is all. Your name is not known in any list of Camerons."

"By what right do you talk to me like this before your menials?" broke out Cameron, shaking with anger.

Colin Robertson sat very erect, looked amazed.

"Menials!" he ejaculated. He pointed to me, stretching his arm out to full length. "I would have you know that that young man there is one of those who held off all the *métis* you called in from Qu'Appelle and the west to desolate the Colony. You cannot call a young man like that a menial!"

"I had a temporary commission," said Cameron, sulkily.

"Then," replied Colin Robertson instantly, "I am in perfect order in addressing you as *Mr.* Menials, indeed! And that young man," he pointed at Currie who had just then entered, "was one of the young men who accompanied Mr. McLeod to Bas de la Rivière not only when he went there to recover stolen furs but when he went there in charge of your officers that I sent over out of harm's way here. That second visit was the occasion when he brought back some of the cannon that you were kindly taking care of for the Colonists and lent to your colleagues there—and elsewhere. I still hope that we shall discover some day where the remainder were distributed, find them too."

"You may!" said Cameron, meaningfully, in threatening voice.

"Yes—as you say, we may. It looks so, not only from all the advice that Governor Semple has had at Fort Daer of renewal of North-

West machinations, but from this correspondence intercepted—intercepted—to-day." He took the letters from his pocket. " Permit me to read a few lines," he suggested, "so that you may know where your people stand. This is from Yellowhead to you : *I have received your kind favour. . . . I remark with pleasure the hostile proceedings of our neighbours, I say pleasure, because the more they do, the more Justice we will have on our side. . . . A storm is gathering in the north-west ready to burst on the rascals who deserve it; little do they know their situation. . . . Last year was but a joke*—a joke, Mr. Cameron, he writes—*The new nation under their leaders are coming forward to clear their native soil of intruders and assassins. . . . Glorious news from Athabasca. . . .* The new nation : by that he means the half-breeds or *métis* out in his vicinity on the plains. And what think you is the glorious news from Athabasca? Eighteen persons in the service of the Hudson's Bay Company, who had gone to trade in Athabasca, have suffered every degree of misery and distress. One of them alone reached Fort Chippewyan. All the others perished and those who survived the longest had been reduced to the necessity of eating the flesh of the dead. Glorious news from Athabasca, you observe. Sweet fellow, this."

He paused.

"Here's another, intercepted," he said, "on the way to a namesake of yours—J. Duguld Cameron—at Sault Ste. Marie. I opened it by accident, seeing the name Cameron : *I am in the fort of Rivière Qu'Appelle, dashing about with my sword and gold epaulettes, conducting and transacting your business.* Another red and gold coat not entitled to be worn, I suspect! *Sir William Shaw*—why Sir I do not know—*is collecting all the half-breeds from the surrounding departments and has ordered his friends in this quarter to prepare to take the field. . . . He has actually taken every half-breed in the country to the Forks of Fort des Prairies. . . . It is supposed when they are collected they will form more than one hundred."*

He opened another.

"This is to yourself from Cuthbert Grant," he explained. *"The half-breeds of Fort des Prairies, of English River, are all to be here in the spring. . . . It is to be hoped we shall come off with flying colours and never see any of them again in the colonising way in Red River. . . . In fact the traders shall pack off with themselves also for*

*having disregarded our orders last spring according to our agree-
ments. . . . We are all to remain at the Forks to pass the summer for
fear they should play us the same tricks as last summer of coming
back, but they shall receive a warm reception."*

" These are letters to me—or to someone else," protested Cameron,
" not letters from me. I do not expect even your Governor Semple
has evidence against me to warrant my arrest—an arrest he has no
authority to make at any rate. Might I ask how long you intend to
adopt this attitude? And how long have I to stay here in this fort you
call Fort Douglas?"

" Till the ice goes out and the rivers are open."

" Oh! Well, do your damndest!"

Colin Robertson looked directly into Cameron's eyes. I glanced at
Cameron but he lowered his eyelids and thus hid all evidence of how
he felt. Then he suddenly looked round, discovered he was being
watched and stared at me with annoyance.

" I trust," said he, addressing Colin again, " I am to be treated as
an officer and a gentleman and not submitted to insolence from the
common Jocks."

" Whether you are, or are not, entitled to be called Captain," replied
Colin Robertson, " we shall treat you as an officer of the North-West
Company and the centre of the conspiracy in the Indian Countries to
annihilate the Lord Selkirk colonists and injure the trade of the
Hudson's Bay Company. If you come with me now I shall show you
your quarters in person," and he gave a bow.

I felt a sense of amusement, and also of annoyance, and also a
touch of shame. I was amused at Cameron objecting to finding himself being scrutinised by one of the " menials," I was annoyed at being
referred to as though I were one of the " common Jocks," I was
ashamed at my snobbery. I wondered if I had dormant in me something of the arrogance of this man. But these emotions were trivial
compared with the effect upon me of the passages in these letters that
Colin Robertson had read to our prisoner. Truly there was a shadow
on Red River Settlement, I considered.

Because of my domestic anxiety at the time—my anxiety due to
Christina's condition—the shadow was magnified to my mind. I
considered that it was wrong for her to remain at the old cabin. I
must find quarters for her within the precincts of the fort itself.

Events of the following days confirmed that view. Some of the men who had been left at Fort Gibraltar, coming across on errands to Fort Douglas, reported horrible talk since the arrival of the mail-carriers there regarding what was being planned against both the Hudson's Bay Company and the Colony. After Robertson and Cameron left the North-Westers had seemed to think it essential to comfort themselves with liquor. There had been a night of bousing among them. The Hudson's Bay men who made these reports hid at first the fact that they had joined the drinkers, then considered that it was absurd to hide it. They might be guards at the fort but whisky and brandy and rum were whisky and brandy and rum, and were to be shared. Besides, most of the "menials," as Cameron would call these employees there, were under the impression that with his seizure guards and prisoners were as cronies.

During the next days more men in the North-West service came in from west. What they blabbed out in their cups was to the same tune as what the mail-carriers had divulged. Great days were coming, these new-comers told our men. It behoved them to quit their Company and join the rivals. The place was to be invaded as soon as the settlers came back from Pembina and the rivers were open. They would kill the men and have the pick of the women. A group of them began, it appears, with lecherous leers to discuss the appearance of this or that girl they had seen.

Sent over to Gibraltar with a note to the man left in charge there, I was gaily called into the midst of one of these orgies.

"There's a woman I've seen several times," said one. "Tall and little hips," and he made a motion in air with his hands.

"I know her," said another, watching these motions.

Apparently these sodden fellows could tell of whom they spoke by a mere wave of the hand and a look in the eye from one to another. But later they named some of the women they desired to cohabit with. At the mention of the wife of a Hudson's Bay employee several shouted approval.

"I'm going to have her!"

"I am!"

"No, I am!"

"Let's all have her!"

I looked from them to one of our men who had been left on guard.

Clearly he had been drinking too but he closed one eye privately to me.

Because of Christina's state my imagination was morbidly fired as I returned to Fort Douglas. I had horrible imaginings of abduction and rape. Arrived at the fort I realised I must show my dread on my face so I controlled myself and made my report with calm. When time came to return home I lingered till the others were gone, hoping the while that Colin Robertson would not suddenly rise and leave.

" Sir," I began when we were alone.

" Yes, Baxter?"

" There is a small cabin within the palisade, towards the north, that is empty and used for nothing so far. Might I be allowed to have the use of it temporarily?"

" What for?"

" For my wife, sir. She is with child and "—I hesitated—" I am anxious about her being alone."

" Baxter," said Robertson, " if you had been out and to and fro in this land as I have it would seem ludicrous to you to talk of a house within sight and gun-shot of a fort as a place where one could be alone!" Then he peered at me. " What do you fear?" he asked.

" An attack. These letters you intercepted——"

" Is that all?"

" No, sir. The talk of some of the men at Gibraltar when I was there to-day——"

" Were they drunk?"

" Yes," and I repeated to him that talk.

He whistled softly to himself a bar of *En roulant ma boule* and then——

" Very good," he said, " very good. Move in by all means, Baxter."

I returned home to Christina, still troubled. I could see anxiety on her face though she strove to hide it.

" Tell me of your day," she requested.

My day!

" Oh, nothing special," I replied. " But there is a small cabin within the palisade and I have been thinking it would be good to have you close there, close to the surgeon soon. It would be better to be in the fort."

She was radiant at the suggestion.

"A half-breed came——" she began, and hesitated.

"What?"

"A French half-breed, a *métis,* came by to-day. He was drunk and——"

"And what? Who was he? What did he say? Why didn't you tell me this immediately I came in?" I demanded.

"He was all right, David. He was drunk but he meant well. He saw me at the door and he said, '*Méfiez vous bien.*'"

Quickly I thought. She must not know the apprehension that I had known earlier as I walked back from Gibraltar. She must not in her condition be alarmed, thought I.

"It was probably only drunken nonsense," I said.

"I do not think so," she answered. "He seemed to be very seriously warning me of something but without telling what. I think he meant well. If he had not been drunk, indeed, he might not have called it to me. He did so twice, in a whispering voice."

"You do not know who he was?"

"I never saw him before to my knowledge. But this is a good thought of yours, David. I would like to be nearer you—in the fort."

And so it was done. The next day being Sunday I was free. By evening all our effects were moved to that small unused cabin within the palisade. The sun was setting as I put the stove-pipe in place. Before the evening's chill came on us the stove was giving its hum of occupancy and sanctuary.

CHAPTER TEN

I

ONE of the older men among the settlers, prone to oracular pronouncements and declamation, had delivered a private address to me after our marriage, telling me that now I was about to play my part seriously in the world. "You will not be alone and a free agent any longer," he had declared. "You will be truly part of the body politic and social, feel yourself a man taking his ordained part in the cosmic life."

On removal between the fort walls I recalled that statement. The older cabin was not many yards aside from the Settlement road, yet much more frequently than formerly was Christina visited in our new home by women—whose men had not gone to Pembina that year—coming to the Colony store. They came to see her, also, not only because she was a little way nearer to them in their transits but because of her interesting condition. She dismissed the grave prophesies of those who told her that agony was in store for her, but though they did not frighten her they troubled me. One had even gone so far as to inform her that though Indians seemed to bear their full-blood children with little difficulty, the native wives of white traders in the land had a very bad time: ". . . and you are part Indian, my dear," the caller ended.

In my life alone with Christina I was always happy. Court Nez was right when he said we had something in common; Madame Lagimoniere was right when she said we were made for each other. In the realm of our minds we were ecstatically happy. When thaws came in April and the melting snow on the roof decorated the eaves with icicles, neither of us could ever pass in or out without looking at them and noting the lights they held.

"They remind me," said Christina, "of a chandelier in the convent in Quebec."

When the river began to thaw and long fissures ran on the ice with a sound as of a cracked whip, we shared the same pleasure, hearing that sound. As April wore on we heard not only the drip of the icicles but the sudden crashing, splintering fall of them and rain drumming on the roof, with a shared ecstasy—an ecstasy hard to describe. It was not due to joy that spring was coming. The winter, cold though it had been, we had not found long, and had been happy in it. Together we were in touch with the elemental and eternal things, together were aware of the gleam of icicles, saw the flashing colour of a passing jay, the quaking of the curtain of the Aurora round the northern sky over Rupert's Land.

I told her of the wintry forests of the north, of mornings I had seen seeping over drifting lakes and hurrying rivers when voyaging inland from York Factory. And she was moved to tell me of her early days. I listened enthralled, picturing her life. What an infancy! She had drawn happiness out of it and retained it. Her father, it appeared, was always good to her—drunk or sober, always good to her. Her mother had loved her and her mother she had loved, still loved in memory.

"Am I tiring you, David?" she asked, pausing once in an account of her early life.

Tiring me! I was living it all with her. I was picturing my Christina as a small child with dark enjoying eyes. How I loved her! And ahead of her was the ordeal of childbirth.

There was slush in Red River. Its ice, southward, was melting more rapidly than there. Water flooded over the frozen surface. Then chunks of ice came thrusting down. These were piled up in places, thumping, sodden, against each other. Water was dammed up. Red River was abrim to its lower bank and the flood crept again up and up towards the higher, among the trees. Suddenly the ice blocks toppled and away they went swirling, colliding, thudding, crashing. Red River poured along in spate, in freshet.

The " trippers " came back to the Settlement.

II

A few days after the return of those who had been at Pembina during that winter, I had to go to the Colony store for information regarding a transaction between the Hudson's Bay Company and the Settlement. There I met Hugh Chisholm and was aware of a subtle change in his manner. Marriage had not made me feel myself as " a man taking his ordained part in the cosmic life," but Chisholm no longer treated me as an unattached male. His somewhat paternal or avuncular manner was gone.

" Yes, we are back again," he said, " and I hope this time to stay. I went out buffalo hunting, and Mairi came along too. She couldn't thole another winter in the cabins and huts by Fort Daer, going over for rations and nothing much else to do but visiting in the afternoons from house to house and drinking tea. She went out with some of the other women who felt as she, and did her share when the camp moved after the kill. We had some cold weather. I came on her once at the gralloching with an old half-breed woman. She was holding her hand into the body of the buffalo for warmth. Oh, I'll be glad when it's over—when there is no more need for tripping for any."

He had not been at Fort Daer when Pangman was arrested but he had been told of that and heard the reasons for it.

" What has been done with him?" he asked.

" He has been released," said I; " by Semple's letter, I gather, all that was wanted was to get him away from Pembina. Colin Robertson has let him go on having a promise from him that he will not return there."

" I hear the agent at Fort Gibraltar—Duncan Cameron—is practically a prisoner here. Is he to be released too?"

" No. He was practically under arrest before, under guard at his own fort, but now he is going to be sent off for trial. Mr. Robertson has a lot of evidence to show that he has again been conspiring against the Colony. I wish we were rid of him. Soon we shall be. But I believe if Governor Semple had been here, and had given the order to make arrest by word of mouth, Colin Robertson would have counselled patience, advised a little delay so that Cameron could be removed from the district immediately after arrest. How is Agnes?" I asked, changing the subject.

" Agnes? Oh, Agnes is fine. She's the happy-go-lucky one. You can always tell where she is by her laughter. *She* "—I realised that *She* meant Mrs. Chisholm, not his younger daughter, by the way the word was uttered—" is getting tired of the tripping too. I don't blame her. Now and then I still blame myself for coming to the Colony. Man, man, I hope this year we have a grand crop and no new troubles and can settle down happy and finally. Come and see us, you and your

R

bonny wife. *She* often speaks of her and so does Mairi. Mairi took a
great fancy to her."

"Thank you indeed. She will not be going anywhere just at present,
but——" I began.

"Is that so? Man, man, an addition! A new-comer expected. That
will make a full man of you, David, make you see life as real."

That remark reminded me of the private address delivered to me
just after my marriage by the oracular elderly settler. I was then
twenty-six but still—so greatly had the dictatorship of my brother at
home affected me—I felt that I was, as it were, on a truancy. I was
enjoying the life I lived as an escape from my former life. I was
married, to be sure; my wife was heavy with child; but I could not,
remembering Mr. Chisholm's words, see life as "real." There was
an impression as of playing a part. There was an impression with
most of those of my age of having escaped from dull serfdom. The
life by Red River being so different from the life we had all led at
home that was, perhaps, inevitable.

III

With Captain Semple's return to Fort Douglas the very atmosphere
there seemed to suffer change. Colin Roberston ruled differently,
demanding attention and promptitude, but there was nothing of the
martinet in his manner. He was nearer to the voyageurs or *coureurs
des bois* than was Semple who, like Miles Macdonell, I must admit,
had been affected by idea of discipline and deportment inculcated in
the army. Semple, in the middle of talking to one of his staff, would
suddenly stare and interject with a rasp, "Stand up, man! Stand
up! You are slouching!" Even Robertson, when the Governor was
present, was more smart and soldierly than at other times, but often
with a twinkle in his eyes. At such moments he seemed also to feel as
one playing a part.

Semple, examining the account books and letter-files after a tour
of inspection of the fort, clipped a few words of approval of the conduct of the place during his absence at Pembina and Colin bowed his
thanks.

"What do you propose, sir," he inquired, "to do with our friend
Cameron? I'll be glad to see him go."

"Send him off to England now," said Semple. "The Hayes River will be open. Off with him at once. That man John McLeod had better have charge of him at least to Jack River, get him so far on the way from here. You will follow, but for the present you must remain here. I have to visit some more of the Company's posts. I shall be gone a month or so."

Colin Robertson went away and Semple continued with his frowning examination of a resume of accounts that had been prepared for his scrutiny by myself and Mr. Archibald, and was so employed when Colin came back. Robertson seemed even larger than usual. There was something almost whimsical in his gait. He caught my eye and looked with mock severity at me. Apparently he was in merry mood.

"Well?" snapped Semple, looking up and seeing him standing there.

"Our prisoner wishes to have the honour of a word with you before he goes."

"Why, Robertson, here is celerity!" ejaculated Semple. "You have all ready?"

"Already all ready," replied Colin. "Mr. McLeod is packing for himself and Cameron's servant is packing for his lordship."

"His lordship—oh, I see, you mean Cameron. And he wants a word with me, eh? All right."

Robertson went off and soon came back, opening the door with a wide sweep. If Cameron saw mockery in his manner he did not reveal annoyance with him but he looked sullenly at me sitting at my table there. He had once before objected to talk in that room before "menials." Even at Archibald he stared sullenly. Archibald Mac-Donald was an officer, to be sure, not a "menial," had been Sheriff for some time and in sole charge, but he was young and looked young. His presence as well as mine clearly irritated Cameron.

Glancing up at him I asked myself why I should be indignant at Cameron's grandeur. When I had heard—long ago it seemed because of all the changes—of Miles Macdonell, on his way to Montreal as a prisoner, dismissing for insolent behaviour the servant provided for him by the North-Westers, I had felt only admiration for him. I had not regarded the incident as illustrative of any arrogance. That Cameron, who had taken Captain Macdonell prisoner, was now to be taken away himself as a prisoner gave me great pleasure; but should I not, I considered, esteem him for his bearing as of one un-subdued?

Cameron stepped ponderously to the table at which the Governor sat, looking this way and that as though expecting a chair to be offered him. The nearest vacant one was at the other end of the room. Close by was a stool. He lifted it and with a swing of his arms set it down near Semple, and seated himself, humped forward. Colin Robertson smiled down at him, but with a tinge of admiration.

"Look ye here," said Cameron to Semple, "at your orders I was seized at Fort Gibraltar and brought here under threat."

"Threat?" inquired Semple.

"Threat! Fixed bayonets are threats, are they not? I was brought here and held here. Even before then I was virtually a prisoner in my own fort, under surveillance, with men posted there by your lieutenant here, "and he wagged his head sidewise towards Robertson. "I am in the position of a man under arrest and yet no warrant of any sort has been served upon me."

"If you care to remain a little longer I have no doubt I can produce a warrant," said Semple.

"Absurd! Ridiculous!" scoffed Cameron. "You will find out in Montreal what authority a governor of the Hudson's Bay Company has for such high-handed measures."

"You are not going to Montreal," said Semple. "You are going to England."

"The devil I am! Have you never heard of the Canada Act?"

"I have. And it does not apply in your case."

"Does not apply?"

"No. It does not apply in murder cases. Murder charges in Rupert's Land, even by the Canada Act, may be tried in England."

Cameron's eyes blazed.

"Murder!" he shouted. "There is no suggestion of murder. Your lieutenant's explanation for my detention was merely that he had heard rumours that half-breeds—half-breeds, sir—on the prairies were planning an attack on the settlers, and that I had some part in it."

"The letters he discovered bore all that out," agreed Semple.

"You gave your orders before these letters were what you call discovered and what I call intercepted," answered Cameron. "That is another charge against your gang. And now you talk of murder!"

"I am talking of the slaying of John Warren, to which you were accessory. Several others, too, were wounded: attempted murder. No, Mr. Cameron, we are taking you to England. Lord Selkirk has had legal advice regarding justiciary rights and it appears that in a case of murder any citizen, even with or without warrant, is entitled —nay, more, it is his duty—to apprehend a murderer or those involved in murder. And murder cases, I repeat, do not come under the Canada Act."

"You might even be able," said Cameron, "to get perjurers to affirm that I shot this Mr. Warren myself."

Semple cleared his throat with three short rasps. He looked up at Colin Robertson, very much the Governor.

"Take him away," he said. "Mr. McLeod is competent to deal with him."

"You are not sending me with that man McLeod?" demanded Cameron.

"Mr. McLeod will get you to Jack River. That will be a change for you. It will be better for you to wait there briefly instead of here. Mr. Robertson will follow soon and accompany you to England, where you will be tried."

Semple returned his attention to the papers on his table and Colin laid a hand on the prisoner's shoulder—not perhaps an entirely arresting hand it seemed to me.

"Mr. McLeod is not a vindictive man," he said in a soothing tone. "He is an honourable man. He has been used roughly by your Company on occasion, has had various experiences at the hands of your colleagues that might make you expect revenge from him, but he will look after you suitably, I feel sure."

Cameron rose, ignored then by the Governor who was still intent on his papers. The incident was finished. Colin Robertson opened the door and the North-Wester preceded him. The door closed softly. Captain Semple sat still, bent to his desk, but under his brows he gazed at that closed door, cogitating.

"Baxter," said he, "I do not know how it is achieved but I have noted it before this: News travels quickly in this country. The people at Gibraltar will, for a certainty, hear that Cameron is going. If there is delay in his departure they may make some sort of hostile demonstration. Do you now go and get some of the labourers about the place prepared to stand by when he is being taken to the boat. Explain to Mr. Robertson and Mr. McLeod, if you see them, what they are there for."

With alacrity I rose.

"A minute!" Semple halted me. "No arms. No show of arms. We can play the game that Cameron on occasion chose to play. There may be a scrimmage but I want no shooting. Numbers will suffice. Yes, tell Mr. Robertson what you are about if you see him."

"Yes, sir."

IV

McLeod had a good deal to attend to in the trade house before he was ready. It was with no slighting intention that Cameron was kept waiting after his packing was finished.

The passage of news over the mere mile between Fort Gibraltar and Fort Douglas, thought I, was not so hard to understand as these other passages that had been, no doubt, in Semple's mind, swift passages over hundreds of miles of prairie and wilderness. Indians, half-breeds, free-traders were all the time coming and going by the riverside, stopping at camps and cabins adjacent to " the forks " to whiff a pipe and gossip; and further, some of us had the opinion that the Colony was systematically spied upon by servants of the North-West Company.

By the time that all was ready for the departure of Duncan Cameron and John McLeod there were many expectant people in the vicinity, not only Hudson's Bay employees and settlers but free-traders also, as well as men from the North-West fort and, of course, a few Indians as if conjured out of the spaces of the prairie. Down the steep bank, in the course of many loadings and unloadings, an incline had been gouged. On either side of that ramp people were clustered. Seeing some of the rival labourers coming closer I signed to the men I had gathered together and they moved lower down, near the river's edge. Two of the large canoes with loads already in them were buoyantly waiting there, and a boat was moored near them with mast stepped.

I had found an opportunity to intrude on John McLeod during his final conference in Indian Hall, to murmur to him that the Governor had arranged for a number of men to be at hand in case of a demonstration by the North-Westers.

"Eh? Oh, yes, quite—quite," he had responded, as though little interested.

Colin Robertson I had not seen but it struck me that he would have the same thought as Semple, and had prepared for the contingency for I saw then, atop the bank, approaching in groups of twos and threes, some of the voyageurs who had come with him from Terrebonne, men who looked as though related to pine-knots. They glanced down knowingly at their comrades who waited in the canoes and in the boat, and as more people began to come from the direction of Gibraltar they had a light of battle in their eyes—perhaps even of hope of battle, thought I.

Out from the fort behind them appeared Robertson and Cameron. In a penetrating voice as they drew near Cameron spoke.

"An expensive business this is going to be to your earl!" he said.

"The earl has had much expense already," replied Robertson, "enough to stop the mouths of those who say he is but a company promoter, an exploiter. A pretty penny your Company has cost him so far."

Down the ramp they went without any sort of demonstration, though eagerly observed. So loudly had Cameron spoken that what he said could be heard by all, as no doubt he intended. He would have it known that he did not go away tamely. Colin's reply was not pitched so oratorically and there was an inquiring murmur among those crowding there of "What did he say? What did he say?" and the quick repetition by those who had heard.

"The cases mount up," said Cameron as he stepped into the boat. "From the day your Miles Macdonell, who was called a governor, made his order regarding the pemican, forbidding its export, they have mounted up. We shall wreck your earl in the courts, whether of England or of the Canadas, and your Colonists here."

"Another threat?" asked Robertson so calmly that—

"What did he say?" the people inquired. "What did he say?"

As he spoke Colin noticed that one of the labourers had brought some things down in an old pemican-sack and emptied them into a canoe.

"Let me have that sack," said he.

When it was handed to him he bent it as if it were a flag to the halliard and hoisted it to the boat's masthead. There was a chuckle from some of the Hudson's Bay Company's men standing by and a rumbling of rage from the North-West labourers who had gathered there. A pemican-sack for flag on the boat was to take Cameron away they saw as insult and taunt. One of these hissed.

Colin Robertson raised his head, looked up the slope, walked back slowly.

"Who made that sound?" he demanded.

They gloomed at him heavily, exchanged quick glances one with another.

"Nobody, eh? I must have imagined it, eh?"

John McLeod was approaching. He laid a hand on my shoulder in passing.

"Good-bye, lad," he said, thrusting me aside. He turned to Robertson. "Good-bye, Colin."

"Good-bye, John."

McLeod went down the slope, sat in the boat.

"All right. Cast off," he ordered.

The men rose at their sweeps, stepped, sank back, stepped and sank back again. The current and the powerful pull took the boat swiftly away. The pemican-sack, heavier than a flag, unwieldy for a flag, swung at the masthead. McLeod's glance was caught, stayed, by it. He studied it, frowning. It puzzled him. Then a slow smile of understanding spread on his face and looking up the bank he caught the culprit's eye and knew him for the culprit by his beam of pleasure that the standard had been noted.

The boatmen began to sing:

> *Rouli, roulant, ma boule roulant,*
> *En roulant ma boule roulant,*
> *En roulant ma boule.*

The paddles of the canoes dug in.

I passed up to the prairie level with a light tread. There went Duncan Cameron who had taken away Miles Macdonell, taken away himself now! I had to tell Christina before returning to work. She heard my step at the door with joy.

"Cameron is off," I told her. "He is off!"

"Already?"

"Yes. John McLeod has him in charge. He is off to Jack River and thence to Hudson Bay and England on the charge of complicity and instigation in the murder of Mr. Warren. I feel it mere justice that he who took Miles Macdonell off should go now himself."

"I am glad to see you, David," she said. "I was asleep and had a dream. I was in Montreal, on my way back here from Quebec—all the noise of the traffic round me. So many houses, so many people! And I thought I would never get back to Red River. I wanted to be here in time to hear the song of the cat-birds after their long flight, and to see the orioles. Then I woke and thought at first it was morning and looked for you and you were not here. Oh, David, we shall always have each other, won't we?"

I stooped and kissed her.

"Always," I assured her. "But I must get back. I just had to come and tell you the tables are turned on Mr. Duncan Cameron."

I hurried to the accounting-room. As I entered Captain Semple looked up.

"Where have you been?" he rasped.

"Down at the river, sir, to help to make a showing of our people there if there was any trouble."

"Quite. But the others, I observe, have been back some time. Mr. Robertson came in to see me, and Sheriff Archibald, both back from seeing that man away. Where have you been since the boat left?"

"I went to see my wife, sir."

"To see your wife! You may not run off to see your wife during hours of duty here," said Semple. "Do not let it happen again."

"My wife is—— " I began on the point of telling of her condition, and then I considered that it was not because of her state, not because of any anxiety I had felt regarding her in that state, that I had gone to see her, but just to share with her my joy in the turning of the tables, in Duncan Cameron being haled away as once he had haled Miles Macdonell away.

"Very good, sir," I answered, and sat down.

Well, Duncan Cameron was off, down the river. The *Rouli, roulant, ma boule roulant* of his departure remained merrily in my ears.

CHAPTER ELEVEN

I

CAPTAIN SEMPLE, setting out again on a spring tour of inspection to the new outlying posts of the Company, left a final order with Colin Robertson.

"While I am away," said he, "I wish you to have Fort Gibraltar dismantled. Have it pulled down and float the logs here to strengthen our Fort Douglas."

"We may need that," remarked Robertson.

To my ears the words hinted expectation of further trouble as a result of such action.

"It really should have been done long ago," said Semple. "I understand that Captain Macdonell gave an order to the chiefs of both Gibraltar and Qu'Appelle—both within the territory of Assiniboia conveyed to Lord Selkirk—to dismantle and evacuate. He gave the order and did not enforce it. Evidence of weakness again."

"Not exactly, sir," objected Colin Robertson. "It was only to comply with a legal requirement. Long duration of occupancy without protest might give them a prescriptive right, according to the earl's lawyers in England."

Semple blew through his nostrils, snorted.

"Well," said he, "the place should be dismantled now. Recent events demand it."

"Very good, sir," said Colin Robertson.

By the time Captain Semple returned from his tour of inspection Fort Gibraltar no longer existed. He came back with many a memorandum of more than rivalry between the Companies, of conflict, bitter conflict. It galled the North-Westers that the Hudson's Bay Company, which once had been satisfied to have its factors sitting on the shore of "the Bay," and Indians going thither to trade, was sending its officers out into remote parts of Rupert's Land and even into the Athabasca country beyond. He came back with some grim stories of outlying posts attacked and furs appropriated, of seizures and

266

counter-seizures, of brigades on their inland voyages on the waterways waylaid, of bloodshed.

He settled down at once to the writing and dictation of reports that would go to the Company's headquarters in London. Colin Robertson would carry these, setting off to catch the ships that came to Hudson Bay that year before they weighed anchor for their return voyage.

"You have done well in my absence," said Semple. "I knew you would have that place down, but I had not expected such celerity in the use of the logs here. I like the watch-tower you have built."

"It may be required," Robertson prophesied.

Semple had no reply to that, unless a blank stare be considered a reply.

"Well," said Robertson, "now that you are here I must be off. I have said my adieux to my various friends. I dropped in on your wife just now, Baxter, to give her farewell. Madame Lagimoniere was there with her youngest, the little Cypress. I am a trifle anxious about Lagimoniere, but would not tell her that. She is trying, I could see, to keep herself from worrying. I had expected him back long ere this. He left here on *la Toussaint,* the first of November. I know a winter journey to Montreal is an undertaking, but this is June—June!—and no word of him, no rumour even coming in among the Indians that he has been seen on his way. I told Madame that I have no doubt he got through safely and that the earl prevailed on him to wait till the rivers open for his return. I suggested he may be travelling with the earl, perhaps captaining a brigade of canoes for him. I said to her that I expect this, that I expect that; but I only hope all is well with him."

We were silent, with the silence that falls between men just before a parting.

"Well," said Semple at last, "you wish to be going. I have to thank you, Mr. Robertson, for all you have so ably performed."

Colin Robertson bowed.

"I am now dismissed," said he.

"Oh, don't say *dismissed*—freed, rather, from your onerous duties here. I am taking great pleasure in stating in my reports how excellently you have performed your duties."

Robertson bowed again.

"Now that I am going may I offer you advice?" he said. "I have not offered any so far. I do so now only because of the knowledge of the calibre of some of the men not far distant, as distance is accounted in this big land. Cameron has been always—or almost always —safe. He erred when he made a personal appearance on the day the Governor's old house was attacked. But he has played safe as a rule from a lawyer's view-point. I doubt if we have. For example, the razing of Fort Gibraltar may raise the devil!" and he laughed lightly over the play on words.

"After all," said Semple, "they had orders from Macdonell to evacuate."

"I know. True. But as I told you, and as they knew as well as we, that was only to comply with a legal technicality. However, the thing is done now—and there is a cousin of Miles Macdonell's out on the plains who has all the military fire of the family. Just as the former Governor had to think of the women and children, so have we— or I should say you, sir. I don't like finesse myself. I like the downright. When men are alone, give me the downright, straight from the shoulder every time. But these North-Westers cling to the notion that they are as a continuation of the old French pedlars."

"That is absurd!" exclaimed Semple. "Quebec fell long ago."

"I know. Still, they have that attitude and though they may be wrong they have it deeply ingrained. They are not fearful people, Captain Semple. They would not be in this land if they were. And to get back to the point I was headed for: Even though we may be sure that by the old charter we have supremacy here we should remember the law courts—and by the law courts I mean the law courts of the Canadas, especially the Montreal courts where we should have less justice than in Quebec, or York, or Sandwich. That is the North-West Company's centre: they have a big pull there. Well, that is all—a counsel of diplomacy, perhaps it might be called."

"Thank you, thank you, Mr. Robertson," said Semple. "I assure you I shall precipitate nothing. If we have further trouble, and you hear of it, you may rest content I have not precipitated it. I realise as well as Captain Macdonell that there are the colonists—the women and children—to remember. I realise that I have to protect them." He put his head back and half-closing his eyes laughed. "But I must say," he added, "that there is a certain humour in advice of propitiation to the enemy from you. I heard of the pemican-sack at the masthead of the boat in which Duncan Cameron was taken away. It had its subtlety, perhaps, to some minds but it was surely blunt and clear as a thumb at the nose to the North-Westers looking on— and to Cameron. There was also that hardly propitiatory interception of their mails by you!"

"Oh, well," said Robertson, and as both laughed together I considered that I had never seen them, so far, so little as senior and junior officers, so much as simply man to man.

Colin Robertson turned to me, holding out a hand and as I rose to bid him good-bye said he : "You have helped me greatly with the clerical work. It does not come naturally to me. I do not easily adapt myself to sitting at a table immersed in accounts."

While he was speaking, Captain Semple and the young Sheriff preceded him out of the room, both going to the river to see him off. Colin delayed, listening to their steps passing slowly downstairs. Then, with a chuckle, he bent closer to me. An incident that had befallen some time back had evidently stuck in his mind.

"'A minute, young man!'" he began, imitating Captain Semple's manner, and he quoted a speech that the Governor of Rupert's Land had made to me, as closely as his memory retained it: "'Your action savours of insubordination and insolence. But I will say this for you— and for the Governor you defend: It is possible that within his capacity he did his best. He was loyal to Lord Selkirk, and you, young man, within your capacity, are loyal to Miles Macdonell.'" He delivered a friendly punch on my chest. "Good-bye, lad, good-bye," said he and, still chuckling, wheeled away after Captain Semple and Mr. Archibald.

11

Early in the morning of 19th June, Christina wakened me with a moaning that she could not suppress. She was in agony.

"It cannot be," she said, "it cannot be so soon. It should not be till two more months."

Her appearance alarmed me. Hastily I dressed. Madame Lagimoniere had told me that I was to send for her when Christina's time came, whatever the hour. Perhaps the recent apprehensions of renewed attack on the Colony had had a hastening effect. I must get help for her, but on whom should I call first—Madame Lagimoniere or Surgeon White?

She drew a trembling breath and attempted a smile of reassurance to me. Suddenly there was a great singing of birds in the night. Every year it was so; the cat-birds seemed to fly all night in their migration and on their arrival did not emit the small mewing cries from which they had their name but announced their advent with roulades of song, somewhat like those of Old Country nightingales. Though still pinched from her bout of pain Christina, at that sound, looked into my eyes.

"Listen!" she said. "They have come. Do you remember the dream I had of being far away, how I was afraid that I would not get back to hear the cat-birds singing, and——" Pain clutched her again.

"I am going for Madame Lagimoniere," I said, and glad I was that arrangements had been made for her to come and live near, in the fort, during her husband's absence.

I was taken out of my own life for a moment by the reception I received from her, had it impressed on me that others had their anxieties. In response to my knock she called out to know who it was, and when I answered there was a drop in her voice, a note of disappointment as she replied, bidding me wait a few moments.

"So early you come," she said, on opening to me, "I wondered who it might be, thought perhaps Jean Baptiste had just arrived."

Having informed her of Christina's pain I hurried back again. The cat-birds continued to sing their ecstatic song. Dawn blazed up in the east. An immensity of space and light was round me. I had been told, I recalled, that marriage would make me part of the body politic and social—or something of that sort—and Mr. Chisholm had remarked that fatherhood would make a full man of me, cause me to see life as real. I felt, instead, very much an ignorant atom of humanity in the midst of mystery in which I had dabbled.

As I passed the Governor's quarters I saw three Indians, after some talk with the sentry on duty, come riding in. They were not local Saulteaux by the look of them. One dismounted and leading his horse by the lines walked towards Semple's house. Arrived there he did not knock. He tried to peer in at a window, shielding his eyes with a hand. It came naturally, spontaneously, to me to do always what I could for these people. I halted.

"You want somebody?" I asked.

From under his tunic he produced a letter, but when I held out a hand to take it, it was at once drawn back.

"Court Nez sent this for big chief here," he said.

The door was opened by Semple's servant, a tall raw-boned Highlander who had obviously just risen.

"What iss all thiss?" he demanded.

"He has a letter for Captain Semple," I explained.

The Highlander held out a hand for it.

"No!" said the Indian, and with a quick intoed stride he shoved passed the servant and padded into the house.

The Highlander tried to grab him.

"Be careful," I warned. "It's all right, Angus. That's not the way to do with them."

But Madame Lagimoniere had followed me and together we went on to my cabin. She had a matter-of-fact manner, buoyant, reassuring. Childbirth to her was, apparently, a trifling affair. It was too early yet to call the surgeon, she said, and set about preparing breakfast. But I had no appetite. How could I eat while Christina lay there in agony? I took what comfort I could in the fact she did not moan again. I went into the bedroom, sat down by the bed, took her hand, and our fingers linked. I sat there a long while, utterly glad that she had freedom again from pain, fervently hoping that she would not have another spasm such as she had already suffered.

"I think you ought to go," she said at last. "It must be time for you to go."

There was a step at the door and Madame entered.

"Yes," she said, "I think you had better go. The Governor is already stirring—out and about."

I stooped and kissed Christina, feeling then a sense of self-reproach. When I went out into the square I saw the three horses of the Indians who had come to see the "big chief" with a letter from Court Nez. I had been by Red River long enough to observe horses, recognise them, remember them with no conscious effort. A buckskin with a white forehead and a white sock on its near foreleg; a piebald; one the colour of smoke; yes, these were the horses, munching hay that had been thrown down for them beside the cook-house. And as I passed its door I had a glimpse of the Indians within, sitting at a table eating. I stopped to speak to the one who had carried the letter.

"How is Court Nez?" I asked.

"He good."

"Where is he?"

He made a very Indian gesture, curving his hand in air, pointing to west. By his manner, a dismissing manner, he found me plaguy. He wanted to eat, not to talk.

"Did he send a letter to his daughter, his girl, to Christina?" I asked.

"No. Just letter for big chief."

"I ask because I marry Christina. Christina is my woman."

He did not consider any comment was necessary in reply to that explanation for my inquiry. His eyes dismissed me. By their blankness it was as though he no longer saw me. I went on then to the administrative building.

Captain Semple was already seated at his desk.

"Good-morning, Baxter," he said, and then: "You have a troubled look. Have you some anxiety?"

"My wife, sir. I was wakened by her in the night—or early morning."

"Oh, let me see—yes, she is a half-breed, I believe. Had she news?"

"News? No, sir. She is about to have a child."

"Oh! Oh, indeed. Congratulations. I hope it will come off easily. Tell me, you have been here some years: Do you know anything of a man "—he tapped a letter which lay on his desk—"I presume a French free-trader by the name—called Court Nez."

"He is my father-in-law, sir."

"He is! Then you can tell me about him. I had a note from him this morning, brought by some Assiniboine Indians. He warns me that yet again the North-West influence is being used on the half-breeds of Qu'Appelle to rouse them against the Colony, soon. I can rely on your father-in-law, can I, not being one who merely wishes to intimidate us?"

"I should say yes, unquestionably, sir. From what I know of him he would not send a message unless—unless "—I hesitated for expression—" unless he felt the need to warn imperative."

"Well, I saw Peguis yesterday and he had the same story to tell me. It is hard to believe an attack would be launched against us now. Yet it might be that the North-Westers are moved to fresh hostility because they have heard Lord Selkirk is on his way here, and hope to wreck the Colony before he comes. My desire for peace will not prevent them from making war. An urgent warning from this man Court Nez that I should promptly be prepared for attack by the half-breeds of the west, and that warning from Peguis: these, I take it, are to be heeded. Peguis has nothing of the scaremonger in him, nor of timidity."

"And neither, I can assure you, has Court Nez," said I.

III

I had never known time to pass so slowly. I sought to comfort myself with the knowledge that Madame Lagimoniere was with Christina and that the surgeon was within speedy call. But I was not successful. I imagined something happening at the Lagimoniere cabin that would bring an urgent summons for Madame to return to her children, and Christina left alone. The thought was torture to me.

At last noon came and I hurried home. I found the surgeon in charge and Christina easier. Also Mrs. Chisholm was there. I had a sense of the heavenly hosts with us then! Mrs. Chisholm and Mairi, it was explained to me, had come that morning to the Colony store and, being near, had looked in on Christina. The surgeon was already there, relieving Madame Lagimoniere so that she could attend to her family, and to relieve him Mrs. Chisholm had stayed while Mairi went back to the farm. Everything was all right. There was no need to worry.

"How long does the labour last?" I asked.

"It varies," said Mrs. Chisholm. "It shouldna be long with her, though, she being part Indian."

I frowned, recalling the statement made by one of Christina's visitors some time ago, that though Indians seem to bear their own

S

full-blood children with little difficulty, the native wives of white traders in the land had a very bad time.

"What's bothering you now?" inquired Mrs. Chisholm, obviously because of my expression. When I told her she snorted away the view as a superstition. "Nonsense! Folk talk nonsense," she declared. "I'd as soon believe you can cure warts by putting a dish-clout under the bed!"

At that moment Surgeon White came from the bedroom.

"If you go in to your wife with that look on your face," he said, "you will frighten the girl. All this has happened before, you know. It has happened frequently in the course of history."

"All what, Mr. White?"

"Childbirth," said he, and slapped me heartily on the back.

"But this is two months earlier than we expected," I said.

"Well, there is nothing unusual even in that."

I laughed and felt as if divided in twain, the one half of me able to be amused, the other half of me sick with suspense. Mr. White smiled comfortingly on me.

"I'm just going over for some dinner," he said.

"There's plenty for you here," I assured him.

"No, no, I'll be back later. I'll not be far away. I can do nothing yet. Don't worry. I'll be back anon."

I left the meal that Mrs. Chisholm had prepared for me and went in to see Christina.

"Have you had your dinner?" she asked.

"Yes."

"Madame Lagimoniere is coming over again this afternoon," she said, "and thinking of her I have been wondering what to call our baby. Hers are la Reine and Prairie and Cypress—the first girl born on the King's birthday, the boy far out on the prairie, and the second girl in the Cypress Hills."

"If it's a girl we'll call her Christina," I said.

"And if it's a boy we'll call him David," said she. "Well, that's soon settled."

I kissed her and went quietly away.

There was no censure that day from Captain Semple for being a little late. As I entered he looked up.

"Boy or girl?" he asked, and then, "Oh, not arrived yet by the look of you, young man."

"No, sir."

A sound behind made us both turn sharply. There in the doorway stood an Indian youth. He was in white man's clothes, his hair cropped short.

"See to him—what he wants," said Semple.

"I want to speak to you, Governor Semple," said the young man in such perfect and easy speech that Semple opened his eyes wide. "I have come from Qu'Appelle. I was at Brandon House for a time. The Hudson's Bay people are my friends."

"Who are you?"

"Mistouche is my name."

"Who sent you here?"

"Nobody. I came myself. I have run all the way."

"That must be about a hundred and fifty miles!"

"Yes, it is. I ran because I had to get here quickly to warn you. Tête Jaune—Alexander Macdonell—is trying again to get the Cree Indians, my people, to come down here and kill the Colony settlers. My people will not come, but he has got some half-breeds not only from la Souris and Qu'Appelle but from the Fort de la Prairie. They are coming. I have run to let you know."

"Well, I thank you," said Semple. "I certainly have to thank you. What can I do to show my gratitude?"

"I do not want anything. I have told you. That is all." He turned away without a word and then at the door evidently remembered the white man's usage. "Good-bye to you, sir," he said, and passed quietly out.

Semple stared after him.

"Well, I'll be damned!" he said. "Back in New York State I have heard an Indian talk English as fluently but I did not expect to hear such fluency up here, nor have I encountered it so far. Mistouche—Mistouche: I must remember his name. Three warnings within twenty-four hours must mean something, Baxter. Do you serve a spy-glass to the look-out in the watch-tower, if there is such a thing procurable."

"There is, sir. Yes, there is."

"Well, pray serve one to the sentry in the watch-tower and tell them to double the guard at the gate. There is no need to create apprehension, but tell them to watch carefully. If any men arrive in numbers have the gate closed till their intentions are known. And the watch in the tower must be watchful."

"Very good, sir."

I had just returned from the watch-tower, sick at heart over these new threats because of Christina, when Lieutenant Holte entered, but to him Semple said nothing of these warnings, merely discussed the matter that had brought him there—which had to do with schooner transport on Lake Winnipic during the coming summer.

The afternoon drifted on, slowly for me. Surely, thought I, if Christina had been delivered of a child someone would come to tell me, despite the name Semple had for strict attention to business in business hours. Madame Lagimoniere, I believed, would dare to. The fact, thought I, that her husband had gone alone to make the winter transit to Montreal with a message to Lord Selkirk, and had not been heard of since, ought surely to give her licence for that! But no one came. I made exit, ostensibly to the latrine, intending to run across to our cabin but seeing, as I glanced up at the office window, that Semple had risen and was looking out, I did not. I returned to my table and considered the Governor's stiff, stout back at the open window.

Should I boldly step up to him and ask leave for a few minutes to visit my wife? He had been very gracious, very human, on hearing of Christina's state. Patience, patience! The afternoon wore on. It would pass; the sun was well down the western curve of that immense blue dome that arched over the Indian Countries.

Suddenly Semple, who had risen again to look out of the window, palms on sill, bent forward in an attitude of alert scrutiny. I heard running feet below and from outside the Sheriff's voice came up.

"Would you come to the watch-tower yourself, sir. The guard has just reported a body of men—they seem to be Indians—as if riding down to the farms."

"Indians!" exclaimed Semple. "To the farms! Not coming here?"

He went out, not flustered by any sign, not running, but with shoulders braced.

Many of the settlers who had arrived only the year before, with him, and been housed and victualled at Pembina during the winter, had not completed the erection of their homes and instead of sleeping in shelters beside their fields came nightly to the fort where various buildings had been arranged as hostels for them. But night was far off yet. They would not have so much as started on their way to the fort. If an attack was imminent they must be summoned at once. And most of the earlier arrivals (such as the Chisholms), whose houses had been destroyed after the eviction of the previous year, had preferred, while rebuilding, or completing the building that had started before going to Pembina, to sleep at their allotments in shelters constructed after the fashion of wigwams. All must be warned, I realised. All must be called to the safety of the fort, if here was not a false alarm.

When Semple had gone I ran to the window. I looked over the roofs of the buildings to the watch-tower.

"That's Mr. Pritchard, I think, coming down the ladder," I spoke to myself. "Now's my chance," thought I, "to run over and see how Christina is doing."

As I ran on my way I saw the young Sheriff and Captain Semple marching on in step across the square. Mr. Pritchard halted and awaited their coming. I ran at a tangent to our cabin, past the cook-house. I noticed there, sitting just outside, the Assiniboines that Court Nez had sent with his message. They were evidently resting, spending the day at Fort Douglas close to the kitchen. As I passed one of them looked up and spoke to me the word "scoutaywaubo." They had received grand meals in return for their ride but before they left they hoped for some firewater. I paid no heed, ran on.

As I reached the cabin the door opened and Madame Lagimoniere came out. Having come out she closed the door behind her and spread her arms on either side.

"A girl," said she. "A healthy, sound little girl, though she is a seven months child."

"A girl." My voice choked. "She is delivered, then. Had she long to wait after I went?"

"Not long."

"Let me in to her, please."

"No." Madame Lagimoniere spread her arms again. "Surgeon White is with her now."

"Is there something wrong?"

"Nothing," she replied. "He saw you coming from the window and told me to keep you out."

"But I must see her—I must see her. Just a look—just——"

"David Baxter," said Madame Lagimoniere firmly, "control yourself. Think of all the troubles of others. If you went in you would but worry her just now. Be brave!"

Looking at her then I thought she was bravery personified. Two of her children had been born in wild places with no help from any surgeon. Yes, she was a brave woman.

"A healthy, sound little girl," she repeated.

"Thank God for that. But promise if she asks for me you will——"

"Yes, yes, if she does that I have no doubt Mr. White will let you see her."

I heard Semple call me and call again, loudly. Turning, I ran back. There was the Governor hurrying across from the watch-tower, not looking my way but up at the office windows. At sight of me coming from another direction he glared and when I drew level demanded: "Where were you?"

"I took the opportunity, sir, to run across and see how my wife fared."

"Could you not have asked me for leave when I was in the room? I know," he ran his words together in his haste to have that over, "how-a-young-lad-must-feel with his first experience. Is she delivered?"

"Yes, sir, a fine, healthy, sound little girl, although premature, a seven months' child—perhaps because of all the apprehension she has had and kept much to herself."

He looked at me sharply, piercingly.

"Oh, well," he said, "that is that. And now, Baxter, I rely on you. Mr. McLeod sang your praises to me, Mr. Robertson has spoken well of you. I rely on you. Do you go now, at once, down through the Colony and warn all to come immediately to the fort. If they argue or offer objection say it is my orders: all to the fort. Bid them when possible to come as far as they may by the trails of the river side and avoid the road, for these men out there going towards the allotments are all armed, we can see. You must take the road going out, I fear, for the sake of speed. It depends on what befalls how you return."

"Yes, sir," said I, and at once broke into a run towards the gate.

"Take horse, man!" shouted Semple. "Take horse! You are not an Indian runner. You cannot keep that gait up for long. Take horse!"

I halted, perplexed. A horse would have to be caught from among those grazing on the plain.

"Any horse!" said Semple, exasperated. "That horse, for example," and he pointed at the piebald horse of one of the Indians who sat at the cook-house door.

I stepped swiftly up to it. It sidled and stubbornly showed the white of an eye to me, but I loosened the reins and prepared to mount. Its owner rose in one motion and with a gruff order in his own tongue came to its side.

"He take your horse," said Semple. "I tell him. All right."

"You give me *scoutaywaubo*?"

"Yes, yes."

"All right. Good!"

The horse pivoted. It raised a hind leg to kick forward like a cow. I pivoted with it, facing the tail. Perhaps the owner mounted on the off-side by a white man's styling of a horse's sides. Indians, I had noted, usually did, though some mounted and dismounted by either side according to need or fancy. Or perhaps the piebald objected to any save its master riding it. At last I made a leap and alighted in the saddle. It was like a small pack-saddle, merely two crotches of wood with a pad of buffalo skin between over something soft, perhaps moss. The stirrups were just two pieces of bent wood depending from broad raw-hide thongs. I got my feet into them as the horse rose on its hind legs.

"There you are. You're up. You're up!" said Semple.

With the long lines I lashed the animal over the croup and it came down, trembling. I drove my heels against it.

"You're off!" called Semple. "You're away!"

IV

I was indeed away. I went out of the gate in a whirl of dust. With the flat of a hand I struck the horse's neck on the off-side. It wheeled as I had desired and rub-a-dubbed northwards. I leant forward and, as I had seen the Indians do, stretched my arms out. The animal responded at once, accelerated, with a nervous galloping that had the sound as much of a runaway as of a horse under control. But it had not bolted. It was merely trained, and perhaps in dread of rougher treatment, giving to the full the pace that I ordered by that forward cant and lunge of my arms. Like many at Red River I had a soft side for the aboriginal people, but too many, I often thought, were cruel to their mounts—as to their dogs. True, one would come on some who treated their animals with kindness, having discovered there were other rules besides those of terror, but . . .

Of what was I thinking? Only a part of me as I rode, the ground wavering back under me, was thinking of horses and Indians. The greater part of me was thinking not even so much of my errand as of getting it over, getting it done, and returning to Christina. A girl. A girl-child. A healthy, sound, little girl-child. It was over. She was delivered. But why might I not see my wife? It was Mr. White's orders, and he was a good surgeon. I must trust him.

I came to the first farm. I bore gently on the lines, or the raw-hide thongs that were knotted round the horse's lower jaw. The pressure won quick response. Within but a few yards the horse slowed down from that urgent gallop, fell into a lope, into a trot, into a quick walk. I saw a man passing from a house to a shed and hailed him, beckoned him. He came running.

"Everybody to the fort," said I.

"Everybody to the fort? Why?"

"Governor Semple's order."

I did not think it necessary to say that the road should not be travelled on, for there were no enemy riders visible yet to west. These people could go direct, thus close, had not need to seek cover among the trees by the river. I touched my heels to the horse's wet flanks and at once it stepped up, fell into a lope again and of its own accord from the lope sprang into the gallop. Bending forward I clapped its neck in gratitude but at the touch of my hand it leapt sideways as it galloped. I balanced quickly in the saddle. Beneath me, through the pad, I felt its muscular movement and had that sense of getting to know it, moving with it. It raised its head and gave a snort that was half-whinny.

"My God!" said I, in a choking voice. "You are a great horse!

I did not like your eye when I mounted you, but you are a great horse!"

I wanted to do this duty assigned to me speedily and to get back —back to Christina. Drawing near the next house I saw the gate open but no one was in sight. At a mere touch on the neck the horse wheeled from the Settlement road into the farm track. Having seen me enter someone came out and stood in an attitude of waiting.

"Everybody to the fort!" I called, wheeling as I spoke.

"What for?"

"Men have been sighted from the watch-tower coming this way."

"But why should——"

"Captain Semple's orders," I shouted over my shoulder and back I went to the road, and on northwards.

At a wigwam a little way farther on my message brought a look of panic to the woman who came out to meet me.

"Are we to be attacked again?" she quavered.

"Not in the fort," I assured her. "Everybody has to go into the fort."

"Is an attack expected?" she asked.

"There is a party of armed men coming in from west. Captain Semple thinks it best to have all in the fort."

As I rode out to the road again I heard her calling and an answering shout from the river bank. At the Chisholms' I had no need to turn aside. Hugh Chisholm was at work close to his fence.

"What's the haste, lad?" he inquired.

"Orders from the Governor," I replied. "Everybody has to go to the fort—men, women, children, everybody, at once. There is a body of men, very suspicious-looking, coming in from the west."

Chisholm's face showed an expression of utter disappointment. His arms fell limp to his side.

"And look at the crops!!" he said. "At last we are—oh, well, this is the end of it if the half-breeds get the best of us again. Finished, finished! It is the half-breeds, I suppose?"

I rode on. As I did so I looked ever and again to west across the open lands, the slight undulation of the plain, the patches of bush, the stretches of grass. The men who had been sighted through the spy-glass from the watch-tower were apparently riding out as if crossing from the Assiniboine River to evade Fort Douglas and arrive at the farms. But I could not see, though elevated in the saddle, any movement there save of some horses, riderless, unsaddled, grazing, stepping and grazing, stepping and grazing.

My horse slowed down of its own accord as I no longer urged it. For a long way it had come at racing speed. The sweat trickled on its neck, every hair damply flattened. As it went on at the quick step of its species I did not press it further. I wanted to save it for the return, the return to Christina.

We came to where one after the other were farms of folks from the Highlands. Many did not have the English, or had only a smattering of it. Some had difficulty in understanding my order. Some, on hearing the reason for it, looked out westward and then again at me dubiously. The fields that had pleased the Chisholms, pleased them. They looked at the growing grain and out over the plain where the sun was dropping into infinite peace. A few thought I was joking, that I was out upon some other errand, amusing myself with nonsense as I rode, and they watched for a laugh, for a smile to come on my face.

" It is nothing to joke of," said one. " It would be no joking matter after all we heard of what happened here before when the half-breeds came round."

" I'm not joking, God knows," I said.

The man looked at the horse. It had come merely at a quick walk but it was wet with sweat. It had been run, clearly. But when I halted it, very wearily it stood, relaxing as these Indians ponies relax. Its sides heaved like bellows. It lowered its head, nostrils distending and closing rapidly. One hind-leg was hip-shot. The man considered it thoughtfully.

" Ah well," he said, " I'll get them gathered."

" Better go by the trails along the river," I advised, " till you get near the fort."

" The road would be easier."

I looked out over the plain. Nobody was yet to be seen there.

" Please yourself," I said.

At the touch of my heels the horse's head rose, its whole body tautened. It moved forward with a sudden lunge and leapt into a lope. I came to the end of my warning ride, to the last group of workers building a log home beside a rustling corn field.

"Listen," I pled, thinking of Christina, anxious to get back to her, my duty done, "I've been sent by Captain Semple to warn all to the fort." I waved to west. "Armed men are coming again from there. He orders everybody to the fort, and you had better go by the river, keep in cover of the trees."

I turned my horse and understood at once why these people looked at me as if incredulous. The scene was peaceful. I had a glimpse, over the slightly sloping vista to east, of fields, of the river, a bronzy reach of it, a tranquil twist between the growing corn on the left bank and the oak thickets on the right. To the west was but empty prairie. Or was it empty? I heard a pounding of hoofs and rose in the stirrups for better view. There came a small herd, galloping, but no riders were on them. They rushed along parallel with the road, mobbed together, slowed, turned to look in the direction from which they had come, heads raised, fidgetting, ready to gallop again.

"Something has frightened them," thought I.

I had not gone far when I saw, crossing the road, a group of mounted men. They were approaching one of the farm-houses. I could see feathers in their hair. One had on a war-bonnet.

"Peguis," I decided, "is having his own way in spite of Captain Semple. He has got his braves together and is going to look after the settlers."

But next moment, reining in, I halted by a cluster of wayside oaks and elms. These riders were acting oddly to my mind. They were surrounding the house. I could hear little quavering whoops as they did so. The old stratagem, thought I, had been resorted to: the half-breeds had put feathers in their heads and had probably also painted their faces so that the Indians would have the blame for the attack. Well, I must get back. I had done my duty. I must get back to Christina.

I flicked the horse aside from the Settlement road, but not to a river trail. A sudden inspiration for tactics came to me. As I rode towards the river. I might be seen by these men. To continue on the road was impossible: they would intercept me there. So I rode out to west, on to the open plain. That group, I suspected, had probably caused the stampede of the horses I had seen. Out on the prairie I rode and then headed south. I could urge the horse no more. It was very tired. Ever and again it stumbled. I was constantly lifting my rein-hand to support its head, to help it in recovery. I spoke encouragingly to it, clapped its neck again and that time it did not flinch but gave a small nicker as in response, tossed its neck and stepped out more vigorously.

" You're a noble beast!" I said aloud.

Suddenly I dropped from the saddle, went down on a knee. Over one of the low rolls of land I descried feathers again, a feathered head or two and then shoulders also of other riders. When I alighted the horse at once took opportunity to snatch grass tufts. If these men glanced my way they would see no rider, only a grazing horse. I rose furtively and peered over the swaying tops of the tufts. The horsemen had ridden on to the road. Perhaps they would find the farm towards which they headed by then uninhabited. I hoped so. I devoutly hoped so. I had done my best to convey the warning of " all to the fort."

I mounted and rode on, thinking then only of Christina, Christina.

v

I came to a small cluster of oak trees, near the place called Frog Plain. To left of me I had glimpses of those settlers who were hurrying to the fort by road instead of using the trails. Passing on beyond that oak grove I saw a great number of mounted men riding from south-west and between them and the road, on which the agitated figures hurried, I observed a body of men marching from the fort.

From the direction they were taking they would soon put themselves in front of these advancing horsemen. I decided that the riders the watch had first espied through his glass must have been those that I, returning from my errand, had seen converging in groups on the settlers' homes, an advance party.

I swerved closer to the road on which were only hurrying colonists. The body of men coming afoot from the fort moved rapidly. That tantalising sense of making no progress that I often experienced on the flat plains, away from tree stands, I felt then although they were marching quickly in my direction and I riding towards them—felt so, perhaps, because of my impatience to be done with interruptions that held me from Christina. They evidently intended to intercept the others. I saw, clearly, Semple in the lead and recognised, close behind him, Mr. Pritchard and Lieutenant Holte.

"Have you warned all?" the Governor shouted to me.

"Yes, sir, all," I called back.

"Then now join us," he ordered, and paid no more heed to me.

I wanted urgently to see Christina but obediently I rode level with them. The duty on which I had been sent was finished, but a dread of seeming cowardly even to myself restrained me from pointing out to Semple that I was unarmed.

"A fool! You are a fool!" I told myself when I joined them. "What good can you do, unarmed?"

A sense as of nightmare was strong then. I was the only one mounted and riding beside them. I had an exaggerated impression of elevation, as if I rode with head in the sky. This was not real, I told myself, surely this was nightmare. Having obeyed the order to warn the settlers, I should be riding back to Christina, but was not. I decided, mutinous, to turn my horse and go. But the half-breeds were then so near that to have gone at that moment would have looked like flight, fearful flight. So I stayed.

The half-breeds were by then, in fact, close enough to be seen individually clear. Either they had full-bloods with them or again, as I had suspected, were desirous to appear as Indians, for many were feathered and painted. Apparently there was uncertainty among them. Those strung out in the lead slowed to allow the ones behind to overtake them, and then all grouped together. There was a quick conference which ended, evidently in a decision to ride on as they had been riding, for they resumed their former loose formation, strung out across the plain, headed again north-east as though towards the middle of the Settlement or thereabouts.

But suddenly, at a sign from a man in the front, they made a circling motion before Semple and his men. Recalling the circling half-breeds of the fights at the smithy, my heart raced. What could I do, I asked myself, unarmed there? The horn of the circle curved. Then one of the riders came forward, holding up the flat of a hand in air.

"What do you want?" he called to Semple.

"What do you want?" Semple shouted back.

"We want our fort!" the man replied, riding nearer. As he did so the others drew closer.

That was a puzzling reply, thought I—— "We want our fort!"—a foolish reply, a mad reply to fit this nightmare. Fort Gibraltar existed no longer. It had been razed. Its logs were built into Fort Douglas.

"Go to your fort," answered Captain Semple, meaning no doubt Qu'Appelle.

The spokesman had a musket in his hand. He had not reined his horse in. It was advancing at a slow stalking walk. At Semple's answer he glanced over his shoulder at those behind and then, near enough, he pushed the barrel down threateningly against Semple's chest.

"Why did you destroy our fort?" he screamed.

For a moment I thought I was going to see Semple shot dead before us. His chin was outthrust. He put a hand up and laying it on the musket daringly—or foolhardily as some might say—pushed it away. Then a shot was fired elsewhere. No one, afterwards, had any clear knowledge of who fired it and it was followed so promptly by others that it would be hard, perhaps, even for one looking on, detached and utterly calm, to say who fired first. From the road on which the settlers were still hurrying came screams that made me think that other half-breeds were molesting them; but no—the sudden discharge of shots had alarmed the women and children and involuntarily they cried out and ran on.

"My God, my God!" I moaned in misery, helpless, unarmed; for Semple's men (there were about thirty of them), being in close formation, clustering behind their leader, were a target that could not be missed.

There was firing on both sides but the evidence of it was only on our side. It seemed that half the company was down, including Semple who lay on his side. I had not been hit, but when another fusillade was fired I dropped from my horse and crawled near to a bush.

"For God's sake lie down—spread out and take what cover you can," I heard somebody shout.

I did not need the advice. I lay pressed to the bush, face to the earth, looking along the ground. There was much moaning round

me. I heard men call on God and on Christ. One rose and, evidently
wounded worse than he knew, fell. I recognised Mr. Pritchard's
voice saying, "Give yourself up—give yourself up!" A moment
later I realised the reason for that urgent advice for the half-breeds
had dismounted and were running towards the fallen, knives in hand.
I saw one of the Company's men—Rogers I believe his name was—
rise to a knee to aim his piece, then sag forward on his face. Mr.
Pritchard, hurrying forward, stumbled over him and as he recovered
and came to his feet a painted half-breed made a stab at him with a
knife. One of the others, however, quickly intervened, stepped
between. Pritchard, I remembered, had been in the service of the
North-West Company. Many of these men must have known him
of old. It was to plead mercy from them, no doubt, that he had been
advancing so.

Then I noticed Semple raise himself on an elbow and look back at
Fort Douglas.

"Has Mr. Bourke not come with the field-piece?" he inquired.
His voice was distressing in its plaintiveness. "I bade him follow
us with a field-piece," he continued, in a tone of extreme dejection.

Some of the men on the ground were not wounded but crouched
there for shelter. A few then stood up together but at once there
was a volley from the encircling enemy.

"Do not keep so close," Semple implored, gasping and coughing
from a wound. "Spread out and take cover and each shoot as he may.
Do what you can to take care of yourselves."

Unarmed, I could only lie still. I looked round and saw a man
staring at me, met the gaze, wondered who he was and why he
should stare so, then realised that he was dead. I crawled towards
him. Beside him lay a musket. I meant to get that and his ammunition
belt. And then, as I crawled along, there came the rattle of wheels and a
renewed shouting among the half-breeds who were riding round and
round in a whirling circle.

I looked towards the road and there was a cart rocking along. The
men in it balanced and swayed. There was a field-piece in it. The
driver was adroit in the handling of horses, bringing them at the gallop
and sweeping them round so that the tail of the wagon was towards
the half-breeds. But they were too mobile. They changed direction
and swept off behind the cart. There was another burst of shooting.

I was troubled then for Christina's sake. The shooting would surely be heard at the fort. What effect might it have on her? The driver of the cart collapsed, fell over the side, hit the ground and lay there kicking, thrashing once or twice, then was still.

Suddenly we were surrounded. Half-breeds afoot ran among us, crazed with excitement. One bent over the dead man whose musket I had hoped to avail myself of, bent over him, demoniacal, gloating, drew the head back as though to look down into the dead eyes, and nearly severed it from the body at one stroke of his hunting-knife.

Then Cuthbert Grant—not painted like the others nor apparently crazed like them—appeared.

"Stop shooting! Stop shooting!" he called to all. "Where's Captain Semple?"

I heard Semple speak in a weak voice.

"Well, Grant," he said, "you have won this. But I am not mortally wounded. If I could be taken from here I might live."

"I shall see to that," replied Grant. He turned and shouted orders to his men. "Let the wounded lie," he commanded. "I will have none of that."

If I lay there longer, thought I, despite Grant's orders I might be brained at any moment. I stood erect. I looked round for the horse on which I had ridden through the Settlement. It had dashed wildly away when I dismounted in the first volley of firing, but there it was in that lull, returning, trotting towards the horses of the half-breeds, its neck elongated, its teeth bared, whinnying shrilly. The sound started them all. All the horses there elongated their necks with a curling of their lips, bared their teeth, and whinnied loudly as in equine laughter.

I moved stealthily towards the Assiniboine's pinto that had served me so well, talked soothingly to it. It did not notice me. It wanted the company of its species and went plodding on, dragging the reins, whinnying again. I had merely, without any fuss, to step up to it and catch the lines, toss them over its neck, swing to the saddle, wheel it about.

"Who's that going? Hie, you!" somebody called.

A musket cracked but I was off. Swiftly again the pinto bore me. The fort gates were closed but inside stood two or three of our people, guns in hand. At sight of who came they opened to me.

"How goes it?" one asked.

I paid no heed. I rode into the square. Groups of the settlers sat there in attitudes of waiting and dread. I galloped past them and had not reined into a standstill before I leapt from the saddle and ran to our cabin.

I opened the door—and at the sight of Mrs. Chisholm's face could not speak.

" How——" I began, and again, " how——"

She shook her head. She bit her lip, tears pouring down her cheeks. I went into the bedroom without another word. Madame Lagimoniere was there. There was an odour of blood in the place, blood and soap.

" She is dead?" I think I spoke, or whispered, the inquiry.

Madame Lagimoniere looked at me without speech.

" The baby—— the baby——?" I asked.

" Agnes Wallace has taken her," said Madame Lagimoniere.

Behind me came Mrs. Chisholm.

" Agnes has taken her," said she. " She will see to her. She is feeding her own."

I knelt by the bed. Christina was already rigid. I laid a hand on her heart and the feeling of her body gave me full sense that she was gone. She had left that body, she was not there.

" Could Mr. White not do anything?" I demanded, looking up at them as through a haze.

" Mr. White was not here," said Madame Lagimoniere.

" Not here!" I ejaculated.

" Not here when the hæmorrhage broke out again. The first one he attended well. It seemed to be over and when he was called away——"

" Called away! Do you mean to say he went?" I asked.

" Word came from the watch-tower that Captain Semple was wounded. They needed him out there and we all thought that she was all right."

" But his duty was here. He could not leave one for another."

" David, David," said Mrs. Chisholm, her voice trembling, " the bleeding had stopped. He left her with us. Then she heard the shooting and we could not keep her quiet. She wanted to know where you were. When the hæmorrhage started again we tried our best to—we—we—we tried our best."

I rose from the bedside and strode violently out of the house. I strode

T

across the square, seeing nobody. I passed on to the gate. I was going to look for Surgeon White out there. I was going to take him by the throat and crush the life from him. As I came to the gate it opened and some wounded men entered. One had a dangling arm that he clutched, another had his head tied in a kerchief, a blot of congealed blood on it.

So the surgeon had left Christina to go out on the plain! And I, riding back, had somehow not seen him. Could not the wounded have been brought into the fort for attendance? Cuthbert Grant was out there, taking control, and had ordered his men not to kill the wounded; and, the fight over, he had promised Semple he would look after him.

"Where is—where is——" I choked "—where is Surgeon White? Is he not coming with you?" I asked the wounded men.

"What did you say?" asked the one with the bloody kerchief about his head.

"Where is Surgeon White?"

"He is dead."

"Dead!"

"Yes, he is dead. He was shot out there."

A feeling of emptiness, sickness, utter weariness fell on me. Unaware of all those round me within the palisade waiting to know what had befallen, I walked back to the cabin.

I went directly into the bedroom where she lay. The sun was setting, the window open, and evening light was splashed on the wall above her head, the passing glory.

CHAPTER TWELVE

I

I WAS as one stunned during those days. I stood at Christina's grave while a Highland voice intoned English words to which I paid little heed and only fragmentarily heard. These were only the ritualistic words for the occasion. What I felt, thinking of her, I could not put into words.

It was Madame Lagimoniere who drew me a little way out of my isolating sorrow by telling me I must go with her to see "the little Christina." *The little Christina* : I did not at first comprehend. In the square of the fort, to shelter the settlers, tents were erected again, recalling the time of the arrival of the families from Ross and Cromarty with Captain Semple. To one of these she conducted me and we found Agnes there. I was aware of her eyes quickly examining me as we entered, and speedily averted.

"Come and see her, David," she whispered. "She is asleep," and she bent over the shakedown on which the new Christina lay.

I looked at the sleeping child and came near to breaking down.

"It is good of you, Agnes, to look after her," I mumbled.

"I can do that easy," she told me.

The canvas walls kept none of the outer sounds from us but they seemed far off to me. As I stood there Mairi came in.

"Am I wanted?" I asked.

She did not understand.

"Am I wanted?" I repeated, striving to pull myself together.

"No, no," she responded. "I just came to speak to Agnes."

I was wondering why Christina should be taken from me, wondering if she no longer existed or if her spirit was near. "I can see the trail," she had said to me once. That day I could see no trail. Suddenly it struck me that I should be doing something, even though I had not been sent for. Captain Semple was wounded. Grant had promised to have him looked after, but I did not know who was in charge there. I must have spoken the thought aloud that I should be doing something.

"That is all right," Mairi said. "Nobody expects you to do anything, David. The Sheriff told my father to let you know that. Later on you can report to him."

"Oh, Mr. Archibald is in charge," said I. "Yes, he would be when Captain Semple left the fort. How is the Governor?"

Nobody answered. Then——

"He was killed," said Mairi in a low voice.

"But he was only slightly wounded. I saw him. And Cuthbert Grant——" I stopped there because of the way all looked at me.

"Grant put him in charge of somebody else," said Mairi. "It was not his fault. Another man came along and would not heed what the guard said, just pushed him aside and shot Captain Semple to death."

"When was that?" I asked.

"The day before yesterday," said she.

"The day before yesterday!" I ejaculated.

"Don't bother to think it out, David," Mairi implored.

I was all astray. I was lost. I did not know how the days and nights passed. But I did, despite her advice, make an effort then to recall all that had happened. I remembered how I had fallen asleep at last, exhausted, on the night of the fight and how, wakening, I had thought at once of Christina, been anxious regarding her as though forgetting she was dead, and a second time had the shock on learning she had gone. Yes, yesterday they had buried her and then Hugh Chisholm had gone back with me to the cabin, sitting there with me till, exhausted again, I slept. On awakening I had leapt up to go to her, then realised yet again that she was not there. The room was empty. The world was empty.

I looked at that mite of humanity asleep on the shakedown.

"I should be at work," I said, and turning to Agnes, "Thank you for looking after our baby," said I.

She just nodded, holding her own sleeping child close to her ample breasts. Only dimly aware of Madame Lagimoniere, who had brought me there, and of Mairi, I went away.

People were carrying dishes of food from the cook-house to the tents. Men stood here and there talking, some subdued, some excited. I crossed to the office buildings and as I came to the door a hand was laid on my shoulder. Glancing round I found Mr. Pritchard beside me.

" My dear boy," said he, " I was sorry, sorry indeed to hear from Archie your news. These are sad days for us all."

I could not at the moment speak but after a space I was able to.

" What has been happening?" I asked. " I have been thinking only of myself, I fear."

" Oh, I have been coming and going between Cuthbert Grant and Archie MacDonald. They took me prisoner, you know." (I did not know.) " I am on parole. They have me to carry messages. Grant has given an order that all leave the Settlement."

" Well, why not?" I demanded. " It is all over here. Somebody told me Semple was shot where he lay wounded."

" That is so. Poor Mr. Holte was killed too. Most of the wounded were killed by them. Only to a scant few of us was quarter given. The knife, axe, or ball put a period to the existence of the wounded and on the bodies of the dead were practised all those barbarities which characterise the inhuman heart of the savage. What would have happened to the settlers if the watch in the tower had not seen them headed across by the Seven Oaks is for the imagination to consider. They took prisoners of some in an attempt to prevent news of them being carried to the fort, not knowing that it was from there the settlers had received the warning. Poor Captain Semple. Some called him a martinet, but I always found him amiable and mild. Bourke is a prisoner. He was shot when he brought out the cart with the field-piece, crawled away, lay hid somewhere. They found him to-day, they tell me, but will not let me see him. I have just been to see his poor wife to let her know he lives. They have no surgeon——"

" They could get Surgeon White——" I began and then got my wits back fully again. " What am I talking of?" said I. " Surgeon White was killed. There is nothing more to say. Why don't we all go, go anywhere—back to Scotland?"

" Some of them—the young men especially," said Pritchard, looking away from me, " want to fight."

" With all these women and children round?"

" That's the point. Because of them the men want all the more to fight. Grant says, on the other hand, that he doubts if he can restrain his *métis* if the settlers do not go speedily. They vow if they have to come again they will kill everybody—men, women, and children."

"Then we'll fight them!" said I.

"Are you there, Mr. Pritchard?" came the Sheriff's voice.

"Yes, here I shall see you later, David," said Pritchard, again putting a hand on my shoulder. "Take hold of yourself, boy. That's the way. It is worse for you than for some. You have had your personal——" he seemed to search of a word "—shock," he ended, and went indoors.

I slowly followed him. There was the door of the accounting-room and there was where I should be at work, on duty, at any duty that might be assigned to me. Going upstairs I found the room full of men. White men and Indians stood there. All were in little groups, conferring, and now and then someone in one group would turn to those in another as though seeking support in a point of view. They made way for Pritchard who passed to the table where the young Sheriff sat. As they moved aside so I saw Chief Peguis by the desk, tears pouring down his face. He was speaking:

"I came to Semple, I say to him I bring my young men and go and meet half-breeds and kill them and take scalps. Semple say, No. Now you see. Now we bury these people. My heart is sad about this. The wolves eat some of these people. Some men out there dead have ears cut off. Some men have——" he plunged into an account of the state of the bodies left there after the attack.

"Yes, yes, chief, we know," replied Archibald, "but there are the women and children to think of. They have more men than us and they are better armed. Well, Mr. Pritchard, there you are. I think this is all we can do. We have been discussing it: some of the men say *fight* but the majority think we should agree to go. We are outnumbered. You can tell Cuthbert Grant we will go but that he must sign an inventory of all in the fort and promise that there will be no burning again."

"I think he will agree to that," said Pritchard. "I feel sure he will be glad to sign an inventory and see all safely gone. There are thousands of pounds worth of goods and implements in the fort and on the farms. I can point out to him that Lord Selkirk's agents can at least realise something on these effects and that to make an inventory and promise to leave all intact does not mean that the settlers will be back this time."

"By God, we will be back!" came the voice of one who was listening.

"Never!" exclaimed another. "To hell with the place!"

A hubbub of talk arose. At the table Sheriff Archibald and Mr. Pritchard exchanged a few more words, then Pritchard elbowed his way through the press and went out again.

Somebody plucked me by the elbow. I turned and found one of the settlers, Livingston by name, at my side.

"Here's a man will do it for us," he said to the crowd. "He's accustomed to copying documents. He writes the real nice script."

Archibald, at that, looked up and saw me. He came forward, holding out a hand.

"I am sorry indeed to hear of your loss, Baxter" he said. "I had word of it so did not trouble you with anything."

Again I was rendered mute. I could only nod my head.

"He could make a fair copy of our letter to the Prince Regent," declared Livingston.

"Yes, that's so," agreed the Sheriff. "He could. Will you do that for them, Baxter? There will be something of real value to put your mind upon."

"Yes, I can do that," I replied. I could do it though it was nothing to me. Nothing mattered to me.

"Then go into the officers' private room there," suggested Archibald. "There is nobody in it. It will help to clear this room too. Go with Mr. Baxter, you gentlemen, and he will make a fair clean copy for your signatures. God bless me," he ended, "there are a lot of things to consider. With all these people here, and so many afraid to go outside the palisade, sanitation has to be thought of, for one thing. Yes, you go in there and get that letter to the Prince Regent ready. We shall take it with us to Jack River and send it on to York Factory to go out with a returning ship."

From a listening group came a snort of disgust.

"Plenty of us," said one, "will be on the boat that takes it."

Only a few followed me but those who did were highly serious. Mr. Livingston had a sheaf of papers in his hand. He put it down on a table and I seated myself.

Many minds apparently had been at work upon the draft of that letter. There were scratchings of erasure and interlinear corrections, deletions, additions; but I could read my way through and that being so I dipped a pen and began:

> To His Royal Highness
> George, Prince of Wales,
> Regent of the United Kingdom of
> Great Britain and Ireland, etc., etc.

We, His Majesty's most loyal and dutiful subjects, natives of Scotland, now settlers at Red River, in the territories of Hudson's Bay Company, beg leave humbly to approach the Throne to lay at the feet of your Royal Highness a brief account of the wrongs we have sustained, and to beseech a share of your paternal protection.

Being obliged to leave the land of our fathers in Scotland, we embraced the proposal of settling under the patronage of the Earl of Selkirk and the Hudson's Bay Company in a British Territory, rather than follow the steps of a number of our countrymen who were emigrating to the United States.

On our arrival here we received allotments of lands, and soon found that in point of beauty, fertility of soil, salubrity of climate, and facility of cultivation, the country far excelled any description we had ever heard of it. We met friendly and hospitable reception from the native Indians.

We cultivated some ground, which yielded returns abundant beyond all we had ever known; and we began to cherish the hope that we had found in His Majesty's Dominions a happy asylum for ourselves and our children after us, but to our misfortune, a few individuals, who engross to the Fur Trade of Canada, under the appellation of the North-West Company, considered our innocent prospects of happiness as incompliable with their views of interest, and determined to effect the ruin of this Colony while in its infancy.

I·made occasional pauses for certainty because of alterations. When I hesitated once Livingston came to my shoulder and peered over, but before advice came I had found the sequence again.

For this purpose they endeavoured to incite the Indians to attack us; but in this they did not succeed, the natives having sagacity enough to perceive that our prosperity would be of permanent advantage to themselves. Not being able to accomplish their object this way, the North-West Company next attempted to deprive us of the means of subsistence. While our crops were yet scanty, our subsistence chiefly depended on the herds of buffaloes, with which the neighbouring plains abound. To deprive us of this supply, horsemen were employed to chase away the animals from our hunters. By this device they distressed our families considerably; but as they did not succeed in driving us away, they had recourse to more decisive measures for destroying our establishment.

In the spring of the year 1815 they collected a number of persons, mostly natives of the country, the sons of Canadians by Indian women, many of whom had previously been our friends, but who were unable to resist the threats, as well as allurements, which were held out to induce them to become the instruments of crime. These ignorant men had been accustomed to believe that the commands of their masters would at least screen them from punishment, or, rather, would entirely absolve them from guilt. But the more effectually to secure their obedience, the North-West Company, by a train of deception, led their servants to believe that in all their measures against the Colony, they were acting under the immediate authority of His Majesty's Government.

There was an increase in the clamour without. Those in the room, curious regarding it, moved away. I was progressing well enough without their aid.

The first object was to get possession of the arms and artillery which had been provided for our defence, of which, by a combination of fraud and violence, they found an opportunity of robbing us. After this they made repeated attacks upon the house of our Governor, in the course of which four persons were severely wounded, and one of them mortally. The ostensible purpose of these attacks was to arrest the Governor, upon a warrant issued against him by a partner of the North-West Company; and we were assured that on his surrender all hostilities would cease. Unable to repel the superior force of our assailants, the Governor at length gave himself up, in hopes that by this sacrifice our peace might be secured. But when the North-West

Company had thus deprived us of our chief magistrate, as well as of all means of self-defence, they renewed their attacks upon our place of refuge, threatening us with a general massacre if we did not immediately quit the country. Compelled to abandon the farms we had cultivated, we were indebted for the preservation of our lives to the unsolicited interposition of the Indians. A band of the Saulteaux nation, under their chief Peguis, assisted and escorted us until we were out of danger, while our fellow-subjects trod our crops underfoot, and reduced our cottages to ashes, as well as other buildings which had been erected for the accommodation of the settlement.

We then retired to the northern extremity of Lake Winnipic, a distance of three hundred miles, where we received information that our enemies had dispersed; and being joined by some additional settlers, we returned, and after a few months' absence reoccupied our farms. Our perseverance redoubled the animosity previously expressed by the North-West Company. In the spring of the year 1816 they collected a still greater force, from various and distant parts, for the avowed purpose of expelling us from the country. In the month of May a number of boats conveying provisions for our use were intercepted and pillaged by command of Alexander McDonell, one of the partners, who openly declared that the North-West Company would not suffer a Colony to exist at Red River, and that if the settlers dared to resist, the ground should be drenched with their blood. The Indians in the vicinity, having heard of the approaching danger, came and offered to fight for us, but our Governor, Robert Semple, declined their services, being unwilling that under any circumstances the arms of savages should be raised against his fellow-subjects. On the nineteenth of June about seventy servants of the North-West Company on horseback, disguised and painted like Indians going to war, suddenly invaded the settlement, and carried off as prisoners such of us as had not had time to escape. Anxious to enable us to retreat to the fort, our Governor came out on foot with about five and twenty men, and proceeded to the settlers' lots. The servants of the North-West Company perceived this small party, galloped up, and having surrounded them, sent a messenger to summon them to lay down their arms.

This demand was soon followed by a general discharge of firearms; our friends were overpowered by the superior numbers of their

*antagonists. The Governor and others, who were at first only wounded,
or having ceased firing, and were calling for quarter, were brutally put
to death and stripped of their clothing, which the murderers put on
their own persons while yet reeking with the blood of their victims.*

I paused there long, staring straight out of the window till I was
blinded by the light. I turned again to the scrawled and altered draft
but could not at first see the words.

"What's the good of all this?" I asked of the empty room. "We
are going. Why petition? This is the end."

I pressed a hand against my closed eyes and then continued with
the copying in my best caligraphy.

*We shall not attempt to describe the situation in which we were left
after this catastrophe—without any adequate means of defence against
the merciless ruffians who had thus butchered our friends and relations
—our lives were spared only on condition of our quitting the country
immediately, and delivering up the property of the Earl of Selkirk and
of the Hudson's Bay Company to the clerk of the North-West who
commanded on the occasion, and who declared that we owed our lives
to his leniency alone, as he had received orders to let none of us escape.*

So far I had reached when several of those who had set me the task
came back.

"How far have you got?" asked Livingston.

"To the end," said I. "I have just this moment finished."

"This is good. There will be more to add. But let me have your
fair copy so far."

After folding the missive carefully he put it in a pocket, gathered up
the original sheets from which the transcription had been made, and
they all hurried out.

II

That task finished, I then put my elbows on the table and bending
forward laid my head on my crossed wrists. The sunlight that had
dazzled me while I wrote slipped away. There was shadow in that small
room, deep shadow on Red River Settlement for me.

As I sat so, inert—how long I do not know—I heard a voice I knew:
" Come in here, then, come in and let us talk together. Semple should
have listened to Peguis."

I raised my head and gave ear. That was surely Court Nez speaking! I heard the Sheriff reply: " I doubt if Captain Semple realised
how virulent the half-breed's animosity had become."

" But didn't I send him word?"

" That is so," Archibald admitted, " and he was grateful.   An
educated Cree named Mistouche came also to warn him."

" Three warnings—Peguis's, Mistouche's, and mine!"   Yes,
Court Nez was out there in the accounting-room.   " See here,
MacDonald, you are not going to sit down under this. Why, the
Indians, your friends so far, will despise you, despise you!"

There came a sound of drums—a *thud, thud, thud*—and a rhythmic
and agitating chanting of voices. I heard quick steps across the floor
of the other room. The Sheriff had evidently dashed to the window
to look out for——

" No, no," said Court Nez, " that's not the half-breeds again. That
is the full-bloods I brought with me. I have my own little following
among the Assiniboines, you must understand. I told them to sit
outside the fort and to give up a war-dance after I was in here for a
spell, lest I required to convince you we mean it." He gave a burst of
thick laughter. " See here, say the word and my Indians, and Peguis
with his, can go out and kill every *métis* on the prairies. Hell, man!"
he continued, speaking then, I think, possibly wildly, perhaps with
too great belief in his influence over the tribesmen westwards, " I
could send runners to some of my old friends among the Blackfeet,
and to my old friends among the Gros Ventre, and if any got away
west as far as their country they would be finished off there.   The
damned half-breeds!"

I shuddered, thinking of Christina—his half-Assiniboine daughter.
And how, I wondered, could I tell this man that she was dead, had
died in childbirth? By his voice he was in grim mood. His manner
of speech recalled that day on which we sat together on a fallen log
by Red River and he had his knuckles skinned.

" It is very good of you to show this personal interest——" began
the Sheriff.

" Personal interest!" exclaimed Court Nez. " It is that!   They have killed my daughter. Do you understand? They have killed my daughter."

So he knew. He had heard.

" Well, not exactly," said Archibald. " She was in the fort and——"

" Not exactly! I know, man. Surgeon White—— I've all the news of that—had left her to go out and see to the wounded. I don't blame him for that. He thought she was out of danger. I blame nobody except those damned half-breeds. Let me have any of your young men who are not white-livered with me. Some of these fellows that Semple regretted were turning into Indians and getting to love the winter tripping, surely they would come and help to annihilate them?"

At the words *white-livered* I felt that it was cowardly for me to sit there listening and making no sign. And, also, I thought that what Court Nez proposed would be bad indeed and would negative all the case that I had just been penning to send to the Prince Regent in England. I passed quickly into the accounting-room.

Court Nez had his back to me. The two men were alone there, standing. Archibald looked at me as I entered and his glance caused his companion to turn. He did so heavily, ponderously. There was a slight stoop to his massive shoulders but it was like that of a boxer. His whole frame suggested power held in reserve and his poise a consciousness of his bodily strength, or belief in his bodily strength. His arms hung loose at his sides. I saw that since our last meeting he had changed. The eyes were more peeping, utter ruthlessness was in the set of that jowl.

" Well, David," he said, " she is gone. I heard. What happens, happens. At least I gave her the best I knew—and you too. They tell me that. I know you did that, for I hear that some of the women said they could not imagine what you did with yourselves, seemed quite contented with each other." He raised his head and opened his cavernous mouth to laugh but instead there was just an ejection of hisses from the back of his throat. " You both had in you what some do not have at all," he added, " and you had the best of it, not the worst of it."

There was a step on the stairs and Mr. Pritchard came in. He was tired. He was dusty. He saw me talking with Court Nez and turned at once to the Sheriff.

"These Indians at the gate," said he, "how long have they been there?"

"They came with Court Nez," replied the Sheriff. "You know him, of course."

Court Nez turned. Mr. Pritchard bowed to him and he to Pritchard.

"Oh, yes, we have met—often," said Court Nez. "Don't worry about the Indians outside, Mr. Pritchard. They are not alarming your people. I explained to them, the poor harried folk, when I came in that all was well."

"What does Grant say now?" asked the Sheriff of Pritchard.

"He agrees," replied Pritchard. "He says you can make an inventory and he will come and check it and sign it all in order."

"Is he not afraid to come?"

"Evidently not. Grant is not a fearful man. I'll say that for him. Of course he may bring others with him. He says he thinks he can keep the half-breeds in check if they show any sign of so much as jostling our people when they go."

"But can he?" asked Archibald. "They went mad out there after that massacre. He promised Semple he would get him to the fort, but Semple was shot dead as he lay."

Court Nez raised a hand and waved it at them.

"Don't worry about that," he said. "If go you must I shall see you are convoyed all the way along the river bank to Lake Winnipic. But why go? Peguis can lead his braves, I can lead mine against them. We could wipe out these damned——"

The Sheriff interrupted him. He had heard this often enough.

"It is the women and children I think of," he said.

"We can protect 'em!" declared Court Nez. "And as for the women—not all of them are for going, I am sure. I listened on the way across the square. Listened? I saw too. A woman can convey much with a glance. I saw the way groups of them glared at the men—and the men saw it too: contempt for them, that's what it was. If these were real men they would do something: that's what the faces showed. You are sure about your majority wanting to go— men and women?"

"Oh, yes."

Court Nez paced heavily back and forth.

"You don't happen to have anything here for a man to drink, do you?" he said.

Pritchard and Archibald looked one to the other.

"Yes, I can get you something," replied the Sheriff, and went towards the officers' room.

But Court Nez swung out an arm rigid before him so that he was stopped by it. The motion was a trick, something like the bringing down of a cupped hand on the thigh. The effect was of a blow on Archibald's chest though the arm was but held firm, as a barrier. He halted and looked sharply into Court Nez's eyes.

"On second thoughts—no," said Court Nez. "I want to be able to *see* my grand-daughter. Can this young clerk be spared?"

"Certainly, certainly," replied the Sheriff.

"Lead the way," ordered Court Nez, catching my elbow. "Where is the child? What a world to bring children into! Still, some can make the best of it—or the best out of it."

III

"The child," said I, as we went out, "is in the tent of a man called Wallace, Bob Wallace. He married Agnes Chisholm. They were very good to me, the Chisholms. I could go in and out of their place as if it was my home."

"Uh-hu."

"Agnes has recently had a baby of her own—about three months ago, I suppose—and so can nurse the little Christina."

"Uh-hu."

"I suppose it had to be," said I.

"Perhaps everything has to be, young man," said he.

"Well, this is where they are," said I.

The front flaps of the tent were laid back so that it was open and I looked in. It was Mairi I saw first.

"May we come in?" I asked.

"Come in, come in," she said.

She was alone. Agnes's baby was lying on a blanket spread on the ground to one side, employed upon counting her toes, marvelling at them, and beginning the count again with small crowings and splutterings. The new Christina, to the other side, was on her back, great dark eyes staring up at the tent roof.

"This," said I, "is Mairi Chisholm, sister of Mrs. Wallace who is looking after our baby. This is Court Nez, Mairi, my father-in-law."

Mairi was staring at the man who came in behind me. Neither made any sign of having seen the other before.

"How do you do, Mr. Courtney?" said she.

That appeared to amuse him.

"Just Court Nez," he advised. "Just Court Nez, Miss Serious Eyes." He chuckled again and looked at the babies, at me, and then went down on a knee to peer closer at Christina. "Aye, aye," he muttered. "So there she is, wondering. I hope she may get an answer."

I glanced from him to Mairi who stood still, looking on. Yes, *Serious Eyes* fitted her then as a name. Court Nez rose. As he came to his feet he lurched slightly.

"Well," said he, "we'll get back to see what Archie MacDonald and John Pritchard are about. Good-bye to you, Serious Eyes."

At that moment her sister arrived.

"Here is Agnes," said I.

"Ah, here is Agnes, nursing her own and yours," said he. "I'm Court Nez, Just Court Nez. You're a fine buxom wench."

Agnes gazed at him with hauteur. I think, by the look on her face, she remembered having seen him before when he turned aside from the Settlement road once, accompanied by two silent Indians.

"My father-in-law," I explained to her.

"Oh!" and she beamed at him. Then, solemnly, she added: "We were all that sad about the wean's mother."

"God's will, God's will," chanted Court Nez, humping his shoulders, his expression gloomy.

Agnes looked then as if afraid of him. He left the tent without another word and I followed him. After a few paces he paused to look round the square.

"Some of them in terror," he said, "some wanting to stay and fight, some of them sick at heart and feeling far from home. And what home have they to go to if they leave here?"

Glancing over my shoulders I saw Mrs. Chisholm, who must have come from the other direction, entering the tent. Then clear came her voice. She had not, evidently, recognised Court Nez, and indeed he had changed much since the day she first saw him and was partly puzzled by his behaviour, partly indignant over it. Clear came her voice with a note of horror in it: " Who is the dreadful-looking man that David is with? What a——" She stopped abruptly, or was stopped abruptly. Mairi, or Agnes, or both, thought I (thought Court Nez also, I do not doubt), had signalled her urgently to be silent. He raised his head as if listening for more. Then he laughed harshly. He brought his hand down with such a thud on my shoulder that my whole back was shaken.

"Come, we'll return to the Sheriff," said he, " and I'll have my dram."

CHAPTER THIRTEEN

I

It was the morning of the 22nd of June. Boats, canoes, and rafts also were being loaded with provisions and tents. The settlers purposed, below the rapids, to transfer these loads to one of the schooners. They could not know then, not being endowed with prevision, that by the time they got so far the schooner would be a charred hulk.

Those who had been taken prisoners by the first body of half-breeds to cross Frog Plain were released. Not only, I heard, had the *métis* killed the wounded and mutilated the dead but had driven off and feasted on the sheep and cattle that had come to us with Semple.

While all were in the midst of the final duties, I again at work though still with part of me absent, Mr. Pritchard arrived. At sight of him the Sheriff stood rigid.

"What now?" he demanded. "What now, Mr. Pritchard?" for he took it that Pritchard was there by request of Cuthbert Grant again, with some new objection to our departure. The faint smile on Pritchard's face might have been one of acceptance at another hitch.

"I'm free to come with you," said Mr. Pritchard. "I am released." He held out a piece of paper for examination. "Grant has given me this. I wonder if he thinks I may need a safe conduct." He read the written words aloud: "*This is to certify that Mr. John Pritchard has behaved himself honourably towards the North-West Company. Cuthbert Grant, Clerk of the North-West Company.* Gracious and condescending of him. I would that I could write as excellent a testimonial for all my recent North-West friends."

Archibald glanced at the slip of paper.

"Well," he said, "I suppose it is a gentleman's signal of appreciation that you did not break your parole. I was worried over leaving you as a prisoner with them. All the prisoners are free, then?"

"All but Bourke," replied Mr. Pritchard. "I am very anxious about him. He is one of the finest young fellows I have ever known. I saw Mrs. Bourke just now. She is being very brave but she is dreadfully upset about him. Through some Indians she has heard something:

306

He lay in a thicket close to the oaks, it appears, all through the night after the slayings. The mutilation of the dead must have gone on close round him. He was probably unconscious next day when Peguis went out with his men to bury some of the gashed corpses, or else he would have called. At any rate, all next day and night he seems to have lain there. An Indian who returned to the scene found him and was dressing his wounds when a party of half-breeds came along and took him prisoner. That is all she knows, poor girl. None of my captors would tell me of him. ' He is not dead ': that is all they will say. They speak vindictively of him. I know that before the driving out of the settlers last year they tried to get him to join them by bribes and liberal promises, and were annoyed when he refused them. And I think they bear him a new grudge for bringing out that field-piece the other day. By the way: I must tell you—a runner arrived at Grant's camp just as I was leaving, with a message from Yellowhead telling Grant not to let us go till he arrived. Grant showed it to me doubtfully, and I said: ' Do you take your orders from him?' I could not have spoken better. He was undecided not a moment longer. He took the note and dropped it in the fire."

" So!" said the Sheriff. " You touched his pride. Well, the sooner we get our people into the boats and away, the better. And everybody seems to be ready."

" There are a lot of them," remarked Pritchard.

" Yes, about two hundred all told. With the later settlers, despite loss of the two-thirds or so of the earlier ones they lured away, we got up again to two hundred souls, as the saying goes. If only it was two hundred men this would never be. Women and children are the big majority of that tally."

As we turned to go down the bank we saw a long file of mounted Indians riding slowly northwards a little way from the fort we were leaving. Pritchard frowned at them.

" It is all right," Archibald assured him. " These are the Assiniboines that Court Nez is leading. He is accompanying us along the river bank some way in case of the *métis* being menacing as we go. Oh—and here is Peguis."

With him were Madame Lagimoniere and her children, to whom I had already bidden farewell. Archibald turned away and left us, walking urgently back towards the fort.

"We are just going across the river," Madame Lagimoniere ex-plained. "Peguis has put up a tepee for me there. Some Hudson's Bay officers may remain in the fort but he thinks it possible that they may be attacked. So he wants me to go across the river to wait for my husband where some of his people can see to my needs. Any day now, surely, Jean will come back. They are watching for him— all his Indian friends are watching for him now to bring him to me."

There was a renewed shouting of men along the bank. There was weeping of women—some women. Others, dry-eyed, wore a look of suppressed rage. Sinclair came down the slope with a load on his back. His wife carried his violin. As he trudged along he whistled his own tune, *The Blue-bottomed Fly,* and Zzz! Zzz! he buzzed in the ears of the most lugubrious. When they swung round and glared their fury on him he chuckled and walked on.

To the officers of the Hudson's Bay Company still at the fort— Mr. Sutherland, Mr. Fidler, and a Mr. MacRae—I had said good-bye. John McLeod was not there then. After taking Duncan Cameron to Jack River he had received instructions to build a new post between York Factory and Lake Winnipic, and when that was completed was going to take charge of the English River district. I missed him.

"Where is Mr. MacDonald?"

The inquiry startled me. I found that the speaker was Cuthbert Grant.

"He was here not long ago?" I answered. "I think he went back to the fort to make sure that all have left. Yes, here he comes now."

Grant gave a small salute to Archibald who, returning it, scrutinised him with much the same expression he had worn on seeing Mr. Pritchard unexpectedly back again.

"There is no need for you to worry in any way," said Grant. "I have spoken seriously to my men. I have picked out several, very reliable, to go in the boats and canoes a little way with you. They have sworn to me that if any of the others dare to go down river and offer indignities, they will see to them. They are armed and I have explained to them how I wish this exodus to be conducted."

Archibald studied him gravely.

"Cuthbert Grant is beginning to realise," thought I, "that there will be a reckoning for the killings by the seven oaks on Frog Plain," and I wondered if he had heard of the petition being prepared to send to the Prince Regent.

"I have not forgotten," said Grant, "that our fathers were countrymen. Perhaps you would be so good as to explain to your people, lest the arrival of these fellows perturbs them."

"These are some of Mr. Grant's men," Archibald called. "They are going a little way with us that there may be no trouble from the —from the others."

There were doubtful glances from a few of the settlers at sight of the *métis,* but Court Nez's full-bloods had drawn near and were riding slowly along the bank to reassure them. If here was treachery they had these Assiniboines to protect them—and there was Peguis being paddled back to the west shore by two of his braves who had taken him across to instal Madame Lagimoniere in her tepee. He also, with a party of warriors, was going to see us well upon our way. The "picked and reliable" *bois-brûlés* that Grant had brought with him scattered along the water's edge and found places in the boats, their leader watching them.

"I myself will ride along the bank," he said to Archibald, and so saying he moved away to where others of his men, mounted, one holding a led-horse, awaited him.

"All ready! All ready!" the Sheriff called.

There was a lull in the clamour of voices. Archibald, at a clear space on the bank, holding a tree-branch, craned out, looking upstream and downstream. Some young men came running from the fort, carrying bundles.

"You are the last, are you?" he shouted to them. "Oh, yes—I saw you there. You are the——"

"Yes, we are the last," one answered in sullen accents. "If we were all armed we would not need to go at all."

Archibald looked after them with annoyance.

"When Captain Macdonell tried to teach musketry and drill," he complained to me, "many rebelled and told him they were farmers, not soldiers. You know that, Baxter. Now there are those who say that arms should have been provided for all. Assuredly we have evidence that a protective force was needed. Well, have you chosen a boat?"

"If you do not specially wish me to come with you I should like to go with my friends the Chisholms," said I. "One of the girls has my daughter in her care."

"By all means then do so."

Court Nez came along and hailed me.

"You will come back," he bellowed. With a sudden movement he wheeled his horse and rode away.

"Was that a prophecy or an order?" asked Mr. Pritchard as we descended to the water's edge.

I saw Mrs. Chisholm waving anxiously to us and, responding, Pritchard and I climbed into the boat in which she sat with her husband, Mairi, Agnes, and Bob Wallace. Agnes had her own baby in her arms and Mairi held the little Christina, who was asleep.

The Sheriff was the last to embark, after those on the rafts had cast loose. There was a plashing of oars and paddles. From ahead came singing:

> "O God of Bethel, by Whose hand
> Thy people still are fed;
> Who through this weary pilgrimage
> Hast all our fathers led."

So the voices rose. On the prairie level the Indians led by Court Nez raised in reply a wavering call, not the high cry of battle in its fierceness but a low musical: *La-la-la-la-la-la-la-la*! From looking at my child in Mairi's arms I looked at Mairi.

"How queer it is," she whispered. "How queer it is," she repeated, whispering, holding the baby closer.

> "Our vows, our prayers, we now present
> Before Thy throne of grace:
> God of our fathers, be the God
> Of their succeeding race."

> *La-la-la-la-la-la-la!*

Mairi stared with wide eyes at the bank where the riders could be glimpsed against the sky between the foliage, feathered figures undulating along.

"How queer it all is!" Her lips shaped the words. She spoke below her breath.

> "Through each perplexing path of life
> Our wandering footsteps guide;
> Give us each day our daily bread,
> And raiment fit provide."

The wavering cry of the Indians came down from the prairie. I sat back, listless. All was over. I was again as one in a trance, carried away under the green web of the overhanging boughs past the play of small ripples at bends, past the dipped branches and the fan of ripples they scratched on the stream.

> "O spread Thy covering wings around,
> Till all our wanderings cease,
> And at our Father's loved abode
> Our souls arrive in peace."

La-la-la-la-la-la-la!

Yes, all was over. Christina was dead. A great sickness was at my heart. I saw again the huts at Nelson Encampment; saw and heard the rapids of Hayes River, saw the expanse of Winnipic, heard Hillier reading from a parchment in his hand, saw the interior of Fort Gibraltar and Christina cross the big room in which I sat attending on Miles Macdonell. Back there, upriver, was the hut in which the Lagimonieres had lived. Back there was the path on which I had walked with Christina. The dusk of a past night returned for me and her voice: "I can see the trail."

She could see the trail. I could see no trail. All was over. Through the trees went the quick dart of a golden oriole. I watched its yellow flash pass among the green foliage, and as I looked it was as though I heard her voice again: "I wanted to get back here in time to hear the song of the cat-birds after their long flight, and to see the orioles."

I must not break down, I told myself. I looked sternly at the banks on either side that seemed to be drifting back as I was carried away, on the flow of the water.

PART THREE

CHAPTER ONE

I

THROUGH occasional gaps in the continuity of the riverside trees, where only bushes dappled the slope, the horsemen could still be seen accompanying us along the left bank, the western bank.

"This conducting of us," said Pritchard, "this protection of us by Grant, of all people, is downright ridiculous. It is superflous for him to have us convoyed by these he calls his reliable men. The chief effect is for himself, a small sop to his conscience for the killings. He is none so bad and he has been used. Some would say he was having us convoyed now in the hope we may put it to his credit when the day of reckoning comes. God help the *métis* if they do make any further attack now! These Assiniboines and Saulteaux would just set to work. Red River would be red indeed then."

When the flotilla was well past the farms, Cuthbert Grant rode down to the water's edge and signalled. At his beckoning the men he had sent in the boats requested to be put ashore. The whole flotilla drew in and the *métis* landed. Indifferently I watched them climbing the low bank.

"They have brought led-horses to take them back," said Mr. Chisholm.

What had he said? I was not sure. Had he spoken to me? I did not care. It did not matter. Then I saw the Indians that Court Nez had been leading. They were a little to the other side of Grant's mounted convoy. I could see the horses' heads tossing, the pivoting riders. There was a gathering, a grouping of the file. As I watched they turned, but instead of going by the way they had come, along by the river, they rode straight out across the prairie and as they went they raised that low, musical *La-la-la-la-la-la-la!*—seven trembling cries.

As the boats and canoes and rafts were pushed off again into midstream, I watched the men Grant had summoned ashore mounting the led-horses. There was a small milling of riders. Grant raised a hand and waved to the departing colonists. Nobody that I could see

paid any attention to him. He waved again. In a boat ahead Sheriff
Archibald stood up and responded.

That was a sad departure. There was not much talk among the
settlers. Gloom was on us all. Now and then a woman, as the banks
receded behind us and we drew near the delta and the lake, would
lower her head and bite on her lip to stem the tears that welled in her
eyes. Young men rowed gloomily; old men, doubting themselves,
tried, I presume, to take what comfort they could in the thought
that even if various efforts of their lives had gone agley their intentions had been well. But none had the heart to sing any more, even
hymns or paraphrases of petition. Our first camp was very melancholy.

On reaching Lake Winnipic we found that the house poor
Lieutenant Holte had lived in while working there had been
destroyed, and a schooner that had lain at a slip there was but a cinder,
a charcoal hull. Some of the enemy, after Holte left for Fort Douglas,
must have played incendiarists there.

We had just lit the cooking fires at our second camp by the lake
when round a promontory came a brigade of canoes from east. It
drew into the shore among our moored craft. There was menace in
the manner of disembarkation of these new-comers. One of them,
wearing a vivid red coat, came striding forward.

"Where is that fellow Semple?" he demanded violently in place of
salutation.

Pritchard, who had voyaged all that way in the Chisholms' boat,
turned to me.

"This is A. N. Macleod, Archibald Norman Macleod, usually
called just Norman Macleod," he said, "a very different sort of man
from our John."

The Sheriff left the camp to meet him.

"You ask for Captain Semple?" he said. "Captain Semple is
dead."

"Ha! He is dead, is he? We arrive too late to see these settlers
given their congé."

"So!" remarked Pritchard, turning again to me. "Out of his own
mouth the evidence! The thing was planned from farther than
Yellowhead's fort on the prairies, as I suspected. East and west were
both to be in at the death of the Selkirk scheme. Poor Grant," he
added, dryly. "When this all comes to the courts, as come it must,

he will have to bear the brunt alone. The organisers will get off scot-free."

Norman Macleod turned and spoke to the men behind him and they called to the others. It was the news of Semple's death they passed round, and as they heard it they cheered. The settlers by the cooking fires were strained of aspect.

"Well," said Macleod, stepping closer to Archibald MacDonald, "we will just examine the cargoes you have brought with you."

"By what right?" demanded Archibald.

"Can you prevent us?" asked Norman Macleod as he glared first at his men, all carrying arms, and then at the unarmed refugees.

So the canoes were ransacked while we all looked on in suppressed rage and chargin. We suffered an emotion that was a blend of helplessness and shame. There was a trunk in one of the boats bearing the name *Robert Semple*. We had brought it with us, intending to ship it from York Factory to his relatives. That was lifted out by Norman Macleod's order. It was locked but he did not ask who held the key. It was broken open for his inspection. They rummaged in it, removed all the papers from it. When every boat had been searched and all letters found had been appropriated, Norman Macleod chanced to observe Mr. Pritchard.

"Ah!" he exclaimed. "An old Nor'-Wester! Happy meeting. I heard you had gone over to the enemy."

"You heard wrong," replied Pritchard. "I retired from the service of the North-West Company and had no desire to leave the country, so when I discovered that Lord Selkirk's colonization scheme made no exceptions for admission to obtain lands I bought there, to settle and farm, as I thought, for my last years."

"Very tolerant of Selkirk, no doubt," sneered Norman Macleod. "So he had no objections to a retired North-Wester settling on his lands? But, my dear Pritchard, you are just the man for me. You will be able to give an unbiased report of what has befallen at the forks. You are not a Hudson's Bay man. You are a retired North-Wester, settled, if one can use the word, at the Red River Colony. Your young leader here might be prejudiced. He might even inform me that I had no power to demand a report from him," and he glanced slyly at Archibald.

"Nor from me," said Pritchard. "But I shall have great pleasure in writing an account of all I have seen since I took up my parcel of land by Red River."

"We shall be camping here for the night," said Macleod.   "I should be glad if you will do so immediately. You have ink?"

"I have no doubt ink can be found."

I had the impression, rightly or wrongly, that in Mr. Pritchard's mind at the moment was a thought of the letter to the Prince Regent, carried by Livingston, to which much would have to be added.

Macleod then moved his men a little way off. The settlers, discussed their arrival with eyes averted from them, stealing only occasional glances at them. Some time later another canoe, one of the large ones, came from east and down to meet it ran several of the North-Westers. They lifted out a small field-piece and its carriage, set it up on the bank, and pointed it at the refugees' camp.

The light, even the lingering light of twilight in these parts, grew dim. Macleod came over to where Pritchard sat.

"You have finished?" he asked.

"Finished, yes," said Pritchard and held up the sheets on which he had been working, wiped his quill with a tuft of grass, closed the inkpot with a snap of finality.

The North-Wester began to read and as he read he scowled.

"You have written a nice report here!" he broke out. "This will do you no good. Do you hold to this?"

"I do."

"Then I fear we must take you with us. You may not go with these settlers."

"Indeed?" said Mr. Pritchard. He felt in a pocket and drew out a paper. I recognised it as the one he had shown us at Fort Douglas on the day of embarkation, when Cuthbert Grant had released him.

Macleod took it and inquiringly read it aloud: "*This is to certify that Mr. John Pritchard has behaved himself honourably towards the North-West Company. Cuthbert Grant, Clerk of the North-West Company.* Well, all the same you come with us. The others can go on to-morrow, but you stay here with some of my men while I proceed to Red River and see Grant."

Pritchard opened his mouth in a yawn, raised a hand to cover it.

"I shall sleep now," he said. "I am a little weary. Might I ask why the field-piece that came in that laggard canoe is trained on us here?"

"Yes, you may ask—and I shall tell you. It is not a laggard canoe. It was sent in pursuit of me from Bas de la Rivière because of news received since I left. I have just had word from there that your so-called Governor, Miles Macdonell, is coming west by our route and is but a little way behind us."

I had to take hold of myself, obliterate a look that I knew must have come on my face.

"They fear he might follow on from Bas de la Rivière?" suggested Pritchard.

"Fear? No. But if he does we are now well ready for him."

"The cannon is trained on the camp of settlers, not on the water where he might be seen arriving," commented Pritchard.

"That is so," agreed Norman Macleod.

"May I ask," said the young Sheriff, approaching "where exactly that field-piece came from?"

"From Bas de la Rivière," replied Norman Macleod, glaring at him.

"One bearing the same surname as you," remarked Archibald, chattily, "went to Bas de la Rivière not so long ago and retook some guns that had got there from Fort Douglas by way of Fort Gibraltar. I wondered, when I saw that piece being unloaded, and noted the calibre, if he had found all that were being housed there, or where it had come from. Some are still missing."

"I do not know of what you talk," said Norman Macleod. "You can take your people on to-morrow morning. Mr. Pritchard here I am retaining," he turned away, "as a witness," he added over his shoulder.

The dusk had fallen. Night, at last, after the slow blue twilight, was not only under the branches in the woods but everywhere. In small shelters of brush most slept, exhausted by all they had been through. A few had put up tents. Hugh Chisholm, John Pritchard, and I had, before dusk, lopped some fir-branches for a mattress and on these we lay down, rolled in our blankets with a buffalo robe to cover us.

But I could not sleep. Miles Macdonell, Miles Macdonell, Miles Macdonell! He was near. He was coming back. He was coming this way. I lay long awake and then realised that Pritchard was also awake.

"Can they force you to stay with them?" I spoke quietly.

"Eh? Oh, that! I cannot sleep for thinking of Bourke. It is of Bourke I am thinking, not of myself. He was badly wounded. I wonder where they have him and if they are tending him, or——"

A baby cried in the encampment, a sudden small outbreak of complaint. I rose on an elbow and listened. Did the sound come from the tent close by in which Mrs. Chisholm, Mairi, and Agnes with the two babies slept? No, it was not my little Christina who cried. I heard, from the far end of the camp, a woman's voice as she consoled her child in Gaelic.

11

The next day all were up and away early, and glad to be away. We did not leave Mr. Pritchard alone with Norman Macleod. Four others he retained, two Hudson's Bay employees who had accompanied us (as they were going on Company duty to Jack River post and thence to York Factory), and two settlers, all in the manner of prisoners but by the name of witnesses and on the strength of his appointment as a justice of the peace.

"What right," I asked, saying good-bye to Mr. Pritchard, "has he to demand any one, whether as witness or prisoner?"

"He is a magistrate," replied Pritchard, with a shrug of his shoulders, "a magistrate—and a major. And besides, by the look of things just now, he has the right of might."

The right of might: the phrase remained in my mind as the boats coasted the south end of Lake Winnipic.

Because of the news we had of Captain Macdonell being on his way, and so close behind Norman Macleod, we did not cut across the estuary of Winnipic River, or Traverse Bay, but followed the coast line and passed into the mouth of the Winnipic to make our next camp in hope of there meeting the returning Governor. It was four years since I had been in that neighbourhood, four years in which I had seen much of the right of might. For the sake of a good camp place we went some way upstream and landed not far from the North-West Company's fort of Bas de la Rivière, though not in sight of it.

The settlers had just finished their evening meal when round a bend, driven strongly on the current, came three canoes. Those in them, seeing the crowd upon the beach, stayed their paddles and swept in-shore. I rose, shaking with excitement. Down the bank hurried Sheriff Archibald MacDonald as out of the first canoe stepped a very tall man and made two or three long strides forward.

Miles Macdonell was back again.

I could not speak to him at once. After all that I had suffered, I could not speak to him at once. The Governor and the young deputy Governor, while the men in the canoes came ashore, stood in deep talk, then sat down just where they had met and talked on. Now and then I saw Captain Macdonell turn and look solemnly at the settlers in their groups.

Not only was I eager to meet him even though at the moment I held back. Others, longing for an end of that discussion, began to move nearer. Then both rose and immediately Miles Macdonell was surrounded by old friends, shaking hands, shaking hands, shaking hands. Many had pressed ahead of me to greet him. I could not so much as catch his eye. Yes, I heard him say, in reply to their words of greeting, he had been gone some time. After leaving them, sur-rendering to Cameron, he told them, he had been taken to Fort William, and there he found Sheriff Spencer who had been held at that place since the autumn of 1815 in what the North-West officers called "private custody." Together they were taken on to Montreal.

"The original warrants," he explained to the listening crowd, "charged us with breach of the peace. New warrants were there served on us for felony. But from session to session our trials were postponed. In October Lord Selkirk, and Lady Selkirk with him, arrived there by way of New York and then we were introduced to further subtleties of law, and heard of Oyer and Terminer, which his lordship ruefully called *interminable*. Farcical—it was all farcical. From September 1815 to May of this year the cases were postponed and bail found. However—here I am, bringing this advance guard to see how all goes at Red River while the earl follows."

He paused and looked round the intent gathering.

"His lordship," he said, "has been doing his utmost to gain per-mission to have a military force for protection of the Colony. Well, it was refused him, but it so happens that while he was in the midst

x

of all these affairs an order was issued for the reduction of the De Meuron and the Watteville regiments, and the Glengarry Fencibles. The first is named for Lieutenant-Colonel the Earl de Meuron, a French-Swiss, and includes many German and Piedmontese soldiers who were forced by conscription to enter Buonaparte's armies. These joined the regiment when it was at Gibraltar, and finally it came to America. His lordship had the notion to offer free grants of land to any of these soldiers who might wish to settle at Red River. In the event of further assult on the Settlement they could turn from plough to sword. Twenty men of the Watteville regiment, all with good character and acquainted with various trades as well as with military service, are coming with their Captain Matthey. More than double that number of the De Meurons, with their lieutenant, Mr. Fauche, and their captain, D'Orsonnens, are coming, and a few of the Glengarry Fencibles are also on the way with some of their officers. At last, you realise, you will have trained and disciplined soldiers at hand for defence if needed."

"Where is the earl now, sir?" asked Hugh Chisholm.

"He is on his way to Sault Ste. Marie. That is at the south-east corner of Lake Superior."

"Will he be thinking to take us back to Red River under the protection of these soldiers?" broke in Livingston, he who had in his care the letter to the Prince Regent.

"We are going home—we are going to Scotland," another interjected, but a chorus of groaning *Noes* followed that remark.

"What is there for us there?" asked one of the women, angrily. "We were evicted from our houses in Scotland."

"In answer to your question, sir," said Miles Macdonell, looking at Livingston, "the earl had not intended coming by this route to Red River Settlement. You must realise he knows nothing of the events of this year. Of the late dreadful massacre, of which the Sheriff has just been telling me, he knows nothing. He has been trying so far to evade the North-West Company's forts so that, if a clash comes, it can be proved he did not seek it. His intention is to continue by the American lands, by Fond du Lac and the St. Louis River, to Red Lake and the head-waters of Red River. He sent me ahead this way merely to give information of his coming, to prepare for it, and to take over management with Mr. Colin Robertson—who, I find now, is at Hudson Bay with that man Duncan Cameron as his prisoner."

"If Captain Macdonell returns at once by the way he has come," said the Sheriff, addressing the crowd, "he should get back as far as Sault Ste. Marie by the time Lord Selkirk reaches there. His lordship must know as soon as possible of what has befallen us here before he is further out of reach of the Governor-General."

"What do you think we should do?" asked Mr. Chisholm of Captain Macdonell.

"I think you should all continue to Jack River," answered Miles Macdonell, "and wait there until you hear Lord Selkirk is at Red River with his forces of trained soldiers."

"And then we would be established," said Chisholm.

"Then you would be established," said the Governor. "You would have your military protection in these ex-soldiers as settlers beside you. By the way, I think your petition to the Prince Regent, of which Mr. MacDonald tells me, should still go forward. There must be enough in that to rouse the home government to action."

"We have more to add," declared Livingston.

Suddenly Miles Macdonell saw me and held up his hand and we came together through the throng. He gave me a searching look.

"It is good to see you again, sir," said I, shaking hands with him. "Did Monsieur Lagimoniere get through with his message from Mr. Robertson?"

"He did indeed," Miles Macdonell replied. "He reached us on the first day of this year. An intrepid man, that. He refused to give the letter he carried to any but the earl. He was in his voyageur's clothes, and torn they were. The servants tried to restrain him, but he would give the missive from Mr. Robertson only to Lord Selkirk, and thrust his way into the ball that was being given on that night."

"A ball!" ejaculated someone.

Captain Macdonell understood the meaning of the tone in which the man spoke.

"The waterways were frozen by the time Lagimoniere came," he said. "His lordship had to wait till the spring before he could move, and there was also a vast deal of litigious detail for him to attend to apart from the arrest of Mr. Spencer and myself. He could not be a recluse over his affairs, bent over them all the twenty-four hours.

There were social obligations—and these," he added, "not without value for his undertakings."

"Lagimoniere left us on the first of November—and you say he arrived in Montreal on the first of the year," said I. "Did he wait there to return by canoe with the earl?"

"No. He should have been at Red River long before you left. He rested only a little while and then started back. He said his wife would be anxious if he was long away."

"His wife is anxious," said I. "He has not yet reached there. Here is June three-parts gone!"

"That is very strange!" exclaimed Macdonell. "That is bad. I do not like it. On the way east he travelled stealthily, but perhaps he was not so careful on his return. Perhaps he has been intercepted. Certainly from what I have heard now from Mr. MacDonald," he continued, turning to the crowd again, "my plans must be changed. It would be best for you to proceed to Jack River as you intended. There is good opportunity there for support—both game and fish. Wait there until you receive word to return to Red River. And then," he inclined his head to Mr. Chisholm, "you would be established."

A murmur of approval rose from the surrounding crowd.

"To Jack River!" they shouted.

"To Jack River!"

"Well, Captain Macdonell," said Archibald, "I see your tent is up and a cloth spread before it for your evening refreshment. Pray you go, sir. We will talk later. This is encouraging news you bring us."

"It is sad news I receive," said Miles Macdonell. "The earl has had enough of sad news already. This will affect him deeply. Later, then," and he turned away. The crowd giving him passage, he strode to where his servant was preparing his meal.

III

Returning the few yards to our camp I looked into the tent that had been put up for Mrs. Chisholm and Mairi and Agnes—Agnes Wallace. In the manner in which the Indian mothers line the cradles for their children with dried moss, Agnes, gathering moss, had made mattresses for her own child, and mine.

I stooped into the low tent and down on a knee looked at the sleeping Christina. Even with no more between me and the others than the thickness of the canvas I was suddenly far from all, though the sound of low talk came in clear to me, set apart from them in a world of my own. The two children lay motionless, breathing quietly. I thought again of my wife until it seemed that she was there in spirit. I heard her voice. I remembered the oriole that had darted its gold by the river as the boats were cast loose, and how it brought to me my lost Christina. I remembered Court Nez's parting words: "You will come back." I saw in my mind's eye the trails along the west bank of Red River, the one along the rim, the other on the lower level: "I can see the trail," came again her voice in memory.

There would be a day, thought I, when all these settlers would find themselves happily restored. This land, this country of Christina's, would be their children's inheritance. I recalled my home in Scotland. No, I could not take Christina's girl there, her girl and mine. This retirement was to be only a temporary retirement. I would not go to Hudson Bay and thence to Scotland again on the returning ships of that year, carrying the little Christina away from her mother's land —and my new land. I would go only to Jack River post and soon would be again by Red River.

A definite, permanent affection for the Old Land endured but life there, certainly for those called "the people"—and I was one of them—as we heard of it from each party of immigrants, grew steadily less happy. The tyranny and evictions in the Highlands, the industrial servitude in the Lowlands, were deplorable. Here was a freer land despite all our troubles! Neither in Highlands nor Lowlands, somehow could the people achieve desirable existence. The spirit in them that resented the conditions of life there, though it did not take rebellious turn to mend it, was not utterly crushed. When the present troubles were over it would create a better social order here. Regrets they might have that in their own loved country a tolerable existence was denied them and with a certain devotion they would always recall that country, despite that regret. But, as one had remarked once when, under stress of opposition here a return to Scotland had been suggested, to return would not only be "out of the frying-pan into the fire" but into the frying-pan again! Here they would stay—and I with them. Here, with opportunity to begin afresh, they would be themselves and never permit a state of things to arise such as had caused them to leave the land of their nationality.

I wondered, so pondering, how much the hectoring and the ceaseless assumption of suzerainty over me of my elder brother caused me to feel exasperation towards all who would be overbearing to those they believed, by circumstances, were in their power. Be that as it might, here was my country and here was my life to be lived, free. That sense of freedom would grow for us all, the initial discord with those who resented our presence over. The spirit that had not risen to rebellion in the Old Country would here at last create a way of life such as all desired. So I pondered in that tent, kneeling beside the slumbering new Christina.

I came out and looked across at the camp of the canoe-men who had brought Miles Macdonell and saw him at the water's edge rinsing his hands, saw him rise up, shaking the drops from his fingers, a silhouetted figure against the flow of Winnipic River, saw him move back to his tent and stand there, drying his hands on a napkin. Then, at a sudden impulse, I went quickly to him.

" Sir! "

He turned, napkin in hand. He seemed to me much older than when he left Red River. While talking with the settlers his age had not shown but in a reverie at that moment he looked so, much older, and there was sadness on his face. It lightened, seeing me.

" I was wondering, sir," said I, " if I might take up my position with you as before."

" Why, surely, Baxter, when all is settled. It is good to see you again. I have heard of your behaviour after the people were ejected last year. Colin Robertson wrote an account of it, among all the other matters. John McLeod is a great man and you who served him deserve some honourable mention."

" I did not want to go then," said I.

" To go *then*. Do you want to go now?"

" No, not now. For a time I wanted to go, but not now. I had a reason, sir, for wanting to leave."

" Not faint-hearted ever?" asked Macdonell.

" I had a reason, sir, a deep reason." I felt sorrow nigh overcoming me and Miles Macdonell realised, I think, by the look he gave me, that I was under some great stress.

"Tell me as you will," he said.

I hesitated, drew a long breath.

"Oh, well, sir," I said at last, "I have a reason now to stay. And I come, at any rate, to ask you: May I take up my position with you as before?"

"Do you want to accompany me to Sault Ste. Marie instead of going on with these poor people to Jack River to wait there till we are ready for them?"

"I do."

"I shall be glad to have you with me, Baxter. You know when people have been through difficult times together how it is: there is a bond of union."

Thinking of Christina, I was moved additionally by that remark.

"Well, well," said Miles Macdonell, as if bringing an end to the talk, "we shall make an early rise. We go back against current for a considerable way. Be at my tent here in the morning at a good hour, Baxter.'

He dropped the napkin with which he had been drying his hands.

"Thank you, sir, and good-night."

"Good-night to you, Baxter."

CHAPTER TWO

I

ALL the way, by Winnipic River, Lake of the Woods, Lac la Pluie, I travelled with Miles Macdonell and his men over the route taken by the settlers who were enticed away from Red River to the Canadas, the route by which Colin Robertson had come west. In after years I would not be able to visualise it in fair sequence. In what order came the multitude of lesser lakes and connecting rivers I would not be able to recall, but whole stretches I would remember clearly.

There was a sense of tranquillity in the woods on either side—to some extent misleading, I knew, aware that the beasts in the recesses of that wilderness preyed one upon another. But there it was, that sense of tranquillity, that ambient peace, something to remember for ever along with memories of that other, earlier, inland voyage from York Factory. There were swirls of water lit with green and orange reflections round wet dark rocks; there were places where little lakes were strung like liquid sapphires through the wilderness, lake after lake. At night there were the owl-calls in cavernous forests; by day there were the plunging fish-hawks and the patient hunched herons standing on one leg. Out of the still woods on either side came the tapping of foraging wood-peckers.

Here was beauty enough, thought I, and why should any one have to die? Here was infinite peace, and why should people be at strife? The patter of rain on the leaves was even part of that sense of peace. Merganser and loon gave there the same cries that I had heard by Hayes River. There were polished green reaches on which lily leaves undulated in the ripples left by the canoes. There were slopes strewn with grey-blue granite boulders, and among the boulders grew berries in great clusters. There were stretches from which there was no foaming white escaping river to pole up or glide down but only a reflection to paddle into and shatter. There were days of thunder-colour, purple woven in the forests, crashings and reverberations, windy lashings of the water. Round a bend one day we came on a swimming moose and gave chase and it was shot as it lumbered up

328

out of the shoaling water towards a slope of yellow pine—and so
we had fresh moose meat next day. There were sickle beaches on
which the fine sand was like powdered ivory. On all sides was delight
for the eye.

Under the stars we slipped past the North-West Company's Fort
William, seeing only a light or two in its houses scattered along the
bank and the twining reflections like snakes of gold in the water.
The sequence of bay after bay, promontory after promontory of that
vast inland sea of Lake Superior silenced me, the grey-blue granite,
the seemingly interminable forest beyond.

We camped one night in a place where the colonists, voyaging east,
had also camped I was told. Against the ragged granite promontories
on either side the water made occasional plashings and guttural remarks as of people talking quietly because of the hush. The woods
curving round the bay had the aspect of watching us under their
drooping branches. A man coughed over his tobacco and the cliffs
answered back. Once they had echoed the evening psalm, thought I,
of those who had accepted Duncan Cameron's offer of lands in Upper
Canada. They had been there and they had gone, leaving no sign
beyond the circles of ash.

In one of the camps on the shore of Lake Superior I had a long
talk with Miles Macdonell. I had been thinking of myself as a very
ordinary person who had been introduced by Captain Roderick at
Glasgow to a very extraordinary series of events. Only five years
earlier I was little more than a boy harassed by the watchfulness and
fault-findings of my excellent brother. Yes, a very ordinary youth
I had been, flung among extraordinary occurrences. I recalled the
dinner at Fort Gibraltar with its unforgettable glimpses of Christina,
at which I had met cousin Alexander, Tête Jaune, and Court Nez.
I recalled the winter of the coteau buffalo-camps and the death of
Jules, and how I heard for the first time the keening of an Indian
woman for the dead.

Most of the men were away fishing on the evening of these
memories. Two camp-fires crackled in a curve of the bay. The light
from them, and the approaching night, danced together on the fringe
of forest. When a burning bough broke asunder it sent up sudden
showers of sparks. From the lake came occasionally small pipings of
sleepy ducks. A persistent rumble some way off was of a river pouring

on through the darkness into Superior. Before long the men would be returning.

Miles Macdonell came and sat down beside me.

" I have asked you nothing, Baxter," said he, " of your own life since I left Red River. It was remiss of me. We all have our own lives, though greatly involved in a multitude of communal and general affairs, but we are seldom allowed furlough, as it were. At times the life that we are forced by circumstances to live seems irrelevant!"

" I know well what you mean, sir. I have been feeling so ever since we left Red River." I paused and then, as one given opportunity to relieve his mind of many pent thoughts, I continued · " It was the same at Nelson Encampment in a way. Oh, so far as that goes it was the same at home——"

Macdonell looked at me with inviting interest and attention.

" But after Christina—my wife—died——" I hesitated.

" I did not know you were married, Baxter."

" I married the daughter of Court Nez," said I.

His eyebrows involuntarily rose, then realising he had shown astonishment he at once looked away.

" He sent her to the Ursulines Convent in Quebec to be educated," said I, that he might know she had acquaintance with more than camps and forts and trading-posts.

" My daughters went there," he said. " Were you married long?" he asked.

" We were married in November last, sir. She died on the day that Captain Semple and all those men were killed near the Seven Oaks. She died in childbirth. Surgeon White was called away to attend to the wounded and she had a hæmorrhage, a second hæmorrhage. The women with her could not stanch it."

" Ah, my dear lad," said Miles Macdonell, " you have all my sympathy. I must tell you—that you may understand how I feel for you—that my first wife, my dear cousin, died after giving birth to our second son. I know all the agony a man goes through at such a time. And the child?" he asked.

" The child is in the care of Mr. Chisholm's daughter, the younger one, Agnes, who married Robert Wallace. I made full arrangements with her before we left to come here. They did not want me to pay them but I insisted on that."

" A boy?"

" A girl."

We did not speak for some minutes.

" Indeed, sir," said I, " we have had shadows on Red River Settlement."

He stared at me.

" How strange you should say that!" he exclaimed. " When I talked with Lord Selkirk in London before coming out in '11 he used that very phrase——"

" That is why I said it," I replied. " The map, and the sunlight drifting off it——"

" Ah, I had forgotten. Of course, I told you myself. To be sure, I told you of that. And you have remembered it."

" I have often remembered it of late," said I.

" You bring it all back to me," said Miles Macdonell : " That room in London and the earl talking of the evictions and of his sympathy with the evicted. I am worried when I think of how his fortune has been depleted so far by all that has happened at the Forks. Well, he has another life, I have discovered. I know more of his private life now. He is blessed with a jewel of a woman for wife. Lord Selkirk, Baxter, has been most grossly calumniated. He is not that visionary and weak character that his enemies have striven to lead people to believe. I imagine he will not readily give in."

" The shadow will pass, sir."

" I pray so. I hope so. I trust so. There was a certain Reverend Mr. Straham in Upper Canada who published a very violent attack on his lordship after the party of settlers arrived there—oh, a monstrous attack on him! I hear that the reverend gentleman begins to regret it, that he says now he made it on the information of the North-West Company. This ruthless killing of Captain Semple and his men, when it becomes public, will give many a new view of affairs on Red River. By the way—you remembered Owen Keveny?"

" Yes."

" He has been murdered."

" Murdered! I recall that some prophesied he would come to a bloody end. He went back to Ireland in '14, I think."

"Yes, and returned to York Factory with Captain Semple last year, but went at once into the Company's service and was appointed to some post in this vast wilderness away up there," and he waved an arm towards the spaces of night behind. "The news came from yonder that he has been murdered. The rumour is that the North-Westers are at the back of that, though I admit that he had a name for being a man not prone to conciliation."

The men came back from the fishing, and talk then was all of the size and quantity of the catch. The woods round the bay were darkness. Beyond the camp-fire night was deep. There came still these occasional slight pipings of ducks dozing afloat on the water a little way off shore, and there was the plashing of the folding and unfolding of the lake's edge along the beach. Lake Superior, we all knew, had taken toll of many a canoe-load of voyageurs and these sounds were good to hear, telling of a placid lake.

They ebbed and returned as I dozed and woke. Half-awake, half-asleep, because of the tenor of the talk with Miles Macdonell in that lonely place I felt a stranger in the world of affairs and feuds; and now and then, thought I, one met those who felt similarly and perhaps on occasion revealed that they also were strangers impressed into a service that was not truly theirs.

II

It was on the 24th of July that we reached Sault Ste. Marie and to our astonishment found that not only Lord Selkirk had already arrived there but had despatched his boats along Lake Superior to Fond du Lac. The earl's physician, Mr Allen, met us on landing and gave us that news. But he would not permit any, not even Captain Macdonell, to see Lord Selkirk that night.

"It is most important," said Captain Macdonell. "He would wish to be apprised at once of what has befallen."

"I do not care what has befallen," said the surgeon. "So much has befallen here of late that he is worn out. He is in his tent; he is asleep. I was glad to see the batteaux sail off this afternoon, for with them gone he can relax. And——"

"But," persisted Captain Macdonell, "with the news I bring he may wish to alter his plans, may wish to bring back those batteaux and change his route, go to the Red River by Fort William instead of——"

"He can send to-morrow to halt them and get them to come back. I tell you, sir, Lord Selkirk is not a well man and he has been taxing himself. As his medical adviser I——"

"Oh, very good. You may be right."

"I am right."

In the morning Mr. Allen came to us where we had encamped by the shore and told us that he had informed Lord Selkirk of our arrival.

"He is considerably rested," he said. "What you have to tell him"—for Macdonell had acquainted the surgeon with much of it on the prior evening—"cannot but agitate him, but a night's sleep, one night's sound sleep at last, will have given him the strength now to hear all. Come and see him."

The tent was open to the lake. Lord Selkirk was reclining on a pallet but rose to welcome Macdonell.

"Well, Captain Macdonell!" he said. "Mr. Allen gave me a surprise when he told me you were here. I am glad I had not gone after the boats. Only the canoe for the transportation of Mr. Allen and myself and our personal servants remains here."

Then he glanced at me and shot a look of inquiry at the Governor.

"This is Mr. Baxter, sir. I have mentioned him to you when giving accounts of our doings."

"How do you do, Mr. Baxter. I am very glad to meet you."

Selkirk extended a hand and took mine with a firm pressure, then addressed himself again to Macdonell. There was a manner of great restraint on the man, I thought. To me he gave an impression of quietness and self-control. He was of my colouring and an inch or two, perhaps, taller than I, nearly as tall as Miles Macdonell but slender and gaunt.

"Let us be seated," he said, and then: "You return because of ill news?" he asked in a voice that might to some ears suggest diffidence. As an aside in my mind came the thought that I had met many diverse men in many years, heard many sorts of utterance from the blustering, or domineering, voice of Owen Keveny to the quiet voice of this man.

"Yes, sir, I do," replied Miles Macdonell.

" To what effect? Do you tell me you have been all the way to Red River and back?"

" Only to Bas de la Rivière," said Miles Macdonell. " There I received the news that brings me here. I met there the settlers—once again on their way from Red River."

" They were leaving the Colony again?"

" Yes. But Mr. Baxter can tell you better than I as he was a witness of the whole dreadful affair. I have heard various accounts from various people, but I think you should hear what he has to say."

I was in the midst of the recapitulation when Selkirk, who had been listening with knotted brows and close-set lips, abruptly spoke.

" I must interrupt," said he. " This will change my plans. Would you be so good, Captain Macdonell, as to order your men instantly to go after the boats and tell them to return here—they are not away long. Or better still," he amended, " my own canoe-men. Yours may be weary. Mine are fresh. They have been resting."

Mr. Allen rose.

" I shall tell them," said he. " You have more to learn from Captain Macdonell and Mr. Baxter."

Miles Macdonell turned to me.

" You have not yet told his lordship," he said, " of the prisoners taken by Norman Macleod."

" Prisoners?" said the earl.

" Yes, sir," I replied, " that is the name for them, though Macleod spoke of them as witnesses;" and I told him of Norman Macleod requesting Mr. Pritchard to write an account of the killing at Seven Oaks, and the result.

" We must have these people released!" exclaimed Lord Selkirk when I came to an end. " This is preposterous. Here is the most detestable system of villainy that ever was allowed to prevail in the British Dominions."

He packed the pillows behind him and leant against them. Part propped on an elbow, part reclining on his camp-bed, one foot on the ground, one leg over the other, he gazed out of the tent door, chin in hand, deep in thought.

" Yes," he said at last, ending his reverie which we honoured with silence, " yes, I shall now write to Sir John Sherbrooke giving him all details of what you have told me, Mr. Baxter, and asking him for further legal powers and, again, for a protective military force for the settlers. It means another delay. So far I have been allowed only six men and a sergeant, and these but for personal protection. A concession? A fobbing of me off! All the legal power I could obtain was a minor magistracy of justice of the peace." His lean jaws tightened. "At any rate, we shall not go by Fond du Lac and Red Lake," he said, vigorously. "We shall go now by Fort William. Have you provisions sufficient for your party?"

"Hardly sufficient," replied Macdonell.

"Then do you see to that, pray. I had closed my account with the traders here, settled all that, but we shall have to reopen again. I have nothing here for your men, they being unexpected. Yes, by Fort William, whatever Sir John Sherbrooke can or cannot do, we shall proceed now."

"Very good, sir."

"And if necessary," added Lord Selkirk, "we shall turn out the North-Westers—turn them out of Fort William as they have turned out the settlers!"

III

A sense of the extent of the land, of its distances and the need for patience, was undoubtedly felt by the earl after he had dispatched couriers with his letter to Sir John Sherbrooke. The ex-soldiers, going out to farm under his auspices, brought back on their way to Fond du Lac, did not share his impatience. For their services in the boats en route they were being paid. What impatience I experienced was for news of my little Christina, of how she fared away off yonder to the north of Winnipic.

When the reply came from Sir John Sherbrooke is was not what Selkirk desired. He was advised to seek the assistance of magistrates in his neighbourhood, Mr. Askin at Drummond's Island or Mr. Ermatinger at Saulte Ste. Marie. As Mr. Askin held the more important position from the earl's point of view then, one giving him wider powers of jurisdiction, he decided to make his representations to him first and retain Mr. Ermatinger as a last hope. Drummond's Island was just next door as it were, at the north end of Lake

Huron; and while waiting for Askin's reply he gave orders for all to be ready for embarkation.

When the messengers returned none could tell by Lord Selkirk's aspect whether the reply was to his mind or not. I was close by at the time and observed his purposed calm. Slowly he read the note, even paused midway to slap at the mosquitoes on his hand and to shake from the sheet the slain ones that fell on it, then folded it and put it in a pocket. Shocked by the news of Captain Semple's end, the affair of Seven Oaks, the last bitter eviction of his colonists, the detention of Mr. Pritchard and others, there is no doubt that he felt he must school himself into preparedness for rebuffs, be ready to accept them without agitation. He had of late been not at his best in health and must conserve his energy to cope with what troubles might still be ahead.

"Ermatinger," said he reflectively. "Ermatinger. I wonder if he is related to the Ermatinger of the express service from York Factory to the Pacific coast of which I have heard. Well, I know the magistrate's residence. I shall be back anon."

He had been sitting at his tent door in his shirt-sleeves because of the heat. Rising then he entered the tent and his servant followed. I was reminded of another occasion when close outside a tent I heard voices come clear from within—of the day when Court Nez, deferring a dram, demanded to see his grand-daughter and we went together to the Chisholm tent at the fort. I recalled how, on leaving, we overheard Mrs. Chisholm exclaim: "Who is that dreadful-looking man that David is with?" On this occasion of overhearing there was not any biting criticism or discouraging or unhappy opinion of anybody, but it nevertheless reminded me of that other one.

There was the sound of the whisking of a brush.

"The edge of this cuff, my lord, is wearing thin," came the servant's voice.

"Why so it is!" said Selkirk with a slight laugh. "I may be out at elbows before all this is over."

"Oh, do not say that, my lord. This blue coat, now——"

"Do you think Mr. Ermatinger is to be influenced by attire?" asked Douglas.

I moved away.

CHAPTER THREE

I

On the 2nd of August, after these enforced, unavoidable, and yet wise delays, from Sault Ste. Marie went the boats again—but north instead of west. Mr. Ermatinger, like Mr. Askin, had expressed his regret for inability to offer any assistance. Sir John Sherbrooke had felt that the best he could do was to send a full report of the affair of Seven Oaks to Lord Bathurst, the Colonial Secretary in London. But Lord Selkirk required immediate and retributive action.

Once or twice we camped at the same places as on the eastern voyage and woods that had heard the old Gaelic songs and evening psalms of the settlers that Cameron lured away heard the rollicking voices of the mercenaries, the ex-soldiers, in lilts to which they had marched in Europe as well as on the western continent to which they had come in the course of their martial lives. As the great majority of these soldier-settlers were from the De Meuron regiment, as time slipped along all were so called: "the De Meurons."

On the evening of the 12th day of August the fleet drew in from the lake at a point that thereafter would be down as Point Meuron. Boats and canoes were beached. Early on the morning of the 13th Lord Selkirk took action. In what he proposed to do he would not employ the regulars who had been accorded to him on the understanding that they were for personal protection; and though their military uniforms would have aided him with the scarlet of authority he abstained from doing so—in my opinion not merely to prevent the possible subsequent charge that he had exceeded his rights but from an honest and direct desire to adhere faithfully to the understanding regarding them.

In command of Captain D'Orsonnens he despatched a party of the De Meurons to make the arrest of the chief partner in residence, William McGillivray, and the warrant he signed as a justice of the peace. Their appearance, by long campaigning, was military enough, I considered as I watched them go. Marching off in step they conveyed the impression of much acquaintance with united and vigorous action. The bearer of the warrant who accompanied them was a Mr. McNab and as those in our camp saw them go someone, of course, had to spill into the approving quiet: "Mr. McGillivray will be nabbed in no time."

And in no time he was nabbed. At sight of William McGillivray walking down the slope with Captain D'Orsonnens and Mr. McNab, even before I could study his face, I had a suspicion regarding the ease of the serving of that warrant. Something in the carriage, the bearing of the man reminded me of Duncan Cameron of old Fort Gibraltar. A dread took me that here there was to be a preliminary policy of submission, of acquiescence, designed to give the appearance of the innocent shamelessly wronged.

"How do you do, my lord?" said William McGillivray with a fine bow as Selkirk came from his tent. "This is very unexpected indeed, but of course I would not question your authority as a justice of the peace. As soon as your appointed constable presented the warrant I made haste to comply."

"Oh, too smooth, too smooth!" I sighed to myself.

"Will you be so good as to come to my tent, sir," said the earl, "that we may discuss certain matters?"

Before the tent door a sentry paced with fixed bayonet. High white clouds sailed through the blue space. The edge of blue Superior broke in foam along the bays and promontories. In the trees near-by winds sighed and passed. I turned and strolled away and as I walked Mr. McNab joined me.

"Well, Mr. Baxter," he said, "that man McGillivray acted as a perfect gentleman. Promptly he prepared to accompany me. Captain D'Orsonnens was out-by with his squad and never required at all, at all. It seems that there are other two partners in residence. One of them was as full as a neep and seemed to find a private amusement in the arrest. Says he, 'Oh-ho!' says he, 'there goes Pomp and Ostentation now!' The other is a wild-looking man. He offered himself as bail and asked the one with the load of liquor in him to do likewise, and despite his jeer at McGillivray being arrested he agreed. All I could say was that I would repeat their offer to the justice of the peace—that is to say to my Lord Selkirk."

We were strolling along the bank as he talked and I suddenly noticed a man walking towards us from the direction of Fort William. He stood on the ridge and there halted to look down on our camp, at the boats and canoes drawn up on the beach. There was something to me very familiar in his gait, glimpsed just before he stopped, and in his posture, keenly remarked when he halted and stood there.

Where had I seen this man before? He was massive, an enormous fellow, considerably younger than the arrested McGillivray. He wore his hair unusually long, longer than most, and it was bunched out round his face much like a wig of his grandfather's day.

"I know him, I have him placed," thought I. "He was with Norman Macleod when the settlers' effects were rummaged through on the way and Captain Semple's trunk was stolen by the North-Westers."

Just as I thus remembered him he turned, his survey of the camp over, and went stalking back by the way he had come. I then had no desire save to return and make report of recognising him. The release of the prisoners taken by the North-Westers was, I had heard the earl say, to be one of his first demands, and there was the man to approach promptly with that demand.

McNab went with me but looked back over his shoulder for a few steps.

"That was one of the other partners," said he. "That's the one Mr. McGillivray addressed as McLoughlin. He's a fierce-looking man when you see him close, with a glare in his eyes under an awful frown. Aye, that's John McLoughlin, a fearsome-looking young man."

"So that's who he is," said I.

"Aye, that s who he is. The other partner, the drouth, is by name of McKenzie."

But I had no great interest in him then, or his name. I wanted to be at the camp to report that a man who had been with Norman Macleod when Mr. Pritchard and the others were held prisoners—allegedly witnesses—was close at hand. I never knew how much, if at all, Lord Selkirk was influenced to his next action by that information. The discussion with McGillivray may of itself have led to it. Be that as it may, on my return I asked the sentry to call Captain Macdonell from the tent.

Macdonell, who came out curious or perhaps even anxious to know why he had been sent for, did not apparently think he had been flippantly summoned when I communicated my news. He listened gravely.

"Thank you, Baxter, for the information," he said, and went back at once to the session.

Warrants, at any rate, were made out after it for the arrest of the other partners.   On that occasion Captain Macdonell accompanied McNab. D'Orsonnens again remained at the gate of the stockade with his men.

A servant at the door of the agents' quarters asked, suspicious, surly, what we wanted.

"We wish to see Mr. McLoughlin and Mr. McKenzie," said McNab. In a moment or two McLoughlin came to the door.

"Yes—this is he, the same man," I muttered to Miles Macdonell.

I had just made that remark when McLoughlin was followed by a man who was perhaps of an age with McGillivray, or even a little older. He peered at us, saw the file of men just outside the gate, and seemed to be of the merry opinion that they were a guard of honour for him. He squared his shoulders, saluted, beamed genially.

"Oh-ho!" murmured McLoughlin over his shoulder. "Here comes Sleepy-head," and then in a lower voice he added : "Let me introduce Mr. McKenzie, gentlemen, Mr. Daniel McKenzie. Mr. McKenzie is a most eager friend of your side, and at the moment very drunk," he finished.

There are situations that can be surmised.

"This man," thought I, looking on, "this man McKenzie may possibly be the best of the partners," and at once I found myself ready to say a word on his behalf.

Mr. McKenzie drew himself up and gave a bow which nearly unbalanced him.

"He speaks truth," said he. "I have always been against the fomenting of feud against Selkirk and his settlers."

"Go to bed, Dan," said McLoughlin.

"To bed! To be rid of me? If Pomp and Ostentation would withdraw and leave Sleepy-head here everything might be more happily executed."

"I have a warrant here for the arrest of baith of ye," said McNab and, in a voice as of an intoning cleric, began to read it.

That was a large fort, much larger than Fort Gibraltar.   The stockade must have enclosed many acres. As his singing voice sounded out men came from various houses, some of them armed with muskets, others with clubs, new-cut cudgels.

Macdonell gave them a sidelong glance.

"We do not wish to have trouble," said he in a level voice. "I trust you will restrain your men from violence."

But they came closer. Some of them, seeing the file at the gate, dashed in that direction, presumably intending to shut it but D'Orsonnens gave the order and his men marched in. Standing to one side of the door of the officers' quarters, I had a glimpse of a De Meuron, evidently at a word from the captain, hurrying away, clearly for reinforcements. It had been Selkirk's policy to send a very small party on the arrests instead of a force that might suggest a wholesale assault on the place.

A mob of North-West labourers dashed at that small party, encircling it, and at the same time two or three came leaping towards the declaiming McNab, Macdonell, and me. There was to be a melee. For a moment I had a sickness at the pit of the stomach. Here, thought I, is going to be a repetition of the bloody affair of Seven Oaks. McNab's voice was raised higher.

"He's like a bellman!" thought I, a wave of amusement meeting the wave of dread.

A big bearded man in buckskin trousers hurled himself at me, sent me staggering backwards. I fell, the giant on top, thrusting my head into the earth. The smell of dust was in my nostrils. I wriggled free, wriggled upwards, jabbed a fist at my assailant's temple, came to my feet. Miles and D'Orsonnens were shouting to the De Meurons, McLoughlin shouting to the North-Westers to stop the scrimmage. The bearded man rose and sought to grapple with me again but my reach was fortunately long. I held out one arm rigidly to fend the fellow off and his nose came in contact with it, violent because of his furious spring. The blood gushed. For a moment he paused, putting his hand to his face, and that pause was my opportunity. I felled him with a swinging blow and let out a yell as I did so, a yell I heard myself as ferine. I suspected that here was an attempt to massacre us. I would fight to the last.

Macdonell was in similar combat beside me, knocking down one of the labourers. And then suddenly there came a lull. It was the most unexpected lull imaginable. The thuds and the imprecations ceased. It was as though a communal decision had come to obey orders to desist. The North-Westers drew off. The one I had felled returned to consciousness, saw his fellows retiring, rose, shook himself and followed them. The De Meurons looked one to another and began to laugh quietly, stood there with their chests heaving, shaking blood from their knuckles, mopping blood from their heads. D'Orsonnens gave the order for them to fall in again and there they waited before the partners' residence, in command after that brush that had been whimsical to them.

In at the gate came the reinforcing party for which a runner had been sent, led by a lieutenant—Fauche. Very much disappointed he and his men seemed to be when they saw that all was over.

11

Lord Selkirk's party apparently had the mastery, though there were many more North-Westers' employees in the fort than on his side. They must have outnumbered the De Meurons and the rest of us by two to one but their officers had accepted the state of affairs: McGillivray, very dignified, was allowed to go back to his residence and join the other partners there.

Afternoon sent the shadow of the palisade stretching over the grass. Lord Selkirk, with Captain Macdonell, another lieutenant, Mr. Graffenreith, and myself, went into the partners' house.

"You gentlemen," said he, "will be permitted full liberty here within your own quarters, on condition that you will abstain from any hostile action."

"I give you the promise," said McGillivray, and looked to McLoughlin.

"I too," said McLoughlin. "Do you want a Bible-oath on it?"

"No, gentlemen. I think the promise will suffice. I look upon you as on parole."

Daniel McKenzie was amused at that and chuckled to himself.

"You may not think it necessary to have my promise also, m'lud," he said, "but I give it. I promise that I shall not order an attack on you and your men in the night. I promise that I shall join in no plots of the dark hours against you," and he waved a hand in air before him while McGillivray and McLoughlin watched him sullenly.

Late that night my thoughts were carried back to a day at Fort Gibraltar, carried back by an odour in the air, an acrid tang from the smoke from the chimneys. Seeing Miles Macdonell emerge from his tent I drew attention to it.

"It is the same," said I, "as when Mr. Robertson sent to Gibraltar to arrest Duncan Cameron. They are burning papers over there."

Miles Macdonnell raised his head, sniffed the air.

"You are right," said he. "Well, it is done now. We can get nothing from the ashes."

But that odour, as well as sounds that had kept Lord Selkirk awake, led to other discoveries on the morrow.

III

At an early hour the earl, accompanied by D'Orsonnens, Miles Macdonell, and me, with a guard of six De Meurons, went into the fort again. The guard was left at the door of the officers' house with Fauche. The manner of our entry caused McGillivray and McLoughlin, seated in the main room, to exchange an involuntary glance as of conspirators revealed.

Lord Selkirk gave them no matutinal greeting. They might have been, in fact, not only prisoners but prisoners to whom their warden was not minded to unbend. Before the broad hearth he stood still, looking at the ashes that lay in it.

"Good-morning, my lord," came a thick voice behind us. There was McKenzie apparently in the same condition as on the past night, ingratiatingly drunk. "Good-morning, gentlemen. Early risers, early risers!"

Selkirk still considered the ashes in the hearth, without commenting on them.

"I think we will take a turn or two about the place," he said to all or to no one in particular. He passed out of the house, D'Orsennens, Miles and I following. "I did not sleep much last night," he explained when we were outside, "and I heard considerable sounds of tramping and comings and goings in the bush. Let us take a turn about in the vicinity."

From doorways of houses we were watched but that was all.

"There has been much recent trampling here," said Selkirk, pointing to the ground. "Let us go and see where all this leads to."

It led into the woods and there beside what might have been a grave it stopped.

"Shall I send the men for spades, my lord?" asked D'Orsonnens. "Do so, please."

When the spades were brought the ground was dug and we came upon several barrels of gunpowder. Following up the broad hint of other marks of recent tramplings we found in the loft of a barn many muskets, loaded and ready to be primed.

"Well!" said Lord Selkirk, "Let us continue."

We had gone but a little way, making a circuit to rear of the main buildings, looking for other sign of recent doings, when we heard a voice hailing: "*Au secours! Au secours!*"

We halted and gave ear.

"*Au secours!* Help! Capitaine Macdonell! Is that the voice of Capitaine Macdonell?"

"This is Captain Macdonell," he gave answer. "Who calls, and where?"

"Here, here. It is I—Lagimoniere."

"Lagimoniere!" ejaculated Lord Selkirk.

"Lagimoniere!!" I gasped.

Hurriedly we all headed directly for the hail, crashing the warm odours out of the scrub, raising agitated butterflies. So we came to a path that led to a small log cabin, or less a cabin than a front of logs against a low bank. The place was what was known as a dug-out—a place much like a root-house. There was a padlock on the heavy door. One of the men, at a sign from D'Orsonnens, prised it off with the spade he carried.

The door opened and Lagimoniere came out, blinking in the sunshine.

"Ah, my dear capitaine!" he cried out, and taking Macdonell by the shoulders kissed him on both cheeks. Then he saw Selkirk: "Milord," and he bowed. "I did not know you were there. Your voice is so quiet I did not hear it. What a journey I have had! And David Baxter! Ah, *mon ami,* what do you do here?"

He embraced me, then swept his hand backwards at the den in which he had been prisoned.

"All lined with logs," he said, "or I would have dug my way out. And every day when they brought my food they came in and looked to see that I had not been trying to dig my way to freedom."

Lord Selkirk left us and entered the dug-out to examine it more closely. Lagimoniere turned to me.

"My wife?" he asked. "When did you see her last?"

"When the settlers left Red River."

"Left Red River!"

"All had to go. They were attacked again. Captain Semple was killed."

"*Sacré!* Captain Semple. And again all were sent away? And they come this way now as these others of last year?"

"No, no. We are going back."

He looked bewildered.

"I do not understand," he said.

"They have gone to Jack River. We are on our way to Red River with many men, over a hundred ex-soldiers."

"Ah, I must control my heart. I am confused. You say you are on your way to Red River—*to* Red River?"

"Yes. I have passed here already from Red River to Sault Ste. Marie where we met Lord Selkirk——"

"Oh, I shall hear all that later. But tell me, tell me of my wife and children. Tell me more of them."

"They are safe," I assured him. "They did not have to go. The free-traders are not in the black books of the North-Westers. Chief Peguis is looking after Madame Lagimoniere. He took her away on the day we left to a tepee he had pitched to east of the river—just across from that cabin in which——"

At that moment Lord Selkirk came back to us from the dug-out.

"My dear Lagimoniere," he said, "how long have you been in that den? How did you come here?"

"Oh, it would not have been too bad, *milord,* if I had not been a prisoner," replied Lagimoniere. "I have lived for months on the great prairies in such a place and with my wife and children, but free. I was brought here. Some Indians of the Ottawa tribe, bribed by our enemies, caught me in a camp. I woke to find I was a prisoner. They took me to some North-Westers who brought me here. There is your question answered, *milord.* And now I must tell you I think there are other prisoners held here. There was one night, some while ago, I could hear when it was quiet a man moaning. He moaned much for two nights and then he moaned no more. Perhaps he died."

"We must search thoroughly, my lord," said D'Orsonnens. "We must search all the buildings and also in the surrounding bush, especially where there is any little knoll, lest there are other places such as this dug-out, more or less hidden away."

"There's some sort of a house," said the earl, pointing.

We made our way to it, D'Orsonnens leading.

"It is just a necessary," said he, opening the door.

Lagimoniere looked in with him.

"Strange," said Lord Selkirk. "There is a heap of hay and it looks as if someone has lain on it. Faugh!"

From the stench and the buzzing of flies we retreated.

"I see another house back there in the bush," said Miles Macdonell.

We did not continue to where a path might be found leading to it, merely passed again, crashing, on through the tangle of scrub. As we were thus thrusting a way for ourselves we heard a sound of scurrying feet, as though someone was taking flight from the half-seen building.

"Halt, there!" called Captain Macdonell. "Halt, there! Why do you run?"

But the feet continued to pound away from us and the noise of breaking bush came to our ears.

We approached the building. It was of heavy logs and had no window. By the door was a stump of wood, much like a chopping-block. It struck me that it was there as a seat. The door was closed. In two massive cleats that had been affixed to it a massive bolt of wood lay, projecting on either side, flush to the jamb-logs. At a sign from D'Orsonnens one of the men lifted the bolt out and pushed the door open.

We all stood there staring as John Pritchard stepped out, blinking in the sunlight as Lagimoniere had blinked.

"Mr. Pritchard!" I cried out.

Behind him came the two Hudson's Bay Company's men and the two settlers who had been taken by Norman Macleod allegedly as witnesses, actually as prisoners. After the excitement of the discovery of Lagimoniere the welcome for these was less emotional, more restrained. Miles Macdonell and I made formal introductions of all these released men.

Pritchard was very controlled indeed, bowing to Lord Selkirk.

" I am in a sense your first settler, sir," he said. " I mean the first apart from those from Scotland and Ireland. Shropshire was my native place."

" To be sure," replied Selkirk. " Captain Macdonell mentioned you in letters."

Pritchard turned to me.

" I have discovered what befel poor Bourke," said he.

" And what was that?" I asked anxiously, unable to imitate his air of composure.

" Because I was formerly in the North-West service I discovered it," he said. " I would never have found out otherwise. I heard of him from a man here who had to guard me when I was taken one day to a necessary. It is agonising to consider that when we were at Bas de la Rivière—when you, Captain Macdonell, got so far—Bourke was quite close."

" Is he alive?" I demanded, but Mr. Pritchard did not hear or else had to tell all in his own way.

" He was in the North-West fort there. He was taken down from Red River a day ahead of us, and then after a halt they brought him on here. I asked for Bourke as soon as we arrived here but they said they knew nothing of him. As I say, when I was out that day my guard, being an old friend in past days, told me the truth."

" He is not dead, is he?" I asked.

" Where is he now?" said Lord Selkirk.

" They have taken him away again," replied Mr. Pritchard. " They prisoned him here in a necessary—had him locked in—took his meals there, never once tended his wounds."

" That would be the man I heard in the night, moaning!" exclaimed Lagimoniere.

" It would be he who lay on the straw we saw in that privy a few minutes ago," said Selkirk. " Come! We shall get back to McGillivray now and hear from him what has happened to Mr. Bourke."

He set off vigorously, his blue coat-tails flying as he strode along. A temper was clearly in him. Back at the agents' house he asked

D'Orsonnens to order the guard to come in with us. Into the main room we all went. There, still sitting together at the central table, were McGillivray and McLoughlin.

I was thinking much of Bourke, recalling him aboard the *Edward and Anne* on the way out from Stornoway, at Nelson Encampment, on the Hayes River, recalling his marriage, recalling him as he was on the day when the *métis* attacked at the administration houses.

"Can you tell me," Lord Selkirk demanded without preamble, "on what charge you were holding these gentlemen as prisoners?" and he waved an arm at the five who accompanied us.

"And where, my lord, is Bourke?" said I, but was not heard.

"Prisoners!" ejaculated McGillivray, as if horrified at the suggestion. "They are not held as prisoners, sir. They are held as witnesses. I had information to that effect from Norman Macleod, who sent them here. That one especially—Mr. Pritchard there—is required because he wrote a very full report of all that befell at Seven Oaks on Frog Plain on the 19th of June."

Mr. Pritchard stepped forward.

"Yes," said he. "And it was that report which made him hold me as prisoner. He told me on reading it that I had written much that might get me into trouble."

"What have they done with Bourke?" I prompted.

No attention was paid to me.

"Well," said Selkirk, "whether prisoners or witnesses, these gentlemen are free now and it is you who are prisoners. I find that so far from keeping to your quarters last night you were secreting arms and ammunition. Also you have, by the way, been burning incriminating letters," and he pointed to the hearth. "You are assuredly prisoners now and we are the warders. I am sending you straight to Montreal."

"Bourke, my lord—ask them what has befallen Bourke," I pled.

"Sending us to Montreal!" ejaculated McGillivray. "This is preposterous!"

"I would send you to England had I the power, but my lawyers, Messrs. Stuart and Gale, will take care of you in Montreal."

"My lord, I beg of you——" I began, desperate.

"And now," said Selkirk, "tell me of Mr. Bourke." They looked one to another, McGillivray and McLoughlin. "Why," he inquired, "was he confined in a necessary, a common privy?"

"He was wounded," replied McGillivray. "He could not be moved to and fro because of his wound."

Selkirk shook his head as in regret over humanity.

"Where is he now?" he said.

"He must be well on his way to Montreal. He will receive attention there," said McGillivray.

"It is a far cry to Montreal for a wounded man to obtain attention," said Selkirk very quietly.

Those accustomed to a raising of the voice, an excitement of manner, a violence of language under stress of feeling, must have marvelled at him. His manner was so quiet that McGillivray and McLoughlin, glancing again one to the other, seemed to think that he might not act on what he had said. But they did not know the man. He turned to D'Orsonnens.

"Captain D'Orsonnens," said he, "will you kindly see that these two gentlemen have their servants pack just what they need for the journey to Montreal. You will select your most reliable men and a boat's crew to take them thither. I shall have letters to send with the officer you put in command, important letters to Lady Selkirk, to Lord Bathurst, as well as to my lawyers on whom on arrival the officer in command will at once attend. So be sure to inform me when all is ready."

"Yes, my lord. And what of the third prisoner here? Has he to go also?"

"I had forgotten him," said Selkirk; "but no—that is unnecessary."

IV

Daniel McKenzie had been bousing for days but there were few abstainers from alcohol in the scattered forts and posts and it was not generally considered that inebriation rendered a man incompetent to do business. So, when the other two partners had been sent off to Montreal, Douglas arranged with McKenzie for a purchase of stores at Fort William.

"They may tell me," he said later to Miles Macdonell, "that a receipt from all three partners here is necessary, but we need the supplies. Our soldier-settlers number a hundred, to say nothing of the rest, our additional boatmen and others. All must be fed."

From Red River Mr. Fidler came and told us that the North-Westers there, armed and numerous, had turned him and the other two Hudson's Bay officers who had remained out of Fort Douglas, ordering them to find quarters elsewhere as they looked upon it as a Colony post. He had come so far to see Lord Selkirk, hearing from Indians that he was there.

Lord Selkirk had a conference with Miles Macdonell, Captains D'Orsonnens and Matthey, and Peter Fidler and the upshot of it was that Fidler departed with some of the De Meurons to demand surrender of the next North-West fort on the way to Red River—the fort at Lac la Pluie. In about a week he returned to report that the officer in charge refused to surrender even when informed of the occupation of Fort William. "Be damned to you!" he had said. "Come and take me—if you can!" So then Captain D'Orsonnens went with the field-pieces. Still it was Lord Selkirk's desire to avoid bloodshed; the milder Mr. Fidler for that reason he had sent first. D'Orsonnens was all for violent assault, but with the earl's instructions for the saving of bloodshed in mind, for preliminary he mounted his pieces and training them warningly on the fort sat down to a quiet siege. It seemed that they had not enough provisions at Lac la Pluie for that and after a few days the agent there came out with a white napkin on a stick and surrendered.

While taking tally of the goods being purchased from the North-West Company through Mr. Daniel McKenzie, discovery was made of a great number of packages of furs bearing the Hudson's Bay Company's stamp.

"Stolen goods," said Selkirk as his men moved them one after the other into view.

"You know what these represent, sir," said Miles Macdonell.

"More evidence of what we have been hearing in London," replied Selkirk, "evidence of robberies, often with violence, sometimes with bloodshed, in the farther parts of the Indian Countries."

"I told them," said McKenzie, looking on, "I told them virtue would have its punishment. I mean wrong-doing. By that I mean that the birds come home to roost. I trust I express myself clearly."

"Yes, yes, quite so," said Lord Selkirk, and taking him by the elbow guided him through the doorway, troubled over many things.

People would say he had made his purchases from a man inebriated, might even say he had kept him inebriated for his own ends. People would say—he could not help what people might say. Already he had had experience of people of cynical or sinister turn imputing base and covert reasons for honest and open action. The flight of time troubled him, the distances in this great land, the sharp differences of the seasons. The summer was gone. Out in the windy day streamers of leaves were scurrying from the deciduous trees. On the 12th of August we had arrived there from Sault Ste. Marie and here was the end of September because of all the delays.

To go on to Red River then, said all his advisers who knew the land, would be unwise. The enemy would be strongly prepared, in occupancy of Fort Douglas. Here he had now, thanks to his deal with McKenzie, supplies for his men. Soon the snow would be falling. Fort Douglas should be assaulted when assault was least expected by its defenders. It should not be attacked by a force coming up Red River before the "freeze up" but after that, when attack was no longer feared, perhaps at the hour favoured by Indians, on some dark winter night when the night was nearly over but dawn not come.

There had been a plan for Lagimoniere to conduct a force across country to Red River. But already he was irked by the delays in continuing his journey home to his wife and children. His precious time was lost while the North-West fort at Lac la Pluie was being brought to the point of surrender. His precious time was further lost while a force went to Lake of the Woods to look for possible stolen bales of Hudson's Bay Company's furs in the North-West post there; and not only such bales, by the way, were found but the rest of the cannon that Duncan Cameron had been "storing" for the settlers. Lagimoniere was eager to be on his way and Selkirk did not try to detain him longer.

"You will travel quicker alone," said he, "than if you had to lead our men. You wish to see your wife again. I owe you a debt beyond your wages and I shall pay it to the best of my ability when I come into my kingdom, so to speak, and those who have trusted in me have their inheritance."

Lagimoniere only smiled in reply. He had faith in his powers of travel when alone. With the posts of the Lake of the Woods and Lac la Pluie in the hands of his friends he would not be ambushed on the way by enemies from them. If the North-Westers dared to molest him when he came to journey's end, because of his service to Colin Robertson in going to Montreal with a letter for Lord Selkirk, they would fare badly. He had plenty of friends there among the free-traders—and among the *métis* also.

He sat for an hour or two in conference with D'Orsonnens and Macdonell, drawing maps for them to make all clear against the day when they would follow to Red River by ways on which they would not be expected.

" I shall be home, maybe, before the snow flies," he said, " but I take snowshoes in case. Once I travelled from Red River to Montreal in two months. This is not half that distance I go, but the snow may fly soon. It is a long way even so." But he took few provisions. " It is better to travel light," he declared. " I will fish. I will make night-line and have breakfast in morning. Good fish. I will make snare for rabbit and rabbits will run in the snare in night and spring the snare. Whizz! Whizz! Up in the air and hang! So I will have my dinner. Good-bye, *messieurs*. Good-bye, *milord*. A Dieu. I shall see you again at Red River."

CHAPTER FOUR

I

NIGHT was over Assiniboia. A chill wind out of the north-east was sending a slight peppering of snow aslant across the space.

A body of men, like so many snowmen, sat upon ladders that they had made in the last dense wood on their way. We were not far from the place where Fort Gibraltar had stood. We were all white in hue, by race as well as by the figures made of us by the snow, all save four: Chippewyan Indians who had come to Fort William shortly after Lagimoniere left there and went on alone to his wife and children. They had come to see the "big white chief," Selkirk, with a message from Lagimoniere who had talked to them and told them to tell Selkirk they knew the ways through the land of lakes to the prairie country, other ways besides the waterways, and might therefore be helpful.

It had been an arduous journey for us under their guidance and on that dark night some of the De Meurons murmured their amazement that any one could wish to live in such a land. But they were seasoned campaigners and their derisive complaints were not suggestive of weakness. Occasionally some rose and trotted quickly round in circles to aid the circulation of the blood.

D'Orsonnens conferred with Miles Macdonell.

"We might go now," he suggested.

One of the Indians replied for Captain Macdonell: "Too soon. You say you want catch all asleep. You wait."

Nobody spoke for some time. We cowered into our scarves and collars, for the snow was determined to sift down our necks.

"If we stay much longer," said D'Orsonnens, and laughed, "we shall have to cross the plains here on snowshoes."

"Would that it were a heavy fall, and wet," said Macdonell. "With this dry frost there will be some scrunching as we advance," and then hopefully he added: "But the whistling of the wind may cover the sound from many who may lie awake."

There was a faint, filtered, eerie light round us, the suffused light

353

z

of the moon through the snow whirls. At last the Chippewa leader spoke. "Maybe time," he said.

"Now remember," Miles Macdonell warned the Indians, "we want to take the place without killing anybody. The big chief wants it that way."

"They kill plenty your people," said the leader.

"Well, that's the way the big chief wants," answered Macdonell. "So when we get in over the walls of Fort Douglas, remember no——" and very softly he imitated the cry: *La-la-la-la-la-la-la!*

They laughed quietly. "No war-cry," said one.

"No. No war-cry."

D'Orsonnens addressed his men.

"Now," said he, "when we get there let there be as little talk as possible. Get into the positions as arranged. Put the scaling-ladders up as quietly and as quickly as possible. Separate into groups inside as arranged. Enter the houses that are clearly dormitories and announce to those in them that they are prisoners and that none must try to resist."

"What do we do if any one fires at us?" a man asked.

"In that case, shoot, but shoot only those who offer armed resistance. Lord Selkirk impressed it on me that he has no wish whatever to imitate the attack that was made on Captain Semple."

I was shaking, part with the cold, part with excitement. Here I was back again by Red River, near the site of the building in which I had first met Christina. We set off across the plain, our heads lowered and canted to the thin drift of snow, our muskets slung from our shoulders, carrying the ladders. Fort Douglas loomed up before us. The ladders were stealthily raised, leant against the wall, and up each one a man clambered. Atop, he bent to catch the last rung of a second ladder then pushed up to him, balanced it on the palisade, canted it down on the inner side, disappeared and was succeeded by another man, and that one by another.

But I was not there only to watch and fix upon my mind a picture for remembering in years to come. I was there to participate. Up I clambered on a ladder, poised on the edge, felt for the top rung of the inner one, fumbled quickly down, my hands numb, though I wore mitts, from grasping the snow-chilled wood. As I came to ground within the square I found Captain Macdonell there.

"Well, Baxter, here we are home again," he muttered, and hurried away with some of the men.

Home again!

Before I got into the place a few of the men had gone to the cabin by the gate. There was no sentry on duty, no attack being expected, but several people were asleep in that guard-house. I heard D'Orsonnens speaking: " . . . and if any man there stirs or cries out till I return here, club him!"

Miles Macdonell, with that remark to me of "Home again," had gone swiftly away. I saw him in the blurred moonlight, with his long stride, leading a group across the square. The snow was not deep. In places the wind had blown it so that there was but a film of white over the ground. Our men, hurrying stealthily on their duty, left the dark prints of their passage there. No light was in any of the windows under the scattered roofs. I could see, dimly, figures moving from house to house, and then they were lost to sight, presumably as they opened doors and entered.

I had been given no special duty, no special orders. I took no active part. There was, as a matter of fact, no specially active part for any unless those who were first to enter the houses might be looked upon as taking a specially active part. Sleepers were awakened to find strangers round them armed, strangers, who told them they were prisoners and, if they had muskets by them, removed them. In the years that were to come people, anxious to have details of those days, were sometimes advised to "ask Mr. Baxter—he was there" about the recapture of Fort Douglas. They were inclined, having inquired of me, to consider me a very matter-of-fact person.

"There was nothing special about it," I would inform them. "We went over the wall and separated into parties. The place was asleep. Oh, yes, there were lots of people there but they were taken by surprise. No, they did not resist. It was all over within half an hour or so and the muskets were collected and put in one of the empty cabins with a guard over them. About the only trouble was that the De Meurons did not only confiscate the arms but the rum too!"

And as I spoke I would be seeing again the white fluttering night, the suffused radiance of the moon, hearing again the whistling wind out of the past.

II

We were installed. The North-Wester in charge—a stranger to me
—and his men were sent off where they pleased, to Qu'Appelle, or
Portage la Prairie, or Fort de la Prairie, or to the devil, as Miles
Macdonell said. I slept in dormitory quarters near the administrative-
house. The cabin in which Christina died was empty but I could not
bear to enter it. Fidler's old place, by the way, in which we had lived
after we were married, was crumbling. I heard him say that he hoped
on his return to Red River to put up another, a larger house, in another
location—a little way to west of Fort Douglas.

Some Indians at once were despatched to Jack River post to cheer
the hearts of the refugees wintering there with the news of our
occupancy. They took with them a letter to Mr. Chisholm from me.
There returned with them a party of settlers who, hearing the good
news, had decided not to remain at Jack River till the waters opened
for boat-traffic. They were weary of body indeed from the long trudge
on snowshoes that wrenched unaccustomed muscles of calf and thigh,
but elated in mind. Their desire was to be back in good time for the
spring tillage. Hugh Chisholm was not of the party but Agnes's
husband, Bob Wallace, was, and good news he brought me of the
little Christina in answer to my letter. All was well with the child.

It was strange for me to be back again at my old desk. A dream-
like quality was given to the events that had taken place since last I
sat there. As soon as the thaw came and ice was out of the river more
of the settlers began to return. The past and present were linked
when Miles Macdonell came to me one day accompanied by Livingston.

"There is a duty for you Baxter," said Captain Macdonell, "for
which I am more than glad to spare you from other tasks."

Livingston was holding some papers which—after a greeting of
reunion and a crushing hand-clasp—he laid on the table. I recognised
them at once for the letter to the Prince Regent which I had disen-
tangled from a web of notes.

"I have had this in care all the while," said he. "You may recall
that I said there would be much to add to it." So saying he took from
a pocket a second sheaf of sheets. "All this," he explained, "must
needs be added to what you have fair-copied for us before. It is to
follow upon these last words: *as he had received orders to let none*

of us escape. I will leave you to it, then. I thank you, Captain Macdonell."

As I sat at the work, transcribing in my best hand, I was aware of voices without as though people were gathering there. They were talking mostly in the Gaelic.

Thus driven a second time from the fields we had cultivated, we set out with our wives and children, unarmed and defenceless, and proceeded with a very scanty portion of provisions to commence our voyage to the shores of Hudson Bay; but we had only proceeded a few miles when we met a number of canoes and boats filled with partners and servants of the North-West Company, accompanied by several persons in military uniform, armed with artillery and muskets, of which the Colonial store had been plundered the year before, advancing to assist the attempt against the Colony, in case the force already sent against it had proved insufficient. They compelled us to wait several days, until they had searched our baggage in quest of papers, breaking open and rifling the trunks, even of our lamented Governor. They imprisoned several of our number, some of whom they tore from their helpless families, without as much as alleging any offence against them. At length, proposing that we should take oaths never to return to Red River, they thus allowed us to proceed on our voyage, but almost destitute of provisions.

Yes, I thought, that is true. In that detention they ate up what would have been their sustenance on the voyage.

More than twelve partners of the North-West Company who came on this occasion to the scene of these atrocities, expressed their approbation, and bestowed presents on those who had engaged in them. They appropriated the Colonial store to their use, caused the breeding cattle and Merino sheep, which had been brought from England with great care and expense, to be killed and served up at their table, turned their horses, as well as those they had taken from us, to graze in our cornfields, and burned a schooner which had been built for the use of the settlement.

They went in company with the men who had achieved the deed of blood to visit the ground where our friends and relatives had been

*slaughtered, and where some of their bodies were yet lying half-
devoured by dogs. Even this, which had drawn tears from those we
call savages, excited no compassion in the partners of the North-West
Company, but was viewed by them with exultation and even with
laughter.*

Somewhile later Livingston returned, looked in and went away
again with a furtive air as though he had come to see if I was finished
and finding me still busy was anxious not to interrupt me in the
task.

*Guided by the hand of Providence, we once more reached our
retreat at the north end of Lake Winnipic, where our only hope of
subsistence through a tedious and severe winter rested on the daily
supply of fish we might obtain from our nets. To the astonishment of
every person of experience in the country, though we had no previous
skill in the business of fishing, famine was not added to the list of
our calamities. Our support was indeed precarious, and our days of
warning were passed in painful anxiety till, on the approach of spring,
we heard that the Earl of Selkirk was on his way back to Red River,
and we determined to direct our steps once more to the ruins of our
former habitations.*

*Those of us who arrived first had to collect and consign to a grave
the bones of our relatives and friends to which our fellow-subjects had
denied the charity of earth.*

*We are now again labouring to re-establish our dwellings and to till
our fields, and if we may be permitted to cultivate them in peace we
entertain no doubt of finding here a happy abode for ourselves and
our descendants.*

*In a country possessed of so many advantages our number would
soon multiply, and we might cherish the hope of becoming, in the
hands of Divine providence, the humble instruments of introducing
the benefits of civilization, with the light of our holy religion, into
regions where they have been hitherto unknown.   But unless the
protection of His Majesty's Government be extended to us, we may be
again exposed to the machinations of the same men whose hands are
so deeply imbued in the blood of their fellow-subjects, and under the
iron domination of a lawless association, oppressive alike to the native*

*Indians and to all other inhabitants, this fine country may be doomed
to lie waste, a scene of crime disgraceful to the British name.*

*Under these circumstances, we must humbly solicit that the effectual
protection of His Majesty's Troops may no longer be withheld from
this part of His Dominions, and that some establishment may be
speedily formed in it for the administration of civil and criminal justice.
And your Petitioners as in duty bound will for ever pray.*

I rose and was stepping to the door to look for Livingston but at the
sound of the chair's movement he entered.

" Finished?" he inquired.

" Finished," said I.

" He's finished!" he shouted.   " Come away!   Come away in.
Come ben!"

The room filled with men.

" You first, then, Mr. Livingston," said one of the new-comers.

Livingston sat down by the table, on the chair that I had vacated,
and taking up the pen he signed. Then each in turn sat there and
signed, some with grim face and heavy hand, some carefully with
accompanying movement of the jaws as though masticating, some
quickly :

> Donald Livingston
> George McBeath
> Angus Matheson
> Alex. Sutherland
> George Ross
> Alex. Murray
> James Murray
> John Farquharson
> John McLean
> John Bannerman
> George MacKay
> Alexander Polson
> Hugh Polson
> Robert McBeath
> James Sutherland

James Sutherland
William Bannerman
Donald MacKay
John Flett
John Bruce
Robert MacKay
William Bannerman, junr.
Roderick MacKay
Alex. McLean
George Adams
Martin Jordan
Robert MacKay
William MacKay
Alex. Matheson
John McBeath
John Sutherland
Alex. McBeath

Alexander McBeath had just signed when from downstairs we heard a woman's voice: " Is this where I have to come, gentlemen, to sign the petition to His Royal Highness?"

" Yess, yess, come up. Make way for Mrs. Gunn."

She came upstairs, entered the room, sat down and signed her name. Her shawl's fringe got in the way so she cast it back.

" I suppose," she said, " on a document like this one should put *spinster*, or *wife*, or——"

" As you please. Yes. Maybe it might be as well," said Livingston.

She cast back her shawl again, added to her name the one word *widow* and then sat for a moment gazing before her, an abstracted moment. The look in her eyes gave me a stab at the heart. She rose and passed the pen to Alex MacKay and the signing continued:

Alexander MacKay
William Sutherland
Donald Bannerman
Hugh McLean
George Bannerman
Donald Sutherland

Two more women came upstairs

> Beth Beathon
> John Matheson
> George Sutherland
> Margaret McLean (widow)

Miles Macdonell entered then and sent me away on a duty outside. When I returned there was no crowd there. Only one or two people remained. Mrs. McLean was just going out. Livingston turned to Captain Macdonell.

"May we leave this in your charge, sir?" he asked. "We are not sure of the procedure for sending it to the Prince Regent."

"Certainly, Mr. Livingston. It should be sent to the Governor at Hudson's Bay House in London who will make sure it gets to the Regent. He will forward it with a covering letter to Lord Bathurst. There should be a copy for the Colonial Office Records also."

"I knew you would be aware of the procedure," said Livingston, and departed.

Then I was lost in a reverie. The expression on Mrs. Gunn's face haunted me and caused me to return in memory to the days of which the petition told. I was abruptly aware of Miles Macdonell sitting very still, observing me.

"Aye," said he, "it has been a very sad business, but we are now on the turn of the tide I feel certain. You are young, Baxter, you are young. You have all life before you. Some day this will be like a cloud that has passed."

"I can never forget her, sir," I said.

"No, no. I realise that," he replied. "Ah, Baxter, it is an adage for us all, that adage of *a stoot hert tae a stey brae.*"

The dropping so into the Lowland Scots by a Highlander had its effect on me. I felt a kinship with this man. Highlanders and Lowlanders were of different races in many ways, thought I, and yet had much in common. A sense of loneliness that had come to me, thinking of Christina, was eased. Miles Macdonell had evidently not forgotten our talk in that bay of Lake Superior. I felt again my old loyalty (it was Captain Semple's word) to this Governor who had been sorely criticised for much. And there were those who even called him arrogant! Yes, the ones who wished to drag him down, the ones who envied his office, the very ones who forced him to be aloof.

" And now," said he, " you might as well return to the petition and make—let me see, yes—four copies of it. Yes, there has been much very sad, but I think the tide has turned."

With my own private excitement I sat down to that work. Any day the rest of the settlers from Jack River would arrive. They had not come all in one flotilla along the lake. Any day the Chisholms would be there and I would see again the little Christina—" Christina's Christina ": that was how I thought of her.

CHAPTER FIVE

I

THAT was a happy arrival. My gaze travelled, searching, from boat to boat. Where—where? Ah, there they were!

There were the Chisholms waving to me. There was Agnes waving to her husband who stood at my side. Despite her condition—she carried a child under one arm, across her hip, and another (it was clear by her contours) within her—she was the first of the women to come ashore. Unaided she straddled, swift and safely, from boat to bank. She kissed Wallace and flung an arm round his neck, then swung impulsively to me and kissed me also—and was unaware, apparently, of the stare of some of the women, scandalised by her disembarkation, her lack of their sense of decorum.

I went closer, to help Mrs. Chisholm ashore.

"O my lad," she said, coming to land, "what a life! What a life! Upon my word I'm getting kind of used to it. But all the same, if I was to find myself waking up in the old home I would believe it was a dream and, 'My, what a dream I have had!' I would say."

Mairi was behind, carrying Christina. Chisholm, still in the boat, steadied her to one side while I aided to the other. With her precious armful she came to the bank. There she turned about that I might see my little Christina, for the child clung close, her chin on Mairi's shoulder.

"Is she awake?" Mairi asked, straining her neck sideways to have a fair sight of the infant.

"Yes," said I.

My baby was examining me very seriously and for what looked out through her eyes I felt a great tenderness. The hope I had then for our child in the queer world was like prayer. Suddenly I laughed happily.

"God bless you!" I said.

"Is she smiling?" asked Mairi.

"Yes."

Mairi guessed what manner of smile it was: little Christina had stared a long while at me and then slowly the smile spread. It came to a climax in a crow, a chuckle of approval. I held out a hand and she grasped one finger, then put her own hand in mind, thrust it into my open palm, and hanging over Mairi's shoulder peered at her hand in mine, seemed highly amused, as though at a comparison of the sizes. At that moment I felt perhaps something of what had been meant by the momiletic elder who had told me that I would be truly part of the body politic and social. I was a man with a duty in life. I must not merely drift in the currents. I had this child to care for, Christina's and mine.

I looked up at Mairi. She was no longer trying to see the baby's face. She was watching me and I surprised in her eyes something I could not understand. Immediately she looked down at the small head on her shoulder.

Mr. Chisholm coming ashore, carrying a great bundle, laid a hand on my arm.

" Well, lad," he said, " we've got to be moving from here. We are blocking the fairway."

It was the passage of Mr. and Mrs. Sinclair we were preventing. I stepped to one side and was on the point of giving these two welcome when there came a diversion : A group of Indians looking on began to talk quietly and quickly together with subdued titterings, and one stole close behind the fiddler. He must have been present on some festive occasion, looking in at the door when Sinclair favoured the guests with his own composition on the uncertainly named fly, for suddenly in the old man's ear he made a hissing : " Zzzz!" Sinclair jumped, wheeled, stared at him, slapped him on the back. Then to the best of his vocal skill he gave the quavering Indian cry : " La-la-la-la-la-la-la!" The Indians standing by took it up and the call went trembling along the bank, laughter following it. Those who drew up the letter to the Prince Regent, I considered, did not make mistake when they wrote of the friendliness of " the native Indians " to the Red River settlers.

As we all walked up the bank together, I carrying Christina, Mrs. Chisholm explained to me what she had arranged, decided.

" We will look after your bairn," she said. " Agnes is to have an addition soon. A Swampy Cree woman at Jack River suckled her when Agnes dried, until she was weaned—which was all in order considering her grandmother's race. O me, we'll manage somehow! We aye have managed so far, extraordinary to relate. What bothers me most—my, my, I lose my breath on this rise—what bothers me most is having to build a home again, having to get the Indians again to help us to build a wigwame."

"Wigwam," called Agnes from behind, following with her husband, he carrying their child.

"That's what I said!" Mrs. Chisholm retorted over her shoulder. "I said wigwame."

"And I said wigwam," Agnes replied gaily.

"O dear!" ejaculated her mother. "I get all mixed."

"You won't have to do any building," said I. "Your house is still standing."

"Bless me! How did that happen?"

"Cuthbert Grant gave orders that nothing was to be destroyed after the last flitting that everybody had to take."

"And how did he find grace?" demanded Mrs. Chisholm, pausing at the top of the bank and looking across the open.

"The general belief is that he realised there would be a day of reckoning—as we are all certain there will be. He got control at last and managed to make the half-breeds understand that affairs are bad enough. The houses that had been rebuilt are just as they were. The ones that were half-built are just as they were also."

"So we have a home, then," said Mrs. Chisholm.

"You have a home."

There was no work in the office that day. Clerks and labourers, all the Colony employees, were helping to get the settlers installed again. Sitting at the door of the Chisholms' house, after they were tidily in occupation, Christina asleep on my knee, I heard of their sojourn at Jack River and was given the gossip they had picked up at Bas de la Rivière when halting there for a night on the return trip: After McGillivray and McLoughlin got bail in Montreal, and told their partners there of Selkirk occupying Fort William, the North-Westers gathered a fighting force and sent them out in canoes to retake it. But most of these were wrecked in the big lake on the way, so then they thought better than to offer force. It seemed, also, that Captain Macdonell and Captain D'Orsonnens had hardly left Fort William with their party for the recapturing of Fort Douglas when a constable came over that cold lake with a warrant for Lord Selkirk's arrest.

"I did not know that," I said, amazed. "No news of that has come this length to my knowledge."

Lord Selkirk refused to admit it, Mr. Chisholm had been told, but wrote his view of the matter to the Lieutenant-Governor who felt he had to inform Lord Bathurst, the Colonial Secretary in London. So they were talking about it even in Downing Street now! Lord Bathurst had replied that the warrant should be enforced but that a commission of inquiry should be appointed. At Bas de la Rivière, Mr. Chisholm went on to tell me, North-Westers and Hudson's Bay men were prisoners together. A Lieutenant Austin of the 16th Regiment had been ordered to take charge of the whole lot of them : both camps. Lord Selkirk was expected there the day the settlers came on to Red River. John McLeod was there already. News had come to him at a post in the north that a warrant was out against him over that seizure of the North-West fort at Pembina that Captain Semple ordered, so being a law-abiding man he went along the lake to answer it, and the North-Westers served it on him at Bas de la Rivière. Warrants for arrest, subpœnas, bails : each against the other!

II

A few days later Thomas Douglas, Earl of Selkirk, came up the river. Along the banks by their farms the people clustered to wave to the boats, to watch for the canoe in which he travelled, to cheer his arrival. Then there was much running to the landing-place below the fort. Pipers were there awaiting him. The ex-soldiers, the De Meurons, were there in military formation. Through cheering crowds he walked up the slope to the fort, the pipers marching ahead.

Sheriff Archibald MacDonald was at the gate to meet him. I was in my place in the office, listening to the sounds of welcome. Looking out of the window I saw a man walking across the square. Was that John McLeod? It could not be! Mr. Chisholm had told me that McLeod was at Bas de la Rivière, a prisoner of the North-West Company.

McLeod saw me, waved a hand, and came running upstairs.

"Well, David," he said as he entered the room and we shook hands, "once again the pipes and the undefeated. They'll come into their own yet!"

"They told me you were arrested."

"Oh, that! I heard a warrant was out for me so gave myself up. True enough! But the earl arrived the one way from Fort William, and Captain Macdonell the other way to meet him, at Bas de la Rivière and these gave bail for me, so here I am to see the celebration before going east."

"But what, precisely, is the charge against you?" I asked. "Mr. Chisholm said it was laid because of the seizure of the fort at Pembina."

"Burglary," replied McLeod, and laughed.

"Burglary!" I ejaculated. "You are being funny!"

"Life seems to be funny whiles," said McLeod. "Yes, burglary. That's the charge—of burglary."

"I hear there are prisoners on both sides."

"Yes, prisoners and witnesses. Warrants and subpœnas are fluttering all over the Indian Countries now." Then, abruptly: "Well, David, I must go. I came up with Lord Selkirk just to see the place before starting off for Montreal."

"You will come back here?"

"I hope so—some day," and he laughed again.

"I may not see you for some time, then," said I.

"You may see me sooner than you expect," replied McLeod. "I cannot imagine, with all you have participated in, that you will not be served either with a warrant or a subpœna. You may be served with both, whatever! Take it philosophically if you are. Consider how much you will see: Little York, Sandwich, Montreal, wherever the courts are held. You may see them all." And then: "Here comes Lord Selkirk in at the gate," he said, looking out of the window. "There's Archibald shaking his hand. Here they come. Here he comes, and the pipers roaring him in!"

CHAPTER SIX

I

On the following day in the accounting-room with me were Magnus Isbister (a young man who had come out in 1811), and Michael Mc-Donnell. The young Sheriff and Mr. Bird, the newly-appointed factor of the Hudson's Bay Company for the Red River district, had been in the room and had just gone out together. There came a slow, shuffling step on the stairs and the thud as of a stick or a peg-leg, a puzzling sound. It was unfamiliar. Something in its very slowness, as well as its strangeness, caused us to raise our heads and listen. Knock and shuffle, knock and shuffle came up the stairs.

When Court Nez entered I did not immediately recognise him. Something had happened to the man. He had a high stick in his hand such as aged Indians are wont to use, but he seemed less lame than stiff, as one suffering from rheumatism, and though he was as heavy as formerly there was a change on his face. The whole man was somehow different. In one of his eyes there was a fixed glare. He did not smile, he frowned, seeing the three there. He came into the middle of the room and made a beckoning motion with hand and head, signalling me to come to him, then walked away into a corner by the window near the Governor's table.

Magnus and Michael looked from him to me as, perplexed, I rose, obeying that odd summons; and both had the decency to become at least outwardly immersed in their work.

With no salutation at all Court Nez declared that he wanted a drink. "I want a drink," he repeated. "That first. And I need your help, David."

"What is the matter?" I asked. As I looked in those eyes they were demoniac to my mind. Yet I felt again, as I had felt before, a sense of pity for this man. "We have no liquor here," I said.

"Look in the Governor's room, his sanctum, in there. The governors usually have the stuff to offer visitors."

"But I could not do that. What is wrong?"

"I need it. I've got to have it. I've had it all my life. I had it in my

368

mother's milk. I've got to have it, I tell you! I am a sick man." He raised his head in the old manner that preceded a laugh, but he did not laugh. Only one side of his face puckered up. The other remained rigid. " I've had a seizure, a stroke," he said.

A stroke! So that was the cause of this stiffness down one side, the slightly dragging gait, the facial rigidity.

" Well," I replied, " I cannot give you any here but I might be able to get you some." I turned towards the door. " Have you seen a surgeon?" I asked.

" What could a surgeon do for me?" scoffed Court Nez, following me and then, as I stood back, going ahead of me.

Downstairs he went, one of his enormous hands hanging at his side, the other wielding his tall staff, and I a tread or two behind. He was just a few steps from the stair-foot, and I had come down level with him, when Lord Selkirk entered from the square, glanced up and, seeing a massive man uncertainly, and with much difficulty, descending, moved aside. At the same moment I halted in the midst of a stride and stepped behind Court Nez that Lord Selkirk might have way to ascend, but he remained where he was. With a roll as well as a shuffle Court Nez came downstairs and Selkirk gave him all the space—and a nod of acknowledgement to me for having offered passage. The old man lowered his head and peered at Douglas.

" You know what I want," he said, as we passed out into the open. " Lead the way. Rum is what I need. And no surgeon."

As we walked away from the door I had the impression that Lord Selkirk had stopped on the stairs but dismissed the thought, deciding that the earl was light of tread in his ascent and had gone up with little sound.

" We might be able to get some liquor at the Colony store," I suggested.

I started off smartly, perhaps with a desire to have it over as it seemed the matter must needs be attended to. But again Court Nez's hand fell on my shoulder with a jar and his fingers closed on it.

" Not so quick, young man," he growled. " Me, I am old, I have lived many snows." He raised his head and there was a hissing sound from his throat, an attempt at a cracking laugh. Aslant, delaying my steps, I saw that he was laughing with one half of his face.

Though with a slight drag of a leg he did not merely crawl and

2A

his clenched hand that held the staff went out and back level with his ear, vigorously. We passed from the bright sunshine into the duskiness of the long low ceilinged store. Only Colin Campbell was there, a young man who had been given the post once held by Bourke —of whom, by the way, scant news was obtainable: but of whom more in place.

"I do not know if you have met Court Nez," said I. "Let me introduce Mr. Campbell, Court Nez."

Colin Campbell looked questioningly at him.

"I did not recognise you!" he exclaimed to Court Nez, holding out his hand. "We have never spoken but I recall well now, when we were going to Jack River House last year, you brought some Assiniboine Indians to convoy us. I only saw you at some distance and—er—you were mounted."

"Yes, and I was strong," said Court Nez, and by the way he crushed Colin Campbell's hand was still so and wished to prove it. "I am in need of some liquor"

"Whisky? Rum?" asked Colin, and furtively flexed the fingers that Court Nez had gripped.

"Rum," said Court Nez. "You can charge it to the account of David Baxter here." When the bottle was produced—"Draw the cork for me," he said harshly. "I am unhandy."

With a look of doubt Campbell drew the cork. Court Nez raised the bottle, gurgled down a great draught, set it upon the counter again.

"Na, na," he said. "Do not drive the cork in too violently. I am unhandy. I may soon want to pull it again."

He turned away with his slight shuffle and I passed out of the store with him. And then, as I had had the impression that Lord Selkirk paused upon the stairs to look after us, I had the impression that Colin Campbell remained rigid, watching our exit.

"Where are you camping?" I asked.

There was no reply.

"Are some of your Indian friends with you?" I inquired.

There was no reply. Having walked a few steps from the store Court Nez stood still.

"I want quarters," he said. "I can hunt no more. My women are dead The old life is over for me. What I used to do I can do no longer. I shall never again be able to do what I used to do. I need accommodation here. You can get that for me. It is the least your Lord Selkirk and your governors can do for me in return for my interest in the welfare of these damned people."

"I think I might arrange that," said I.

"I am sure you could," replied Court Nez in a voice that reminded me of the day when we sat on a fallen tree near the river and I had let him know that I was not afraid of him.

"You would not object to a small cabin, and to being alone?" I asked.

"You might prefer for me to be alone, and I would not object to it," he answered. "I have been alone all my life, even when I have been with others. I have come to like to be alone, but now—now—well, I am unhandy."

"I will get the surgeon——" I began.

"You will get the devil!"

Once again, despite the fact of his evident comparative failure of bodily power, I felt resentment at his hectoring accents. I looked round and saw Campbell in the doorway of the store as though trying to draw my attention.

"Just a minute," I said to Court Nez, and turned back.

"I couldn't but hear what he bellowed at you," Campbell whispered. "There's one of these cabins where some of the De Meurons were living if you want to get a roof for him."

"But the De Meurons are still sleeping there, are they not?"

"No. The ones who were there are camping out on their allotments already, while building." He pointed across the square. "There's a small one over there where there were only two or three of them. They've taken their bedding away but the bunks are there. I know who he is—I've got it all now: Court Nez; I remember about him. Your wife's father. Here's a buffalo robe—you could throw that on one of the bunks for the time, until you get some blankets."

"This is very good of you, Colin."

"It is nothing."

With the buffalo robe flung over my shoulder I returned to Court Nez.

"You have got to look after me," he said. "You have reason. You married my daughter. You——"

"I know, I know!" I exclaimed. "Do not speak to me as if I am inhuman. There is a cabin over here you can go to. The man in the store has just given me this robe to start with."

Again side by side we moved upon our way. The cabin door was open. It was a small place, unglazed, but with a parchment window at one end. I walked in and cast the robe over the frame of saplings in one of the bunks. But still it seemed that he had to hector me. In many ways this encounter was reminiscent of that other near the Lagimonieres' cabin, when it was difficult to impress him that there was no treachery in me towards Christina.

"See here," he said, and sitting on the edge of that bunk he slipped his hand half-way down the tall staff and repeatedly smote with it on the floor violently, as though to accentuate his speech. "See here, there is more reason than your marrying Christina for taking care of the old man now that he is poor and sick, and you've got to know it all."

I stood before him, puzzled.

"I happen to be both your father-in-law and your uncle," said Court Nez.

"You happen——" I could say no more. My mind—if I may use regarding the mind a word used of the stomach—could not injest what he said, or otherwise, as the saying goes, I could not believe my ears.

"Don't goggle at me like that," he said. "Get it into your understanding, David Baxter. My brother—that is to say your father—married the girl I wanted. That was the girl I told you about. That was why I went to Georgia. You never heard of me, eh?"

I shook my head for only negative answer. And then I remembered how on more than one occasion he had spoken my name oddly to me, and how he had asked me questions regarding my old home and my mother and brother. These recollections helped me to get it into my understanding, as he had demanded of me. There came back to me our puzzlement over a remark he had made on the day of his arrival from the prairies at the Lagimonieres' cabin. My readers will recall it: "The only trouble, the only trouble, is that streak. Oh, well, you both have it, no doubt, and so can make the best of it." Of our consanguinity he had been thinking then, long aware, by what I had told him of my home, that I was his nephew, Christina my cousin.

"No, quite so. Never heard of me!" he said. "Well, there is no use saying this might not have been if that had not been, and all that. Your father and I both often did not know what we wanted. Something came in and bothered us. Among people, listening to them, we would suddenly wonder if they were interested truly in what they talked of, and if they were amused truly at what they laughed over. We had to pretend interest, pretend amusement. It depends which way that feeling, that streak " (there was the word again!) " leads one, or urges one—I can see that now—what one makes of life. I believe you understand what I'm talking about—and you and Christina (you both had a bit of it) slipped away from all the nuisances and stillness the right way. Your father ran away, deserted, after he had committed himself. Yes, I see what you are thinking: he left it all after there were two sons, two children born. He ran away. He left her. He tired of domesticity. He tired of respectability. He married to reform himself—and it did not work."

The hissing, humourless laugh came from him again. I still stood before him, staring.

" I met him in Virginia," he said. " I had gone up there from Georgia. He confessed it to me. The queerness in us got the better of him—or the worse of him. What a tragedy! He admired her and then—snap! he could stand no more. He went back to his old play-fellow, the devil. She must have known of it for he went back before he left her. Liquor—and women. And she bore it, she put up with it by what he told me. A woman of that kind must feel it, feel her very soul wounded if she has to play wife to a man living such a life. And then, mark you, if she has an affection for him—and she may have in the face of it all; it is an unreasoning thing sometimes—she will be cut to the quick. When you think how short life is, does it not seem sad that lives should be wrecked, people broken——"

" You say you met him. What happened? Where is he now?" I demanded.

" Dead. Died in a great bouse. And God knows he was not happy. He whimpered at times. He threw the blame on others at the end. I told you to-day I had had it—bouse—in my mother's milk. That's the first time I've said that, and under stress, you'll admit. A man who has lived my life feels badly when he becomes so damned unhandy."

" You were saying," said I, " you were telling me——"

"Oh, I was saying and telling enough," he interrupted. "But there is the other reason for you to look after me—for I presume," and there was a look in his eyes both gleeful and devilish, "that you are of those who think that blood is thicker than water."

I felt very cold although it was a sweltering day.

"This is all truth?" I asked, and my voice sounded strange to me.

"This is all truth. And now, get this cork out for me. I am so unhandy now and that fellow rammed it in with the heel of his hand as if it was never to come out again."

"I will only get the cork out," I said, "if you will let me send the surgeon to you."

"You have no surgeon," said he. "Your surgeon was killed at the Seven Oaks."

"There is another," said I. "He came from Jack River with the people, and Lord Selkirk has his own physician with him who might——"

"Send the surgeon, send my Lord Selkirk, send Satan, send the Almighty, send any one you like. But get that cork out!"

I looked at him doubtfully but as I did so he raised the bottle to his mouth, drew the cork with his teeth, spat it out, tilted back his head and drank. Then he relaxed, tried to laugh once more, and having laughed sat forward. The staff dropped to the floor. He put elbow on knee, head cupped in hand, and moaned.

"Why did you not tell me all this before?" I asked.

"There was no reason to bring up the past. The links were all broken. But now I am helpless. One of my hands has no grip, one side is nigh useless. I need someone to look after me, and who better than one of my own flesh and blood?" Then he moaned again.

"I shall be back," said I.

Feeling utterly cold, even out in the warm sunshine, shivering in the sweltering day, I hurried to the administration house. On the way I thought (it was one of many whirling thoughts) it was remarkable that twice, in one family, and so closely—in two immediate generations—had been that odd occurrence: for there was my brother James, at home, married to Janet. But I had not loved Janet, I considered, as this Court Nez, when young, had evidently loved my mother. As much to be gone from the temptation weakly to put myself in Janet's power as to escape from my brother's small tyrannies

I had left Renfrewshire. Court Nez, I gathered, had gone to the American colonies after his brother had won the girl he loved, as many a young man did in like pass: the colonies, the navy, the regiments all held such. It was not by mere chance, as I had imagined, that his daughter bore my mother's name—Christina.

I hoped I would find Miles Macdonell in the office. Sweeping through my mind were memories of various incidents which, linked, made me feel that I could go to him as to a friend.

At the door of the administrative building I hesitated. No, I would go to the surgeon. If my absence from the office was questioned later I would make explanation. As I paused there Lord Selkirk appeared on the threshold, coming out.

"My dear young man," said he, stepping towards me. He was but slightly taller than I but he bent then, looking at me with more than kindliness, with kindliness and anxiety. "My dear young man," he repeated, "is there anything I can do for you?"

I shook my head.

"I do not think so, my lord," I answered.

"Oh, come, come," said Douglas, and then: "What hold has that man upon you? It is not right that one with a look upon him such as he has should have a hold upon a young man such as you. Come, come." He extended a hand and laid it on my shoulder. "I have heard great accounts of you from Captain Macdonell. I observed you at Sault Ste. Marie, and in the camps on the way, and at Fort William I saw your conduct. Tell me, what hold has that dissipated man upon you?"

I was silent. Selkirk waited and, because of his friendliness, when I spoke I came to the root of the matter. I came so abruptly that Lord Selkirk was startled.

"He is my father's brother," said I.

"Oh, pardon, pardon!" said Selkirk.

I drew a deep breath. I was shuddering. My spine was cold. Rigors ran upon my loins.

"There is no pardon needed, sir," said I. "But there is more than that relationship to bind us. There is another reason why, when the man has come to his present pass, I must look after him."

"Oh? You have not told me all?"

"I married his daughter." And then suddenly returned to me that feeling which had made me think of going to Miles Macdonell not only for leave of absence to attend to Court Nez for the day, but as a confidant. " He was good to her," said I. " She——" There I stopped.

" He may go and trouble her," said Selkirk. " I could not but over-hear how he was talking to you when we met in the doorway here."

" She is dead, my lord," I told him.

Selkirk again inclined his head.

" She died," said I, " on the day that Captain Semple and his men were slaughtered."

" Died? They did not kill women, did they? I never heard——"

" Oh, no, sir. She died after giving birth. Surgeon White was in attendance on her and thought all was well—I am resolved from what I have heard since that he thought all was well—and left her, intend-ing to return after seeing to the wounded. And he was killed."

" Did the child live?"

" Yes, my lord, the child lived. She is in the care of a family of settlers."

" Well, may he not go and trouble these good people, then, demand-ing this or that from them in that demoniac—in that manner of his, perhaps terrify the women at least?"

" No, I do not think so, sir, but I was coming to ask Captain Macdonell if I might have leave of absence for a little while, perhaps for the rest of the day, to see to him in various ways, to get the surgeon to him if only to advise him—well, of how to take care of himself in this pass, in his state."

There was a step behind me and, aware of someone approaching, I moved aside. It was Miles Macdonell who was entering. Lord Selkirk held up a hand to him.

" Captain Macdonell," he said.

Macdonell wheeled in his soldierly manner and came to attention.

" May Mr. Baxter have leave of absence from his duties for a little while?"

" Why certainly, sir," said Macdonell.

" Perhaps for the day—for private business," suggested Selkirk.

" Certainly, sir."

Selkirk turned to me again. Miles Macdonell saluted and went up three stairs at a stride.

"This is very good of you, my lord," said I, hardly knowing what to say.

"It is nothing. If there is anything I can do for you, Baxter, do not hesitate——"

He did not finish, stood there nodding his head up and down and I, unable to answer, saluted and turned away.

II

It did not take me long to make the cabin comfortable for Court Nez, or Mr. *Courney* as some of the settlers later began to call him: "Mr. Courney, David's Baxter's father-in-law." As Courtenay or Courtney he was also named by others: Kortny, phonetically.

"And now," said I, "the Colony surgeon is in attendance on a case and I could not see him but there is Mr. Allen, the physician who has arrived with Lord Selkirk, and I think——"

"Think no more of him! He could do nothing for me," said Court Nez vehemently; and as I thought then that to call any surgeon might only infuriate him into worse apoplexy, there ended talk of medical advice.

In the afternoon I went back to the office. Stacked on the table were the account-books that Archibald had carefully carried with him to Jack River on the last eviction. Lord Selkirk, seated by the table, looking at the array, was speaking.

"I know the tenor of them," he was saying, "but, even so, they will have to look worse for me soon. These people have suffered too much. Many of them I am determined, in return, to absolve from their indebtedness. I am not going to hold them responsible for debts incurred for provisions. And from what you have reported," he turned to Macdonell, "of some of them and their misfortunes, I am resolved to give them grants of land and extinguish, for them, the original plan. It is distressful for people in adversity to have the knowledge of arrears of debt hanging over them. These accounts I can consider later. Now I wish to be out and about visiting."

During the next days he visited all in their locations, sat long in this house and that house conferring with the occupants. When Lagimoniere and his wife, with their children, came to see him he asked if there was any special parcel of land for which they had a fancy. At first Lagimoniere was for pshawing aside the suggestion but——

"Oh, well," he said at last, "perhaps it is time for us to have a settled place. My children have been born in odd corners of the Indian Countries. My wife is not as young as she was. A home—yes. Well, *milord,* there is a place we all love: it is across the river, opposite this point that has been named for you. There are trees there. It is very beautiful."

"Let us go and see it," suggested Selkirk.

When he had gone off with them, accompanied by Mr. Fidler, Archibald, who had been in attendance on the earl that day, very seriously looked to Captain Macdonell.

"He has already to-day made grants of land to a great number," he said. "But you know human nature. There will be some who do not deserve free grants, some to whom he will, obviously, not make such concession, and a portion of these will consider themselves unfairly treated. They will charge him with discrimination."

"You are young to realise all that!" said Miles Macdonell.

"I know, I know. I think he knows too. There are some in the world who hate a benefactor. We encountered one of that order to-day and he was aware of it. I know by his additional quietness as we went on. Then he seemed to throw off the depression the man had caused and bade me admire the colours to west."

They were bright, blazing, and colourful days; but the farmers wanted rain and on the 5th of July rain came and, on the same day, the commissioners—Lieutenant-Colonel Coltman and Major Fletcher —appointed by Sir John Sherbrooke (who had succeeded Sir Gordon Drummond as the Governor-General of Canadas) to inquire into the events that had culminated in the slayings of Seven Oaks.

They arrived, to Lord Selkirk's chargin, aboard North-West Company canoes and were carried past Fort Douglas to the Assiniboine River, where a party of North-Westers had recently pitched a camp near the site of their one-time Fort Gibraltar and, by local reports, were going to build again there. A day or two later, however, Coltman and Fletcher, as though to show their impartiality, slipped away from our enemies' hospitality and pitched their tents half-way between the Assiniboine and Fort Douglas; and there Coltman sought, with benevolence and fairness it seemed to me, to gather all the evidence he could regarding the local discords. He had been a legislative councillor of Lower Canada, Fletcher had been a political magistrate of Quebec and had the rank—whence I never discovered—of major. His bombast made D'Orsonnens, to all who had considered that officer somewhat quaint or, not to mince matters, somewhat comic with his highflying deportment, no longer so, or not worth mentioning.

"He's *non compos*. He's crazy. He's daft," said Mr. Bird. "The major is a maniac!"

Coltman—"a laugh and grow fat person," Surgeon Allen called him once—patiently spent long days in his official tent interrogating all who were brought to him by both parties, all who came uncalled, taking depositions. Major Fletcher, liquor-laden, managed their military escort with amazing parade. Lord Selkirk came in to Fort Douglas one day, after a visit to the commissioners' camp, and remarked to Captain Macdonell that as an old soldier he might find it amusing to watch the evolutions conducted by Fletcher.

"The men," he said, "have a broad grin upon their faces all the time."

I noticed, at that, Magnus exchange a glance with Michael and knew its significance. There were those—there were many, in fact—who had seen Captain Macdonell as similarly amusing or even ridiculous in the days when he still clung to the hope of inculcating military manners in those selected to prepare a way for the settlers, and had organised drills in which I had taken part.

After the rain that had poured down on the commissioners' arrival was over, and the crops were blessed, the sun shone again and one sunny day—the 18th to be precise—many Indians came by appointment to the fort to see the "big white chief." He had a document ready for them, a written promise to pay to the Chiefs and Warriors of the Chippewa and Saulteaux Nation an annual quit-rent consisting of one hundred pounds weight of good merchantable tobacco to be delivered on or before the 10th of October at the Forks of Assiniboine and Red Rivers, and to the Chiefs and Warriors of the Knistenaux or Cree Nation a like present or quit-rent of one hundred pounds of tobacco to be delivered to them on or before the said 10th of October at Portage la Prairie in return for them letting the settlers remain unmolested on the lands by Red River which they had cultivated.

For two miles back from the river, to west, stated the Treaty, these lands were to be estimated as possessed by the settlers. But what, the Indians wanted to know, was two miles?

"You come and show," said Peguis.

So out they all went on to the prairie. Mr. Fidler produced his chains and with a party of labourers to aid him he measured off two explanatory miles for them, back from the river. But how could they estimate the distance? One of the chiefs had an inspiration. There were horses grazing out on the plain close to where Fidler had placed a man holding a tall staff with a pennant atop that they might have a gauge.

"I know," he announced. "This *two miles* is as far as a man can see light, see day, under belly of horse."

They puckered their eyes to the western glare, the setting sun. Huh! Good! Good enough! That would serve: as far as a man could see day under the belly of a horse. On the other side of the river a smaller strip was granted to the white people, a wooded strip where they could gather fuel. It was not much, the Indians thought, to allow the white people for so much tobacco every year. And the white people often gave them sugar and tea in exchange for fish, and when they made more pemican than they needed they could trade it at the store in the fort. Good! Heap good!

Southwards from the allotments of the settlers the ex-soldiers were formally given their parcels of land. There they would, if required, be within easy call of the fort. Those lovely July days were vastly different from the chill whistling night of their arrival. Here, most felt, was a land in which they might stay though a few were discontented. Already many of them had their eyes upon brides to be. Among the winding trails by the side of Red River they strolled with comely Highland wenches on their arms, causing anxiety thereby to some because of a generalising view these held regarding the ways of a soldier with a maid. When the swains delivered their charges at the farm doors long after dusk there would be furtive but searching looks by parents into their faces in the quaking light of candles and cruises, looks that were at variance with the pleasant greetings. Mr. Sinclair expressed himself forcibly and bluntly in my hearing to one dubious elder who had seen, walking along the upper trail, a De Meuron with his arm round the waist of a girl.

"Well," said Sinclair, "you have what you always wanted. You have men here at last who have seen military service and are prepared, by the term of their grants as I understand it, to be soldiers again and defend the Settlement at need. And all you can see is the possibility of a bastard or two."

"I said nothing of the kind, Mr. Sinclair!"

"You did not, but that is what you meant to be inferred."

III

They were busy days for me at the office. But nightly, again, I went along the Settlement road to the Chisholm farm. There was a feeling of well-being there. Never had Mr. Chisholm known such crops. There was a feeling of security also with the De Meurons, at work on their allotments, within call from the fort. Their mere presence there should be enough, all believed, to prevent any more attempts at hostile attacks.

But soon I realised that the prophecy was true that the fight would be transferred from Red River in the west to the courts of the east. There came to the fort one day an officer with a second warrant for Lord Selkirk's arrest. He marched up from the river and into the square as one with authority. He stamped up the stairs after a colloquy with someone below, and strode into the accounting-room.

"Thomas Douglas, Lord Selkirk?" said he.

"The same," replied Lord Selkirk, sitting there to one side of his letter-writing, close to reference files.

"I have a warrant, sir, for your arrest."

The earl sat back in his chair, an expression of ennui on his face: just that, just ennui, boredom, tedium.

"Is bail to be permitted?" he inquired.

"Yes, m'lord. I have been authorised to state that it will be to the sum of six thousand pounds," and the man's mouth twisted in a smile. But that smile was checked and gave place to a stare of astonishment by Lord Selkirk's quiet answer.

"Six thousand," he said. "Very good." A faint smile showed on his face, the smile as of a disappointed man yet one not defeated.

The constable then took it upon himself to remark: "Your lordship may consider yourself lucky that the warrant is only for felony,

for seizing of guns and fusils, and not for your resistance to legal
process, as that offence is not bailable."

On the evening of that day, visiting my good friends the Chisholms,
I was unable to get that scene from my mind.

" Of what are you thinking?" Mairi asked me.

I started at the question. It took me back to days in Fidler's house
—Fidler's old house; he was then building the new one west of Fort
Douglas—with Christina. When I tried to keep to myself this or that of
the Colony affairs that might have troubled her: " Of what are you
thinking, David?" she would ask.

Mrs. Chisholm and her husband had also been aware that I was
not wholly with them. They awaited explanation. I told them everything.

"Ah well," said Mrs. Chisholm, " it is to go to the courts now
instead of being fought out here. Here we are and here we bide. We
are protected now. I thought once I could never bide here, all so flat
and all so strange, and the Indians coming in and sitting down without
so much as chapping at the door. Yet I can see now that it I was
younger I would never have had any wish to go, just the wish to
stay here. Well, it looks as if our troubles were over but I am indeed
sorry for the earl. Our inheritance, I'm fearing, is going to be his
loss."

There had been a change in Mairi since the Semple Massacre. All
were horrified by that atrocity and some had been eager for retaliation,
some upon shaking the dust of the place from their feet for ever.
Here they were back again in the turn of events but for some, and she
was of these, there had come a distrust, or an increased distrust, of
life. The killings had depressed her. The mutilations had shocked
her. It seemed to her, by occasional remarks she let fall to us, that
the psalms of supplication that rose on Sunday from the worshipping
settlers went out only into unheeding space. She was at a loss for a
final verdict on life. I often surprised an expression on her face, when
she considered Christina, very pensive indeed. What, no doubt, she
was wondering, was ahead in life for that mite of one year?

" I hear," said Mr. Chisholm after a lull, " that the earl has deputed
Mr. Pritchard the job of getting a minister for the kirk that's to be
built."

Mrs. Chisholm gave a snort of disapproval.

"It is a pity he could not see to it himself," said she. "Mr. Pritchard is an Episcopalian, I think. He'll maybe not bestir himself greatly to get a Presbyterian."

"Oh, I wouldn't say that!"

"Maybe not, but I would!" she retorted.

"Captain Macdonell," I remarked, "is going to see about getting some priests in."

"They'll be needed," she ejaculated. "I don't hold with mixed marriages," she added. "Why should good Scots lassies marry these ex-soldier Europeans? It's as bad as the factors and clerks marrying Indian women!"

Mairi cast her a glance, the warning import of which was plain enough to see. So did Mr. Chisholm, and cleared his throat violently.

"Eh?" Mrs. Chisholm inquired combatively.

"I didna speak," Mr. Chisholm replied severely.

"No, but you looked at me as if—oh, I see! Oh, well, of course there are exceptions to every rule." She paused a moment and then —"Some, I think, will be just as glad there is no priest to untie them," she declared.

"They are all having civil marriages," Mairi reminded her. "They are going before Mr. Bird of the Hudson's Bay Company and——"

"What kind of a marriage is that?" demanded her mother in a tone of contempt.

"It proves them genuine," said Chisholm. "You'll see, you'll see. When their priest comes they'll run to him to have the church-marriage."

"Aye—and the children baptised, I hope," said Mrs. Chisholm.

At that, both because of the remark and the manner, we all laughed, Mrs. Chisholm too. The air cleared. Mairi, lest I felt aggrieved over the thoughtless inquiry of "What kind of a marriage is that?" laid a hand, very friendly, on my shoulder in passing. I understood the significance of that touch. "A very dear lass is this Mairi," I mused. I was glad to notice that since Agnes's marriage, Mrs. Chisholm had seemed kinder to her elder daughter.

CHAPTER SEVEN

I

DOUGLAS went about his final duties with great serenity and by his conduct won the esteem of both Lieutenant-Colonel Coltman and Major Fletcher. But on the subject of their report Miles Macdonell was not very hopeful. The North-West Company was busy formulating as many charges as it could against both the Settlement and the Hudson's Bay Company. Alone in the counting-house with me one day he spoke his mind on all that.

"Justice is not to be expected," he said. "The scales will be coggled. I have a dread that his lordship may be on the way to financial ruin. Thousands upon thousands of pounds he has spent already over this scheme of his and now, to my mind, there is something in the nature of an earl-hunt started."

News came that the *Edward and Anne*, on which Colin Robertson had sailed in the summer of 1815 with Duncan Cameron in his charge, taking him to England for trial, had been ice-bound in Hudson Bay or, more precisely, in James Bay, whither it had drifted. Those on board eventually had to walk ashore and spend the winter at Moose Factory. The ship did not reach England until after Lord Selkirk left for New York on the way to Montreal and his lawyers there made no charge against Cameron, with the result that he was back in the Canadas, back in Montreal, and had instituted a claim for damages against Colin Robertson and Lord Selkirk.

Douglas in those days often appeared to be a tired man. He had a cough that caused the old people to throw a furtive look of anxiety one to another, a cough of a sort they had heard before; and they knew its omen. A definite uneasiness in his manner, I noticed, after his return from one visit to Coltman. He had just heard that a protest had been sent to the commissioners regarding Red River settlers cutting sun-dried grass, natural hay, in a place that the North-West Company considered that it owned. Here was something that would cause inquiry to go a century back beyond Selkirk's purchase, to the Hudson's Bay Company's charter.

"If a claim to ownership by the North-West Company of a meadow where the settlers cut hay is to be acknowledged at law, then I shall have to consider the alternative," said he, "of removing them out of reach of that Company altogether. If the government is going to be thus partial to them, perhaps the most prudent course to follow would be to seek an asylum within the American lines."

"Yet one of your reasons, I recall," said Miles Macdonell, "for considering settlement here was that you felt a regret that so many of your compatriots went to the American colonies, from the region of Lord Baltimore's old settlement to as far as Georgia. Your desire, I remember, was that they should be under the British flag."

"That is so, but if they are to be under the menace—legalised—of the North-West Company, they would be better on American soil, find better asylum within the American lines where at least they would not have to apprehend hostility from subjects of the same govern-ment——" and he paused there.

"I know how you feel," Macdonell admitted, depressed also. He had a brother long resident—and apparently happily resident—in Boston but, for himself, as he used to say, he preferred to be under the old flag.

"—and there," went on Lord Selkirk, "if they be liable to attack, it will not be considered as an offence to be prepared for resistance!"

That remark all of us understand to refer to the refusal to allow him a military force to protect the Colony, the granting to him, when he asked for that, of only six men and a sergeant on the understanding that they came with him but for his personal protection.

II

It was Lord Selkirk's desire to gather the people together that they might hear his plans and arrangements on their behalf. The place chosen, beside a small creek that ran into Red River, was about midway between the fort and those oak trees on Frog Plain where Captain Semple and his men had been killed.

It was on a sunny day, through which small winds ran ruffling the trees along the river bank, that the settlers gathered in groups and awaited what had to be said to them. I shall never forget Lord

2B

Selkirk standing before them with his back to the trees. He bade them sit down and while they took their places on the grass he pondered, for a moment or two, on what he had to say.

He spoke a little while of his deep regret for all the vicissitudes and hardships that especially those who had been there for some years had been fated to experience. He explained that he thought it fair to the ones who had lost their all through the machinations of the enemies of the Colony to give them free grants of land and absolve them from their indebtedness. He told them that it was his desire that all should enjoy the services of a minister of religion who would be of their own persuasion, that it was his intention to have a market in the Colony for all surplus produce, that all were to enjoy the privileges of British subjects.

There were times when he seemed to me a very tired man standing before them, hat in hand, the breezes stirring his hair. When these breezes came his voice failed against the leafy murmur. He was aware once of those on the outskirts of the crowd cupping their hands to their ears. He raised his head as if listening to the wind, waiting for a lull.

Then firmly he spoke of how on his arrival, when the pipes had welcomed him, he had considered their fortitude and had been pleased with the thought that by their fortitude they were still there and under the British flag. The sound of these pipes was heard in many parts. There were men and women and children of the Highlands and the Isles all over the continent, he said, people of Perthshire, Badenoch, Strathspey specially in New York and in settlements by the Delaware, the Mohawk, the Connecticut Rivers. In Georgia there was a settlement of people chiefly from Inverness-shire. From Argyllshire and its islands and the Island of Skye and the Long Island and Ross and Sutherland too had gone many to form the settlement of Cross Creek, noted in the history of the American war for its loyalty—he paused—and its misfortunes. Fayetteville it had been named later. Men and women from Lochaber and Glengarry who had been in New York had removed thence, because of the disturbance of that war, to the Canadas. From Moydart had come many to Nova Scotia. He spoke of his own attempts, elsewhere, to make a resting-place for those driven from their homes in Scotland. There had been much hardship for those at Baldoon, in his first attempt. For those in

Prince Edward Island, that used to be called the Ile St. Jean, although there had been preliminary hardship, the tide had turned.

"It seems the tide here, for you, has turned," said he, looking round the throng. "I thought, however, that a portion of the ancient spirit might be preserved among the Highlanders of the new world, that the emigrants might be brought together in some part of our colonies where they would be of national utility and where no motives or general policy would militate as they certainly may at home "— heads nodded as he spoke these words—"against the preservation of all those peculiarities of customs and language which you are your-selves so reluctant to give up and which are perhaps intimately con-nected with many of your most striking and characteristic virtues."

He paused again as another wind went sighing through the tree-tops, looking up at them as though a part of him, abstracted, admired the day and had pleasure in the uproar of the leaves.

Chiefly Highland people were there but there were some from the Lowlands and some from Ireland, and many of the De Meurons were there. Seeing these last he would briefly, he said, recapitulate his promises to the ex-soldiers and that being done——

"This lot," said he, inclining his head towards where a group of Highlanders sat, "on which we meet to-day shall be for your church and a manse. The next lot," he raised a hand, pointing in a slow gesture, "on the south side of the creek here shall be for your school and for a help to support your teacher, and in commemoration of your native parish," he looked at those who had come out in the last contingent, "it shall be called Kildonan."

III

His work near an end, Selkirk was planning to depart by the way he had come, down Red River and up Winnipic River to Lake of the Woods, Lac la Pluie, Lakes Superior and Huron. He had just made all arrangements when some Indians from Lake of the Woods, relatives of the Saulteaux, arrived in haste. They had news of bribes being offered to have him killed on his way back. He rewarded them with rolls of tobacco and strings of beads and took them to the camp of the commissioners to repeat an account of what had brought them, accompanied by me and by John Pritchard who was then acting as

his secretary. Miles Macdonell, to my great regret, had already left
Red River for Montreal where he was to wait his lordship, travelling
over the regular route.

"It may be of interest for your reports," the earl said to Coltman
with bitterness in his voice. "I shall, of course, change my plans and
go by American territory."

Coltman advised him to risk "the regular route," pointing out
that people would think he was fleeing from the courts, forfeiting
bail by going across the line. They might also think he was adread of
other warrants awaiting him on the way.

Lord Selkirk smiled at that.

"It may interest you to know," he remarked, "that this very day
I have heard—as the saying goes *a little bird told me*—that that is
actually so. There is a process-server awaiting my passing of Fort
William with another warrant. As you know, they have the place
back in their hands again. I just held it for the winter, did not leave
any of my party in occupation when I came away. What between
lurking warrants and lurking assassins I think I will take the advice
of those who suggest that I go out over American soil. And, at any
rate, I have to be in Washington sometime to confer regarding some
of my territory here which, I am informed, by the terms of the Treaty
of Ghent is actually south of the boundary line. Also a few of the
ex-soldiers wish to return to Switzerland and they are going by the
Mississippi. I may as well go myself to St. Louis to arrange their
passage. Oh, no," he added, noting a look on Coltman's face, "I
did not bring them merely as additional soldiers for protection on
the trip to the west and for service here if hostility met us. They
came out on these terms: If they were not satisfied with the place,
and did not wish to stay, I would be responsible for their repatriation."

. "I was not personally suspecting any ruse on your part, my lord,"
replied Coltman. "I was only thinking that some might imagine
it."

"And give me the discredit of the doubt, add it to the charges they
are eager to pile up against me;" and Selkirk laughed gently.

The news travelled through the Settlement of the dual menace on
the usual route and all were eager for him to avoid Winnipic River
and give the slip alike to rumoured bailiffs, process-servers, constables,
and bribed would-be assassins.

On the day before he was to leave, I had arranged to go to the Chisholms' for supper instead of supping at the employees' mess in the fort. I was preparing to leave the office, the others already gone, when something—I could not have told what, it did not seem to be a sound—made me glance up. Peguis was well into the room, was almost at my side, and smiled at the look of astonishment on my face. He held a piece of stiff paper in his hand and offered it to me. "You speak me this," he said. "Big chief give me this. He speak it me. You speak it now. I want to hold it in my heart."

I took the sheet from him and read it aloud:

The bearer, Pegewis, one of the principal chiefs of the Chippeways, or Saulteaux, of Red River, has been a steady friend of the settlement ever since its first establishment, and has never deserted its cause in its greatest reverses. He has often executed his influence to restore peace; and having rendered most essential services to the settlers in their distress, deserves to be treated with favoured distinction by the officers of the Hudson's Bay Company, and by all the friends of peace and good order.

Selkirk.

"Good! good!" exclaimed Peguis, and taking the paper back he put it carefully away under his buckskin tunic. Then withdrawing his hand he held out to me what at first glance appeared to be but a sphere of birch-bark atop a short stick, with strings of beads depending from it.

"What is it?" I asked.

Pegius shook it before me. Within the sphere of birch-bark was a noise of rattling.

"For your papoose," he explained. "I bring for your papoose. My woman make it."

"Well, that is very good of you, chief. Thank you indeed, and thank her."

"Huh!"

I took the rattle and Peguis suddenly turned and departed as silently as he had come.

I then set off to keep my appointment at the Chisholms'. I walked out of the gate, turned sharply on the road, my head down, thinking how Christina would have liked to see this toy, how pleased she would have been to receive the gift from Pegius and his wife. Chin on chest I walked on. It was a hard world in some ways, hard with its feuds, its hates, and yet what alleviations there were! Constantly one was encountering kindness. I thought of the house to which I was going, pictured Mairi and Mr. Chisholm, Mrs. Chisholm and Agnes—in that order pictured them—looking at the rattle in my hand, and smiled, thinking of little Christina and of her eyes that were like her mother's. As I meditated I lifted the rattle and shook it.

A light laugh made me start. There by a cluster of trees to which I drew near sat Lord Selkirk on a small stool, an easel before him, a paint-box spread on one knee, brushes in hand.

"I see, Baxter," he said, "you have your distractions," and he laughed again, very gaily.

"An Indian gave it to me, sir, for my little papoose."

Selkirk nodded.

"Distractions," he said. "There are times when they seem more important than the demands and entanglements. What a heavenly evening is this! What an ingratiating light! I may never return here so I am trying to make at least an amateur's recording of it, of the peace of it. A lovable light it is on the trees and the bushes."

"And on the walls of the fort," I observed.

"Even on the walls of the fort," he agreed.

Unwittingly I gave the rattle another shake. At that we laughed together. Selkirk returned to his painting. I walked on, thinking I understood why Miles Macdonell would brook no aspersions on the earl. And as I went I made small unconscious dabs of the rattle in air, rattling along to see Christina and Mairi and the others also.

IV

There was no shadow on Red River Settlement. There was no cloud in the sky on the day that Lord Selkirk went away. The soldiers he had been granted for personal protection stood in the square, the sergeant and the six privates, to bid him good-bye, under orders from headquarters to return there by the regular route. The ex-soldiers who had decided to go home were arriving in twos and threes, some of them, after all, in a fuss of uncertainty, swithering between to go or to stay. Saying adieu to the friends they had made was not easy for all. A tassie or two of what Mr. Sinclair called heather-dew did not help them to a decision one way or the other. Lagimoniere was there. The earl was not going by canoe up the flow of Red River but on horseback across the plains. Lagimoniere had requested that he be allowed to see to the loading of the packstring and to act as guide as far as to the Mississippi. From their farms came many of the settlers, Highlanders, Lowlanders, Irish. Indians were there also with chief Peguis and the chief called le Sonnant.

Looking at the throng from the window I was sick at heart. Behind me Lord Selkirk, with restraint in his voice, was giving instructions to the Sheriff. The cough, that the older people had noted, I was aware of that day.

"He will never come back here," I thought. "He will go away and remember the light on the prairie and the woods and even on the walls of the fort, but he will never return."

A melancholy of the sort that had often held me since that dreadful 19th day of June of the year before assailed me again. I wondered, seeing the last of the preparations for that journey, if at the end of the terrestrial journey there was another life though the body was left behind with its eyes and its ears, another life for the spirit, with substitutes for these channels of apprehension beyond mundane guess or imagining, another life in which would be reunions with those loved here.

"Well, good-bye, Baxter"

I wheeled from the window and took the hand that Selkirk held to me.

"And thank you for all your assistance," he added.

"Good-bye, my lord. I hope you have a good journey."

"Thank you." He paused as if with more to say, then nodded, went quickly down the stairs and out.

There was the hum of many voices, several languages. People pressed forward to shake hands with Douglas and it was clear that he was deeply moved.

"You have a fine day to start, sir," I heard Mr. Pritchard say.

"I leave you on a fine day," I heard Selkirk reply—and there was that sickness at my heart again.

I went down into the square after the Sheriff and Mr. Bird, feeling the accounting-room suddenly as a place forsaken.

"Oh, damn these farewells," I muttered. "I do not like them."

I was aware of someone at my elbow, turned my head to see who stood there and found Mairi and her father at my side. When I met her gaze she did not then look away but smiled into my eyes. She was standing with her fingers linked before her and on the impulse of the moment I caught her hands, held them, ardently pressed them. Mr. Chisholm craned this way and that, looking between heads and over shoulders of the throng, all intent on seeing what was going on.

"There he goes," said Mairi, gently withdrawing her hands.

There he went. He was in the saddle. All the horses were moving. There was a stirring, sidling, edging into some sort of order among the mounted men. Lagimoniere was riding back and forth, starting the string of pack-horses.

"Haste ye back!" called Mr. Sinclair.

The others took up the cry: "Haste ye back! Haste ye back!"

Douglas turned slightly in the saddle, looking over his shoulder, and shook his head—a negative gesture, a sad gesture. He raised his hand and waved to them.

"Haste ye back! Haste ye back!' and there were calls in Gaelic that I presumed were to the same effect.

Selkirk did not shake his head again. He did not look round again. He had gone. A horse whinnied, another and another. They tittupped out and left a haze of settling dust. A feeling of loneliness clutched me.

"Come and see us to-night," came Chisholm's voice in my ear. "You will feel kind of lost."

"I will indeed," said I. ' I will indeed feel lost; I will indeed come," and then I laughed, I remember, a foolish-sounding laugh, as one may who is by no means jocund in an attempt to gain for himself, and prove to others, that he is master over saddening emotion.

Just in time had Lord Selkirk gone to have a happy going, to go full of hope for the future of his people, for that night there came an early frost that ruined much of the root-crops and a few days later a lashing gale that ruined much of the grain.

V

Court Nez sat in his cabin, visited not only by me. He was some what in the nature of a spectacle, a show. Young men would go into his place cheerily with a " Good-day, sir," and explain they had just looked in to see if they could do anything for him. Had he wood for the stove? The cabin was not one built after the fashion of those that recalled Old Country houses. There was no hearth under a cavernous chimney with pendent pot or kettle over the fire, broad mantel for the tinder-box and the candlesticks, the snuffers and the tea-caddie to live on, and bellows hanging alongside. It had a stove in it (of the Franklin or Swedish variety) and the stove-pipe was not even set in a cobbled chimney but projected through a sheet of tin in the sod roof.

Was there anything, the young men would inquire, that they could do for him? His stroke had given one eye an odd stare. It was as though it saw through them. Sometimes they could not get a word out of him and, rendered at last embarrassed before that steady stare, would withdraw, followed by a wheezy cackle or a hiss of a laugh. The surgeon—who had at last visited him despite his vetoing of medical advice—allowed him, to prevent an outburst of tantrums that might rise to fury, a daily dram or two, but I had a suspicion that some of his callers, with views of their own regarding the need for alcohol and the fitting quantities, made further contributions.

I went to see him the day after Lord Selkirk went and found him shuffling and staggering round the cabin.

" Sit down, sit down, nephew," said he, seating himself on the edge of his cot and signalling me to a chair. " You haven't brought the brat to see me yet," he said.

" The brat——"

" The baby. How does she go?"

" She is very well."

" Growing, eh?"

" Yes."

" Well, don't let her walk too soon. You don't want her to be bow-legged. Some of these days when it is not too cold—these are early frosts we have had this year— you might bring her over to see me now that we've all settled down. Is she growing like Christina?"

" Yes, she is."

Court Nez laughed.

" You'll see her so anyhow," he said. " You'll see her so. I thought her so myself when I saw her in that tent, and she but recent-born then! Well, she comes of good stock—on her mother's side. The mother's side is good. Who looks after her now?"

" The same people," I replied.

" I would like to have a look at her. This other leg—oh, I don't know. It doesn't seem much good either."

But the visit of little Christina with me to her grandfather was deferred. Next day an officer arrived armed with further warrants and subpœnas, one of the latter for me, calling me as a witness in the case of the killing of Robert Semple and twenty men at the place called Frog Plain near to the wood known as Seven Oaks on the 19th day of June in the year 1816.

As I read it I recalled John McLeod's warning, or prophecy: " I cannot imagine, with all you have participated in, that you will not be served either with a warrant or a subpœna."

CHAPTER EIGHT

I

To Michael I entrusted the care of Court Nez in my absence and spent my last evening in the Colony, for that year, with the Chisholms. With an easy mind regarding both Christina's father and her baby I went down river.

I did not go, all the way, to Montreal by the route on which Lord Selkirk had come west. I did not go all the way down blue Lake Huron and by Lake St. Clair but, with the others also served with warrants and subpœnas, coasting its north shore, to French River and by Lake Nipissing to the Ottawa, on the way down that river passing a place that less than ten years later, for the sake of Miles Macdonell, I was to visit again.

On my arrival Captain Macdonell at once claimed my assistance in secretarial work. Macdonell was troubled over the fact that Lord Selkirk had not yet reached Montreal.

"His enemies here," said he, "are crowing over his non-appearance and saying that he has fled the country and forfeited his bail. I understand he left you in September to go down the Mississippi?"

"Yes, he left Red River on the 9th of September. The commissioners left two days later but they, of course, were coming east by the usual route."

"Her ladyship knows him better than to be upset by these calumniating rumours—or lies. She is working hard for him. In his absence at Fort Douglas she has been doing all she can to show him as he is, and to defend his case. The North-Westers wanted to have all the cases tried here in their stronghold but now, finding the tide of public opinion running against them here, thanks to Lady Selkirk, they are straining every nerve to get them moved to Upper Canada. They are such able negotiators that they may obtain their object notwithstanding the obvious convenience, apart from all machinations, and the facility of this place."

He was interrupted there by the entrance of John McLeod.

"Good-day, Captain Macdonell, and—well, well! Ha-ha, Baxter!

There you are! I warned you that they would require you. I wonder how long we have all to be kept waiting here for our trials. Is there any word of the earl yet?"

"Not yet," replied Miles Macdonell.

Each looked at the other long and steadily and then——

"No," said McLeod.

"No," said Macdonell. "He has not run away. They need not imagine it."

"Have you told Baxter of how they treated you on the way here?" asked McLeod.

"No."

"What is that, sir?" I asked.

"Let me see," began Macdonell. "Well, it was on August the twelfth that I reached Fort William on my way back here but there I was served with a warrant for arrest. It was not, after all, only the earl they were watching for. I gathered between the lines, as it were, more evidence of the truth of the rumour that others were awaiting his passage in the hope of serving him with more than a warrant—of doing away with him. I remained in the hands of the Philistines till I reached Sandwich, the sixth of November—What time is wasted and lost!—and there and then I gave bail to answer the charges of which I was accused by the perjured clerks of the North-West Company. I took passage at Detroit for Black Rock and reached here by the route of Buffalo and Albany."

"Despite your lingering chagrin over the final victory, in their war for independence, of those I believe you still look upon as the rebels in the American colonies," remarked McLeod banteringly, "you preferred to travel through their country to continuing through the Canadas."

"So does his lordship," said Macdonell.

At that moment a boy came into the parlour where we sat. He had a letter in his hand.

"Captain Miles Macdonell?" he inquired.

"Yes, here, boy," and taking the letter from him Macdonell announced, "It is in her ladyship's handwriting." Then: "Ha-ha!" he exclaimed.

"What?" demanded McLeod.

"The earl is here. He has come."

" That is a relief," said McLeod.

Captain Macdonell turned sharply on him.

" You did not doubt he would?" he said.

" No, no," McLeod replied, " not for a moment did I think he had slipped away, but I grew weary of hearing it suggested by his enemies that he had—though I know none of them who would go beyond the aspersion and make a wager on it!"

II

Something of that lack of confidence in life that Mairi had felt after that dreadful day of June, 1816, came upon me during the following days, weeks, months. The ground, as it were, that I had believed was solid under my feet, was quagmire, muskeg; the ice presumed sound for a crossing was honeycombed, rotten, and one might anywhere fall through, and beneath were swift cold currents, destructive eddies.

" Law does not seem to be justice," I said one day to Miles Macdonell.

" No, not always," he agreed. " There are moments when I am moved to be extreme and say that I have lost faith in humanity. But Lady Selkirk alone prevents the words from being said. There is a great woman, a noble woman if ever there was one. There is true fidelity. There is true devotion with no thought that she is acting nobly. And she remains brave though she has seen what we have all seen."

" What exactly do you mean by that?"

" That Lord Selkirk is not well. But he is indomitable. He will see all through before he goes away to——" he paused.

" To what?"

" I fear it is to die, Baxter. Mr. Allen is in constant attendance on him now, but I fear he is to be broken in health as in purse. The costs mount up. He has his counter-cases, of course. There are now filed against him by the North-West Company a matter of thirty cases: larceny, false imprisonment, assault chiefly. Laid by him against them are one hundred and fifty."

" One hundred and fifty!"

" Yes, and worse ones, as you will realise: murder, malicious shooting, arson, grand larceny, and—oh, well, we shall see how all goes in the courts."

Soon we saw how things were to go in the courts. Mostly the verdicts were against Lord Selkirk and his officers.   There were occasional mitigations. John McLeod, impeached with others on that charge of burglary at Pembina, went free. Their lordships of the courts stated that there was no case, considering that the gates of the fort and the doors of the houses were not locked.

Some aspects of the trial of McLennan and Reinhard for the murder of Owen Keveny occasioned similar considerations regarding the letter of the law. That trial was held at Quebec. There appeared to be definite evidence that the murder was instigated by North-Westers but there was evidence also that Keveny behaved so tyrannically to his crews that they rebelled. Still—murder is murder : so there was more discussion. It went off at a tangent. The issue was evaded by argument on where, precisely, the alleged murder had been committed —whether in Upper Canada or in the Indian Countries. In the end McLellan was exonerated, Reinhard was found guilty, but the next doubt—linked to the earlier one—was where, precisely, he should be hanged. After the trial a dinner was given in the gaol at Quebec by the North-West Company, a dinner at which Reinhard was present, specially invited and specially permitted to be present. It seemed, in fact, to be a dinner of celebration, with him for the honoured guest.

" What will happen?" I asked.

" What will happen? He will be forgotten—completely forgotten and allowed some fine day to slip out and away," said Miles Macdonell.

Without altering my view that Duncan Cameron had worked hard against Selkirk and the Settlement scheme, I could not but feel that in the verdict on the case of *Cameron versus Lord Selkirk*, relating to the arrest of Cameron, the carrying of him off to England, the winter's delay at James Bay, the release in England, there was some justice although the verdict went against Douglas.   For illegal detention Cameron was awarded three thousand pounds damages. Colin Robertson, who had been his warder on the way over, tried on a charge of riotously destroying Fort Gibraltar (and a great, gay, riotous lad he looked in the court!) was found not guilty.

I had a desire to ask him about that winter on James Bay when the ice drove them back to Moose Factory. What was the attitude of prisoner to captor, of captor to prisoner? Did they scowl at each other all winter? Did they crack jokes? Did they sit to the table over cards together? But the opportunity to inquire was lacking. Trying to imagine it all I sat in the hotel-parlour with folded hands, motionless a while. I recalled what I had heard of the Hudson's Bay Company's men and the North-Westers herded together at Bas de la Rivière on the way to Montreal and Court of King's Bench for trial on various charges, and decided, considering what I had seen of both men, that Colin Robertson and Duncan Cameron would call a truce and perhaps even swop yarns of their adventures in Rupert's Land, sitting by the open fire or closed stove (I did not know which they had there) at Moose Factory.

In the case of the seizure of the cannon from the Colony stores, and removal of them to Fort Gibraltar, all the North-Westers implicated were acquitted. I listened, wide-eyed, to the summing up:

" It must be proved satisfactorily that at the time of taking there existed what is called a *felonious intent* in English and in Latin the *animus furandi,* because although property may be taken away, unless the *animus furandi* is clearly established it is not a felony but a trespass that is committed."

Thus was the jury advised and counsel drew forth from the witness that there was " no desire to steal but to prevent the cannon being used to prevent the settlers who desired to go from doing so." Purely, they would have us believe, on behalf of those poor settlers had the North-West Company officers and servants been thinking! And the Colony's officers were shown as tyrants who would hold the colonists to their lands by terror.

" You never know what's going to happen," said John McLeod.

III

When, in a corridor of the hotel in which most of the Colony men were lodged, I met my friend John Bourke I did not recognise him. The change on Lord Selkirk when I saw him in Montreal had shocked me. The change on Bourke—who halted me with " Why, David, you do not know me!"—shocked me even more. Bourke was only a year or two older than I but looked old enough then to be my father. Yet he was not broken. I admired him tremendously. Always I had admired John Bourke.

He made no great song about all he had passed through. When I asked if what I had heard was true——

"Yes," he answered, "yes, that's what happened. All the way from Bas de la Rivière—or Fort Alexander, as they are beginning to say—to Fort William I lay on a wooden box exposed to a burning sun."

"How long did they keep you in that horrible privy?" I asked.

"Three weeks," he told me. "Or three weeks and a day to be exact."

"What happened when they brought you on to Montreal?"

"I was released."

"And what then?"

"I tried to make my way back to Red River. I got as far as Sault Ste. Marie, averaging, I suppose, about thirty miles a day for over three weeks. Some Nor'-Westers there recognised me and I was nabbed by a constable and brought here again. I suppose they want me at the Court of King's Bench to give evidence that a field-piece was taken out to Seven Oaks. My wife, they tell me, has been very brave over it all, poor girl. I have now been away over a year from Red River."

When the day came for the case in which we were both to appear as witnesses, the sight of Bourke, cadaverous and yet utterly calm, gave me calm.

Cuthbert Grant and seventeen others were charged with being principals or accessories in the murder of Robert Semple and twenty settlers on June 19th, 1816; but the principals were absent. Cuthbert Grant and Tête Jaune Macdonell when last seen, so went the report, were in a distant part of the Indian Countries towards the western mountains.

The court was very quiet. An occasional cough and its echo accentuated the quiet. The ruffling of papers by one of the lawyers sounded loud as a crackling campfire to my ears. A door banged at the end of an outer corridor, like a gun-shot. "Take it philosophically," John McLeod had once advised me. I took it all as philosophically as I could.

Against John Bourke in that trial the animus of the North-Westers' counsel came to be chiefly directed. Why did they hate him so? I wondered. Was it because it was impossible to fluster him? Questioned by Lord Selkirk's counsel, Bourke was able to tell of his part in the affair—of how Captain Semple, setting out to inquire into the intentions of the armed force crossing the plains towards the farms had, they being so numerous, ordered him back to the fort for a field-piece, how he had arrived with it too late for service (the major part of Semple's men by then being either dead or wounded), how he was immediately wounded himself but managed to crawl into a bush; of what he had seen thence: the killing of the wounded, the mutilation of the dead; of the Indian who had come upon him after he had lain out two days and two nights and of how, while the Indian was tending him, they had been seen by some *métis* who had taken him away and, with no more attention to his wounds thereafter, they had left him hidden at Bas de la Rivière, then carried him to Fort William lying on a box in a canoe, his wounds torturing him, the heat sickening him; and of how, at Fort William they had confined him in that privy where his meals were brought to him and put upon the seat, his wounds still untended; of how from there he was hastily taken out one day and carried on to Montreal, there to be set free; and—of all the rest that I had already heard from him.

But when Bourke was ordered again to stand up and the eye of the North-West Company's counsel was on him, all knew that he was to have a stern ordeal. Question after question he was asked regarding the Settlement, the Colony, the Selkirk scheme; and these words, *Settlement, Colony, Selkirk scheme* were always prefaced by disparaging adjectives which, by his quiet replies, he might not have noticed. When he was led on to the account of what befel on Frog Plain by Seven Oaks he came to the worst moments of the cross-questioning.

"Yes," he said, in reply to the inquiry if he saw Captain Semple fall, "I saw him murdered."

"Murdered!" exclaimed the counsel and ordered him to be more careful, asking him, were he a soldier and commanded to shoot in battle, if he would care to be called a murderer.

With perfect hold upon himself Bourke explained that he saw Captain Semple rise on an elbow, saw a half-breed come up to him and with a pistol shoot him in the heart.

"To me," he finished, "the word for that is—*murder*."

His bearing gave courage to me when my turn came.

" When did you first go to this ill-advised Settlement?" I was asked.

The same sort of question, with similar disaparaging adjective, had been put to Bourke and I imitated my friend's way of dealing with it, which was the simple one of ignoring it.

" I arrived at Red River in the summer of eighteen hundred and twelve," I replied.

" In what capacity was you induced to join the miserable and ill-planned adventure?"

" As a writer," I replied.

" On the nineteenth day of June, eighteen hundred and sixteen, what part did you take in its affairs?"

" I was ordered by Governor Semple——"

" Governor!" interrupted the counsel. " Who told you he was a governor?"

I very nearly answered that I had heard a similar question asked several times by North-Westers, but controlled myself.

" We all knew he was Governor," I replied.

" You knew? You mean you thought!"

" No. I knew."

" Be careful," I was warned. " How did you have your knowledge? Who authorised this Robert Semple as Governor?"

" I presume the Hudson's Bay Company."

" You presume! So, on a presumption, you took orders from him, presuming he was a governor. What did he order you to do?"

" To go and warn the settlers to come to the fort."

" Did you go out armed?"

" No."

That was not the answer that was hoped for. But in similar questioning of others later the desired answer was obtained. Captain Semple and his men were armed and the word *massacre,* the counsel explained, which had been applied to the deaths of these men, was therefore erroneously applied. Armed men, he contended, could be killed but not massacred. That was a contention that helped him on his way.

There were times when I thought that the application of derogatory adjectives was overdone, that the jury would realise the intention of these and suspect there were no better ways to lead them towards the verdict desired. Several times the Attorney-General interrupted with objections, though not to the imputing adjectives but to the questions asked. But it seemed to me that the jury were dotterels, or partisans of the North-West faction. There was something to me almost sickening in the sight of their heads wisely atilt, while counsel explained again that *animus furandi* must be proved against these people who had killed Captain Semple and his men.

Animus was not clear to that jury. They did not take long to decide that Semple and his twenty men were not murdered. No one was guilty of their deaths. What to many was the Massacre of Seven Oaks was apparently at law but an accident. To me, listening, it seemed to be fortunate for the people of the Settlement that none of them had been arrested on a charge of having murdered the one half-breed who was killed at that time and to Mairi I wrote, in a letter she kept and produced with others, for my aid in writing this narrative:

. . . I wonder why no settler was arrested for that! I should think animus furandi could be proven against whoever it was who shot the one half-breed that was killed! Well, here I have to stay with Captain Macdonell at least till the opening of the water-highways next year. Poor Bourke looks years older, but you need not tell his wife that. It has been arranged by Lord Selkirk that he is to return to Red River Settlement with me and others when the waters open. Captain Macdonell has much to do on the earl's behalf. Lord Selkirk and his lady will soon leave here on the way to New York, the battles over. He is indeed a sick man. Captain Macdonell tells me he believes that the legal costs and all the accumulating costs of sustenance and transport of witnesses, etc., etc., will ruin him financially. Take even a minor instance: All the while that Sheriff Spencer was held by the North-Westers as what they called a private prisoner the earl has to pay for his sustenance. His purchase of provisions at Fort William from Daniel McKenzie there, after the departure under arrest of the other two agents of the place, has been declared illegal. Both he and McKenzie have been found culpable. We hear, however, on good authority that the coffers of his enemies are depleted also, although in the vast majority of cases they have been victorious in the courts. But now that it is all over in the courts the tide turns here again. In all public places one hears constantly the words " travesty of justice." I write this to-night as we are in hopes that letters for Red River may

yet go forward this year. I trust that Michael continues diligently in his care of Court Nez. Kiss my Christina for me. I shall not try to express my sense of gratitude to you and Mr. Chisholm and Agnes for all kindness to her and to me.

There I paused, uncertain how to subscribe myself and in the uncertainty wrote only my name, *David*.

IV

There came a day on which I had to accompany Miles Macdonell to the house in which Lord Selkirk had a suite during the proceedings. The earl was lying on a couch in a state of exhaustion. Lady Selkirk received us with much charm and graciousness. While Captain Macdonell, seated in a chair drawn up close to the couch, was conferring with Douglas, she talked to me.

"Poor Dan McKenzie," said she. "He has been so badly treated by his fellows of the North-West Company that I cannot but feel sorry for him. They have never forgiven him for his criticisms of them."

Then she glanced beyond me at her husband who had risen on an elbow and was laying a hand on Macdonell's arm as though intimately to impress on him some evidence, some course of action.

"You know, dear," she said, quietly, "you must rest. Remember what Mr. Allen said."

"I am resting, darling," he replied. "Just look at me! But I must discuss these matters with Captain Macdonell against to-morrow."

She turned back to me, worrying showing in her eyes.

"O dear!" she sighed. "I do not know now whether to regret or be grateful for the interludes of travel, this necessity to go from one court to another through both Lower and Upper Canada—Montreal, Quebec, Little York, Sandwich. My husband was so weary the last time that a court was held in Sandwich that I prevailed on him to let an attorney take his place, but while staying here he did not rest. He was in constant conference with one of his lawyers, with Mr. Gale. He might as well have gone. Some of the travel by road is rough and jolting but the river travel is—pardon me."

Again she was looking beyond me. Captain Macdonell had risen.

"I am glad you came," she said to him. "I think after all it was as well, as things are, for him to see you to-day. He would have fretted so greatly had you not come that it would have spoiled his rest. Now you will rest," she added to Lord Selkirk.

His face was grey with weariness.

"God bless you, yes," he promised, and lifted a hand in parting salute to Miles Macdonell and then to me. Just as we moved away he lifted his hand again and shook it, as though shaking his fist at me.

His lady, Macdonell, and I showed that we were puzzled. Even I, for whom the gesture was made, did not understand it.

"He knows!" said Selkirk, nodding. "You know, Baxter—you remember. The rattle! You haven't forgotten the rattle?"

"Oh, no, sir, I have not!"

"What's all this?" asked Lady Selkirk.

"He knows. He kens!" said Douglas. "I'll tell you after they have gone. It will not weary me to tell you of that, I do assure you. Good-bye."

"Good-day, sir."

"Good-bye, my lord."

We passed out into the noisy street where the carts clattered by and walked in step back to our hotel without a word for a considerable distance.

"What was that about the rattle?" asked Captain Macdonell at last.

I began an explanation but as soon as he got the gist of it, he was absent of manner, thinking of the man as he had left him that day.

"He is a sick man," said he as I came speedily to an end. "I have a dread he will not last long. What a fine woman his lady is! There is devotion. There is loyalty for you. She gives one back one's faith in humanity."

"When will you be returning to the Settlement?" I asked.

"I think I am getting past such appointments, Baxter," he replied. "I am not as young as I used to be. But talking of Red River: Do not consider yourself tied to the Colony service. If on your return you would rather, for some reason, go into the Company service, do not consider you must remain with the Colony administration. There may be great changes out there before long. Mr. Bird, who is at present the Company's factor at Red River, seems to be a very fine man. Let me recommend you to him when I write."

That was not an answer to my question, though arising out of it, but some diffidence kept me from repeating the inquiry. Instead I began a speech of thanks for the interest shown in my welfare and future, which Miles Macdonell pshawed aside.

CHAPTER NINE

I

IN the summer of 1819 I returned again to Red River. Nearly two years I had been gone. I went within the palisade at Fort Douglas only to leave my luggage at the clerks' quarters and without any formal announcement that I was back made haste to see the little Christina. Thoughts of her mother had been keenly in me during the last stretches, where I could see the riverside trails undulating along, though the trees were not as she had ever known them in summer, being leafless because of a recent visitation of grasshoppers, and consequently songless.

In sight of the Chisholm farm, as I strode along excited by the thought that soon I would see the little Christina, came another thought—that Mairi I would also see; and I wondered if in my long absence any had come courting her. The emotion that followed came as a shock to me. I surprised myself, had myself revealed to myself by it; but it was dispelled by another that came at sight of a child playing near the gate.

"Christina!" I called to her, turning in from the Settlement road.

She did not know me. But, to my relief, she had no dread of me, suffered me, without a wail, to pick her up and carry her to the house.

From the kitchen Mrs. Chisholm hurried to meet me, Mairi a step or two behind, and from the stable came Mr. Chisholm. Surrounded by the three, and with Christina in my arms, the reunion was confused and hilarious. My free hand Mrs. Chisholm caught in both of hers and held; over her shoulder I dabbed a kiss on Mairi's cheek, which startled her, brought a flush to her neck and face; and on my shoulder I received a merry thwack from Mr. Chisholm

"Did she know you?" asked Mairi, looking at the child in my arms.

"No, she didn't know me.'

"Don't you remember him? Why, Christina, this is your father come back. Here is your father, Christina."

At last we were all in the kitchen. When we sat down little Christina went to Mairi and leant against her, studying me, the new-comer she was expected to know. Then up went her hand, out went the forefinger pointing at me. I gazed into her dark eyes and, as I looked, slowly the smile spread on her face just as it used to when she was a baby in arms.

"I like that man," she said, and leaving Mairi she ran to my outstretched arms and let me lift her up again, settle her on my knee.

Of affairs at the Settlement since I left I then heard, affairs fortunate and unfortunate, of good crops and of the assault of the grasshoppers, of the result of the petition to the Prince Regent: proclamations by him had been distributed through the country ordering that peace be kept between the rival Companies.

Later I went over to the fort and found Michael McDonnell in the writers' dormitory, and in the course of our preliminary talk he remarked: "Since you went east, subpœnaed for the trials, the men in charge of the Colony affairs have been——" he paused, lifted his right arm in air, elevated the elbow. "Bottle-cronies in place of counsellors is a bad business."

That remark brought back to my mind—and very vividly—my talk with Miles Macdonell in Montreal. How much did he deduce, or suspect, or know? Spencer, I believe, had gone into the Company service. Perhaps a wise plan would be for me to see Mr. Bird, the Company factor, and discover if I could begin work with him. But that must wait.

"You'll be going to see the old man?" asked Michael.

"He's still in the same——"

"Yes, still there, just as when you left him."

Just as when I left him I found Court Nez. The door stood open. He was sitting in the big chair. Aslant between his knees, leaning against a shoulder, was his long staff. He sat erect, his great thighs slack, his hands lying open on them. He might have been waiting for me to crack some joke to him. That rigidity to one side of his face, and the stare of one of his eyes, gave him the appearance of a man restraining mirth.

"So there you are," said he.

"Yes, sir, here I am back again."

His fingers fumbled for his staff as though to rise but apparently he only wanted something to hold.

"Well, be seated," he suggested. "What's kept you?"

"The case for which I was subpœnaed in the late summer of '17 was not called till well on in '18. After the earl went to New York in November I remained through last winter till the waterways would be open this year, assisting Captain Macdonell——"

"I don't mean that. What's kept you since your return here?"

"I went to see Christina."

"Quite right."

Seeing him again I found I had to get accustomed to the ambiguous aspect of that face.

"And how is the little brat?" he asked.

"The child is well," said I.

"Mrs. Chisholm brings her to see me sometimes. Well, there are changes here. A lot of French-Canadians came in last year. The trials down in the Canadas advertised the place," and Court Nez hissed a laugh. "They brought in a brace of priests with them, Provencher and Domoulin—Sévère Domoulin, if I have the name right."

"Yes, Captain Macdonell and John McLeod had something to do with that——"

"So I heard. The De Meurons have gotten remarried now and had their brats baptised, so that's all well. I hear there are still hitches in attempts to get a minister for the Presbyterian folks. They had hoped to have one—by the name of Sage, if I have the name right—who used to minister to some of them in Ross or Cromarty, or some place up there, but he resigned from the church after his flock was exiled. It is queer how folks seem to need the clergy to officiate for them one way or another, to baptise their children when the brats don't know what's being done to them, to spout over their bodies when they're dead. But you tell me something now. You tell me about these trials. I hear the dice were loaded for most of the throws."

"They were indeed."

"Tell me, tell me!"

I began to talk and continued with growing fervour. Court Nez sat rigid. Because of his mask-like face I was not certain that he was paying heed. His eyelids drooped. Was he asleep? No, he was slowly twirling his staff between thumb and forefinger, head back.

"Go on," he ordered.

I told him then of the questioning of Bourke and from that passed into an account of the whole case of the Seven Oaks slayings. Suddenly I stopped.

"I am exciting you, I fear, sir," I said.

"You cannot excite me," replied Court Nez. "And it is absurd of you to be excited yourself. God, how young you are still! Did you think we lived in the garden of Eden? That whoreson counsel was quite right: Semple and his men were armed. Semple sent Bourke back for a field-piece. Semple and the others were not massacred, not murdered."

"Not murdered!" I ejaculated, thinking of how they were outnumbered.

"No. They died in fight, an unfair fight it is true. But I see what he meant by saying that as they were armed they were not massacred, not murdered."

I drew a deep breath.

"I am glad you can take it so easily," I said, and not entirely with ironic intent. I really was glad that the old man remained calm, because of his bodily state.

"The man who came and up and shot the wounded Semple in the heart—he was a murderer," said Court Nez, speaking slowly. "He could not be identified, I suppose?"

"I do not see how that could be done," I answered, and added: "The Nor-Westers say an Indian did it."

"Oh, yes—an Indian," sneered Court Nez. "They would say that. The journals in the Old Country have accounts of the settlers being attacked by savage Indians. I would that I knew who that man was who shot Semple. If I knew—if I knew——"

He rose up out of his chair with a thrust of the tall staff.

"I am unhandy," he said. "I am unhandy but, by God, I believe I could still at a pinch get on a horse. This arm is all right. This hand still has a grip. And if I could get a grip on that man——"

"Don't excite yourself," I begged.

"Excite myself!" Court Nez shouted. "Do you realise that I sit here thinking it over? If it had not been for that surgeon being called away we still would have Christina." He was breathing heavily. "I know there are proclamations out from the Prince Regent," he continued, "through Bathurst, or some of these government people, requesting the Companies to live in peace. They have been sent all through the Indian Countries to the forts and posts. All is peace here now, but away out there it is not. They are not obeying."

"That's all right, sir, that's all right," I sought to soothe him, distressed by his appearance.

"It's not all right!" he said. "I could gather a party of Indians together yet. I could go and see them and say to them, 'Look here,' I'd say to them, ' across the Big Water they are lying about you, saying that you killed the settlers. They are telling them in the courts of the Canadas that one of you shot Captain Semple after he had a promise from Grant of help.' And I would say to them, 'We'll go and kill all these damned half-breeds.' No, no—better still! I could lead them against the instigators of the half-breeds. We could wipe out all the Nor'-Westers in the land!"

"I beg of you, sir," I said, in growing alarm, "to restrain yourself."

Court Nez was quaking from head to foot. The veins on his forehead stood out, one side of his face was contorted, the other was blank, as always. As I stood up, imploring him again to keep calm, he suddenly collapsed. I hurried forward to grasp him, leapt forward in an attempt to stop the fall, but the man's weight was too much for me, knocked me down. His feet tangled with mine and we fell together. There was a dull thud as his head hit the floor.

I extricated myself, scrambled to my feet, bent over him. His enormous body had utterly sagged. There was not even the twitch of a muscle.

"I can never lift him alone," I muttered, and hurried out.

Across to the mess-house I ran. There was no one within. Then suddenly I saw Michael at the door of the administration house.

"Come and help me," I called to him. "He's fallen."

We went back to the cabin and on the way I gave Michael a brief description of what had happened.

Court Nez still lay on the floor, apparently stunned. He had not moved. Together we stooped to raise him.

"What a weight!" exclaimed Michael. "Up with him, up with him. I think he's dead."

We lifted him on to the bunk. Suddenly I leapt aside.

"What's that?" I exclaimed.

It was only a grasshopper in the unexpected, unreasoning spring of its species. It had dashed against me.

"Oh, these damned things," said Michael, seeing what it was.

I flicked it from Court Nez's chest on to the floor and crushed it underfoot. Then I felt his heart while Michael stood by, tense as I.

"Dead?" he inquired, very quietly.

"Yes," said I.

It was as though Death were a presence, invisible, but felt there and hushing us.

"Even so," said Michael. "I had better go and get the surgeon. He warned me once or twice to expect this. We very nearly had it a month or two ago when something was lost at the fort and one of the men who came in to see him said he supposed an Indian had stolen it. We had to quiet the old boy." He looked down at him. "Well, he's quiet enough now."

II

Mr. Bird, chief factor of the Hudson's Bay Company at Red River, graciously dismissed my apology for not having gone to see him sooner.

"I know, I know, Mr. Baxter," he said. "You have had domestic anxiety and a bereavement since your return. Accept my sympathy. Pray be seated. I had a letter from Captain Macdonell in the voluminous mail-delivery of this summer, in which he mentions you. Quite a heavy mail," and he waved a hand to the table. "Books as well as letters, books and journals. I am glad to see the last numbers of *Blackwood's* and the *Quarterly*. I do not know how a man can live without reading. You saw his lordship just before his departure, I believe. Captain Macdonell tells me he is not well."

All this was in a portion of the strong two-storey house that John McLeod had built for the Company during the first absence of the settlers at Jack River. The Hudson's Bay Company's office was still in the lower part, the Colony's administrative office still in the upper. At that moment uncertain steps sounded in the entrance and passed to the stairs. As they stumbled upwards I thought of what Michael

had told me of those in charge of the Settlement affairs and was glad
I had decided to take Miles Macdonell's hint and seek work with the
Hudson's Bay.

"I was hoping," said I, "that you might have a place for me in
the Company's service. Captain Macdonell assured me that I must
not feel tied to the Colony if I was minded to change."

"For myself," replied Bird, "I have always had the impression that
Captain Macdonell saw a lot—a lot more than some imagined. His
advice to you was well-intended. Frankly, I should like to have you
with me, especially because of your knowledge of the Colony affairs.
We have here a vast number of accounts that have nothing to do with
the fur trade, that are relating entirely to the dealings between the
Company and the Settlement. There is now additional need to keep
our books clear, to have our side of the transactions all in order—
and you need not flatter yourself, I am afraid, Mr. Baxter, that if you
returned to your old stool you could keep the accounts less chaotic."

"This is hard news for Lord Selkirk's sake," said I.

"Yes, indeed, and his lordship has had sufficient exterior trouble
during these years. It seems somehow the last straw that now he
should have to suffer from bousers in charge. But I hear that the settlers
are planning a protest which no doubt he will pass to his lawyers if
unable to attend to it himself. As for yourself, I should be glad indeed
if you would come into the Hudson's Bay Company's service in the
special capacity I suggest." He paused and added: "At least you
could feel that you were helping to keep clear records, at our end, of
the transactions between Colony and Company."

With the news of that change I went to see the Chisholms next
morning across the plain where leafless and brittle bushes gave a
suggestion of autumn in the peaceful August day.

As I walked I thought of Christina my wife, of Christina my child,
of Mairi, of Miles Macdonell, without consciousness of connecting
links. I saw Macdonell again in a camp on the way to Sault Ste. Marie,
fire-light flickering on his face, heard his voice as he said that his first
wife had been his cousin. At that time I had not known that I was
related by blood to Christina. As I went along the road slowly,
meditating, it struck me that I had not, neither at the Settlement nor
in Montreal, mentioned to him that Christina and I were cousins. I
recalled the occasion on which, talking with him, in a sudden ardour

I had declared that I could never forget her. We had not been speaking of her but Miles Macdonell had understood what was in my mind. No, I could never forget her.

Then I thought of various evidences of old of Mrs. Chisholm's partiality for Agnes, patiently accepted by Mairi, of Mairi in the kitchen with my child leaning against her, and considered that little Christina could not always live with these people. How old was she? Turned three. At seven, I cogitated, I would have her going for lessons to the new dominie a mile on beyond the farm yonder. Some day I would send her to Montreal or Quebec to finish her education, Quebec, for preference, where her mother had gone to school. I must give her the best.

So pondering I came to the farm. There was Mairi at the gable-end washing clothes in a big tub set on a trestle-table, Christina on tiptoe beside her. Beyond them a blue haze rose into the air from a fire under a tripod from which a kettle hung. As I drew nearer Mairi looked up and saw me. Had I had any doubt if I was welcome there by her, her smile then should have routed it.

"Here's your father," she told Christina, and Christina came running to meet me.

Beside the tub I drew happily to a halt, looking from one to the other. The soap-suds winked and were dispelled as Mairi plunged in her arms and continued with her work. Some of them splashed up on her. Crooking an arm she wiped them from her eyes with the back of a hand. Little Christina strained up to get her fingers into the water.

"I'm helping Auntie Mairi to wash," she announced.

"So I see," said I.

"My Granny's away at Auntie Agnes's," she told me.

Her granny! I looked down at her and realised that she considered herself as belonging to that household. And I, it came to me, considered myself as belonging to it. I glanced from Court Nez's "brat" to Mairi and again, as she had done on our meeting after her return from Jack River post, she quickly extinguished something in her eyes, or evaded me. She shook her head away from the moisture over the tub. She laughed.

"This is warm work," she said.

"Mairi." My voice was serious.

"What?" she asked, a look close to one of alarm on her face.

"This can't go on," said I.

"What can't go on?" But there was a sudden rise and fall of her breasts. She knew.

"Christina living here," I said.

"Oh! No, I suppose not. Some day—I suppose——'

The child glanced from one to the other, anxiously.

"She'll have to come and live with me before long," said I.

Christina had something to say to that.

"Why?" she demanded, and, "I don't want to leave my Auntie," she declared.

Mairi was suddenly flustered.

"Your Auntie," she explained, violently kneading the clothes in the tub, "could come and see you when you were living with your father, just as he comes to see you when you are living here."

"You could come and live with me, with him too," suggested Christina.

Mairi's cheeks were crimson. She laughed again, but with all her attention on the washing.

"Would you come and live with me, Mairi?" I asked, speaking very slowly, definitely.

"What did you say?" she inquired, for that—she told me long after—was all she could think of to say at the moment apart from what was in her heart.

"You heard what I said," I replied. "You know what I mean."

She ceased her rubbing, her scrubbing, her kneading. She stood erect before the tub, her shoulders still raised, her arms rigid, the suds bursting round her wrists.

"You will never forget Christina," she said. "I mean her mother," she added, unnecessarily.

I had a feeling as of being stabbed by her. It was as though she charged me, by reason of my words to her, with some sort of infidelity to Christina.

"No," I said, as in self-defence, "no. I am glad you said that. I won't, I can't, I won't ever forget her."

"I would not want you to, David," said Mairi.

By her voice I knew that I had not understood her former remark and again felt a surge of wondering admiration for her.

" What a dear you are," said I to her, I who once, on leaving her, had said to myself: " What a dear she is."

Little Christina, we discovered then, had lost interest in our talk, just when we did not know. She was hopping, skipping, jumping off towards the gate.

" She told me," said I, " that if anything happened to her she knew you would be good to me."

" Did she say that!"

It was an ejaculation of gratitude, not an inquiry for fuller assurance of the statement's truth. But I nodded in response. Still she stood rigid, shoulders raised, hands in the tub, gazing into distance. Then abruptly up came her arms in a motion that set the suds dancing and holding her hands to me she looked me full in the eyes.

" I have always loved you, David," she said.

CHAPTER TEN

I

It was difficult for me to realise that a decade had not passed since I left my home in Scotland, so much had happened, so much that at times I felt as though I had lived several lives. In 1819 when I returned from the Canadas to Red River I had not completed my twenty-ninth year. Few of those who came out with me in 1811 were many years older than I, yet they and I were almost as ancient to those who had more recently arrived.

During my absence there had been more building going on and in a roomy cabin, between the fort and the new Company house that Mr. Fidler had built, Mairi and I settled after our marriage. The service was conducted by one of the old Ross-shire kirk-elders.

There was a sense of settlement being at last accomplished for all by Red River. The grasshoppers, because of the destruction of crops by them, had again caused more tripping of a few to Pembina and the buffalo hunting, but the old feeling of menace from man was gone. By Red River, and by the Assiniboine, where the North-Westers were building again, the Prince Regent's plea for peace was honoured. News of failure to honour it far out in the Indian Countries, of duels in lonely places, was as thunder from over the horizon. The younger folks could not be depressed. The elder folks looked forward again hopefully.

"It's all bells and ribbons," said Mrs. Chisholm, visiting us one winter day after the first snow had fallen, the skies cleared, and the sun shone.

The shadows of the houses lay blue in the snow; the parallel lines left by the sledge-runners were blue and, as Mrs. Chisholm had seen, and heard, ribbons fluttered and Hudson's Bay Company's trade-bells rang from the harness of the horses that drew the sleighs. There were a few among the older generation—but our friend Sinclair, by the way, was not of these—who deplored that the young had no sense of the Seriousness of Life. Along the Settlement road on crisp days, after work was done, these young ones would go driving, just for the fun of driving. *Jingle-jingle* sounded the bells from Point Douglas to the farthest farm and back again. Parties, of an evening, would put hay in the bottom of sledges to keep the feet warm and when the horses fell in step with crisp tread and the ribbons fluttered they were entranced, entranced with the thudding and the gliding, the ringing and the stars. Even on Sunday afternoons they would spend hours so, less often (to the regret of the pious) singing psalms on the way than harmonising such songs as that one of " Young Molly who lives at the foot of the hill," or a lilt of the French voyageurs, such as *Malbrouke* or *A la Claire Fontaine,* or that one that I never heard without recalling Colin Robertson whistling it at Fort Gibraltar when examining the intercepted mails, and the boatmen singing it when McLeod took Cameron away : *En roulant ma boule.*

With freedom from trepidation books were again in demand. Mr. Fidler was a buyer of books; five hundred volumes there were in his new house—for the times, and the place, a library. There was a great happiness in my own life with Mairi and the little Christina. We had many visitors, the Lagimonieres, the Bourkes among these. Poor Bourke never recovered full health after his cruel experiences. They marked him for life but his valiant spirit remained. Greatly did I always admire John Bourke. The winter sped. Geese and ducks came back from the south, honking the spring into Rupert's Land. The ice screamed, cracked, banked, and was swept downstream; the freshet rose.

Mairi and I were talking much one summer evening of Lord Selkirk. Next day a brigade of canoes arrived. Always there was a relaxing of discipline at the fort when the coming of canoes was reported; and usually the voyageurs paddled upstream singing lustily in a brave final spurt. But here was an arrival without song. As we people clustered on the bank that day of 1820 we began to be troubled. Why this lack of the wonted singing?

" I do not like this," said Mr. Bird to me. " I fear something tragic has happened to them on the way," and he passed down the ramp very solemnly to welcome them.

The canoe drew in. Out of the first stepped the leader of the brigade and took the factor's hand. They exchanged a few words, both very grave.

" There's something wrong," said Bourke, standing beside me.

" Something wrong," said Magnus Isbister to the other side.
Mr. Bird came up the bank.
" What is it?" I asked.
" Lord Selkirk——" he paused.
" Yes?"
" He is dead. He died in France. He died in April."
The people who had gathered to meet the canoes pressed round
closer.
" What is it?"
" What does he say?"
" What's the matter?"
" Why are they so quiet?" whispered Mr. Sinclair in my ear.
" Lord Selkirk is dead," said I.
There was a shadow on Red River Settlement that day.

II

Back in the office again, while Factor Bird read letters, I was lost
in thought. Strange to think that man was no longer in the world.
From the very beginning he had been to me a great man; his quietness had not deceived me into any foolish fancy that he was not strong
of character. Again I saw him, in memory, in the doorway of that
very house and heard his voice : " My dear young man, is there anything I can do for you?" I thought of the day when, with the rattle
that Peguis had given me for the " little papoose," I was snatched out
of my walking reverie by the earl's light chuckling laugh. The voice
came back out of the past as though past and present were strangely
one : " I see you too have your distractions." He was dead. He was
only a memory, but a vivid memory.

By some series of thought-links that followed the news of Lord
Selkirk's death I sat meditating at my table not only on him but on
Miles Macdonell, Robert Semple, Colin Robertson, Court Nez. I
thought again of what Court Nez had told me of my parents and
was glad that my mother's letters were cheerful. Time had helped
to heal her of the disappointment of which she had never spoken to
me—nor, I believed, to my brother James. By what I had learnt from
Court Nez she had known great unhappiness, disappointment, before
my father went off ostensibly to attempt a fresh start in an American

colony. Well, her letters were not despondent. She was living, it seemed, in a world made of scripture texts, texts consolatory and promissory, that she quoted when writing to me for my edification.

"Baxter!" It seemed to me that Mr. Bird more shouted than spoke my name.

"Yes, Mr. Bird?"

"I have spoken to you thrice, Baxter, and you have not heard."

"Pardon me. I was thinking of these past few years."

"These past few years!" said Mr. Bird. "Thoughts of them are enough to make a man deaf to the moment. It has just come to me: Do you please, immediately, give instruction to have the Company flag at half-mast. Strange," he added, "strange to think he has been dead close on four months and only now we know."

Other news had come to Fort Douglas that day, news of the death of Sir Alexander Mackenzie of the rival Company. Just six weeks before Lord Selkirk died away from home, in France, Sir Alexander Mackenzie had died on his way to his Highland home from London.

There was much discussion in the Settlement regarding the possible effect on Red River of these two deaths. Far from London, we were unaware of what was going on there. Lork Selkirk, we learned later, had lost most of his fortune founding the Settlement; the North-West Company, though victorious in the battle-ground of the courts, was near to bankruptcy; so perturbed North-Westers in London were in conference with the Colonial Secretary in the hope that they might be able to effect an amalgamation with their rivals that would save them.

The following year that amalgamation, greatly desired by the Colonial Secretary for the sake of colonial peace, was accomplished. The Companies were merged—under the name of the older one: *The Governor and Company of Adventurers of England Trading into Hudson's Bay*. Immediately, with the consequent reduction of trading posts in the Indian Countries, no fewer than seventy North-Westers came to the Settlement and took up land.

John McLeod (who had been in many parts of Rupert's Land during the years) at that time was appointed to what was considered a very important charge on the Pacific coast, and on the way thither by Saskatchewan and the mountain passes, after a visit to the east, he turned aside up Red River to see his friends of the Selkirk Settlement.

"And here's the end of their persecution of the settlers, of Lord Selkirk, and of the Hudson's Bay Company," said he to me. "The end of it all is coalition, with some individuals remaining—but their firm broken and the name obliterated, whatever!"

For a time the vast estate that Lord Selkirk had purchased was administered by the heirs who, partly in response to the settlers' protest of mismanagement—but more, no doubt, from direct evidence of it—installed a new Colony chief to take the place of him they called "the Grasshopper Governor"; and anon the estate was purchased back from them by the Company.

CHAPTER ELEVEN

In the year 1827 I was in Montreal on affairs of the Company and decided to snatch an opportunity between two appointments to go up the Ottawa River to Point Fortune where Captain Macdonell had retired and was living in the home of his elder brother. On landing at the wharf I had directions regarding my way to Poplar Villa, as the house was called. I had no difficulty in finding it. His brother John, a highly religious man, had erected a Calvary before the house, and there he frequently assembled people of his faith in Point Fortune for prayers.

I walked up the driveway and in answer to my knock the door was opened by a man-servant, whose accent was of the Hebrides whether he had been born there or in the Canadas. Yes, he told me to my joy—for I had a dread, the house sitting there so quiet in the sun and leaf-shade, that my visit was in vain—Captain Macdonell was at home. He led me through an entrance hall in which I had a passing glimpse of what seemed like military commissions and engravings of family homes. He entered a room, the door of which stood ajar, and announced me.

Miles Macdonell was standing with his back to a sideboard, a goblet in his hand, and it flattered me, or I should say it gladdened me, to see his expression of astonishment and pleasure. It was clear that he had to put a restraint upon himself. A soldier should be a stoic.

"Baxter! My dear Baxter!" he cried out, and having shaken hands with me stood back a pace and studied me. "This is hard to believe. I was thinking of you this very moment. I tell you true—and there is the proof," and he waved to where a map lay unfolded on a table.

"A map of Assiniboia," said I. "Well, I have been thinking of you, sir, these many days. I have been looking forward to this meeting ever since leaving Red River, ever since I knew I must come to Montreal on some business."

"Oh, well, be seated, be seated," said Macdonell. "I am alone to-day. But wait, before we be seated. To this reunion we must drink standing." He opened a cupboard in the sideboard and took out another goblet. "I'm alone here to-day. I was just on the point of having one with myself and the ghosts when you arrived."

He poured a dram for me and having handed me the goblet remarked, " This is a great occasion." He elevated his own and bowed over it. " Slainté!" said he.

" Your health, sir," said I, and we drank.

Then, sitting down, said he: " Tell me your news, all your news I pray you."

" I came to Montreal on legal business for the Company," said I, " which I joined, as you know by my word to you at the time, on your kind advice and recommendation."

" I am glad there was something to bring you here. And yourself? Tell me of yourself. How is your daughter?"

" She is eleven years of age now," said I. " By the way, I never told you of an extraordinary discovery I made: That man Court Nez was my uncle. My father and he were brothers."

" He was your uncle! So your wife, like my first wife, was your cousin!"

" Yes—my first wife, Christina. I also married again. Not long after my return to the Settlement I married Mairi Chisholm, Hugh Chisholm's elder daughter. You may remember her."

" Indeed I remember her. I remember all of the family well."

" We have two boys now," said I.

" Their names?" he asked.

I paused before replying.

" Perhaps I should have written to you of that but—well, I did not!" I answered. " The first one we called David Hugh, and the second—Miles."

" Oh, but this is good hearing!" Macdonell exclaimed. " Better than you know, considering my thoughts of to-day. I had my name, oddly enough, not from our family but because, during the wars in Spain, my father's life was saved by a Miles Macdonell from Ireland, of a different family. Well, you did not disesteem your first Governor to call a son after him."

" What do you mean by that?" I asked. " How could any disesteem you?"

" Some have," he replied, " and there are times, as to-day, when it all comes up in my mind again. Semple spoke scathingly of my governance—of my surrender."

I sat back, saying nothing, meditating on whether to speak what came to my mind then or not to speak.

"Why that long thought?" inquired Captain Macdonell. "And to what tune was it?"

"I must tell you," said I, after a pause. "I was in the accounting-room one day shortly after Captain Semple took over and he was, I admit it, criticising some of your actions, criticising, as a matter of fact, your final acceptance of that warrant for arrest."

"So!" said Macdonell, with a shrug.

"Even at the risk of him saying that we writers had not been disciplined by his predecessor, I rose from my place and stepping to his table told him my views. Mr. Robertson was standing by and I could see that he was with me. I told Captain Semple that you would not have acknowledged the warrant were it not that most of the officers, and a deputation of the majority of the people, advised you to."

"What—exactly—did he say?" inquired Macdonell, dryly.

I laughed then, at myself.

"It is the exactness of it that bothers me in the repeating," I admitted, "but I will tell you. He said to me, as exactly as I can recall: 'I will say this for the man you defend—within his capacity he was at least loyal to his employer: he was loyal to Lord Selkirk. You, young man, within your capacity, I realise, are loyal to Miles Macdonell.'"

Captain Macdonell laughed.

"That's what he said!" he ejaculated. "Well, well, he said true —within his lights. But God rest his soul. He had his troubles. I bear him no ill-will."

"I think he discovered in course of time," I remarked, "that you had not been as at first he imagined. Colin Robertson was with you, and I remember that John McLeod, when these matters were once under discussion, was all for you."

"These two—enough! These two—Colin Robertson and John McLeod. You lift the black mood that has been upon me, Baxter. But tell me of the Settlement."

"You would hear of the flood?" I said, why beginning with mention of an unfortunate matter I do not know, perhaps because it happened just the year before my visit to him.

"I heard of the flood," said he. "It was thinking of that to-day that made me take out the map again," and he turned slightly to lay a hand upon it.

"That is the worse of our news," I said. "People who visit us from other parts are greatly taken with the district. Just before coming here I had the duty of conducting Mr. David Douglas, the botanist from Kew, and he told me, when we were riding round for him to view the land, that he thinks very highly of the Settlement— the homes, the fields."

"That is very good hearing," said Miles Macdonell. "The Settlement is truly accomplished, then?"

"Yes, it is truly accomplished."

"And the people can never be driven out again," said he.

"No," said I.

"They have got their inheritance," said he.

"Their inheritance," I agreed, "in a goodly land."

"What a great man Lord Selkirk was," said Macdonell then. "He was a fighter to the last. Some news you may not have heard. You know after you left me in Montreal and returned to Red River I had a great deal to do regarding Selkirk's affairs. When Lord Bathurst, urged thereto by the Prince Regent, got in touch with Ellice of the North-West Company in London, to see what he could do towards an end of that trouble in the west, Ellice had the effrontery to say that he would be willing to arrange for a removal of the remaining settlers to the Canadas. Selkirk was on his death-bed when that news came to him and he spurned it. He spurned it. And he was right. The North-West Company was by then itself broken. The victors were the vanquished. I hope he realised before he died that all would be well for his settlers."

He rose and paced to and fro in the room.

"Who knows but what now he may realise, that now he may know?" said he. "My brother would be sad over my doubt. He is a man of faith." He sat down and calmed himself. "It is wonderful to see you, Baxter," he added. "I cannot tell you the good you have done me. I was in a black mood to-day before you came."

A clock struck in the hall.

"The time flies," said I.

"You will stay the night?"

"No, no, thank you. I must not. I asked at the jetty regarding the hour of the boat's departure. I must get back to Montreal."

"You must have a bite," said he, "some oatcakes and cheese at least. And another dram."

"I must watch my time," said I.

"How the time does fly!" said he.

He strode to the door and looked out into the hall and I, watching him, noting that stride, was taken back in memory to earlier days on Red River, days at Nelson Encampment. It was the same stride as of old, but the shoulders, as is the way with very tall men, were slightly bowed in years.

He glanced at the clock and turned back.

"Well, if you must, you must," he said. "It will then be but a *deoch-an-doruis*."

Silence possessed the room then. There was a mitigated light in it from under the outer window-shades, a suffused radiance, a reflected green brightness from the outer world. He took up the decanter and poured the noggins into the glasses, standing back as he did so and looking at each in turn, then dribbling a little more in this one, a little more in that, to have the drams level.

"It comes to the *deoch-an-doruis,* then," he said. "That is yours."

He handed it to me, took up his own, and stood there reflectively while the world, as ever, was rolling round. As we stood there a long shaft of sunlight slipped into the room, afternoon advancing, and spread and blazed upon the map of the Red River Settlement.

"How extraordinary!" said Miles Macdonell. "That reminds me. That reminds me! Did I ever tell you——"

"Of a day in London," I interrupted him, "when you had your talk with——"

"Yes, to be sure," he interrupted me. "I recall you spoke of that to me once and I had clean forgotten mentioning it to you."

The sunlight lay bright upon the map. From the hall, *tick-tock, tick-tock* spoke the clock.

The Governor raised his glass.

"To the memory of the man we served."

". . . the man we served."

THE END

AUTHOR'S ACKNOWLEDGMENT

My thanks are due to:

Dr. W. Kaye Lamb, provincial librarian and archivist, British Columbia, for the loan of several volumes;

Mr. J. L. Johnston, provincial librarian and archivist, Manitoba, for his interest in my researches relative to this story, and for a chair and a suitably spacious table in Parliament Buildings, Winnipeg, and a sight of many more books than I asked him for;

Mr. John Murray Gibbon, for lending me, from his private library, two or three volumes now hard to discover at the booksellers';

Mr. Franklin F. Appleton, for the happy jog he provided by writing to ask me for such a book as this (unaware I was already employed upon it), and enclosing in the letter, as weight to the plea, a fine list of volumes relating to its period; also for giving me the title: *Mine Inheritance*.

F. N.

BIBLIOGRAPHY

Adams, Mrs. Ann. *Reminiscences of Early Days at Red River Settlement and Fort Snelling.* (Minnesota Historical Society).

Anderson, Rev. David. *Notes of the Flood at Red River.* (London, Hatchards, 1852).

Ballantyne, R. M. *Hudson Bay.*

Barrow, John. *The Geography of Hudson Bay.* (London, for the Hakluyt Society, 1852).

Begg, Alexander. *The Great Canadian North-West.* (Montreal, 1881; Toronto, 1894; London, 1895).

Begg, Alexander. *History of North-West.* (Toronto, 1895; London, 1895).

Bell, Charles Napier. *The Earliest Fur Traders on the Upper Red River and Red Lake* (Minnesota, 1783-1810. Winnipeg, 1926).

Bell, Charles Napier. *The Old Forts of Winnipeg.* (Winnipeg, 1927).

Bell, Charles Napier. *The Selkirk Settlement.* (Winipeg, 1887).

Branch, E. Douglas. *The Hunting of the Buffalo.* (New York and London, D. Appleton and Co., 1929).

Bryce, George. Brief Biographies of Selkirk, Simpson, Mackenzie, Douglas, in *The Makers of Canada.*

Bryce, George. *The Remarkable History of the Hudson's Bay Company.* (Toronto, Briggs; London, Sampson, Low, Marston and Co).

Bryce, George. *The Romantic Settlement of Lord Selkirk's Colonists.* (Toronto and Winnipeg, 1909).

Bryce, George. *The Scotsman in Canada.* (Musson Book Co.).

Butler, Sir W. F. *The Great Lone Land.* (London, Burns, Oates, and Washbourne, Ltd., 1923).

Catlin, George. *Manners, Customs, and Conditions of the North American Indians.*

Catlin, George. *The North American Portfolio.*

Charters, Statutes, Orders in Council Relating to the Hudson's Bay Company. (London, Hudson's Bay Company, 1831).

Cocking, Matthew. *Journal of, from York Factory to the Blackfeet*

Country. (Royal Society of Canada, with introduction and notes by Lawrence J. Burpee).

Cowie, Isaac. *The Company of Adventurers.* (Toronto, Briggs, 1913).

Davidson, Gordon Charles. *The North-West Company.* (University of California Press, Berkeley, 1918).

Douglas, David. *Journal kept during his Travels in North America.* (Royal Horticultural Society, 1914).

Douglas, T. *A Narrative of Occurrences in the Indian Countries of North America since the Connexion of the Earl of Selkirk with the Hudson's Bay Company.* (London, printed by B. McMillan, Bow Street, Covent Garden, 1817).

Douglas, W. *The First Days of Red River Settlement.* (Winnipeg Free Press, 1937).

Dugast, M. L'Abbe G. *The First Canadian Woman in the North-West.* (Transaction No. 62 of the Historial and Scientific Society of Manitoba, Winnipeg, 1902).

Ermatinger, Edward. *Ermatinger's York Factory Journal.* (Transactions of Royal Society of Canada).

Five Fur Traders of the North-West, edited by Chas. M. Gates, introduction by Grace Lee Nute.

Garry, Nicholas. *Diary of* (Transactions of Royal Society of Canada, 1900).

Godsell, Philip H. *Arctic Trader.* (New York, Putnam, 1934).

Gunn, Hon. Donald and Charles, R. Tuttle. *History of Manitoba.* (MacLean, Roger and Co., Ottawa, 1880).

Hamilton, J. C. *The Prairie Province.* (Toronto, Belford Brothers, 1876).

Hargrave, J. J. *Red River.* (Montreal, John Lovell, 1871).

Harmon, Daniel William. *A Narrative of Voyages and Travels in the Interior of North America.* (Andover, 1820).

Healy, W. J. *Women of Red River.* (Women's Canadian Club, Winnipeg).

Hill, Robert B. *Manitoba.* (Toronto, Briggs, 1890).

Irving, Washington. *Astoria.* (London, Geo. Bell and Sons, 1877).

Kitto, F. H., D.L.S. *Athabasca to the Bay.* (Ottawa, 1919).

Macdonell, Capt. Miles. *Letter Book of* (Canadian Archives, Report for 1896, p.p. 187-326).

Mackay, Douglas. *The Honorable Company.* (Bobbs, Merrill, Co., Indianapolis and New York, 1936).

Mackenzie, Alexander. *History of the Highland Clearances.* (Glasgow, P. J. O'Callaghan).

Martin, I. C. *The Hudson's Bay Company's Land Tenures and the occupation of Assiniboia by Lord Selkirk's Settlers: With a list of grantees under the Earl and the Company.* (London, Wm. Clowes and Sons, Ltd., 1898).

Martin, Chester. *Lord Selkirk's Work in Canada.* (Humphrey Milford, Oxford University Press, Toronto, 1916).

Martin, Chester. *Red River Settlement.* (Papers in the Canadian Archives relating to the pioneers, selected by) (Ottawa, Archives, 1910).

Masson, L. R. *Les Bourgeois de la Compagnie du Nord-Ouest,* edited by (Quebec, de L'Imprimerie General a Coté et Cie, 1889).

McGillivray, Duncan. *The Journal of, with introduction by Arthur S. Morton.* (Toronto, McMillan Co. of Canada, 1929).

McKeevor, Thomas. *A Voyage to Hudson's Bay during the summer of 1812.* (London, 1819).

McLeod, John. *His Diary of Affairs at Red River.* (MS. copy and with marginal notes by his son, Archives, Winnipeg, Manitoba).

Minutes of the Councils of Red River and the Northern Department Rupert's Land.

Montreal, Bishop of. *Journal of, during a visit to the Church Missionary Society's North-West American Mission.* (London, 1845).

Morice, Rev. A.-G., O.M.I., M.A. *The Macdonell Family in Canada.* (Reprinted from the Canadian Historical Review, September and December, 1929).

Munro, W. F. *The Backwoods of Ontario and the Prairies of the North-West.* (London, Simpkin, Marshall and Co.; Manchester, John Heywood; Glasgow and Edinburgh, John Menzies and Co., 1881).

North Dakota Historical Quarterly Vol. V. (State Historical Society of North Dakota at Bismark, D.N.).

Oliver, E. H. *The Canadian North-West, its early development and legislative records, Minutes of the Councils of the Red River and the Northern Department of Rupert's Land.* (Ottawa, Govt. Printing Bureau, 1914).

Papers Relating to the Red River Settlement. (House of Commons, 12th July, 1819).

Pritchard, John. *Letters or Diary.*

Pritchett, John Perry. *Selkirk Purchase of the Red River Valley.* (Reprint from Journal of Economics and Business History, Vol. VIII, No. 4, August, 1931).

Red River Settlement, Papers Relating to the, 1819-58. (House of Commons).

Reinhard, Trial of Charles de, to which is annexed a summary of Archibald McLellan's, indicted as an Accessary. (Montreal, 1819).

Robinson, H. M. *The Great Fur Land* (New York, 1879).

Report of the Proceedings connected with the disputes between the Earl of Selkirk and the North-West Company at the Assizes held at York in Upper Canada, October, 1818, from minutes taken in council. (Montreal and London, 1819).

Robson, Joseph. *An Account of Six Years' Residence in Hudson's Bay.* (London, 1752).

Ross, Alexander. *The Red River Settlement.* (Smith, Elder and Co.. London, 1856).

Russell, Alex. J. *The Red River Country, Hudson's Bay, and North-West Territories.* (Montreal, 1870).

Ryerson, Rev. John. *Hudson Bay.* (Toronto, G. R. Saunderson, 1855).

Selkirk, Earl of. *A Sketch of the British Fur Trade in North America with observations relative to the North-West Company of Montreal.* (London, 1816).

Selkirk, Earl of. *Observation on the Present State of the Highlands of Scotland with a view of the causes and Probable Consequences of Emigration.* (London, Longman, Hurst, Rees, and Orme; and Edinburgh, W. Constable and Co., 1805).

Shuttleworth, E. B. *The Windmill and Its Times* (printed privately by Edward A. Apted, Toronto, 1924).

Simpson, Sir George. *Peace River, a Canoe Voyage from Hudson Bay to the Pacific.* (Ottawa, 1872).

Southesk, Earl of. *Saskatchewan and Rocky Mountains.* (Toronto, 1875).

Statement Respecting The Earl of Selkirk's Settlement on the Red River, its destruction in 1815 and 1816; and the massacre of

Governor Semple and his party, with observations upon a recent publication entitled " A Narrative of Occurrences in the Indian Countries." (London, John Murray, 1817).

Taché, Mgr.   *Sketch of the North West of America.*   (Montreal, 1870).

Trémaudan, A. H. de. *The Hudson Bay Road.* (Dent, 1815).

Wallace, W. Stewart. *Documents Relating to the North-West Company.* (Champlain Society, XXII, 1934).

West, Rev. John.   *The Substance of a Journal during a Residence at the Red River Colony.* (London, 1824).

Wood, Louis Aubrey.   *The Red River Colony.* (Chronicles of Canada, Vol. XXI, 1915, edited by Geo. M. Wrong and H. H. Langton).

Lake Athabaska

Ft. Wedderburn

Ft. Churchill

Ft. Prince of Wales

Hudson Bay

Nelson Encampment

York Factory

Athabaska

L. la la Crosse

Nelson R.

Hayes R.

Grand Rapids

Norway House

North Saskatchewan R.

The Prairie Fort

L. Winnipeg

L. Winnipegosis

Bas de la Rivière

Ri.

L. Manitoba

South Saskatchewan

Qu'Appelle R.

Assiniboine R.

Ft. Douglas

Lake of the Woods

Ft. Gibraltar

Lac la Pluie

Brandon House

Portage la Prairie

Ft. Daer

Pembina

Mandan Town

Missouri R.

Red R.

Fond du Lac (Duluth)

Mississippi R.

N

W   E

S

C.W. JEFFERYS